UNTOLD

NANCY ANN HEALY

ISBN-13: 978-0692913512 ISBN-10: 0692913513

PROLOGUE

"Where are you going?"

Kaylee Peters turned to her friend and smiled. "You guys go ahead. I want to walk into the foundation stones and take some pictures."

"Kay," Jenna Dean scolded. "Don't take all day. You must have a million pictures of this place by now."

Kaylee laughed. "Yeah, well every picture is different even if it's taken of the same thing."

"You know, you are not going to get rich and famous by taking pictures of old stones," Jenna told her friend.

Tom Montgomery grabbed his friend's hand. "Let her go, Jenna," he said. "She's heard Donovan's ghost stories so many times she thinks she is going to find one in a picture."

"Oh, ha-ha," Kaylee replied. "Just go; I'll catch up with you."

"Just be careful climbing around there," Tom warned.

Kaylee rolled her eyes. "I won't fall in any ditches; I promise."

"Yeah, well, don't go getting any poison ivy this time either. Last time you gave it to me, and it sucked," Jenna reminded her friend.

"Uh-huh, how do you know that mangy mutt didn't give it to us both?" Kaylee challenged her friend.

"Fenway is not mangy," Tom defended his dog. Jenna and Kaylee both laughed at his indignant tone.

"I won't take too long. If I don't catch up to you on the trail, I'll see you back at the car," Kaylee promised.

Jenna let Tom begin to lead her away. "No poison ivy!" she called back.

Kaylee watched her friends go and chuckled. "It was that dog," she mumbled as she ambled off the trail.

AUTHOR'S NOTES

The return of Alex and Cassidy happened unexpectedly. *Untold* is a story whose origins are found in daily hikes with my husky, Jameson. Walking amid old ruins for miles without seeing another soul made me wonder what tales the woods had to tell. And, who better to explore the story of a serial killer than Alex Toles? It's been a joy to walk with these characters again and explore their lives ten years after *Conspiracy* ended. This story allowed me to bring my two writing worlds together and introduce the cast of J.A. Armstrong's By Design series into Alex and Cassidy's world.

Untold features passages from Mother Goose's Nursery Rhymes. Over many centuries, the original Mother Goose rhymes have been adopted and altered by different cultures. I imagine that will continue to be the case for the rest of time. This book is no exception in exploring Mother Goose, albeit it with a different flare. One of the most amazing things about art is that it has the ability to inspire creativity in those who interact with it. Sometimes, we find ourselves transported back to another time by the sound of a song, a movie, or reading a rhyme to our children. Indeed, each of us is part of a unique story. We carry the stories of others along with us as we write our tale.

Thank you to my beta readers, Jeannie, Lori, CJ, and Nadine for their feedback, honesty, and diligent work. Thank you to LJ Reynolds for being a sounding board and resource when I needed it. Most of all, thank you to each of you who picks up this tale and travels with these crazy characters. I hope that they bring you a fraction of the joy that they continue to bring me. Remember this; everyone has a story to tell. Don't let yours go untold. ~ Nancy

CHAPTER ONE

"Kenzie!" Alex Toles called up the stairs. "If you are coming with me, get a move on!"

Alex's wife stepped into the hallway and pursed her lips in amusement. "Troops not falling in line?" Cassidy teased Alex.

Alex turned to Cassidy and shook her head. "Why is it that they ask to go and still can never be ready?"

Cassidy shrugged. The sound of Mackenzie's feet pounding the upstairs hallway echoed down the stairs.

"I'm ready!" Mackenzie declared halfway down the staircase.

Cassidy turned away to hide her amusement. "Oh, she's yours," she muttered.

"Kenz?" Alex pointed to her daughter's attire.

"I borrowed your shirt," Mackenzie explained.

Alex glanced in Cassidy's direction just as Cassidy turned to face her. Cassidy's body shook with laughter. Alex rolled her eyes and turned back to their daughter. "You can't run in that," Alex pointed out.

"Why not? You do?" Mackenzie challenged Alex.

Had Alex not already been running behind schedule; she might have found the display amusing. Mackenzie looked both adorable and ridiculous sporting one of Alex's FBI T-shirts. The youngster had attempted to tuck it into her shorts. Half of it hung out the bottom, while the other half spilled out the back. The sleeves reached Mackenzie's wrists. Alex wondered for a spilt-second if she should get the camera. The fact was, she was dangerously close to being late already.

Alex looked at her daughter and smiled. "Kenz, you could get hurt running in that."

Mackenzie put her hands on her hips in protest.

Alex took a deep breath. At seven-years-old, Mackenzie seemed to have an answer for everything, and in Mackenzie's mind, her logic was completely—logical. Alex's thumb instinctively reached for her temple and began massaging it in frustration.

"Mackenzie, if you want to go with your mom, you have to wear something that fits you, not her," Cassidy told their daughter.

"It fits," Mackenzie argued.

Cassidy fought the urge to smack herself in the forehead. Mackenzie was not trying to be difficult. Cassidy recognized that, but Mackenzie was a willful child who sometimes struggled with the reality that she was not in charge of everything, particularly herself. "Mackenzie," Cassidy's voice took on its motherly warning tone.

Mackenzie groaned and turned to stomp back up the stairs.

"No stomping," Cassidy called out sternly. "Or you can go with me and the twins to the store instead." She heard Mackenzie grumble, and she chuckled. "She *is* your daughter," Cassidy repeated.

Alex scratched her brow. "I don't think I was ever that difficult."

"Yes, you were," a voice came up behind the pair.

"Oh, thanks, Mom," Alex laughed.

"Just telling it like it is," Helen Toles said. She turned her attention to Cassidy. "I think Bonnie and Clyde are plotting something in the family room," she said, referring to Alex and Cassidy's twins.

"They don't want to go to the store," Cassidy surmised. Helen grinned. "Do I want to know what they are plotting?"

"Probably not, but safe to say Kenzie gave them some good ideas," Helen said.

Cassidy pinned Alex with a stare and shook her head.

"What are you looking at me for?" Alex asked.

Cassidy's eyebrow shot up. "They are not even five yet."

"Two weeks, Cass."

"Yes, I know," Cassidy replied. "Giving birth to twins is not something one generally forgets."

Helen laughed. Cassidy's playful reminder had made Alex go

pale in an instant. Cassidy had survived an unusually long, grueling labor with their two youngest children. Twins had not been on either Alex or Cassidy's parental radar. Both had learned that nothing prepared a person for twins, at least not for their twins.

Connor and Abigail were twins in every sense of the word. They were each other's best friend. And, they enjoyed concocting what Cassidy called "little conspiracies." Those included hiding under Dylan's bed to avoid going shopping and hiding in Mackenzie's closet to try to scare her. Attempting to hide in the backseat of Alex's car so that they could go to work with her was the stunt that nearly gave Cassidy a heart attack. Quite frequently, the twins enjoyed stowing their favorite items in the shopping cart behind Cassidy's back when she took them to the store. Mackenzie delighted in egging the pair on. While it was rare, when conflict arose between Connor and Abby, the situation could become volatile. Mischief times two could be exhausting. Alex often wondered how Cassidy handled their children all day. She was just about to try and placate Cassidy when Mackenzie came barreling down the stairs.

"Ready!" Mackenzie declared.

Cassidy chuckled, leaned into Alex, and placed a soft kiss on her cheek. "Saved by Kenz again," she whispered.

Alex wrinkled her nose in reply. Cassidy giggled.

"Acceptable?" Mackenzie asked, sounding more like an adult in a business meeting than a seven-year-old.

Helen covered her mouth to keep from laughing. Cassidy smirked at the expression on Alex's face, certain that she would never grow tired of watching Alex with their children. Watching Alex and Mackenzie together consistently amused Cassidy. Mackenzie and Alex shared a special bond. Alex became enthralled with Mackenzie the moment that Cassidy told Alex she was pregnant. When Mackenzie finally arrived, Cassidy immediately noticed their daughter's attachment to Alex. She often pondered how different their daughters were. Abby was attached to Cassidy more than any of her other children had ever been, even their eldest, Dylan. As a baby, Abby would cry when Cassidy attempted to put her down. Even now, when illness or upset struck the toddler, Abby sought out Cassidy. As much as Alex or her grandmothers tried, Abby was often inconsolable until she was in Cassidy's embrace. It was ironic. Abby resembled Alex more than any of their children did. She had clearly inherited the Toles' genes. Mackenzie on the other hand, looked so much like Cassidy that Alex had dubbed her Mini-Cass. And, as much as Cassidy knew Alex adored Mackenzie, Mackenzie could get under Alex's skin faster than any of their kids. Cassidy wondered if Alex would ever realize that Mackenzie prided herself on that ability.

"Better," Alex finally answered Mackenzie's question. She watched as Mackenzie skipped down the steps and toward the front door. "Kenz," Alex warned gently. "Aren't you forgetting something?"

Mackenzie turned in the doorway and waved. "Bye, Mom."

"Have a good time, Kenz," Cassidy replied with a smile.

Alex leaned in and kissed Cassidy on the cheek. "Love you," she whispered. "See you later tonight."

"Yes, you will," Cassidy agreed. "Go on, Coach," she said with a pat to Alex's backside. "And, I love you too."

"Mom!" Mackenzie called from outside the door.

"Think I should pretend I don't know who she's calling and let you answer?" Alex joked.

"Mom!"

Cassidy laughed. "Go on, Alfred."

"Accurate," Alex playfully groaned as she made her way toward the door. "Hold your horses," she yelled to her daughter.

Cassidy closed the door behind Alex and leaned back against it to face her mother-in-law. "Guess it's time to round up Bonnie and Clyde," she laughed.

"You really think this warrants our involvement? Seems like an issue for the local police," Detective Jared Brown asked his partner. David Siminski exited the car and kept moving. "Dave?"

"I don't know," Siminski replied honestly. "But, when Michael calls—I answer."

Brown nodded his understanding and followed his partner across a grassy parking area toward a small cluster of picnic tables where law enforcement and a few bi-standers had gathered. Jared Brown was a relatively new addition to the Connecticut State Police's Major Crime Squad. His partner, Detective David Siminski was a veteran—one of the investigators other officers talked about and aspired to become. Siminski had spent six years with the Federal Bureau of Investigations in Washington D.C. He'd opted for a role back in his home state when his mother had become ill seven years ago. One thing Brown understood, if David Siminski thought there was a reason to be here, there likely was.

Siminski approached the small group, keen to listen to the conversation as it unfolded.

"I don't know," a young girl's despondent voice answered. "She wanted to take some pictures of some of the old buildings—you know—the ruins?"

Detective Jerry Daniels nodded just as he captured Siminski out of the corner of his eye. He smiled at the girl. "Okay, Jenna. Why don't you and Tom have a seat?" he suggested. "I'll be right back," he told her, turning to his old friend. "Take a walk?" he asked Siminski.

"So?" Siminski asked as they strolled.

"You know; three kids out in the woods, one goes off on her own," Daniels began. "We're looking, but by the time they thought to call anyone—Well, we're already losing light."

"What makes you think this is anything more than a kid looking for an escape?" Siminski asked.

Daniels groaned. "The kids," he replied. "They're rattled."

"You think her friends know something?" Detective Jared Brown asked. Daniels looked at him curiously.

"Sorry, Jerry," Siminski apologized. "Detective Brown is a bit curious as to what we are doing here," he confessed. "To tell you the truth, so am I."

Daniels stopped moving and faced the pair. He nodded his understanding and looked directly at Siminski. "Call it my gut," he said honestly. "Let's say that I doubt that this will stay a local case for very long."

Siminski released a heavy breath and scratched his brow. He had worked with Daniels for five years before accepting a position at the FBI. Jerry Daniels was an astute investigator. Siminski had often pondered suggesting that his old friend join the bureau, but Daniels had always been clear that he had no desire to leave his department, nor his family ties. Daniels' father had served in the same town as the Chief of Police for thirteen years. The detective felt a sense of pride in continuing that service to his community, albeit in a different role. Glastonbury, Connecticut remained more small-town America than it had ever reflected city life. It was not the type of place that dealt with kidnappings, homicides, or violent crime with regularity. Nonetheless, Siminski knew Daniels to be an adept investigator. Sometimes, investigators needed an informal consultation before a formal collaboration with another agency ensued. Siminski respected that.

"So, give me the basics," Siminski said.

"Seventeen-year-old girl out with her friends for an afternoon hike in the woods. Near as I can tell that is exactly what it was. No indication of any partying, skipping a few classes maybe," he smirked. "Seems she and her friends over there have been doing this since they were kids; the hiking part, not the cutting class," he interjected. "So, they are familiar with the landscape," he explained.

"How long has it been?" Siminski asked.

"Four hours," Daniels answered. "They waited for two before they called."

"Why so long?" Brown inquired.

Daniels shrugged. "Well, she said she was going off to take some pictures—of the trail, that is—and, she'd catch up to them. Took them a bit to get back here. They just figured she was behind them, maybe took a different trail out. That's the story. The young man over there, he went back to where they had parted company to look for her—didn't find her. When he got back here, they called us. Like I said, they know the area. To tell you the truth, they didn't seem all that rattled until the sun started to set. Jenna over there says that's just not like Kaylee. We've got a small team out there now. A larger team is coming in at daylight. We'll bring in some dogs in the morning. But, you know the drill. There's no evidence of foul play."

"Except that a seventeen-year-old girl is suddenly missing," Siminski commented. Daniels nodded.

"Runaway?" Brown asked.

"Possible," Daniels conceded. "Anything is possible," he said flatly.

"Maybe she fell out there," Brown offered another possibility.

Daniels jaw tighten. "Lots of maybes," he replied. "That's possible. Like I said, anything is possible. We've combed the area she was in and the trail back. The kids seem pretty sure that she would have gone the same way."

"And, you trust them?" Brown asked.

"Their stories match. They're genuinely worried. They called. I don't have any reason to think they aren't telling me the truth. Hell, they told me they cut class," he said.

Siminski glanced over at the two teens. Jenna's face was in her hands while the young boy rubbed her back. He's spent years learning to read people. Neither of the kids was acting as if they wanted to hide anything. That worried Siminski immediately. If

Kaylee hadn't given them the slip, and if she hadn't met with an accident, there was only one other possible scenario; she had met with someone else. "The parents?" Siminski asked Daniels.

"Down at the station now," Daniels explained. "We'll be taking both kids down to meet their parents shortly."

"So, you don't suspect her friends?" Brown wondered.

"I don't suspect anyone specifically of anything," Daniels replied flatly.

Siminski smirked. Brown had only been in his position for six months. He was intelligent, but he had a great deal to learn. "And, you suspect everyone as capable of anything, and any scenario is possible," he offered, looking at his partner rather than his old friend. Siminski took a deep breath and looked back at Daniels. "Well, let's see what you've got so far."

Alex stood at the side of the high school track, trying not to laugh. Mackenzie was determined to try and keep up with her older brother. "Well, she never quits. I will give her that," Alex muttered as she watched her daughter pump her arms ferociously to gain speed. She laughed. "Oh, Kenz, I didn't deem him Speed for nothing."

Dylan rounded the final turn and glanced back over his shoulder. He looked down the last stretch at Alex and received the wink he knew gave him permission to slow his pace. He chuckled. "I'd have to crawl backward to let her catch up to me." Dylan shook his head and turned deliberately on his heels, increasing his speed in the opposite direction toward his little sister. Mackenzie squealed when Dylan reached her. He lifted her in one fluid motion and guided her onto his back.

"Dylan!" Mackenzie tried to protest through her giggles. Dylan kept running toward Alex.

"He is strong," Alex's assistant coach, Doug Meyers commented as the pair rounded the final turn.

Alex looked on affectionately. "Yeah, and he'll want extra credit for running with weights," she commented.

Dylan was out of breath by the time he reached Alex. Mackenzie vaulted from his back, and Dylan bent over to try and catch his breath. "You're getting heavy," he looked across at his sister. "Pretty soon, you'll be passing me," he told her. Mackenzie looked up at Alex and smiled proudly.

"You were keeping a good pace there, Kenz," Alex complimented her daughter. It wasn't lip-service. Mackenzie would likely never keep pace with Dylan. Alex hated to admit that she could barely keep stride with her son when he pushed his pace. He was taller and stronger than her. But, Mackenzie was nothing if not determined. That was an attribute that Alex hoped the youngster would retain throughout life.

Alex watched as the last three runners on her team rounded the home stretch. "Stretch it out and get some water," she directed the team. "Tomorrow, be ready for me to press you."

"We done already?" Dylan asked Alex with a mischievous glint in his eye. "I mean, I'm sure you're tired after sitting behind that desk all day," he teased.

Alex lifted an eyebrow at the teenager. Dylan enjoyed challenging her. "Starting line in five," she challenged him.

"Oooo," Mackenzie teased her brother. "Mom's gonna teach you a lesson," she goaded him.

Dylan swatted Mackenzie playfully on the backside. "We'll see."

Mackenzie took a seat on the bleachers and readied herself for the race between her brother and her mother. It was a common occurrence. She'd yet to witness Dylan beating her mother, and she doubted that he ever would. She loved them both. They were her heroes. But, Alex? Alex was invincible in Mackenzie's mind. She sometimes wondered if her mother was made of steel. It seemed to Mackenzie that Alex could handle anything and master everything.

Dylan stretched his back as he walked toward the starting line. Alex finished some last-minute notes with Doug and began making her way toward her son. “You up to this?” Alex asked him.

“Are you?” Dylan returned.

Alex smirked. “Wise ass.”

“Worried?” Dylan poked.

“Mmm. For you,” she replied as they took their positions.

“Last chance,” Dylan goaded Alex.

Alex kept her eyes forward. “Uh-huh. Winner buys pizza.”

“Fine by me,” Dylan laughed. “Either way, you’re paying.” Alex looked at her son for an explanation. Dylan shrugged. “Well, my money is your money if you think about it.”

Alex laughed. “So, in other words, I lose either way.”

“I’ll take it easy on you,” he promised.

Alex pursed her lips. “Don’t,” she ordered him. She called out to Mackenzie. “Call it out Kenz!”

Alex and Dylan resumed their starting positions. Mackenzie stood up and cleared her throat. “Ready! Set! Go!”

“God, help me,” Alex thought when she heard Mackenzie bellow her final command.

“Quiet,” a raspy voice whispered. “Shhh. Big girls don’t cry. Shhh.”

Frightened eyes peered over a piece of electrical tape, pleading for mercy. The man smiled and stroked the young girl’s blonde hair as if she were his pet. He cocked his head to one side and contemplated her. “Shhh,” he repeated, his voice hovering slightly above a whisper. She flinched at the sensation of his hot breath in her ear. His lips wrinkled into a satisfied smirk, delighting in the waves of fear that poured off his captive. He breathed it all in, savoring the intoxicating aroma of terror. Slowly, he placed his cheek against hers, breathing steadily, wanting to prolong his time with her, desiring to feel the palpable energy that terror provided—power. She felt it—his power. He could taste it. "Sh. Sh. Sh. Sh," he cooed to the young woman. He watched as her eyes closed in resignation, and he moaned softly.

She had struggled more than he had expected. It had taken him some time to calm the rage within him. He glanced at the angry, red marks on his arms. It only made this moment more satisfying. Struggle required power. He would take hers, and she would know his. Again, his hand caressed the blonde head, and he breathed in the scent of her body close to his. His hand traveled over her neck, down a breast that strained against its will toward his touch. He'd never stopped marveling at the reality of these moments. Fear caused a body to bend. As much as he had encountered resistance, there inevitably were moments when he tasted submission. It was as if the body understood its helplessness before the mind could comprehend. He would take what he wanted. His fingertips brushed over the cord that wound around small wrists, binding them in a painful twist. A sadistic hiss rolled from his lips into her ear and lingered. He felt her shudder and closed his eyes to savor the moment.

"Intoxicating, isn't it?" he cooed. "Fear," he continued. "The adrenalin as it drips through your veins. What does it taste like?" he asked her, lust coloring his voice.

Green eyes fluttered closed, and a single tear slipped over a bruised cheek. She whimpered, the taste of blood and glue mingling in her mouth. She had fought for escape. She'd battled for control. Now, she prayed for release.

He sniggered maniacally. He had felt her cross the threshold of resistance. She was his. Like all the others, he would lay final claim to her. He leaned in and pulled her closer. He plunged the knife into her side first, just enough to make her scream against her restraints.

He pulled back, and his eyes gleamed with satisfaction. He grinned. Her body bucked and her legs kicked in one final desperate attempt to save her life. His eyes narrowed, and she met them with a stoicism that surprised him for a second. He cocked his head and offered her a sympathetic pout laced with sarcasm. She held his gaze, and he followed through with the next blow, and the next, and the next until she went limp in his arms.

The man let out an exasperated breath, closed his eyes, and craned his neck, enjoying the pop that followed. He inhaled deeply. He traced his lips with a fingertip, removing the spatters of wetness he found there. Instinctively, his tongue snaked out, and he basked in the tinny taste as it traveled down his throat. The scent of blood filled the air, mixing with a lingering aroma of fear. He gradually opened his eyes. His head moved from side to side as he considered the huddled form on the floor. He sniffed the air one last time, made his way to the bathroom, and shed his clothes. One swift twist of the shower dial and he was standing under a steady stream of hot water. He lifted his face to greet it and began to hum a familiar tune. "A hunting we will go," the words sprang from his lips. "We'll catch a fox, and put her in a box. And then, we'll let her," he stopped singing and laughed. "Know."

CHAPTER TWO

"Abby, no," Cassidy told her daughter. Abby looked up at Cassidy and pouted. Cassidy shook her head and raised her brow. "No," she repeated firmly.

Abby's eyes began to fill with tears and Cassidy sighed lightly. Abby was the most sensitive of any of Alex and Cassidy's children. Cassidy sometimes found herself at a loss dealing with the toddler. Unlike Mackenzie or either of her brothers, Abby's sensitivity was always genuine. That was not to say that the Toles children were not softhearted—they were. But, Cassidy understood that all kids could be manipulative—even hers.

As a teacher, Cassidy had reassured numerous parents over the years that a child's inclination to manipulate situations did not equate to becoming a deceptive adult. She had spent her first two years in elementary education. It had taught her a great deal about the way children navigated their world. Cassidy had always been grateful for that short stint, believing that it had helped prepare her for motherhood in tangible ways. Children needed to learn how to fulfill their desires and goals as much as they required limits placed upon them. A simple pout, an angry tantrum, faking the occasional stomach ache—these were all a part of discovering both how to leverage the world they lived in and how to accept boundaries. Cassidy had always tried to walk a fine line with her children. In most cases, she easily recognized genuine hurt or anxiety. And, it followed that Cassidy was usually able to discern when one of her children was putting on a show for her benefit, hoping to get his or her way. While Abby happily engaged in innocent toddler schemes with her twin brother, Cassidy continued to be amazed that the little girl had not seemed to develop a sense that she should pretend to feel any certain way. With Abby, what she displayed was what she genuinely felt.

Cassidy smiled compassionately at Abby. "Oh, sweetheart,"

she said calmly. "Not today, okay?" Cassidy tried a different tactic. Abby nodded.

"Mommy!" Connor called for Cassidy's attention.

"Yes, Connor?"

"Blue flakes!" he pointed to a box on the shelf.

Cassidy rolled her eyes. She was not sure where Connor had come up with the name Blue Flakes, although she suspected if she grilled Alex hard enough she would likely find out. "Corn Flakes?" she asked Connor.

"Blue," he told her.

"Connor," Cassidy began. "Why do you call them Blue Flakes? They aren't blue," she pointed out. Connor shrugged. Cassidy pursed her lips and raised her brow at him.

"Momma likes 'em blue," Connor said adamantly.

"Momma likes her Corn Flakes blue?" Cassidy tried to understand. Connor nodded.

"Yep," he replied. Abby nodded her agreement.

Cassidy shrugged just as Helen came up behind the threesome. "What's going on?" she asked Cassidy.

"Sometimes, it's better not to ask," Cassidy said, throwing a box of Corn Flakes into the basket with her children, and pushing the cart forward.

Helen looked at the toddlers in the cart curiously and received two identical smiles. She shook her head. "Good thing you two stopped at four," she commented to Cassidy. Cassidy smirked. Helen immediately noted the amused twinkle in her daughter-in-law's eye. "Oh, no. You're not. Are you?" Helen stopped Cassidy's progression. Cassidy offered her mother-in-law a smile. "Does she know?" Helen asked. Cassidy shook her head. "Oh, my God. You're not kidding. Are you kidding?"

Cassidy laughed. "No, I was going to tell her this weekend. You just uncovered the secret first," she said.

"I didn't know you two were even trying again."

Cassidy sighed. "We didn't want to get anyone's hopes up—not even ours."

Helen nodded. She was genuinely surprised to learn that Alex and Cassidy had decided for one more try in the children department. The fact that the pair wanted another child was not shocking to her at all. For years, Cassidy had teased Alex about trying to field a football team. Family meant everything to the couple. That was an undeniable fact to anyone who knew them. Cassidy was forty-three, and Alex would be turning the corner to forty-seven in a few months. It wasn't uncommon for women to have children later in life, but it also was not something Helen had expected to receive as news from the pair. She patted Cassidy's arm as they walked. "She'll be over the moon—again."

Cassidy nodded. She was positive that Alex would greet the news that they were expecting with excitement and emotion. She was equally certain that Alex would have concerns. They had not made the decision to try one more time lightly. Dylan was about to finish his junior year of high school. It wouldn't be long and he would be headed off to college. Mackenzie was in second grade, and the twins were finally becoming more self-sufficient. Cassidy had thought that she would be ready to head back to work soon. Ironically, it had been Cassidy who had driven the decision to try and conceive one more time. She understood that people were all built for certain things. Alex, Cassidy knew, had a need to fix things—to solve puzzles, to try and erase what Alex deemed as danger from the world. Cassidy? Cassidy had grown to understand with each passing year that while she loved teaching, motherhood was her calling. She continued to tutor part-time, and she enjoyed it immensely, but raising the family she and Alex had built was her passion. She wasn't ready to let that dwindle just yet.

Alex had expressed concerns. They had tried not long after the twins' first birthday for another baby. Cassidy had miscarried just days after Cassidy's first prenatal visit. It had devastated them both.

Now, the clock was ticking against them. At first, Alex's biggest worry had surrounded Cassidy's potential disappointment. Their doctor had been honest and forthright about the difficulty they might face in conceiving. And, the doctor had stressed that regardless of Cassidy's excellent health, her age made a pregnancy considerably higher risk. After months of discussion, Alex had acquiesced to Cassidy's wishes. She'd always greeted Cassidy's teasing about wanting to start a football team with their children good-naturedly. A football team might have been pushing the envelope a bit, but Alex would never have denied that having children with Cassidy had been the single most meaningful part of her life. The thought of losing Cassidy or any of their children was unthinkable to her, and Alex did not care for the word 'risk' as it pertained to her wife or children.

"Cassidy?" Helen called for Cassidy's attention.

Cassidy smiled at the older woman. "She will be—over the moon," Cassidy agreed "But, she'll probably lock me up and throw away the key at the same time."

Helen chuckled. "Don't worry; I know how to pick locks."

"Nothing," Jerry Daniels groaned. "It's like she just disappeared into thin air."

"Maybe she doesn't want to be found," Jared Brown suggested.

Daniels glared at the younger man, and Dave Siminski decided it was time to cool the tension he felt building. "Possible," Siminski conceded. "Possible, but not likely," he said. "Doesn't fit."

"You think someone took her? Abducted her?" Brown guessed.

The muscles in Siminski's jaw twitched perceptibly. He looked at his old friend and saw the same concern in Detective Jerry Daniels' eyes. "I'd bet on it."

"There's nothing here to indicate that," Brown pointed out.

Siminski looked up at the sky. Sunshine had given way to indigo. He wiped a hand over his face in frustration. The state forest covered nearly two-hundred acres. There was no way to be certain which path Kaylee Peters had taken. If she had met with foul play, which Siminski felt certain was the case, she'd likely been dragged off any marked trails. That would make a search for evidence daunting beyond belief. He shook his head. "I don't like it."

"I agree," Daniels said. "We're going to lose light soon," he observed. Siminski nodded. "Thoughts?" Daniels asked.

"Start with the usual suspects, the normal protocol," Siminski replied.

Daniels' narrowed his gaze at his friend. "This is not going to be my case for long; is it?"

Siminski chuckled. "Hard to say," he answered. "She could turn up at home in an hour."

"Or?" Brown asked.

"Or she could never turn up at all," Siminski said bluntly. He smiled apologetically before taking in his surroundings a final time. "There's someone I want to consult," he said. "Before you officially bring us into the equation."

"Who?" Brown wondered.

Siminski grinned. "The only person I know who has ever captured a ghost."

"Pizza, huh?" Cassidy wrapped her arms around Alex's waist.

"I figured that you could use a break," Alex replied as she loaded the last dish into the dishwasher.

Cassidy kissed Alex's back and made her way to lean against the counter beside her wife. "Almost beat you, didn't he?" she laughed. Mackenzie had regaled the family over dinner with the story of Dylan and Alex's impromptu race that afternoon.

Alex nodded. “He did beat me,” she told Cassidy. Cassidy’s brow furrowed with confusion. “He would have if he’d given it his all,” Alex explained.

“Took it easy on you?” Cassidy surmised. Alex nodded again. “Alex, you’re still his hero; you know?”

“I wish he would trust that I am okay with the reality that he is faster than me now.”

“Maybe it’s Dylan who isn’t ready to let that be the case,” Cassidy suggested.

“Why?” Alex asked.

Cassidy shrugged. “He’s the same way with me when we ski,” Cassidy said. “He can ski circles around me but he doesn’t.”

“Cass, I don’t know many people who can ski circles around you.”

Cassidy laughed. “You’re biased.”

“Nope. Just honest,” Alex disagreed. “I guess we’ll both have one more season with Speed around to feed our middle-aged egos—me on the track, you on the slope,” Alex said. Cassidy smirked and looked at her feet. “What’s funny?” Alex asked.

Cassidy looked back at Alex. She hadn’t intended to tell Alex about her pregnancy until the weekend. In fact, Cassidy had planned a night at the beach for them as a surprise. It seemed as if she kept getting caught in her attempt to keep the secret, or maybe she decided, she just didn’t want to keep it to herself. She smiled at Alex.

“Cass?”

“I think the slopes will be out for me next season,” Cassidy replied.

“Why?” Alex asked curiously. Cassidy raised her brow. “What am I missing?” Alex asked.

Cassidy took a step toward Alex, and wrapped her arms around Alex’s neck. “Well, there’s a chance we might be unwrapping presents in the hospital this Christmas,” she said.

Alex remained confused. Cassidy rolled her eyes. “Holy shit,”

Alex gasped. "Cass? Are you telling me that you're pregnant?" Alex asked. Cassidy smiled. "Seriously?" Alex asked again.

Cassidy laughed. "Not the reaction that I expected."

"Really?"

Cassidy nodded. "Got the call about the blood test yesterday morning. Sometime mid-December," she explained. Alex smiled and kissed Cassidy tenderly. She pulled back and let her forehead fall softly against Cassidy's. "Happy?" Cassidy asked.

"Of course," Alex replied emotionally.

"Worried?"

Alex pulled back and smiled. "A little," she confessed.

Cassidy nodded. "Me too."

"Cass…"

"I am," Cassidy admitted. "Just a little. I think this one is meant to be," she told Alex.

"You do, huh?"

"Yeah, I do."

Alex nodded. "Dylan bails just in time," she chuckled.

Cassidy laughed. "You know, somehow I think he will be a bit disappointed about that."

Alex agreed. Dylan loved his younger siblings. She and Cassidy had always been grateful for their son's desire to spend time with Mackenzie and the twins. They rarely needed to ask Dylan for his help. He seemed to revel in his role as a big brother. Alex had thought that when Dylan began dating, that would change. It hadn't. Dylan had been dating the same girl for the last two years. Maggie Nolan had become as much a part of the Toles clan as any of Alex and Cassidy's children, nieces, nephews, or siblings. She was an only child who delighted in all things Dylan. Those things included spending time with any and all members of the Toles family.

"He'll have a few months before he leaves us," Alex said, her voice trailing off.

"You know, Jane offered to take them down for a tour of the

academy next weekend," Cassidy told Alex. Alex sighed. "It's what he wants, love."

"I know. I know it is. I just wish he'd…"

"Choose something other than the military?" Cassidy guessed. Alex nodded. "It's part of who he is."

"I know that too. He's got a lot of his father in him."

"He does. He's got a lot of you in there, Alex."

"I don't think…"

Cassidy took Alex's face in her hands. "I know you don't think so. You don't see what I can see. He wants to be like you. He always has."

"You wouldn't catch me dead trying to fly a plane," Alex replied.

"You know what I mean," Cassidy returned, receiving yet another sigh from Alex. "He's always loved planes and cars."

"Well, how about he becomes a race car driver? Safer," Alex offered.

Cassidy shook her head. "I think I'd prefer The Naval Academy."

"You just like the uniforms," Alex poked. One thing Alex knew; Cassidy loved to see Alex in her uniform.

"I like you in yours," Cassidy admitted. "I like you better out of it, though," she flirted.

Alex burst out in laughter. She pulled Cassidy to her and kissed her slowly. "Hard to believe he'll be leaving."

"Hard to believe we'll have one in diapers and one in college at the same time," Cassidy chuckled.

Alex smiled. She was about to answer when her cell phone startled her. She looked at it, surprised to see the caller's name. "Sorry," she apologized to Cassidy. "I think I need to take this. Dave?" Alex answered the call.

Cassidy winked. "Anything to get out of bathing the twins," she teased. She placed a kiss on Alex's cheek. "I'll see you upstairs," she whispered.

"Hold on one second, Dave," Alex spoke into her phone. She grabbed Cassidy's hand and pulled her back.

"Yes?" Cassidy asked.

Alex leaned in and kissed Cassidy deeply. "I love you. I can't wait for one in diapers. One in college, I could do without."

Cassidy understood. "I feel the same way," she said. Cassidy kissed Alex on the cheek. "I love you too. I'll see you upstairs.

"I'll get the twins ready," Alex promised.

"Finish your call," Cassidy replied knowingly. "I've got the kids covered. Just don't make me wait too long or I'll be asleep," she said as she left the room.

Alex watched Cassidy go and grinned. "I'll wake you up."

"Don't count on it, Alfred," Cassidy called back, already down the hallway.

Alex chuckled. Cassidy could hear a pin drop three rooms away. "I wonder if this one will be the one to inherit that ability."

"Never know!" Cassidy's voice boomed back.

Alex laughed. "It never gets old." She glanced down the hallway before returning to her call. "Dave? What's going on?" Alex asked.

Dave Siminski chuckled. Alex was never one to mince words. Right now, he didn't have time for casual niceties either. "I need you to look at something."

Alex took a deep breath. "I'm listening."

"Look, I got called out to look at something."

"And?"

"Alex, listen, I can't explain it. I have a bad feeling about this one."

"Homicide?" Alex asked.

"Missing teenage girl," Siminski replied.

"Missing for how long?"

"Hours," he told Alex.

"Hours is hardly cause for the major crime squad," she said. "How do you know she didn't just take off with friends?"

Siminski groaned. He didn't know if Kaylee Peters had taken off with someone. It wouldn't be the first time a teenager sent the police on a wild goose chase. He'd worked enough cases in his life that he had developed an ability to read between the lines—to see the truth in a person's eyes. Kaylee's friends were scared—not only worried—scared.

"Okay? I don't understand what makes you think I can help."

Siminski kept his chuckle in check. Alex was an investigator who had a talent for seeing what no one else did. Part of that stemmed from her ability to concentrate amid confusion. He had witnessed that a few times when they had both worked at the FBI. Insanity could surround Alex: noise, movement, questions, and somehow Alex Toles seemed to be able to focus with razor precision.

"I need your eyes."

"Where?"

Siminski laughed. "There's no point in you coming here. She's not here."

"Okay? But, that is where she was last seen."

"Yes," Siminski agreed. "Alex, that's why I need you. There is nothing here. I mean nothing. It's like she vanished."

"Well, Mulder, we both know that isn't possible," Alex replied. "Either she walked away or someone took her away. That much we can be certain of, and as much as I enjoy a good fantasy, I'm not betting some alien ship beamed her up."

"I hear you. I'm telling you, we have walked these woods for the last three hours. Nothing where she was last seen. This place is approaching two-hundred acres and there is barely light left."

"Where are you?"

"State Park on the Glastonbury side," he replied.

Alex had been to the park a handful of times with her older brother. Krause loved to hike when he was restless—hike and drive.

She combed her memories of the place. “There’s something there,” Alex said assuredly. “There is always something. You just aren’t looking in the right place.”

“Which is why I need your help,” he said.

“Is this even our case?”

“No, but it will be,” he said. “And, if I had to bet we will be revisiting some folks from the past.”

“You think it’s going federal?”

“I feel it.”

Alex sighed. "Dave, I haven't worked an active case in over five years," Alex reminded her friend.

"No, only all the old dormant ones you've got everyone in that classroom piecing together."

Alex groaned. "Your point?"

"Maybe you can take the investigator off the case; you can't banish the need to solve the puzzle," he said. Alex grimaced. "Come on, Alex; I could use your help on this one."

"You don't even know if this is one," Alex replied.

"No, but if it is we've got a ticking clock that is winding down against that girl."

"Fine. Have your buddy send me what you’ve got—all of it. I'm not making any promises. If I don't see anything that seems..."

"Deal," Siminski stopped Alex's offer in its tracks. "Call me when you've got something."

Alex chuckled. "I'll call you if there's anything to find."

Alex groaned as she perused the documents on her laptop. There wasn’t much to look at—pictures of trees, stone walls, and barely discernable remnants of buildings. She rubbed her temple in frustration. Dave Siminski possessed a trait that Alex seldom encountered in her years as an investigator—instinct. In Alex’s experience, people often scoffed at the notion that instinct played a role in solving cases. She didn't need scientific evidence to support that idea. It wasn't an idea as far as Alex was concerned. It wasn't a possibility. And, it was never dumb luck that solved a case. Many times, the driving force that led to a trail of evidence was instinct. Something in an investigator's gut said to keep pushing.

Instinct also had risks attached to it. At times, a gut reaction could be motivated by an emotional response. That sometimes led to witch hunts and ghost chases. Alex has seen that as well. Siminski was a veteran. He'd worked everything from serial killer cases to bank robberies. He would push when his gut told him to, but only until he found hard evidence. If he had thought to call Alex, it meant that something about this case had gripped more than his interest, it had twisted his gut.

Alex pulled up the initial police report and combed through it for what she was certain had to be the tenth time. Young girl. Big forest. No signs of foul play. Well, none that anyone had detected. She rested her face in her hands and sighed. "Where did you go?" she muttered.

"I went to bed," a voice answered from behind her. Alex lifted her head when Cassidy's hands began to massage her shoulders. "What are you doing down here?" Cassidy asked. Alex swiveled in her chair. Her eyes had narrowed to slits, and her forehead was creased in concern. Cassidy shook her head, recognizing the familiar set of Alex's jaw. It was an expression that indicated Alex was in pain. "Headache?" she guessed. Alex closed her eyes and nodded. "Sit tight," Cassidy directed her wife.

Alex heard Cassidy's footsteps as they padded down the hallway and turned back to the computer screen.

"Close the laptop, Alex," Cassidy called back. Alex huffed. She barely had the chance to sit back in her chair when Cassidy reentered that room. "Take these," Cassidy handed Alex some pain reliever and a glass of water. "What are you doing?" she asked Alex.

Alex sighed. “That call was from Dave Siminski earlier.”

“Yes, I gathered that.”

“He asked me to look at a case. To be honest, I’m not sure why he asked me. It’s not even our case.”

Cassidy licked her lips as she studied Alex. Reading Alex had never been difficult for Cassidy, not since the first day they had met. They had shared a powerful and unique connection from the moment that Agent Alex Toles had walked into Cassidy O’Brien’s home. That had been over ten years ago. Cassidy’s ability to understand Alex had grown with each year. She took a deep breath and prepared to tread what she knew could become treacherous waters quickly.

“Our case?” Cassidy asked gently.

“Yeah, The State Police.”

Cassidy nodded. “Do you want to talk about it?”

“Not much to talk about. I looked. I didn’t find anything.”

“Mm-hum.”

“What does that mean?” Alex asked.

Cassidy sighed again. “Alex, you have been down here for nearly six hours.”

“No, I haven’t.”

“Yes, you have. It’s almost two in the morning.”

Alex looked at her phone. “Shit,” she grumbled. “No wonder I have a headache. I’m sorry, Cass.”

“Don’t be.”

“I guess, I lost track of time.”

“I guess so. So?” Cassidy prodded Alex.

“What?”

“If you spent six hours looking, that tells me you think there is something to look for.”

Alex smiled. “There’s always something to look for, Cass. That’s why detectives and agents have jobs. It’s just that there isn’t always something to find. At least, not something that requires our involvement.”

Cassidy listened to Alex thoughtfully. This was not the first instance of someone asking Alex's input on a case. It didn't happen often, but it was hardly unheard of. Alex generally dealt with anything work-related at work. Something about whatever Dave Siminski had called to her attention was different. Cassidy could see the wheels spinning in Alex's head as Alex attempted to put the scattered pieces of a puzzle together.

"Why are you looking at me like that?" Alex asked.

Cassidy raised an eyebrow. "You know why."

"Cass, I'm just helping Dave out, and I'm not sure that I am going to be much help at all. Who knows if this is a case? And, even if it is a case, who knows where it will land?"

Cassidy nodded, reached over, and shut Alex's laptop. "Well, for now, it is landing in sleep mode—just like you."

Alex smiled. "Is that an order, Mrs. Toles?" she asked. Alex's smile did little to conceal the evident pain she was in.

"Come on," Cassidy said as she stretched out her hand.

"Cass?" Alex asked as Cassidy led her toward their bedroom.

"Yes?"

"Do you think a seventeen-year-old girl would run away from her best friends?"

Cassidy stopped and turned to Alex. She considered the concern she saw in Alex's eyes. "That's what Dave sent?"

"Sort of. You taught high school. What do you think?"

"I'm not a detective, Alex."

"I'm asking you as a teacher—as a mom."

"I think it depends," Cassidy said. "What do her friends think?"

"What?"

"You just said she ran away from her friends. What do those friends think?"

"They don't think she ran away," Alex said.

Cassidy nodded. "Then chances are she didn't."

Alex sighed.

"Is there any more you can do tonight?" Cassidy asked.

"Not really."

"Then leave it until morning, love."

Alex sighed again. *If she has that long.*

Cassidy leaned in and kissed Alex on the cheek. "You can't help her if you can't think straight, Alex."

"I'm not sure I can help at all."

Cassidy smiled and gently led Alex up the stairs without comment. *Yes; you can. And, something tells me that you will.*

CHAPTER THREE

Alex stretched her back until it popped while she waited for her coffee to brew. She felt Cassidy's arms surround her waist and smiled. "You're up early," Alex observed.

"Don't remind me," Cassidy grumbled.

Alex turned and placed a light kiss on her wife's lips. "Are you feeling okay?"

"Tired," Cassidy admitted.

"Why are you up so early?"

"Kenzie has that field trip today; remember? Mom will be here shortly. Bus leaves at seven."

Alex grimaced. One thing that Mackenzie did not take after Alex for was rising early. She seemed to have inherited Cassidy's propensity for sleeping late whenever possible. While Cassidy occasionally grumbled in protest about early mornings, waking Mackenzie often felt like walking into a sleeping lion's den.

"Want me to get her up?" Alex offered.

Cassidy patted Alex's chest. "No," she said. "Raincheck."

"You sure?"

Cassidy nodded.

"Coffee?" Alex asked. "No offense, you look like you could use a cup," she teased.

Cassidy raised her brow. "I wish."

Alex mentally slapped herself. There would be no caffeine for Cassidy for the next few months. "I didn't forget. I just…"

"Forgot?" Cassidy laughed. She leaned in and kissed Alex's lips. "It's okay, love. You have a cup for me. I'm sure once the beast wakes, so will I."

Alex snickered as Cassidy plodded out of the kitchen. She grabbed a mug and filled it, savoring the scent before sipping it. She was surprised when Dylan rolled in, stretching his arms.

"You have a field trip too?" she asked him.

Dylan laughed. "No."

"Went for a run without me? How did I miss you?"

Dylan shrugged. "Didn't sleep much."

"Everything okay?"

Dylan nodded. "Yeah. Besides, no practice today; right?"

"Nope. Today you get a free pass. Tomorrow…"

Dylan nodded.

"You sure you are okay?" Alex asked.

"Yeah, totally. I promised Mom I would take over with the twins after school. Grandma has dinner plans," he explained. "Mom won't be back until after six. I didn't want to miss a workout."

"Worried about the meet at the end of the month?" Alex guessed. Dylan was slated to compete in three events at the state-wide track meet.

"I'd like to place in at least one event," Dylan said.

"You will."

"I hope so," he said. Cassidy walked into the kitchen shaking her head. "Morning, Mom."

"Morning." Cassidy patted her son's back.

"Kenz up?" Alex inquired.

Cassidy rolled her eyes.

Dylan laughed. "I'm on my way up anyway," he said. "I'll move her along."

Alex watched Dylan leave. She sipped her coffee slowly, wondering what was traveling through his teenage brain.

"What's wrong?" Cassidy asked.

"Do you think Speed is okay?"

"I think he's seventeen."

Alex sighed. "Something is bothering him."

Cassidy had a guess as to what was on Dylan's mind. She had pondered talking to Alex about it. This was an instance that Cassidy felt called for Dylan and Alex to learn to communicate without her intervention. She would intercede if she felt it was necessary, but she intended to give it a little time. Dylan had always considered Alex his hero. What Dylan had yet to realize was that Alex felt the same way. Alex had always marveled at Dylan. Right now, they were standing at an impasse, neither expressing what needed to be said clearly.

"Cass? Did he say something to you?"

"No. If you are really worried, Alex just talk to him," Cassidy suggested. She made her way to Alex and kissed her on the cheek. "I need to shower and get Kenzie on the move. I'll see you tonight."

Alex nodded. "Something is bothering him," she muttered.

"Talk to him," Cassidy called back.

"Momma!" Connor called out to Alex.

Alex set down her computer bag and squatted to meet her son. "Hey, where are you running to?" she asked.

"Blue Flakes?" he asked.

Alex laughed. "You want Corn Flakes?"

"Blue!" he giggled.

Alex chuckled and lifted Connor onto her hip. "Where is your partner in crime?" she asked him suspiciously as she made her way back toward the kitchen.

"With Gandma."

"With Grandma?"

Connor nodded.

"I see he caught you," Rose laughed.

"No. I caught him," Alex winked and tickled the toddler in her arms. Connor squealed and wriggled in her embrace. Alex put him in a chair beside Abby and kissed Abby on the cheek.

"Mommy went bye, bye," Abby told Alex.

Alex forced herself not to laugh at the expression of concern in her daughter's eyes. "Yes, she did," Alex said. "Mommy is spending the day with Kenzie. You get to hang out all day with Grandma."

"Can you stay?" Abby asked.

Alex smiled. "No, honey. I have to go to work. But, someone told me that D. is going to be here to play with you later this afternoon."

Abby brightened. She and Connor had taken to calling Dylan, D. Alex wondered if Dylan might just have to learn to answer to anything. She certainly had. She chuckled at the thought.

"D's the best!" Connor cried out excitedly.

Rose shook her head while Alex moved to pour cereal into two bowls.

"I can't believe they won't let me get them their cereal," she said. "What is it with you?" Rose questioned Alex.

Alex shrugged.

"Give it up, Alex. You know, sooner or later I will figure out this secret you have."

"I don't have any secrets."

"Yeah? Not one of these kids will eat cereal unless you put it in the bowl. I'm watching you."

Alex turned and faced her mother-in-law. "You've been watching me for how many years? Don't become a detective," she advised lightly.

"Mmm."

"Sorry," Alex apologized when her phone rang. "I need to…"

"Say no more," Rose replied. She picked up the two bowls from the counter as Alex made her way into the hallway. Connor and Abby looked up at their grandmother skeptically. "Oh, now don't you two look at me like that. She made it. I just delivered it."

"Good morning," Alex answered her phone.

"Not really," Dave Siminski replied.

"I don't like the sound of that."

"They found a girl matching our description."

"Where?" Alex asked.

"In the woods."

"Where she was last seen?" Alex inquired.

Siminski sighed.

"Dave?"

"No. New York State."

"Shit," Alex muttered.

"You up for a ride?" Siminski asked.

"Yeah," Alex said tacitly. Her stomach had dropped in an instant.

"Might not be her," Siminski offered a glimmer of hope.

"Where do you want to meet?"

"Your front door. I'm about three blocks away."

"Weren't going to give me a say, huh?" Alex chuckled.

"Nope."

"I'm here," she sighed and promptly disconnected the call.

Alex took a deep breath and walked into the kitchen to say a final goodbye to its occupants. Rose immediately noted the pallid tint of her face.

"Alex?"

Alex's strained smile told Rose to let her questions lie for the moment. She nodded.

"Well, I am off to the races," Alex told the twins.

"Racing?" Connor asked excitedly.

"Not that kind of racing," Alex chuckled. Her children's ability to shift her mood in an instant always amazed her. "Work," Alex explained. She turned to Rose. "Would you do me a favor?"

"Sure."

"Let Dylan know it might be a late night for me," Alex said. "I'll let Cass know."

"Do you need me to cancel tonight?" Rose asked. "Helen and I can stay here with the kids if..."

"No, you and Mom have had these plans for months. You two go and have a good time. Dylan can handle the Wonder Twins here until Cass or I get home."

"You call if…"

Alex winked at her mother-in-law. "Go get your granny on," she teased.

Rose threw the dishtowel in her hands at Alex. Alex caught it and tossed it back. "At least, I know where Cass learned that trick," Alex laughed. "You two have fun with Grandma."

"Oh, we'll have fun. YaYa will be here later," Rose said.

"YaYa!" Abby exclaimed with delight.

Alex snickered and left the room with a wave. If Abby had a second favorite person in the world, it was Alex's mother. Alex laughed as she made her way to the front door. *Those four together spell trouble.*

Alex stepped out of David Siminski's car and was met with a pair of familiar eyes.

"Well, I'll be damned," FBI Agent Bill Hanson greeted Alex. "That hibernation thing finally got boring, huh?"

"Just helping you old farts out for an afternoon." Alex pointed to Siminski.

"Yeah," Hanson replied skeptically. "Tell you what, Toles; this ain't exactly what they meant by afternoon delight."

"Not afternoon yet," Alex deadpanned. "So? What have you got?"

Hanson led Alex and Siminski under a line of yellow tape that had been wound around several trees. Alex let her eyes roam over the space. She scanned up and down, noting the scene that surrounded her. To most, the height of the trees, the placement of bushes and plants might have seemed insignificant. Alex had learned early on in her career that something that might seem mundane at first glance often held the unusual clue that cracked a case wide open.

She took a deep breath and readied herself. She'd seen death more times than she cared to count. Seeing death—particularly death brought about by violence was an experience Alex hoped she would never get used to. There was a drastic difference between familiarity with a situation and a feeling of comfort in it. Her eyes drifted to Agent Hanson's hand as he peeled back a dark blue tarp.

Siminski took a step forward first and hovered over the slumped form beneath it. "Fuck."

Alex closed her eyes for a minute—confirmation. "Are you sure?" Alex asked. Siminski pulled the tarp away and Alex sighed. "You got some gloves around here?" she asked Hanson.

Hanson called to one of the police officers on the scene. Alex crouched down beside the young woman. She scanned the area surrounding the body thoroughly.

"Here," Hanson handed Alex a pair of gloves. "Playing botanist?" he teased Alex who seemed to be studying a small cluster of leaves that partially covered Kaylee Peters' arm.

"Or what," Alex replied dryly. She snapped the gloves into place and carefully moved a strand of bloody hair from Kaylee Peters' eyes. Alex's forefinger traced the outline of a bloody cheek and let her eyes travel down Kaylee's body methodically. She picked up Kaylee's right hand and groaned inwardly at the abrasions on her wrists. "Fucking SOB," she muttered. Alex shook her head. Kaylee Peters' shirt was soaked in blood—not stained—soaked from the slices and stabs in her flesh. She grimaced as she lifted the bottom of the teenager's shirt. "You found her just like this?" Alex inquired.

"Not exactly. Park ranger tripped over her early this morning. Seems this asshole picked the wrong place at the wrong time to dump a body. She was covered in that clump of brush," he pointed a short distance away. "Haven't moved her yet. Sadistic son of a bitch, that's for sure. We've counted ten wounds without moving her. I can't imagine once the M.E. gets hold of her."

Alex looked back at Kaylee's face one last time; committing it to memory. She straightened to her full height and silently paced past her colleagues toward a leafy dirt path.

"Didn't find much," Hanson commented. "Not even a shoe print."

A lack of evidence did not surprise Alex. She made no reply. She let her eyes track left then right, up and back down again. She shook her head. Whoever had deposited Kaylee Peters here had not been overly concerned that she would be found in short order. Alex let her gaze fall ahead down the trail. There were a few things that Alex Toles understood. Every puzzle had pieces. As an investigator, a person hoped to find a few obvious ones—a place to frame the picture, or at least, to start. There was no doubt in her mind that there were clues to be found. She pivoted back toward Hanson and Siminski, her eyes taking in the sight of Kaylee Peters' lifeless body again.

"M.E. is on his way. We'll have a clearer picture when he's through," Hanson said.

"Dogs?" Alex asked him.

Hanson nodded, following Alex's train of thought. Whoever had killed Kaylee, it was unlikely this had been his first go-round. "There's a team out now. So far, nothing that has led us to anything."

Alex licked her lips and crouched down next to the young girl in the dirt. Instinctively, her eyes tracked back to Kaylee's wrists. She felt anger boiling in her veins. Steadily, Alex lifted a hand to Kaylee's eyelids and traced lightly. She groaned. The small red blotches told Alex that Kaylee had endured more than a brutal slashing. What had led to her death would be up to the medical examiner to determine. Regardless of that conclusion, nothing would change the horror that Kaylee Peters had endured. It turned Alex's stomach.

"Hanson," the FBI agent answered his phone.

Alex sighed and resumed a silent contemplation of her surroundings.

"Toles? What do you think?" Siminski wondered.

Hanson approached, holding out his phone to Alex. "It's for you," he said.

Alex groaned softly as she and Siminski made their way down the corridor of the FBI's New York Office. Alex looked ahead and captured the gaze of Charlie Hawkins as she approached—Assistant Director Hawkins.

"Alex," Hawk smiled.

"What the hell are you doing in New York?" Alex asked.

"Nice to see you too."

"Oh, come on; cut the crap. What are you doing here?"

"Dealing with some business," Hawk replied calmly. "How are you, Detective Siminski? Are you missing your roots too?"

Siminski smiled. "Good to see you, Assistant Director."

"Drop the formality," Hawk told him with a wink. "I hear you two have stumbled into a bureau investigation."

"Nope," Alex said. Hawk looked at her expectantly. "The bureau wandered into Siminski's case." Hawk nodded. "So?" Alex continued. "You want to explain your interest?"

Hawk grinned. "Crosses state lines, Alex. You know the drill."

"Uh-huh."

"You doubt me?" Hawk challenged. Alex stared at her blankly. Hawk finally chuckled. She looked at Siminski and smiled. "Dave," she said. "A moment?"

Siminski understood. "I need to call the family and let them know we will be on our way shortly. I'm assuming you want to make the notification with me?" he looked at Alex. "I can call Brown and have him make the notification if you would rather not."

"No," Alex put the thought to rest. "I'll go with you. Just give me a minute."

Siminski nodded.

Hawk directed Alex down the hallway to a small conference room and closed the door. "Back in the saddle, I see," she commented.

"Helping a friend is all," Alex replied. Hawk nodded. "So? Spare me the line about jurisdiction. What's your interest in this case?" Alex asked directly.

"What's yours?"

"I told you already."

"Oh, come on, Alex."

Alex bristled. "What do you want me to say, Hawk?"

"I want you to tell me what you are hiding from in that classroom."

"I'm not hiding from anything."

"Bullshit," Hawk replied.

"Excuse me?"

"You know damn well that you might be the best chance of catching this son-of-a-bitch—whoever he is."

"You have hundreds of qualified agents that can work this case."

"Qualified? Yes. Exceptional? No. And, you know it."

Alex shook her head.

"You're telling me that you are perfectly fine with handing this case over to some agent you know nothing about? You can just walk away and do nothing?"

"Don't you dare," Alex's voice grew menacing.

Hawk's temper was about to reach a boiling point. She knew Alex Toles better than Alex liked to admit. Unlike most people in Alex's professional circle, Charlie Hawkins had both a personal and professional past with Alex. She had no intention of backing down with Alex now.

"I'm not an agent anymore," Alex said. "Hopefully, I can help teach…"

"Oh, save me your sanctimonious bullshit, Alex. Use that on someone who doesn't know you."

"What the hell is that supposed to mean?"

"You, cowering in some fucking classroom, digging up old, unsolved cases or ones you know were taken in the wrong direction so that you can play..."

"So that cops can learn how to look for more than they are taught to see."

Hawk rolled her eyes. "Come off it—so you can get back in the game in a safe little hideaway."

"You have no idea what I…"

"I have every idea what you went through," Hawk reminded Alex. "I saw the fallout; remember? I live the fallout. What are you so afraid of?"

Alex kneaded her temples. "It's not who I am anymore."

"You keep telling yourself that and maybe one day you'll believe it."

"It's true."

"It's bullshit," Hawk disagreed. "You are one of the most talented investigators I know. It's not something you do, Alex; it's who you are. It's in your God damned DNA."

"What do you want from me?" Alex bit back.

"Come back."

"To the FBI?"

"Take this case. Solve it. If you want to quit and go back to hibernating under that desk of yours afterward, I won't fight you," Hawk said.

Alex's temple twitched. "Why me? Why this case?"

"Because you are already in the middle of it," Hawk answered. "And, because you are the best we've got."

"You haven't got me," Alex reminded her old friend.

Hawk threw down a photo of Kaylee Peters' body. "Does she?"

Alex closed her eyes. "That's not fair."

"You started this, Alex."

"I agreed to help a friend."

"Well, now another friend is asking for your help."

"Why is this so important to you?" Alex asked.

"Maybe you should ask yourself why you are so determined to walk away instead."

Alex pinched the bridge of her nose and groaned.

"You go home and think about it tonight. Talk to Cassidy."

Alex sighed. "Hawk…"

"AD Bower is here in New York. You know Ben. He's the best. If it matters; I'll make sure you get whatever you need."

Alex shook her head. "I have a job."

"Yeah? That's what it's all about now, Alex—paying the bills?"

"Fuck you, Hawk."

"That didn't work for us, remember?"

Alex chuckled despite her frustration.

"Don't walk away again," Hawk said.

"Again?"

Hawk nodded. "There's a reason this landed in your lap."

"That's what worries me," Alex said.

"Yeah, I imagine it does. You gonna let your fears rule your life? This psychopath is still out there. You and I both know this is not some simplistic, drug addict who got his rocks off and panicked."

Alex grimaced. She did know that. "Hawk…"

"You call me in the morning. Sleep on it."

Alex stared at her friend for a moment. She nodded at Hawk and turned to leave.

"Alex?" Hawk called after her. Alex looked back from the door. "You're the best. Don't bother with false modesty around me. We both know it should be you sitting behind my desk."

"Yeah. Me and desks, Hawk…"

Hawk smiled. She doubted that Alex realized what her

statement had given away. She nodded. "I'll expect your call."

Cassidy opened the front door. Mackenzie dropped her backpack and bolted up the stairs. "Slow down, Kenz!" Cassidy called out. "Good Lord," she chuckled.

"I have to pee!" Mackenzie called back.

"Oh boy, wait until Alex realizes you have that hearing," Cassidy laughed. She picked up Mackenzie's backpack and hung it in the foyer closet. Cassidy stretched her neck and rolled it side to side. It had been a long day—one that she had enjoyed immensely, nevertheless—long. Being surrounded by a horde of seven-year-olds could exhaust anyone. Organized chaos; that was Cassidy's specialty. She giggled at the thought when Connor's voice bellowed loud enough to filter through the house.

"Boo!" Connor screamed in the distance.

"I'm not sure I want to know," Cassidy mused as she made her way to the back door. She was about to step through when she heard Dylan's voice speaking softly to Maggie. Eavesdropping was not something Cassidy engaged in. She felt paralyzed by his words. Unable to pull herself away, she hovered just inside the kitchen and listened.

Dylan laughed at his brother and sister as they ran around the backyard. "No wonder Mom is tired at night," he observed.

"They do have a lot of energy," Dylan's girlfriend, Maggie agreed.

"Well, hopefully, they will be tired when she gets back with Kenz."

"Are you worried about your mom?" Maggie asked.

"No, not really. I just think there's something she hasn't told us yet."

"Like what?"

"I think there might be someone else coming to live here."

"Who? You think one of your grandparents is moving in?"

Dylan laughed. "No, I think this one will be a little younger," he said. Maggie was confused. "I think Mom is pregnant," he said.

"What? Seriously?"

"Yeah."

"Why?"

"I don't know. She has that look."

"She gets a look?"

Dylan smiled. "Yeah. I remember when she was expecting Connor and Abby. She was always smiling—well, except those few weeks when she was puking."

Maggie shuddered. "Why wouldn't she tell you?"

Dylan sighed. "A few years ago, Mom miscarried. It happened right after she told us that they were expecting. I'm not sure I've ever seen her so sad," Dylan explained.

"That's awful."

"Yeah, it was. I think they are probably being cautious," he said.

"What do you think about it?" Maggie asked.

"About what?"

"About having another brother or sister? I mean—wow. You'll be like eighteen years older."

"Close," he agreed.

"Does that bother you?" she wondered.

"Only that I won't be here so much," he replied honestly. "I'll miss them."

Maggie clasped Dylan's hand. Connor was hiding under a lawn chair. Abby was searching for him and beginning to get frustrated. "She looks just like Alex," Maggie laughed as she watched Abby's face grow pensive. “But, that expression?” Maggie shook her head. “That looks just like you when you are worried.”

Dylan chuckled. “YaYa always says that we get certain things from our parents. I guess that's true. Like Mom, she loves teaching, so did Grandma. Alex and Uncle Pip? They're a lot alike—just like Kenzie," he laughed. "She'll probably grow up to rule the world. She's a lot like Alex."

"Does it bother you?" Maggie wondered.

"You mean that I’m not related to Alex? It did at first, I guess. I mean they're all kind of like Alex; you know? Just like I'm like Mom and my father too. Kind of made me feel strange sometimes."

"Did your parents tell you? I mean, who their father is?"

Dylan shook his head. "They didn't have to," he chuckled. "Just like I already knew when Mom sat me down to tell me about mine. People look so hard they don't see what's in front of them sometimes."

"So, you do know."

"Yeah, but it doesn't matter, Maggie."

"It would matter to me."

Dylan shrugged. "Maybe. You aren't us. This isn't the family you have. Alex is our mom. Alex is my mom. I guess I have always felt that's the way it was supposed to be. I might not look like her, but I don't want any other parents than the two I have. Biology is biology. It doesn't necessarily make someone family."

Maggie considered Dylan's words. "Do you wish you'd known him?"

"My father?" Dylan asked. Maggie nodded. Dylan smiled. "I did—sort of. And, I feel like I do. Alex has told me so many stories, and so have Alexandra and Steph. But..."

"But what?"

"My Aunt Jane talked to me not long after Mom sat me down to tell me who my dad really was. She told me that my father was happy for Mom and Alex; happy that they had found each other. To tell you the truth, I think he and Mom had more than me in common."

"Like what?"

"I'm pretty sure he was in love with Alex—like for a long time."

"Mrs. Merrow told you that?"

"Nah. Aunt Jane wouldn't tell me that. Like I said, some things you can see if you don't look so hard."

"You know that doesn't make sense, right?" Maggie joked.

Dylan shrugged. "Yeah, it does. It's like you asking me all these questions; thinking they're my questions," he said. "I don't really think about any of this. Everybody else worries about it more."

"I guess it's just hard for me to understand."

Dylan laughed. "I'm not sure you need to understand. I sort of feel like Mom—well, like we were just waiting for Alex. I just know once she came, everything changed."

"Yeah, I would bet finding out your mom was gay was a shock."

Dylan laughed raucously. "Sorry. I was six. I didn't even think about it until Mom and Alex explained it."

"Really?"

"Think Kenzie's brain," he tried to explain. "On second thought, don't," he joked. Dylan grew quiet for a moment. He smiled and looked back at his girlfriend. "Mom laughed with Alex. She still laughs with Alex. Alex was there. I mean, it never mattered. No matter how much work she had or even when Kenzie came; Alex was always there. Every soccer game, anything that mattered she has been there. If she was away? She'd call. I don't ever remember it being different."

"You're worried what she'll say about the academy," Maggie observed.

"I don't ever want to disappoint her," Dylan replied honestly. "She's never disappointed me."

Cassidy closed her eyes and bit her lip gently. She wiped away a tear as it fell over her cheek. "Oh, Dylan," she whispered. "If only you knew how impossible that would be."

"Mr. and Mrs. Peters," Dave Siminski greeted the couple. "This is Alex Toles," he explained. "She's been assisting me with your daughter's case."

Don Peters extended his hand and offered the pair a seat. He took a deep breath and looked Siminski in the eye. "Tell us."

Siminski squared his shoulders. "I'm sorry," he began. "A girl matching Kaylee's description was found earlier today in New York."

"Was it her?"

"Yes, Sir, I believe so. But, we will need you to make the final identification. I will be happy to escort you," he said.

Jan Peters erupted in a wave of uncontrollable sobs and fell into her husband's embrace.

"Do you know?" Don Peters asked. "Do you know…"

Alex sensed Siminski's hesitation. She had developed a belief that honesty was the best policy when dealing with a victim's family. She stepped in.

"I think that some of your questions will be best answered by the medical examiner," she said as gently as she could. "Kaylee's injuries were extensive."

There was no way to soften the blow. Alex hated it, but there were no words, no tone of voice, and no tactic that could ever make the horrific news that a child had been brutally murdered more palatable—none. She watched as Jan Peters trembled in front of her. The anguish and fury in Don Peters' eyes made her stomach churn. She'd occupied this seat numerous times in the past. One major thing had differed then—Alex had not been a parent. Pain that she had once thought she understood took on new meaning for her. She struggled to remain the investigator in the chair; her parental protectiveness reared its head as Don Peters held her gaze firmly.

"Who would do this?" Jan Peters cried helplessly.

Siminski closed his eyes momentarily. He would never get used to this. "I think that you should know," he said. "The FBI will be running point on this investigation. We will, of course, assist and cooperate in every way that we can, as will your local police department."

"The FBI?" Don Peters questioned.

"Kaylee went missing here," Alex began. "She was found in New York. Any time a crime is committed that crosses state lines it becomes federal jurisdiction."

Don Peters nodded. "That's why you're here," he looked directly at Alex.

"Me?"

"It's what you do; right?" Peters asked. "I remember…"

Alex nodded. She sometimes forgot how much she and Cassidy had been in the spotlight in the past. "I'm not an agent any longer, Mr. Peters. I work with the state police now."

"But, you'll find him? Whoever…"

"We will do our best," Siminski interjected.

Alex felt her stomach roiling.

Jan Peters looked at Alex. "You have children?"

"Four," Alex said, offering the woman a smile.

"Then you understand," Jan Peters said.

Alex stood and nodded. "I'm sorry for your loss," she said earnestly. God damned empty words.

"Are you up to making the ride?" Siminski asked the couple.

Don Peters nodded.

"Will you accompany us?" Jan Peters looked to Alex.

Alex found it impossible to refuse and nodded. *This day sucks.*

CHAPTER FOUR

By the time Alex had arrived home, Cassidy had already gone to bed. Alex made her usual rounds, checking on Mackenzie and the twins. She'd found Connor sleeping in Dylan's bed and laughed. He loved his big brother. She let him be. Dylan wouldn't mind; she was sure of that much.

Once she felt comfortable that everyone was safe and sound, Alex made her way to the kitchen. She hadn't eaten since morning. The truth was, she didn't have any appetite. Nothing she did to distract herself seemed to succeed in banishing the images of Kaylee Peters. Little about the case set well with Alex. She kept trying to convince herself that it wasn't her problem; it wasn't her case. An eerie feeling had come over her that she couldn't shake. It was a sensation she had not experienced in quite a few years. Darkness—that is what Alex labeled the feeling coursing through her. It was cold—colder than death. It chilled the blood in a person's veins and left a hollow feeling in a person's gut. Emptiness—a void—that is what Alex felt. It sent a shiver down her spine.

Alex massaged her temples and went to open the refrigerator. She smiled at the note she found awaiting her arrival that was pinned to the door by a magnet. She gently tugged on the piece of paper and unconsciously traced the image on the magnet with her hand. "Speed," she muttered. She gazed at the picture affectionately. How old was that magnet? Alex laughed. Dylan was eight in the picture. His face was lit by a bright smile, one missing tooth in the front as he proudly held his soccer trophy. How on earth had nine years passed; Alex wondered? Seventeen—Dylan had just turned seventeen two weeks earlier. Kaylee Peters was seventeen. Alex sighed heavily and looked back at the note in her hand.

Hi Love,

It sounds like you had quite the day from your message. Please eat something. There is leftover lasagna in the fridge. There's also some pizza that Dylan had ordered. Eat some. Please. Dylan went to Maggie's to study. I imagine he will be home after you. Wake me up when you come to bed.

Je 't'aime,

Cass

Alex smiled. Cassidy knew exactly where Alex would head when she got home, and she also knew what Alex would avoid. "If I don't at least eat a piece of that pizza, she'll ground me," Alex chuckled. She grabbed a can of Diet Coke and opened the lid of the pizza box to retrieve a piece of pizza. Her thoughts immediately traveled back to Kaylee Peters. "How the hell did you land in New York?" Alex mused aloud. She took a bite of the pizza and washed it down with a swig of Diet Coke.

Rest was not going to come soon for Alex and she knew it. Time to pour over the statements Kaylee's friends had given again. She made her way into the living room where she had dropped her bag and flopped onto the sofa. She set down her food and opened her bag, spreading out several files in front of her. Alex opened the first folder and met with the image of a smiling seventeen-year-old girl.

"Son of a bitch," she muttered. She bent down to grab another file from her bag and caught a glimpse of the family photo album Cassidy kept under the table. Alex picked it up and placed it in her lap, opening the cover with a smile. She shook her head as her eyes studied the photos of Cassidy and Dylan when he was a baby. "So, beautiful," Alex commented as her fingertip traced a picture of Cassidy holding Dylan.

Alex took a sip from the Diet Coke beside her and sighed. Her eyes strayed for a moment to Kaylee's picture. "Fuck." She threw her head back and closed her eyes, her fingers reaching for the bridge of her nose.

"Alex?" Dylan stepped into the room.

Alex's mind was spinning with images of her family that inevitably morphed into Kaylee Peters. How could she walk away from this case? Alex silently argued with her conscience. How could she walk into it at all? She'd made her choice; made a promise to Cassidy—to herself. Kaylee could have been Dylan. Dylan could have been Kaylee.

"Dammit," Alex continued her inner battle.

"Alex?" Dylan called a bit louder. He observed Alex as her temple twitched in thought. He wondered what she was concentrating on so intently that she failed to hear him calling to her. "Alex," he tried one more time. Alex sighed, lost to her private battle. "Mom!" Dylan finally called loudly.

Alex's eyes flew open and met with Dylan's. "Dylan?"

Dylan smiled. "Sorry. You were deep in thought, I guess."

Alex nodded. "Did you just get home?"

"Yeah."

Alex regarded Dylan silently for a moment. He had grown into a handsome young man, one that looked slightly down on her despite her considerable height. He was poised and carried himself with a quiet confidence much as Cassidy did. Right now, Alex saw shadows of the six-year-old boy she had met ten years ago. Dylan was looking at his feet, shifting his weight from side to side.

"What's up?" Alex asked.

Dylan looked up and shrugged. He nodded to the photo album in Alex's lap. "Does it bother you that much?" he asked.

Alex was confused. "Does what bother me?"

"Me wanting to go into the Navy," he said.

Alex let out a long sigh. Dammit, Toles, he thinks you're upset about this trip to the academy. Alex waved him over and patted the cushion next to her. "I think we need to talk," she said.

Dylan nodded sadly.

Alex smiled and flipped the pages back in the photo album. "See this?" she pointed to a photo.

Dylan nodded again. “That’s my seventh birthday party.”

“Yeah.”

“We had just moved in here.”

“Yeah,” Alex confirmed. “And, you were obsessed with the tree out in the front yard.”

Dylan laughed. “And the pool table downstairs,” he recalled.

“And that,” she chuckled. Alex felt herself becoming emotional. She had remained reserved in her dialogue whenever Dylan mentioned entering the military. It wasn’t because she disapproved. It was simply her protective nature. She flipped the page in the album, considering how the conversation should progress.

“You’re disappointed in me,” Dylan said.

Alex startled. She turned to Dylan and grabbed his arm tenderly. “Disappointed in you? Dylan, is that what you think?”

“I don’t know. I know that you and Mom would rather I go to a university somewhere—like Mom did.”

Alex pinched the bridge of her nose and groaned. “I’m sorry, Speed.”

“Huh?”

Alex shook her head. “That’s not true at all,” she said. “I just know what can come with enlisting,” she continued. “I know where it can lead, and I know what you might see. I don’t want you to see that,” she said honestly.

Dylan nodded. “You saw a lot.”

“I did. More than I ever wanted to—far more than I ever hope you have to.”

“Do you wish you hadn’t done it?” he asked.

Alex sighed heavily. “You mean, do I wish I’d never gone into the army?” she asked. He nodded. Alex shook her head. “No. I wouldn’t change it.”

“Even with everything that happened?”

“Even with that. I wouldn’t have you or your mom, or your

brother and sisters," Alex smiled. "I know you want to fly, Speed. I know it's in your blood—wanting to fly, service—all of it. Your father…"

Dylan shook his head. "Maybe. Who knows? Do you know what I think of when I think about him?"

"Your father?"

"Yeah."

"No, I don't," Alex confessed.

"You," Dylan said. Alex was perplexed. "Somehow, whenever I start thinking about him, I always end up thinking about you."

"Dylan, I…"

"No, Alex… Mom," Dylan changed midsentence. Alex's eyes welled up with tears. "I'd like to think he'd be proud of me."

"He would be," Alex assured her son.

"But he isn't you," Dylan said. "Maybe I should care more what he would think, but I don't give it much thought."

Alex listened quietly. Somehow, she understood that there was more Dylan needed to say—more he wanted to say.

"I remember the day you came home from seeing him the last time," Dylan told her.

Alex closed her eyes as her chest tightened at the memory. The day he died.

"I'd never seen you look sad. You looked so sad," Dylan said.

Alex nodded. "He was my best friend, Dylan. In many ways, he was my best friend."

"I know," Dylan replied. "Then what I remember most was seeing you standing in the doorway in your uniform."

"That's the first time you saw me in uniform."

Dylan nodded. "I think I sort of knew ever since then."

"Knew what?"

"That I would follow you in my own way."

"Dylan…"

Dylan shook his head. "I don't want to work for the FBI," he chuckled. "I don't really want to think about serial killers and criminals," he said. "I want to fly. I've always wanted to fly."

"I know."

"Yeah, and I want to serve—like you."

Alex released her breath slowly. "There are a million ways to serve," she said. "Not every way requires a uniform."

"Maybe. I just know that this is what I am meant to do."

Alex smiled. "Then that's what you have to do," she told him.

"You won't be disappointed?"

Alex looked at Dylan proudly. "Dylan," Alex took a deep breath. "You know, I've always admired you."

"Me?" Surprise lighted Dylan's face.

"You are so much like your mother—kind, patient, thoughtful, intelligent—more than that; you're strong and resilient. You were that way at six-years-old," she chuckled. "I haven't said this in a long time to you," she began.

"What?"

"Remember when I asked you if I could marry your mom?"

Dylan chuckled. "Yeah, you were so nervous, you stuttered."

Alex laughed. "Thanks for reminding me," she winked. "I think about that night a lot."

"Really?" Dylan asked.

"Yeah. You might not remember how sick you were that day."

"Yeah, I do. I don't think broken bones compare to that ear infection," Dylan shuddered.

"That was the first time you were sick. I mean, the first time for me." Alex explained. "I remember thinking there had to be some way I could make it go away for you."

Dylan listened as Alex continued. Her eyes strayed from his—a weak attempt to conceal her burgeoning emotion. He'd always been close to Alex. From the moment, he had walked into the kitchen to see the tall agent standing with his mother, Dylan had felt safe in her presence. He wondered where her thoughts were traveling. He'd always known how to talk to his mother. He could tell Cassidy anything. Alex? Dylan wanted to impress Alex, not because she required it, because she was his hero. He doubted that would ever change.

Alex steadied her breathing. Why do they have to grow up? She let her eyes track back to Dylan's. "I couldn't do anything to stop it," Alex said. "All I could do was be there for you," she recalled. "Your mom reminds me of that all the time," she chuckled. Dylan smiled. "I guess what I am trying to say is that I don't want to see you hurt. I know you're seventeen. I know someday you'll be forty-seven. The truth is, Dylan it won't matter how old you get. To me, you are still that little boy rubbing his ear, standing at the side of the bed asking me to make it better somehow. You might not ever understand this, but you're my son. I told you a long time ago that I never thought I would have a son. I didn't. I didn't think I'd ever have kids—a family. I didn't even think I wanted one."

"For someone who didn't want kids, you sure hit the mother lode," Dylan laughed.

Alex chuckled. "That's one way to put it," she agreed. "The thing is, you never stop wanting to protect your kids, Dylan—not ever."

"I get it. But something bad could happen no matter what I do."

Alex nodded. She smiled again affectionately. So much like your mother. "True," she conceded. "Also, true that I will support whatever you want to pursue. I wouldn't be any prouder of you if you chose a university or a military academy. Just like if you wanted to be an actor or a playwright—if you wanted to be a mechanic or a pilot; I would love you just as much," Alex said. "You're right. What I hit was the jackpot. No one could ask for a better son, Dylan."

Dylan pushed back his tears, even as a few trailed over Alex's cheek. He nodded and closed his eyes for a moment.

Alex moved to embrace him. "Too old for a hug?" she asked. Dylan shook his head. Alex took him into her embrace. "I love you,

Speed."

"I love you too, Mom."

"Good evening, sir," the security guard greeted a well-dressed man as he left the building.

"Brandon. Nice night."

"Finished for the evening?" Brandon asked.

"I am," the reply came.

"Off again or will we see you tomorrow?"

"I'll be back on Monday," the man replied.

"No rest for the weary."

"None at all," the man agreed with a smile. He made his way to the white van parked a few feet away, turned and waved to the security guard. "See you next week, Brandon."

"Not me, I'm afraid. Another job next week."

The van started and the man gripped the wheel tightly. "No rest for the weary," he said. He turned to look at the long silver box in the back of the van. "No rest at all."

Cassidy rolled over the minute she heard Alex close the bedroom door.

"You're awake," Alex commented.

"So, it would seem. You okay?"

Alex flopped onto the bed beside her wife. "I don't know."

"Want to talk about it?"

"I don't know," Alex chuckled. "Dylan thinks he's disappointing me."

Cassidy nodded. "Did he tell you that?"

"Yeah."

"And?"

"I told him that he couldn't disappoint me. Shit. Cass, I can't believe he would think that."

"You're his hero. What you think about what he does means more to him than what anyone else has to say."

Alex sighed. "I don't know why."

"Yes, you do," Cassidy disagreed. "You two have had a special bond from the day you met."

"I love him so much, Cassidy," Alex said as she looked to the ceiling. "I just want him to be safe."

"I know that, love. He knows that too. He just needed to hear you say it."

Alex looked at Cassidy. She shook her head sadly. "I want you all to be safe."

"What happened today?"

Alex grimaced.

"I know it was bad. I don't need the details. What happened with you?"

"I don't know," Alex admitted. "They found her in the woods, just thrown in a pile of leaves. Jesus, Cass… He restrained her. He stabbed her so many times that the," Alex shook her head. She would spare Cassidy the gory details. "Crazy? Maybe he is. Evil? If there is such a thing, this is it. I don't know what to think. She was seventeen, Cass. Just a kid like Dylan. I sat there with Dave when he told her parents—her mother's eyes…"

Cassidy reached over and took Alex's hand.

"What the hell can you say?" Alex asked rhetorically. "I've sat in that seat dozens of times—telling a family that their loved one is gone—murdered. Today…"

"I'm sorry, Alex."

"The FBI is taking over."

"So, you won't be involved at all?"

Alex took a deep breath and blew it out slowly.

"Alex?"

"Hawk was in town."

"Here?"

"No. She was in the New York bureau office this morning."

"Huh."

"She wants me to come back," Alex looked back at the ceiling.

"Excuse me?"

"To the bureau."

"She wants you to go back to the FBI?" Cassidy sought clarification.

Alex nodded. "And, take this case under AD Bower."

"Are you going to do it?" Cassidy asked.

"No."

"Why not?"

Alex turned back to face her wife.

"Well?" Cassidy urged Alex to answer.

"I… Cass… This case… I… I haven't been in the field for a long time."

"So?"

"What do you mean—so?"

"Do you want to go back?"

Alex closed her eyes. "I can't get her face out of my head."

Cassidy squeezed Alex's hand. "Then you have your answer."

"I can't go back, Cass."

"Alex, it's who you are," Cassidy said.

Alex shook her head. "No. It's what I do. It's what I did."

Cassidy nodded. She watched as Alex's fingertips pinched the bridge of her nose. Cassidy reached over and gently removed Alex's hand. "Alex, all of us are made for something, some purpose in this life."

"Maybe that's true," Alex agreed.

Cassidy smiled at Alex, noting the battle raging within her wife. She waited patiently for Alex to continue.

“Mine is you,” Alex told Cassidy. “It's always been loving you.”

Cassidy closed her eyes, the truth in Alex's words washed over her in a warm rush. She breathed in the emotion that coursed between them and opened her eyes again. “I know that,” she confessed. “Just as loving you is what I was always meant to do,” Cassidy said. “It's loving you that gives me the strength and the courage to be all the other things I was meant to be. To be the mother I am, to teach what's inside me—to make the difference I can make. Loving you, Alex, for all its ups and downs, it's the centerpiece that anchors everything else. But, it isn't the sum-total of my purpose. Loving me is not the sum-total of yours either.”

Alex huffed in frustration. Cassidy had always possessed a powerful command of words. Alex admired that, but at times it could frustrate her. She struggled to express the competing thoughts and emotions that collided inside her.

“Alex,” Cassidy called softly.

“What if it had been you, Cass? Or Mackenzie or Abby?”

Cassidy had anticipated the wall that held Alex back. “What if it was?” She threw the question back to Alex. Alex was stunned. Cassidy nodded and continued. "Wouldn't you want to know—need to know who had done that to me? Wouldn't you want that person found so that they could never do that again?”

“Maybe,” Alex said. "There are lots of people who can do that. I teach them how. That's how I make a difference now."

“Because that's what you feel called to do or because you think it's a way to continue while keeping us safe?” Cassidy challenged.

“We’ve been having this argument for almost five years!” Alex’s temper flared and she jumped to her feet.

Cassidy remained calm. “It's not an argument, Alex. It's a simple question that you insist on circling. Maybe you've finally come to a point where the circle has broken.”

“What the hell does that mean?”

Cassidy sighed heavily. “It means that you have to make a choice.”

“I made my choice.”

“You did. Choices change, Alex. Life isn't static. You know that. Things get thrown into our path for a reason. When they do, we each need to decide what to do about them. Isn't that what you told me once about Dylan?”

“That's not the same thing and you know it.”

“Of course, it is,” Cassidy disagreed. “I slept with someone other than my husband. That misstep gave me one of the greatest treasures in my life. I made the decision to pretend that Christopher was his father. Dylan spent the better part of fifteen years believing he was someone else.”

Alex groaned. “You made the only decision you could at the time. We made the only decision we could...”

“No. There are always choices, Alex. I made the decision I felt I should. We made a choice to tell him when he was older because we believed it was best. It was not the only choice we could have made.”

“It was the best choice. And, it all worked out.”

Cassidy lifted her brow and smiled.

“Oh, don't think I don't know what you just did,” Alex said. Cassidy shrugged. “Cass—Just my being in the fray again could put you back at risk.”

“We're always at risk,” Cassidy said pointedly. Alex grimaced as Cassidy continued. “Look at that young girl. What did her parents do? What did she do that put her at any greater risk than me or you or anyone we know?” Cassidy challenged Alex.

“That's not what I'm talking about and you know it.”

“Maybe not, but it's the truth. Alex, when I was sitting in that chair in New Rochelle and Carl Fisher had that knife to me,” Cassidy began to recall her abduction.

“Cassidy—don’t.”

Alex was in no frame of mind to revisit the horrors of the past. The case that had brought her into Cassidy's life had nearly taken Cassidy from her. She vividly recalled learning that Cassidy was being held against her will. Seeing Kaylee Peters' wrists had instantly conjured memories of the angry red circles that had once twisted around Cassidy's. Alex had found her thoughts drifting to memories of the knife mark on Cassidy's thigh, and the fear in her lover's eyes that Carl Fisher had left as evidence of his transgression. It made Alex sick.

"You need to hear this," Cassidy said flatly. "I thought for a moment that I was going to die—just for a moment. Then? Then I thought of you. I knew if I could just hold out, just be smarter than he was for a little while, you would get to me. I knew you'd figure it out. I knew."

"You have too much faith in me," Alex said.

"No, but I do have every faith in you."

Alex sat back on the bed with a thud. "I'm not sure I have it in me anymore."

Cassidy took Alex's hands. "You do or we wouldn't be having this conversation."

"Cass, I need to be here for you. Who knows where this case will lead?"

Cassidy kissed Alex's lips. "The only way you will know is to follow."

"What about you? This pregnancy… I…"

"You worry too much, love. We will all be okay, and we will be right here for you—all of us, even this little one. I promise."

"And, if I decide not to follow?"

"We'll still be here."

"I don't know what to do."

"Yes, I think you do," Cassidy replied, pulling Alex into her arms. "Just stop thinking and let it come to you."

"I don't want to lose you."

"Alex, we've been to hell and back again. I would do it all over without a second's hesitation. We have a basketball team here to manage. It might be short of your original plan, but I still need a coach."

Alex chuckled. "Or a butler."

"That too, Alfred. One more kid always equals a dozen more dishes and a lot more boxes of cereal for some reason."

Alex snickered.

Cassidy looked down at Alex and wrinkled her nose. "Alex?"

"Hum?"

"Why does Connor think you like blue corn flakes?" she asked. Alex coughed a bit. "Alex?"

Alex started laughing. "I never called them blue," she said.

Cassidy looked at her curiously. "Why do Connor and Abby think that?" she repeated her question. Cassidy noted the sheepish grin on her wife's face. "I don't want to know. I know I don't, but tell me anyway."

Alex shrugged. "I never said they were blue. I said they taste like poo."

"What? You used to have Corn Flakes almost every morning."

"No, only when Dylan insisted."

Cassidy's gaze narrowed suspiciously. "Alex," she drew out the name slowly.

"What?"

Cassidy lifted her brow. "Just how did you get Dylan to eat that cereal?"

Alex suddenly found the ceiling of great interest.

"Alex?"

"Okay, so maybe I put a little sugar on them."

Cassidy shook her head. "Is that right?"

"Well, they taste like poo! Who wants to eat a bowl of poo with milk?"

"Is this still your preferred method of getting our children to eat breakfast?"

Alex shook her head. "Not anymore."

"Really?"

"No way. Kenzie full of sugar?"

"And, here I thought I was deficient all these years."

"You do use too much milk. Slightly crunchy with sugar—trust me."

Cassidy rolled her eyes.

"Am I in trouble?" Alex asked.

Cassidy's eyes twinkled. "Maybe you need a time-out," she offered suggestively.

"Oh?"

"Mm." Cassidy moved to straddle Alex's hips.

Alex closed her eyes when Cassidy's lips began a tender assault down her neck. "Cass?"

"Settle down, Agent Toles."

"You just want me to go back to the FBI so you can call me that again," Alex remarked.

Cassidy's hands were methodically mapping out the curves of Alex's body. "Makes me think of the day you showed up at my door," she whispered in Alex's ear.

Alex sucked in a ragged breath. "I remember. You had Playdoh on your foot."

"Yes, I did."

"Blue, in fact," Alex commented playfully.

"Mm-hum," Cassidy said. She placed her lips on Alex's and kissed her gently.

Alex sighed into their kiss. Her hands traveled softly over Cassidy's back, drawing Cassidy closer. She smiled at Cassidy when Cassidy broke their kiss, and shook her head.

"What?" Cassidy asked.

"I love you so much, Cass."

Cassidy kissed Alex's forehead. "I love you too."

"It's funny; I think somehow I knew the moment you opened that door and peeled that Playdoh off your foot."

"Knew what?" Cassidy asked.

"Sounds crazy."

"What?"

"I think I fell in love with you at that moment."

Cassidy stroked Alex's cheek. "You are such a romantic."

"No. It's just…."

"What is it?" Cassidy asked, seeing a myriad of emotions play across Alex's face.

"I'll never get used to it," Alex said. "I mean it. I will never get used to this. I still can't believe it some days."

Cassidy smiled. "I hope that's a good thing."

Alex cupped Cassidy's face in her hands. "The best thing. You are the best thing that ever happened to me, Cassidy."

Cassidy's reply came in the form of a reverent kiss. "Let me love you, Alex," she said.

Alex closed her eyes and let herself begin to fall away under Cassidy's tender caress. Cassidy's lips softly danced over Alex's throat and back up to claim Alex's lips with a searing kiss. Alex's hands held onto Cassidy's hips, pulling her closer.

"Cass…"

Cassidy pressed two fingers to Alex's lips. Her eyes twinkled with affection and admiration as she touched her lips to Alex's sweetly. "Always thinking." Cassidy smiled and slipped her hand under Alex's shirt and tugged it free. She bit her lower lip to quell the moan she felt building in her throat. The feel of Alex's skin instantly sent her soaring. Her hand glided lovingly over Alex's abdomen and up to her chest. She cupped Alex's breast through the bra Alex wore, raised an eyebrow at her wife, and sat back on her knees.

Alex stopped herself from chuckling. Cassidy was issuing her a silent order. She took the opportunity to sit up and remove her shirt.

Cassidy gazed at her appreciatively, and raised her brow in challenge again. Alex held Cassidy's gaze firmly as she released the clasp of her bra and tossed it aside. This was a dance that had never become familiar. Each time Cassidy touched Alex, every time Alex made love to Cassidy, it felt like a new beginning for them both. Making love had never been about seeking momentary satisfaction between them. It had always served as an expression of love, desire, and commitment to the life they sought to build and share.

Cassidy pushed Alex back on the bed and hovered above her. She kissed Alex's forehead gently, then her nose, then her lips, so softly that Alex barely felt the connection. Yet, when Cassidy pulled away, Alex felt the loss acutely.

Cassidy's lips and tongue began a graceful dance over Alex's flesh, down her throat to her cleavage. She glanced up at Alex before tasting a straining nipple. Cassidy held Alex's gaze as her lips descended steadily lower. She unbuttoned Alex's pants and pulled them off steadily, her kisses leaving a trail over Alex's legs until Alex was free. She kissed her way back to Alex's stomach, over her breasts, and claimed Alex's lips once again with hers.

Alex's hands worked to free Cassidy of the tank top she was wearing. Cassidy decided to help her wife. She sat back and removed the top and tossed it to the floor. "So, beautiful," Alex spoke the words reverently.

Cassidy smiled at Alex and gently pushed her back. Captivated—Cassidy had always been captivated by Alex. The surge of emotion that coursed through her required nothing more than Alex's presence. She seldom stopped to consider the reality. Cassidy accepted their connection as part of the life she shared with Alex. Still, Alex's ability to stir passion within Cassidy continued to astound her. Every time Cassidy made love with Alex, she felt a sense of gratefulness, and a need to convey the place Alex held in her life.

Alex reached out and caressed Cassidy's cheek. Cassidy leaned into the touch, reveling in the simple gesture. She lowered her lips back to Alex's and spoke softly. "Just feel me, Alex," she requested. She heard Alex's sharp intake of breath and kissed her tenderly. "No thinking," Cassidy whispered in Alex's ears. "Just feel me," she repeated her request.

Alex closed her eyes. Cassidy understood her like no one else ever had or could ever hope to. Only Cassidy had the power to quell Alex's spinning thoughts and competing emotions. Cassidy centered Alex, created both escape and focus in Alex's life. Love possessed many contradictions. Alex had learned that contradiction did not need to equate to confusion. At times, opposite ideas and opposing realities could collide in unexpected ways, even fuse together. Love was the catalyst at those moments. Cassidy had always been able to lift Alex away from the swirling of her thoughts. Alex understood that quieting her questions, and carrying her away was what Cassidy intended to do now; knowing that when Alex eventually fell into her, all the whirling and wondering would slow. When she landed back in Cassidy's arms, Alex would see the picture before her clearly.

Cassidy watched Alex close her eyes as she began to let herself go. Cassidy's fingertips lovingly caressed Alex's skin, slowly spiraling down Alex's body, memorizing each sensation as they wandered over every inch of Alex's skin. She placed her lips against Alex's again and whispered one last time. "I love you," she reminded Alex.

Alex's mind stilled in an instant. Cassidy's kiss began tentatively; tenderly reminding Alex of their connection. Alex felt Cassidy's hand drifting toward her breast and she deepened their kiss.

Cassidy responded to Alex's urgency gently. She cupped Alex's breast and enjoyed the moan she felt reverberate through her body when Alex responded.

"Cass," Alex pleaded with her wife when Cassidy pulled away from their kiss.

Cassidy's lips traversed Alex's shoulders, and meandered across her chest. She kissed a circle around Alex's breasts, teasing her until Alex's hips arched in a silent plea. Cassidy answered the request with a faint kiss across Alex's nipples. Alex groaned in frustration.

"Easy," Cassidy said. She sucked gently at first, feeling Alex's hands reach out for her, and grip her back firmly.

Alex marveled at Cassidy's touch. It often became insistent, almost demanding, but it never ceased to be sensual and loving. She pulled Cassidy closer to her, needing to feel connected. Cassidy's hands kneaded the muscles on Alex's abdomen as her mouth left its prize and descended lower. Anticipation consumed Alex. Cassidy's descent came in a painfully slow exploration that covered every inch of Alex's body, lingering whenever Alex's breath would hitch in response. Cassidy glanced up at Alex's face. Alex's eyes had closed and her head was back. Intoxicating—watching Alex, feeling Alex was intoxicating. The way strength and softness existed simultaneously in Alex's movements and expressions aroused Cassidy unlike anything else ever had. She marveled at the woman beneath her. Alex possessed the gentlest soul of anyone Cassidy had ever known. Most people saw Alex's power. They admired her intellect and her determination. Cassidy cherished all those parts of her wife. She'd felt their presence in Alex's touch, in Alex's words, and in Alex's kiss. But, more than anything it had always been the underlying tenderness that Alex often tried to disguise that drew Cassidy to her.

Cassidy reached for Alex's hands. They would serve as Alex's tether when Cassidy carried her away.

Alex called out for her when Cassidy's kisses reached their intended destination.

"Cass…"

Cassidy lost herself in Alex; in the way Alex's hips moved, the sound of Alex's desperate sighs, and occasional pleas for release. She teased Alex mercilessly, wanting Alex to fall away from reality and into her.

"Cass, please," Alex begged.

Cassidy answered Alex's request and brought Alex over the edge of sanity, carrying her along until she fell in ecstasy, calling out for Cassidy.

Alex gripped Cassidy's hands as her body disobeyed any command she might issue, responding only to Cassidy's will. Cassidy refused to let her crash. She carried Alex higher until Alex thought she would drown in a sea of pleasure and emotion.

Cassidy gentled her touch until slowly she felt Alex's shuddering give way to faint quivering. She crawled back up Alex's body and kissed her lovingly.

Alex's hand began to wander over Cassidy's hip, and Cassidy stilled its movement.

"Cass…"

"Shh," Cassidy placed a sweet kiss on Alex's lips. "I just wanted to love you."

Alex looked at Cassidy in amazement.

"What?" Cassidy wondered.

"I don't know what I would do without you," Alex confessed.

"I'm not going anywhere, love."

"I'm serious," Alex said.

Cassidy smiled. "I know. So am I." She laid back beside Alex, and enjoyed the warmth of Alex's embrace.

Alex sighed. "How did you know?"

"What?" Cassidy asked.

"That I feel like I need to go back."

Cassidy smiled and pulled herself up to look in Alex's eyes. "I know you."

"I never thought…"

"I know," Cassidy put Alex's thought to rest. "I've always expected this day would come."

"I hoped it never would."

"You can't run from what you are called to do," Cassidy said. "I would never want you to. Neither would the kids."

"I hope so."

"I know so," Cassidy replied. She kissed Alex and stroked her cheek. "I fell in love with all of you, Alex, not just the easy parts."

Alex nodded. "I want you to promise me something."

"If I can."

"If you need me," Alex said. "I mean for anything; if this gets to be too much, you tell me."

"Stop worrying."

"I mean it, Cass."

Cassidy sighed. "I promise."

"Good."

"Will you do me a favor?" Cassidy asked.

"Anything."

"Don't tell this one that I use too much milk."

Alex laughed. "Anything for you, Cass."

CHAPTER FIVE

"Are you taking me?" Mackenzie asked Alex.

"No, Mom is taking you to school this morning."

"Why?"

Alex took a deep breath. "Because I have to work."

"You always work."

"Kenzie…"

"Mackenzie," Cassidy's voice called for her daughter's attention. "Let your mother breathe, please."

Mackenzie grumbled and started to stomp away.

"I know you aren't stomping down that hallway," Cassidy called after her.

Alex shook her head. "Cass, I can…"

"No," Cassidy held up her hand. "No, Alex. She'll be fine."

"I've always taken her."

"Yes, well, now she will have to suffer my driving or take the bus like Dylan did."

Alex chuckled. Cassidy loved their children, but she was no pushover. Alex had to admit, Mackenzie could test the patience of a saint at times. She was about to offer to talk to their daughter when her phone rang. Cassidy offered Alex a wink and kissed her on the cheek.

"I'll take care of it," Cassidy assured Alex.

Alex looked at the phone and sucked in a deep breath. "Hawk."

"Morning, Alex or can I call you Agent Toles?"

Alex was tempted to answer, "bite me." Hawk would have had an immediate comeback for that. "That depends. When do I get paid and how much?" Alex replied.

Hawk laughed. "When everyone else does and the same shitty wage you'd expect."

"Great."

"You're welcome," Hawk said.

"So? What's next?" Alex asked.

"I'm glad you asked. AD Bower asked about assigning you a partner. I told him you deserved the best. I expect your ride should be there any minute."

"My ride?" Alex asked.

"Right; your ride. I imagine your new partner is a few blocks away."

"Why does everyone assume that they can just show up at my house?" Alex asked.

Hawk chuckled. "You are so predictable sometimes."

"Cute, Hawk."

"Just do me a favor?"

"What?" Alex asked.

"Give this a chance."

Alex groaned. "I'll do my best, Assistant Director."

"Hey, you could've had this job a long time ago."

"No, thanks," Alex said. She heard a car pull in the driveway and Mackenzie scream for Cassidy.

"Mom! Someone's here!"

Cassidy made her way to the door and opened it. She grinned from ear to ear when she saw a familiar face emerge from the black sedan in the driveway. "What on earth are you doing here?" Cassidy stepped outside and pulled the woman into a hug.

"Hi, Cass."

"Hi, Cass? I didn't know you were coming. Why didn't you call?"

Alex trotted down the stairs, following Cassidy's excited voice.

"I guess your chariot has arrived," Hawk said.

"I don't think so," Alex replied as her feet hit the bottom stair. "Sounds like it's a friend of Cassidy's."

Alex stepped into the front door and stopped cold. "You have got to be shitting me," she muttered.

"Agent Toles." Claire Brackett broke from Cassidy's embrace

and ambled toward Alex. "Are you wearing that?" Claire looked at Alex incredulously.

"What's wrong with what I'm wearing?" Alex pointed to Brackett's partially unbuttoned blouse. "Button that shit up."

"Why? Do you find it distracting?" Claire grinned.

Cassidy rolled her eyes and made her way toward the pair. Some things never change.

Alex held up a finger and turned her back to Brackett. She lifted her phone back to her ear. "Brackett? You sent Brackett here?" she asked Hawk.

"She is the best we have," Hawk replied.

Alex lowered her voice. "This is not over."

"Have a good day, Agent," Hawk said cheerfully and disconnected the call.

Alex looked at the phone in disbelief. She pinched the bridge of her nose forcefully, and took a deep breath before pivoting back to the woman behind her. "Okay, joke's over," Alex said.

Claire stared at Alex for a moment and then offered a sickly, sweet smile. "You mean, you're not my chauffer for the day?"

Alex took a deep breath.

"Claire!" Mackenzie's voice rang out.

"Great," Alex muttered. Cassidy made her way to Alex's side.

"Hey, kid," Claire greeted Mackenzie.

Dylan appeared behind Alex and smiled. "Hi, Claire," he waved.

"Hey, Dylan."

Alex grumbled something unintelligible and Cassidy giggled. "It's not that bad," Cassidy whispered in Alex's ear.

"It's Brackett," Alex whispered back.

Cassidy kissed Alex on the cheek and patted her chest lightly. "Well, look at it this way, you've always said that she needs direction."

"I didn't mean…"

Cassidy winked. "I have every faith in you."

"Great."

Cassidy turned back to Claire. "Are you two going to be here for a while?"

Claire shook her head. "Sorry," she apologized to Cassidy.

"Well, I guess it's safe to say I will see you soon," Cassidy observed.

"Great," Alex mumbled again. Cassidy whacked her gently.

"I have to get Kenzie to school. Play nice," Cassidy told the pair of FBI agents.

"Bye, Claire!" Mackenzie waved.

"See ya, kid."

Alex rolled her eyes. How Claire Brackett had managed to become a family member still puzzled her. Cassidy—it had been Cassidy. Alex still wasn't sure what Cassidy saw in Claire Brackett, but the strange truth was, Cassidy loved Claire like a little sister. Stranger still, Claire worshiped the ground Cassidy walked on. It had been that way for the better part of five years. At first, Alex had tried to convince Cassidy to keep her distance from Claire. Cassidy held her ground. That did not surprise Alex. What did surprise Alex was the fact that the relationship between her wife and the younger agent was undeniably genuine. It was almost as if they had been meant to find each other. She watched as Cassidy leaned in and whispered something into Claire's ear. Claire nodded and smiled. Alex found it fascinating. Brackett's bravado virtually disappeared. Cassidy looked back at Alex. Alex didn't need any words, she understood Cassidy's silent message. Give her a chance.

Once upon a time, Claire Brackett had been determined to undermine Alex at every turn. While Cassidy had been able to forgive Claire, Alex still struggled to let go of the past. Claire had jeopardized more than an investigation; her actions and her alliances had put both Alex and Cassidy in danger. That was something that Alex had a difficult time letting go. She found herself recalling a conversation she and Cassidy once had about the younger woman's presence in their life.

"How can you trust her?" Alex asked. "Trust is earned, Cass."

"No, it isn't," Cassidy disagreed. "Don't look at me like that."

"Like what?"

"You know, like what. Trust is given until it's broken, Alex. That's the truth. We don't come into this world knowing that we should doubt people. That's something we learn through the disappointments and betrayals we face."

Alex sighed heavily. Cassidy was referring to her father. "You mean your father."

"I do. But I don't only mean my father. When you met Claire did you trust her then?"

"I suppose. She was a fellow agent."

"And, what made you stop trusting her?"

"You know that answer. She was put in the FBI to undermine me. Jesus, Cass, she was sleeping with Carl Fisher. She was traveling with O'Brien! How am I supposed to trust her?"

Cassidy smiled and took hold of Alex's hand. "Alex, Claire followed someone she wanted to trust."

"You mean her father."

"I do."

Alex huffed. Claire and Cassidy's bond oddly enough had been formed by betrayal; not by each other, by the person they each had once revered as a hero—their fathers. Cassidy's father had disappeared for more than twenty years, allowing his family to believe him dead. Claire's father had spent most of her lifetime filling her head with lies, trying to convince her that what she knew was real was only the active imagination of a child. It hadn't been Claire's imagination. She had watched her father choke the life out of her mother. That day had instilled fear and hopelessness in Claire that would manifest in dangerous ways in her adulthood.

"Alex," Cassidy began. "When you learn that everything that

has shaped who you are is a lie; you have to question who you are at all."

"You didn't."

"Yes, I did."

"No. You never changed, Cass. As much as it hurt you when your father came back; you held your ground."

"I had you," Alex said. "I had Mom. I had Dylan and Mackenzie. I had something—I had people I could trust and believe in. That's not what Claire had."

Alex sighed.

"She saved your life, Alex, not because she had to, because she cared enough to."

Alex couldn't argue with that. It was true, although part of her still questioned Claire's reasoning. "How can you let her so close after everything?"

Cassidy shrugged. "I'm not sure I can explain it to you. I just understand. Maybe I see the little girl behind all the bravado."

Alex smiled. Cassidy was the consummate mother. It was in her nature to nurture. "You really trust her?"

"I can't explain it. I do; yes. Claire is…"

"I know, she means something to you. I can see it. I just find it hard to understand."

"Maybe it isn't something that needs to be understood. Maybe it just is."

Alex nodded and kissed Cassidy's forehead. "I'll try, Cass. I promise; I will try."

Alex looked at Claire as she approached. Okay, Cass; I'll try.

"So? You ready to drive or what?" Claire asked Alex.

"Me?"

"Well, yeah. Technically, you are the newbie now," Claire goaded Alex.

"Not really."

"Fine by me either way," Claire said as she headed to the car.

Alex ran inside the door and grabbed her bag. "Oh, no," Alex said. "Give me the keys."

"And, here I thought you always liked it when I drove."

"Very funny," Alex said. "As I recall, you get a little too eager," Alex quipped.

Claire tossed Alex the keys. "Age before beauty, I guess. At least, I know we won't get stopped for speeding."

Alex pressed on her temple with her thumb and opened the car door. *I'm going to kill Hawk.*

"Where are we going?" Claire asked. "I thought we'd be headed to watch the autopsy?"

"I want to talk to Kaylee Peters' brother."

"What about the autopsy?"

"I don't expect it's going to tell us anything new; do you?"

Claire looked out the window and chuckled.

"That's funny?" Alex asked.

"No, I just never took you for one to break protocol."

"I'd ask what you did take me for, but I think we both know that answer."

Claire chuckled again. "Do you think her brother knows something?"

"I'm sure he knows lots of things."

"Ha-ha."

"I don't know," Alex admitted. "From what I understand, they spent a lot of time out in those woods together."

"And?"

"And, what? I want to know why."

Claire rolled her eyes. Alex would forever be a mystery to her. "You're driving," she commented.

"Yes, I am."

Alex paced around the room slowly, taking note of the pictures on the walls, the collectibles on the small desk, even the color of the bedding. She listened to the conversation as it unfolded between Claire and Donovan Peters. Her eyes tracked to a collage that hung over Kaylee's desk.

"How long has she been taking pictures out there?" Alex wondered aloud.

"Ever since she got her first camera," Donavon replied.

Alex's gaze remained fixed to the collage on the wall. She took a step closer, scanning it thoughtfully, committing it to memory as she went. At first glance, the pictures looked remarkably the same. One location appeared on the right side of the collage, a second on the left. Picture after picture of the same place, under each a date marked in red.

"Old rocks," Claire commented. "She had a thing for old rocks?"

Alex shot Claire a look of disgust.

Donovan took no offense to Claire's question and chuckled. He moved to stand beside Alex. "You sound like everyone else," he told Claire.

Claire shrugged. She could think of a million things more interesting to study or hang on a wall than pictures of old rocks.

Donovan pointed to the pictures on the right. "They look identical; don't they?"

"Only at first glance," Alex replied.

"That's what Kaylee would say," Donovan said. He closed his eyes and Alex put a comforting hand on his shoulder. "Sorry," he apologized.

"Don't be," Alex told him. "I'm sorry that we have to barge in here like this."

Donovan shook his head. He loved his little sister. He hadn't begun to process the reality that she was gone, and he was carrying a tremendous amount of guilt about that fact. "She shouldn't have stayed out there alone," he muttered.

Alex gripped his shoulder. "Tell me about the pictures," she encouraged him.

He smiled at Alex. "She loved that place. I think all my ghost stories got her imagination running," he explained. He pointed to a picture on the wall. "See that?"

Alex focused on the point underneath Donovan's finger. She nodded.

"Weeds?" Claire peeked over Alex's shoulder.

Donovan laughed. "That's what I said too," he looked at Claire and smiled. She shrugged again. Donovan pointed to the picture beside it. "Now, look," he told Alex.

Alex's eyes moved to the next picture. She studied it carefully then tracked back to the first, noting the date underneath each.

"Two days apart," Donovan said. "Crazy, huh?"

"What is?" Claire strained to see over Alex's shoulder.

Alex ignored Claire's musings and narrowed her gaze, moving back and forth between the two pictures.

"Weeds and rocks," Claire commented and rolled her eyes.

"Weeds that are almost two inches lower in the second picture than the first," Alex said.

"So?"

Alex took a deep breath and let it out slowly. "So, the ground doesn't just sink overnight."

"Maybe there was a storm," Claire offered a suggestion. "Or maybe some kids were in there messing around," she said. "You know, like taking pictures, or whatever else they do in the woods."

"Maybe," Alex conceded. One thing Alex did know, the ground didn't shift that dramatically without outside intervention—not in two days. She turned to Donovan. "How many pictures like this are there?"

"Thousands," he told Alex.

"Thousands?" Claire asked.

Donovan nodded. He made his way to Kaylee's bed and pulled out a large plastic storage bin. When he lifted the top, Alex was amazed. The entire box was filled with picture scrapbooks. From what she could see, each had a date emblazoned on its front.

"This was her thing," Donovan said. "She said that no matter how many times you took a picture of the same thing, something was different."

Alex smiled. *Smart kid. Probably would make a decent investigator.*

"Anyway," Donovan continued. "Kaylee used to make up all kinds of stories about it. Why did something change? Who changed it?" He sighed with sadness. "I never should have planted those stories in her head. Faeries and elves," he berated himself. "Ghosts." He chuckled caustically. "I had her chasing ghosts," he said with disgust. "Now, look."

"It's not your fault," Alex told him. "What happened to your sister is not your fault, Donovan. Put the blame where it lies, not on yourself," she advised him.

"I wish I could."

Alex smiled at him gently.

"You'll find him, right? Whoever did this?"

"We'll find him," Claire said assuredly.

Alex fought the urge to turn around and smack Claire. She kept her attention on Donovan instead. "It would help if we could take these for a while. I'd like to look them over, maybe have some people analyze them."

"Sure. Dad said whatever you need."

Alex nodded. "We'll need a release signed." She turned to Claire.

"What?" Claire asked. Alex stared at her. Claire rolled her eyes. "At your service," she batted her eyelashes.

Alex chuckled softly.

"Have you two been working together a long time?" Donovan asked.

"Not exactly," Alex told him. "Listen, Donovan; I need to ask you something."

"Yeah?"

"I know Detective Siminski asked this before, but is there anyone or any reason why someone might want to hurt Kaylee?"

Donovan shook his head. "I don't know why anyone would hurt Kaylee, Agent Toles."

"Alex," she grabbed his hand. "You can call me Alex."

Donovan nodded. "Can I ask you something?"

"Sure."

"Do you have any sisters?"

"Brothers," Alex replied. "I have two brothers—one older and one younger."

Donovan nodded. "I should have been there."

Alex's heart lurched in her chest. This was the part of being an investigator she hated—pain. Once upon a time, Alex had thought she could distance herself from that pain. She had empathized with families. She had not sympathized as she could now. Being a mother, being someone's wife, sister, daughter, having a family gave Alex a new perspective on loss.

"Just find him," Donovan said.

Alex nodded. She knew better than to make that promise. Her eyes started to trail back to the pictures on Kaylee's bedroom wall and she stopped abruptly at a picture that rested below on a bookshelf. Donovan and Kaylee in the same location, smiling as if they had not a care in the world. It reminded her of her brothers. *I will find you, you son of a bitch. I will.*

The road seemed never-ending. He'd been driving for hours

after leaving his original destination—hours along a road with nothing but farmland. Occasionally, these stretches of road became interesting. So far, this trip had been disappointing. He reached for the coffee beside him and sipped greedily. He swallowed the cooled liquid and cringed. "Disgusting." The radio blared seventies music and he tapped the steering wheel in time to the beat. "Fields and farms," he muttered.

He turned the wheel with the bend in the road and his eyes narrowed at a sight in the distance. He sighed and picked up his cell phone.

"Hi," he began. "Think I might be later than expected. You know how it is," he said. "They send me where they need coverage. I know. I'll give you a call when I know how long I'll be. Yeah someone called out. Sure. Talk to you later. You too," he said.

He slowed the van to a crawl, pulled over toward the side of the road and rolled down his window. "You look like you could use a ride," he smiled at the young woman walking.

She looked up and met his gaze.

"Where are you headed?" he asked.

"No place in particular," she told him.

He smiled. "I think I know that place," he said. "Want a lift?"

The young woman looked at him skeptically.

"It's a long walk to the next town," he told her. He glanced up at the sky. A few gray clouds passed overhead. "I need to stop for a bite anyway. I can drop you there."

She looked at the van and noted the writing on its side. He smiled at her again, painting reassurance onto his expression. She nodded, deciding he might just be her savior. He pulled over and waited for her to open the door.

"Thanks," she said, heaving herself into the passenger seat with her backpack.

"No, thank you," he said. "I was beginning to think this day was a total loss."

She smiled at the perceived compliment. "At least, I won't get caught in the storm," she said.

He grinned. *There's always something to be grateful for.*

"Don't you think we should be overseeing the autopsy?"

Alex ignored Claire.

"Toles?"

"No."

"I thought you loved protocol."

"What gave you that idea?" Alex asked as she scanned the woods around them.

"You're Agent By The Book, right?" Claire quipped.

Alex shook her head. "You might not know me as well as you think you do."

"Really? I think I know you pretty well," Claire gloated.

"Don't go there."

"Testy much?"

Alex groaned and continued forward. Dealing with Claire reminded her a bit of dealing with Mackenzie. For some reason, Claire felt a need to see how many of Alex's buttons she could push until Alex would explode. Alex had no intention of granting any of Claire's wishes—ever. She had a long, not so cheerful history with her new partner. Why anyone thought it was a good idea to pair the two went beyond Alex's comprehension. She had learned to tolerate Claire Brackett over the years. Hawk was Alex's friend, and Hawk loved Claire. There was no one Alex loved more than Cassidy, and for whatever reason, Cassidy loved Claire too. Claire Brackett had become an unexpected, at times unwanted presence in Alex's life. Until now, Alex had been able to keep her distance. *It's going to be a long day.*

"Toles, what are we doing out here? Don't you think if there was anything to find they would have found it by now?"

Alex stepped over a cracked stone wall that ran along their path.

"Toles, if there was anything to find the dogs would have smelled it."

"I agree."

"So, why am I trudging through a forest? Are you looking for the elves too?"

Alex stopped and strained to focus on something in the distance.

"Toles?"

"I agree. They would have found anything here to find if there had been any dogs."

"What?" Claire asked.

Alex turned to her. "The police didn't get out here until late afternoon. By the time they started searching it was dusk."

"And?"

"And, Kaylee Peters' body was discovered at 5:30 a.m. the next morning in New York. No one came back here with dogs. No need to after that."

Claire considered the information. "Okay, but there was a team out here. They didn't find anything from Kaylee Peters. What is it that you hope to find?"

"I'd love to find that camera," Alex admitted. She kept her eyes set on something in the distance.

"Better hope those faerie stories were real then," Claire commented.

Alex didn't expect she'd ever find Kaylee's camera. She did have a feeling it would tell the story she needed to hear. She started forward again through some brush.

"Where are you going?" Claire called after Alex.

Alex ignored the voice behind her and kept moving.

"Now, she's a fucking Girl Scout too? She'd better have some cookies at the end of this."

Alex heard Claire's muttering and chuckled softly. She'd loathe to admit it to anyone, but at times Claire amused her. She moved a branch out of her way, stepped over a tree stump and stopped.

Claire caught up with Alex and finally saw what she had been focused on. She groaned, immediately understanding what Alex was thinking.

"Do you think we could have at least changed our shoes?"

Alex looked at Claire with a smug grin. "Stop watching Charlie's Angels. No sensible agent wears heels like that," she looked at Claire's feet.

"Doc Martin and I don't have the storied history you two do."

"No, I imagine Doc Johnson has taken up most of your time," Alex deadpanned. She looked away from Claire and at the pond that sat about 100 yards away.

"Did you just make a joke?" Claire asked.

"No, just an observation," Alex replied. She looked back at the hole in the ground beside her. Her eyes circled the remaining stones of an old building's foundation. She couldn't help but wonder what had originally stood in this place—a house, a business, a tavern? She retrieved her phone and looked at the pictures she had snapped of Kaylee's collage. "Something shifted that ground," she mumbled. She started to move toward the edge of the foundation and Claire grabbed her arms.

"Let me," Claire said. She jumped into the pit.

"Brackett, it's full of poison ivy down there."

"Yeah? I'm not sending your itchy ass back to Cass. No thanks. She'd kick mine."

"Oh great, and she'll be thrilled when I bring you home scratching."

"You won't."

"You mean I get to leave you here?" Alex quipped.

"Funny. No. I'm not allergic. I could roll in the shit and never get a bump."

Alex nodded. "That's your superpower?"

Claire looked up at Alex and grinned suggestively.

Alex rolled her eyes. "If that's your superpower, Brackett, you really need to stop seducing kryptonite."

Claire shrugged and turned her attention to the ground beneath her. Alex's eyes swept over the pond. She could easily imagine what had attracted Kaylee to this place. It was quiet. Alex had learned that a quiet place is where anyone keen to listen could find answers to the most puzzling questions. The mere idea of silence was deceptive. There was no silence. There was quiet. Quietness granted the sound of breath, the subtle sounds of life that revealed untold secrets and yet to be revealed mysteries.

Alex closed her eyes and listened. She focused on the sound of her breath and placed it aside. Leaves rustling in the wind—that is what she noticed next. Birds in the distance, faint, but she could hear their song. A trickle of water—Alex honed on the sound. It was close. She tried to picture Kaylee in this place, standing in the same spot, looking at the pond, turning to the cracked and crumbled stones at her feet, clicking her camera.

"What the hell? Toles," Claire called to Alex.

Alex took a deep breath and let it out slowly.

"Alex!"

Alex opened her eyes and turned back to Claire. Claire looked up at her with an expression that Alex recognized immediately as apprehension. She sighed. She had hoped she was wrong. She had hoped.

"What is it?" Alex asked cautiously.

Claire had used the spike of her heel to dig the earth away from the far side of the foundation. She pointed down.

"What?" Alex knelt to see what Claire had discovered.

Claire shifted a patch of earth and pointed. "Does that look like it belongs?" Claire asked.

Alex shook her head. About a foot beneath the soil, a wooden plank was wedged into the rock foundation. Any original boards had long since rotted away, and while nature's toll was evident, it was also apparent that the board had been positioned far more recently than anyone had lived or worked in this place. Alex stood to her full height, stretched her back, and pulled out her phone.

"Who are you calling?"

"Reinforcements," Alex said. "Get Bower on the line," she told Claire.

"What do you think is under there?" Claire asked.

Alex was sure that Claire had already made a guess. She stared at Claire blankly.

"Aww, fuck. I hate those paper suits."

Alex sighed. Me too.

He looked at her; a predatory grin inviting her to shudder. "Shhh," he hissed in her ear. Terror lit her blue irises in golden hues as if he had struck a match to her soul. He stood upright and tilted his head to consider her. Her chest rose and fell dramatically. He savored the sight, enjoying the way droplets of sweat pooled in her cleavage. He could sense that she wanted to close her eyes—look away—somehow deny his presence. She couldn't. He smiled soothingly at her. They never could. There was no way to avoid his advances. He had made certain of that long ago. Unsuspecting, even gratefully they would follow him here. He would pretend to be entertained by their tales. He would appear their momentary savior; he had been her momentary savior. He heard her whimper and leaned back over her.

"Shhh," he cooed in her ear. "Why so many tears?" he asked her. He brushed her hair aside. She still didn't believe him. He could sense the underlying fight she still wished to wage. At first, resistance had frustrated him. In time, he had learned to allow it to run its course. The fight had become almost as intoxicating as he knew her submission would be. He licked a trail from behind her ear down her neck and felt the shiver that passed through her body. So, close—lust and aversion were a breath apart from one another. Her aversion invigorated his desire. He chuckled at her feeble attempt to pull away.

"It's like being hunted," he told her. "We're all being hunted," he said. She shuddered. "It's only a matter of time." His hand trailed over her breast. "Only a matter of time until the hunter captures his prey," he explained. "Only a matter of time until the hunter becomes the hunted," he said with a sigh. Her eyes widened with fear tinged by hope. He sniggered and pressed his body against hers. "Not today."

CHAPTER SIX

"Mom?" Dylan's voice pulled Cassidy from her thoughts. "Are you okay?" he asked her.

Cassidy smiled. "I'm fine." She patted the sofa to indicate he should join her. "I thought you were going to Maggie's?"

"I did. She has a paper due," Dylan explained. "Are you sure that you're okay?"

Cassidy grinned. She was sure that Dylan's repeated inquiries were a deceptive line of questioning. Dylan was observant. She nodded at him. "I don't want anyone else to know yet," she told him.

"Another brother or sister?" he made his guess.

Cassidy smiled.

"I thought so. I'll bet Alex is a nervous wreck."

"Alex is excited," Cassidy said. "She's got a lot on her mind right now."

"Yeah, I gathered that," Dylan said. "What was that about with Claire this morning?"

"I think Alex is planning to tell you herself when she sees you."

"She saw me this morning."

"You know what I meant," Cassidy said.

"Mom?"

Cassidy sighed. "Hawk asked her to take a job back at the FBI."

Dylan stared at his mother.

"Dylan?"

"She's doing it?"

"Yes."

"Why?" Dylan asked.

Cassidy gauged her son's reaction thoughtfully. She was surprised to see apprehension, perhaps even a bit of anger in his eyes. "Because she can help."

"Or get killed."

Cassidy nodded.

"You're okay with that?" Dylan asked.

"Dylan, Alex was an agent when I met her," she reminded their son.

"Yeah, and look what happened."

"Lots of things happened in our lives," Cassidy responded.

"Mom…"

"What?"

"Seriously? You're okay with her doing this?"

"I love Alex," Cassidy said bluntly. "Just like I love you. Part of that Dylan—loving someone—is accepting who they are and letting them be that person." She watched as he shook his head, feeling his fear. "Why do you think Alex is worried about you attending the Naval Academy?"

"Not the same, Mom."

"Isn't it?"

"Not really. No one will be shooting at me."

"Not while you are there."

"Mom."

Cassidy shrugged. "You are so much like her," she mused. Dylan's eyes watered. Cassidy sighed. At the moment, Dylan reminded her of a frightened eight-year-old boy. She took his hand. Some images in life were indelible. Alex coming home after being shot was one of those for Dylan. "Alex loves you."

"I know."

"Mm-hum. She wants to keep you safe. She's always wanted to keep you safe. That's why she's done everything she's done. That's even why she quit."

"Quit?"

"Quit being an investigator."

"Mom, it's not like she quit yesterday. Alex was running Carecom for years."

"Dylan, you know that Alex was doing more than running Carecom. I know you do."

"Still…"

"No. This is part of who Alex is," Cassidy said. "And, if you are honest with yourself, you will realize that you love Alex because of who she is—all of it, even the risky parts. Just like she loves you."

"Aren't you worried?"

Cassidy sucked in a deep breath. "Every time she walked out that door, all those years—yes, I worried. I knew that there was the possibility she might not come back."

"How do you live like that?"

Cassidy smiled. "I trust her. I know that she will always move heaven and earth to get back. These last few years I worried too."

"About what?"

"That she walked away from something that matters to her because of me, because of this family. And, part of her has been lost all that time," Cassidy said knowingly. "The truth is, Dylan, none of us is ever safe from the bad things in the world. Maybe it isn't a gun or a murderer. Maybe it isn't a criminal. Maybe it's a car or cancer."

"Not the same."

"No. But, it hurts every bit as much," Cassidy said. "Loss is loss, Dylan. The way you lose someone doesn't make you miss them any more or any less. One day something will happen to one of us—to me or Alex. It's part of life. You do the best you can to live as honestly as you can. Safety is not something life grants any of us."

Dylan sat quietly for a minute. "Are you glad she's going back?"

"I'm glad that someone will have Alex to help them the way we did. She can make a difference. And, maybe she can help make the world just a little bit safer."

Dylan chuckled.

"What?" Cassidy asked.

"If she doesn't end up in jail for killing Claire."

Cassidy laughed. "They'll be fine."

Dylan shook his head. "I don't know anyone who can get under her skin like Claire, not even Kenzie."

Cassidy nodded. "It might be good for them both."

Dylan laughed.

"I said it might," Cassidy started laughing.

"Mom?"

"Hum?"

"What's their deal? Alex and Claire, I mean?"

Cassidy took a long, deep breath and released it slowly. "They have history."

"You mean like they dated?"

"Something like that," Cassidy said.

"You're not kidding."

Cassidy smiled.

"And that doesn't bug you? I mean, Claire is like part of the family now."

"It did bug me, as you put it, a long time ago. But, no, it doesn't bother me. That was before Alex and I had even met."

"Wow."

"Claire's life hasn't been the best," Cassidy said. "Deep down, underneath it all, she's one of the most sensitive people I have ever known. In that way, she and Alex are very much alike. They just don't see it."

"Can I ask you something?" Dylan looked at his mother.

"You've asked me a lot of things," Cassidy winked.

"Ha-ha."

"You know that you can."

"Do you think Alex is disappointed about my decision?"

Cassidy smiled brightly. "Dylan, Alex loves you more than you will ever be able to understand. I think she fell in love with you the moment you held up your Field Day ribbon in that kitchen. All she wants is for you to be happy and safe. And, that's the hardest part of being a parent."

"What do you mean?"

"I mean that you can't make anyone else happy or guarantee they'll be safe. All you can do is love them and guide them. That's it. That's hard for her. Seeing you? Seeing you as the man you are now, that's hard. She misses that little boy who wanted to run with her in the morning. It was easier to protect him and make him happy. All she had to do was sprinkle sugar on his cereal and play Legos," Cassidy chuckled at the thought.

"You knew about the sugar?"

Cassidy rolled her eyes. "I'll tell you what I told her. You're so worried about Alex being safe, you forget about what makes her happy. She needs to solve puzzles, Dylan. That's who Alex is. She needs to try and make things better by putting the pieces together. You? You want to fly. You've been obsessed with planes since you were born. It's what you are meant to do. Neither is safe. Both are meaningful."

Dylan nodded. "I get it. At least, I think I do."

Cassidy's phone buzzed and she smiled.

"Let me guess; Alex?" he said.

Cassidy winked at her son.

"Tell her I said she owes me a run."

Cassidy nodded. "Hi," she answered the call.

"Hi."

"Uh-oh, bad day?"

"I've had better," Alex replied.

"Want to talk about it?"

Alex groaned. "Do me a favor and try and keep Speed and Kenzie away from the T.V. until I get to tell him about…"

"He knows."

"Shit."

"He's okay. What's going on?"

"I'm not totally sure yet," Alex admitted. "Let's just say I have a bad feeling."

"Which means it's going to be a long night," Cassidy guessed.

"Probably."

"Just be careful."

"Oh, I think it's safe to say nothing where I am can hurt me. Except maybe poison ivy."

"I'm sure that I don't want to know what that means."

Alex snickered. "Well, Claire did promise to protect me from itching."

"I won't even ask."

"Maybe you could convince her to get some sensible shoes," Alex said.

Cassidy laughed. "I'll see what I can do."

"Cass, I…"

"It's okay, love. I told you; we'll be here."

"I love you."

Cassidy closed her eyes. "I love you too. See you later."

"How's the missus," Claire asked.

Alex sighed.

"Toles? Is Cass okay?"

"Yeah."

"Hey, maybe we won't need those suits," Claire offered. Alex's unconvincing smile told Claire what she already knew. That was unlikely. *Fuck. They do not match these heels.*

"What've you got?" Dave Siminski asked Alex.

"I hope nothing." Alex pointed to site in the distance where Claire was standing.

"New partner?" Siminski asked.

"Mmm."

"What? She's a rookie?"

Alex smiled. "I wouldn't call Brackett a rookie. A royal pain in my ass, maybe."

"So? You didn't call us here for nothing. State Police, FBI—come on, Alex. Tell me before we dig."

"Dig is the word," Alex said. She led him the short way to Brackett's location.

"What the hell?" Siminski narrowed his gaze. "What made you look here?"

"Kaylee Peters took a lot of pictures out in these woods," Alex replied. "Thousands."

"And?"

"Some of them were interesting, to say the least."

Siminski pulled his focus to Alex. "You think she stumbled on something?"

Alex shrugged.

"More likely, she stumbled on someone," Brackett walked up to Alex. Alex nodded.

"Well, we know that," Siminski commented. "The question is who? And, where? You think she strayed this far off that trail?" he asked Alex. "This is over a mile from where her friends last saw her."

"No," Alex said. "Maybe someone else did."

"Come again?" Siminski asked.

Brackett stepped in. "Maybe someone saw an opportunity before he realized she'd seen him."

Alex couldn't help but smile in acknowledgment. She had said little to Brackett. The fact that Claire Brackett's thinking followed the same course as Alex's assured her that Brackett was the adept investigator Hawk had promised. Most people would not have considered the possibility that Alex was mulling in her brain. Brackett had.

Siminski shook his head with confusion and looked down at the pit below their feet. "I assume you have a team on the way as well?"

"We do," Brackett said.

"You want us to wait so they can take point?" he asked.

Alex looked at Brackett for confirmation and shook her head. "No. AD Bower agrees. Your forensics team is equipped. Nothing new in this partnership. You have more resources locally. Agent Brackett will supervise," she said, surprising both Claire and herself with the overture. Siminski nodded and waved to his team.

Claire looked at Alex and grinned. "Call me Poison Ivy," she chimed.

Alex chuckled. "Their team is solid," she said. Claire nodded and started toward the hole in the ground. "Claire," Alex caught her by the arm. Claire looked at Alex curiously. "You lead down there. You think we need to stop to preserve anything—stop them."

Claire surprised Alex by responding with a silent nod. Alex looked up to the sky and took a deep breath. *I hope to God there is nothing in there.*

A deep breath followed by a long, audible sigh, and he stretched the soreness from his muscles. He closed his eyes and savored the adrenalin as it rushed through his veins. A fingertip gracefully fluttered over his lip, wiping away a sprinkle of blood. He opened his eyes and regarded the lifeless form on the bed. Another sigh, not of regret, but rather of acknowledgment. One more step he would need to follow carefully. He moved to her side and shook his head. They were always so innocent. Hadn't anyone taught them to be wary of strangers who promised salvation; who promised pleasure? He shrugged as the thought evaporated from his mind, and pulled the sheet around her, tying it with a piece of rope to keep it closed.

He rolled his neck from side to side until he heard it pop and paced to the bathroom that adjoined the room. With one swift turn, the water began to flow. He discarded the remainder of his clothing and tossed it to the floor. Such a mess. Why did it always have to leave such a mess? He sighed; this time with exasperation. Steam wafted through the small room leaving a faint mist on his skin. He adjusted the shower head and stepped in. A deep groan escaped his throat. Pleasure took on many forms. Power was pleasurable—control and then release. He let the hot spray soothe his tired muscles and began to hum his favorite tune. "A hunting we will go. We'll catch a fox, and put her in a box. And never let her go."

Claire squinted and waved her hand. "Light!" she called out. Alex immediately moved to stand above Claire's location. Claire looked up at her. Alex grabbed a flashlight from one of Siminski's team and hopped into the pit beside Claire. Claire motioned with the tip of her head and Alex shined the light.

"Fuck," Alex muttered. She heard a faint, but dismal sigh fall from Claire's lips.

"What is it?" Siminski asked, certain he did not want the answer.

Alex closed her eyes for a split second. She opened them again and looked at the skull below. It had a large crack running along its side. She shook her head. "Fucking son of a bitch," she muttered.

"You kiss Cass with that mouth?" Claire asked.

Alex made no comment. She looked up at Siminski. "It's going to be a long night," she told him.

Siminski nodded his understanding.

Alex focused on the scene in front of her. She understood that she was looking at someone's child, someone's friend, maybe even someone's parent. Whoever it was lying here in this pit; they hadn't come here willingly. That was clear. Now, Alex would need to find out who she was looking at, put aside all her emotion, and find the person who had led them here.

"Are you thinking what I'm thinking?" Claire asked. "There

are more," Claire commented.

Alex felt a mounting pressure gathering in her temples. *I'd count on it.*

Cassidy looked at the alarm clock when she heard the bedroom door open. It was 4:30 a.m. She rolled over and flipped on the light. Alex unbuttoned her blouse and threw it aside. She exchanged her slacks for a soft pair of sweatpants and massaged her temples. She looked beaten. That was the only word Cassidy could find to describe the sight standing before her. "Alex?"

Alex sat on the edge of the bed. Her fingertips brushed the hair from Cassidy's eyes. She leaned in and kissed Cassidy's lips tenderly.

Cassidy reached up and cupped Alex's cheek. "Want to talk about it?"

Alex shook her head.

"Did you eat?"

Alex closed her eyes.

Cassidy sighed. She scooted over and pulled Alex down to lie beside her. Alex let her head come to rest on Cassidy's breast and breathed in Cassidy's scent. She closed her eyes, feeling the first bit of solace she had in hours. Cassidy's fingers released Alex's ponytail and played with her hair.

"Tell me why I am doing this," Alex said.

"Because you care."

Alex sighed.

"Talk to me, love."

"I'm not sure what to say," Alex confessed. "I've seen a lot of things, Cass—a lot of things. Some things you never get used to."

Cassidy kissed Alex's head. "I'm sorry."

Alex took a deep breath and tightened her grip around

Cassidy's middle. "We found something in the woods where Kaylee Peters went missing."

"Do you think it will lead to the person that killed her?"

"Probably."

"Isn't that a good thing?" Cassidy asked.

Alex pulled herself up and groaned.

"Alex?"

"You didn't watch the news tonight."

"No."

Alex smiled weakly. "We found two more bodies."

Cassidy stared at Alex in disbelief.

"Who?"

"I don't know yet," Alex said. "They've been there awhile—a long while, I suspect."

"Oh, God. Do you think it has something to do with her death?"

"Hard to say," Alex admitted. "I think she stumbled upon something without realizing it. The question is whether someone else realized it."

"Alex…"

Alex anticipated Cassidy's next question. "It's not going to be easy to identify them. I have a feeling we aren't done yet."

"What does that mean?"

"It means I'm pretty sure we're dealing with a serial killer and Kaylee Peters was photographing his dumping ground without knowing it," Alex explained. Cassidy felt sick. Alex kissed her on the forehead, laid back and pulled Cassidy into her arms.

"You don't sound surprised," Cassidy observed.

"Not much surprises me, Cass. Not when it comes to this anyway."

"You've seen this before?"

Alex nodded. "Similar."

"I don't understand," Cassidy admitted.

Alex remained silent. She could launch into a diatribe, but she knew it would be hollow. It was her job to think like a monster at times, to climb into the head of a killer. She had learned to discern a killer's thoughts and actions, even a murderer's reasoning and appetite. Understanding how someone could lack complete empathy; that was not a skill Alex had mastered. She knew it. She accepted it. She hoped she would never come to understand it.

"I love you, Cass," Alex said.

Cassidy nestled closer. "Are you okay?"

"I will be."

"Alex, are you sorry that you said yes to Hawk?"

Alex had been asking herself that for several hours. "No."

Cassidy nodded against Alex's chest.

"I might have to bill her for Brackett's lodging though."

Cassidy finally smiled. "Claire is here?"

"Sleeping on the couch in the family room."

Cassidy resisted the urge to tease Alex.

"No comment?" Alex asked.

Cassidy moved to look at her. "Was she that bad?"

Alex chuckled. "No."

Cassidy smiled. "That was painful to admit; wasn't it?"

"You have no idea."

Cassidy kissed Alex sweetly. She did know. "Well, if she gives you a hard time in the morning, bribe her with sugar on her cereal," she said as she collapsed back into Alex's embrace.

Alex rolled her eyes. "I'm never going to live that one down, am I?"

"No."

Alex laughed. "Thanks," she said.

"You're welcome, love. Now, shut off the light and hold me."

"Is that an order?"

"Yes, it is, Agent."

Alex complied. "Yes, ma'am." She closed her eyes and tried to clear her mind.

"Stop thinking," Cassidy commented knowingly. "It will still be there when you get up."

Alex smiled. She doubted that she would succeed in banishing her questions or the images of the day from her mind. She would try. If anything could help her to rest, it would be the woman lying in her arms.

As if sensing Alex's thoughts, Cassidy moved and gently placed her lips against Alex's temple. "Rest, Alex," Cassidy said. "Think about the good stuff."

Alex took a deep breath and pulled Cassidy closer. That had always been Cassidy's mantra. "Think about the good stuff." There was a lot of good stuff. Alex closed her eyes. *Yeah. There's a lot of good stuff.*

"Where are we going?" Claire asked Alex.

"I want to talk to Donovan before we visit the M.E."

"You think her brother knows something?"

"I think he knows that area. I think he knows Kaylee."

"You really think we're going to find more bodies," Claire said.

"You don't?"

Claire shrugged and looked out the passenger window. "We will."

Alex nodded.

"Toles?"

"Yeah?"

"You know, we might never find out who they were."

Alex had considered that possibility. At best, skeletal remains took time to identify. At worst, the victim was never identified. She felt sure that the FBI's team would be able to give them the rough age of the victims, possibly even some thoughts on the cause of death. How long they had been out there? That ballpark might be considerably large. And, without a clear idea when the victims were murdered, it would be hard to cross reference missing persons. Cases took time to solve. Alex feared that time was not on their side. She'd made a call to an old friend; an expert in forensic facial reconstruction. She'd deploy any resources she could. All the resources in the world never amounted to a guarantee. One thing Alex was certain of; whoever killed Kaylee Peters had killed before and would kill again.

Alex glanced at Claire. "That's not an option, Brackett."

Claire noted the resolve in Alex's eyes. She shook her head and looked back out the passenger side window. Alex was nothing if not determined. That was a quality Claire Brackett had always admired in the woman beside her. She'd heard her peers and her mentors reference Alex's intelligence, her talent for seeing minute details that others missed, for memorizing a crime scene, and Claire had listened to more than one agent comment about Alex Toles' ability to draw information from witnesses and perpetrators alike. It had been the former president, John Merrow who had warned Claire about Alex's two greatest strengths; Alex Toles was more tenacious than a pit bull, and she was loyal to a fault. Claire had scoffed at those assessments back then. Then again, once upon a time, Claire had scoffed at nearly every warning she was issued. She'd had the chance to observed Alex at a distance and up close for years. She'd played the role of adversary and ally in Alex Toles' life. In that way, she and Alex Toles were an unlikely pair. A slight chuckle passed Claire's lips. It also made them a formidable team.

"Something funny?" Alex asked as she turned the engine back over.

Claire looked back at Alex. "He doesn't have a prayer."

He groaned as he heaved the large weight at his feet into the large silver box—one more stop. He closed the back door with a thud and made his way to the driver's seat. Coffee—he would need coffee to survive this day. He pressed the button and watched the door roll up. With the twist of his wrist, the engine started and he pulled into the driveway.

"Hey!" a friendly woman waved from across the street.

He smiled at her and waved back, slowing so that she could walk to his window.

"On the road a lot again, I see," she commented.

"It's a good problem to have," he told her.

"I'll bet business is going to get better for you now," she commented. He tipped his head curiously. "You must be traveling a lot if you haven't see the news," she said.

"I tend to like the quiet when I get home," he said. "Sleep at home. Coffee and music on the road."

She nodded. "They found some girl out in Ashland-Pinnacle. Now, a couple of bodies down in Connecticut. They're saying they might be related. You know; like a serial killer."

"Really?"

"Yeah. Sounds spooky," she said. "Like a bad TV movie. The FBI is involved, so the police won't say much. You know that means it's bad."

He smiled at her. "I wouldn't worry too much," he said. "This is a safe neighborhood."

She smiled back gratefully. "Well, it's nice to know we have neighbors to look out for us."

"Absolutely," he agreed.

"Well, travel safe."

"I will. Lock your doors," he said. "Just in case." He rolled up the window and offered her a wave. "Another detour," he groaned. He glanced in the rearview mirror. "I hate detours."

"I don't know," Donovan said.

"Think, Donovan," Alex pressed him gently. "Anything… Think about anything that you thought felt out of the ordinary when you and Kaylee were out there."

"We haven't been out there together in a while," he told Alex.

"I don't care if it was ten years ago," Alex replied. "When you were walking or camping, did you ever meet someone that just felt off? Ever hear something that didn't quite fit?"

Donovan shook his head in frustration.

Claire paced the room slowly, looking at the Peters' home with interest. It reminded her a bit of Alex and Cassidy's house. She stopped and took hold of a picture that sat on the mantle. "Hunters?" she asked.

Donovan looked over at Claire. "More my dad than me," he replied. Claire remained focused on the picture. "He's been known to bag a buck or two."

Claire set the picture down and looked at the young man. "Ever hunt out there?" she asked.

"Once in a while," Donovan said. "It's a short season. Most of the state forest is closed off to hunting."

Claire nodded. "But not all of it?" she asked. He shook his head. "So, if you saw someone dragging, say a tarp? That wouldn't concern you."

"Depends on the time of year," he answered.

"November, December?" Claire offered.

"Yeah," Donovan said. "For deer."

Claire nodded. "Ever get one out there?" she asked.

"No," he said. "Not me. I was never very good. I don't like killing things, to be honest."

Claire shrugged.

Alex rolled her eyes and pulled Donovan's focus back to her.

"Just think about it," she told him. "Anything out of place that comes to your mind; you call me right away—anything."

Donovan nodded. "Kaylee would say that's dangerous," he tried to joke. "Me thinking, that is."

Alex smiled. "Pretty sure my brother would say the same about me."

"Agent Toles," he grabbed Alex's hand. She lifted her brow. "Sorry. Alex… Those bodies—they were there; I mean when we were there? I mean, we were walking on them all that time."

Alex noted the fear in Donovan's eyes.

"Don't sweat it, kid," Claire chimed. Alex turned with astonishment. "Well? Listen, we're all walking on somebody's grave every day," she said as a matter of fact.

Donovan swallowed hard. Alex glared at Claire.

"What?" Claire threw up her hands. "I'm just saying that he doesn't need to be freaked out," she said. She looked back at Donovan. "Listen, kid; if it wasn't for you, no one would probably have ever known to look there," Claire said.

"How could we not know?" he muttered. "I should have been with her."

"Nah," Claire said flatly. "So, what? So, maybe we'd be digging you up to?" she said.

"Brackett," Alex gritted her teeth.

"Aw, Jesus, Toles, give me a break. I'm just telling the kid the truth," Claire said. She looked at Donovan and smiled. "Stop beating yourself up. It's not going to do you any good. Maybe is pointless," Claire told him. "There aren't any maybes in life—trust me. Just like there aren't any ifs. If I did, maybe when," Claire shook her head. "Did you love her?" she asked Donovan. He nodded. "Then that's what you need to hang on to," she said.

Alex could hardly believe what she was hearing. Claire's observations, while less than gentle in delivery, were honest and accurate. She surprised herself with her words. She surprised Claire even more. "Agent Brackett is right," Alex said. Brackett smirked. Alex shot her a look of stern warning.

"I feel like I should do something," he said.

"You are," Alex assured him.

"Doesn't feel like it."

"Call me," Alex said. "Any time at all, anything at all."

"I don't want to bug you with some stupid…"

"Nothing you tell me will be stupid," Alex stopped him. "And, what you think is trivial might be the most important clue we get. Call me. If you can't get me; you call Claire."

Claire shrugged again. "I'm always up."

Alex suppressed a chuckle. "Donovan, one more thing. If you come across any more of Kaylee's pictures, any camera she used; you let us know right away," Alex said. He nodded. "Good. If I don't hear from you, we'll be in touch."

"Do you think whoever killed Kaylee killed those people you found?"

"I don't know," Alex answered truthfully. Claire mumbled something.

Donovan chuckled for the first time. "She does," he pointed at Claire.

Alex nodded. "We try to keep her from thinking at all," Alex whispered. "Safer for all of us that way."

"Yeah," Claire agreed. "I let her do the thinking and the driving."

"What do you do?" Donovan asked.

"Make her look good," Claire smiled.

Donovan laughed. "Thanks," he said to the pair of agents.

Alex gripped his shoulder in reassurance and followed Brackett out the door. She opened the car door and waited for Claire to claim the passenger seat. Alex took a deep breath. "You know," she said. "You're right. Maybe and if are empty concepts," Alex agreed.

Claire listened attentively, waiting for the punchline.

"You helped that kid just now," Alex said. "More than I did."

"Did you just give me a compliment?"

"I just made an observation," Alex said as she pulled the car out of the driveway. "Guess you forgot; I do the thinking and the driving; you just make me look good."

Claire stared at Alex for a minute and then laughed. "That must have fucking killed you."

Alex bit back a smile. *You have no idea.*

CHAPTER SEVEN

Alex sat quietly, listening to the FBI's Forensic Examiner as the agent recapped the county medical examiner's findings, and explained the process of trying to secure any DNA evidence. None of her information was helpful, and none of it surprised Alex. She glanced over at the long metal table that held a woman's skeletal remains, wondering who she had once been; wondering who might be missing her.

"No evidence that she was stabbed?" Claire asked.

"If she was, it wasn't deep enough to cause any damage to the bone," Agent Sandra Eaves replied.

"Huh," Claire muttered. "But, the Peters' case…"

Agent Eaves nodded. "The injuries in the Peters' case were extensive."

"I'd call finding yourself a pile of bones in a ditch pretty extensive," Claire offered.

"Can't argue with that," Agent Eaves said. "But, near as the M.E. could conclude, and based on my examination, whoever this woman is; she was strangled." She moved to the table. Alex and Claire followed. Agent Eaves pointed to the neck area. "See that? It's faint. It is a fracture."

Alex nodded. She leaned in and examined the hyoid bone of the victim's neck. It was clearly fractured. Whoever had killed this woman had applied fierce pressure to her neck. Alex glanced over at Claire briefly. Claire had taken a step away toward the door. Alex groaned inwardly and looked at Agent Eaves. "What about the skull fracture?"

Agent Eaves shrugged. "Can't say definitively," she admitted. "But, I think there's a strong possibility that occurred post-mortem."

Alex nodded. "And, the other victim?"

Agent Eaves moved a few steps to the left and pulled the sheet covering the second set of remains back. "Female."

"And?" Alex urged.

"And? It's almost impossible to say what killed her."

"Almost?"

Agent Eaves sighed. "The only fracture is to her left femur. We both know that could have happened at any point. I can't say with any certainty when she sustained that injury."

"Best guess?" Alex asked.

"Yours is as good as mine, Agent Toles."

Alex nodded. "Any idea how long they were out there?"

"Not my specialty, Agent Toles."

Alex smiled. "Off the record, Agent."

"Alex," Agent Eaves softened her tone. "Wait for Daniel to look at this. That's his field, not mine."

Daniel Lambert was a forensic anthropologist; one of the best the FBI had ever employed in Alex's opinion. She was certain that his team would be able to ascertain a date for the remains. That would take more time than she had. Sandra Eaves had been at this for two decades. She had some idea; Alex was sure of it.

"Sandra," Alex looked at her colleague. "If this is related; I need to know."

Sandra groaned. "Alex…"

"It stays here."

Sandra glanced over at Claire.

"You can trust Agent Brackett."

Sandra looked at Alex in disbelief. "Do you?" she whispered. Alex smiled. Sandra huffed in resignation. "Look, based on where they were found and the condition of the bones, I would guess they had to be out there at least eight years—at least, that long. Could be substantially longer. It's not less than that. I feel confident about that much."

"Define substantially."

"I can't. I suspect where you found them and how you found them might garner more clues than I can discern. Near as I can tell, they were placed there naked. And, Alex? There is nothing left from that scene. They sent dirt samples. I mean, nothing at all that they found in the lab; not even a thread. Still sifting, hoping to find some hair—anything."

Alex sighed heavily.

"Look, let Daniel do his work. It might not have anything to do with the Peters' case," Sandra said.

Alex nodded.

"It does," Claire's voice echoed through the room.

Alex turned to see Claire standing over the first victim, staring at her neck. "Brackett, why don't you go see if you can get an ETA on Agent Lambert's arrival?"

Claire stood still.

Alex moved a few paces to her side and put her hand on Claire's shoulder. "Claire," Alex called to her partner gently. Claire's eyes closed. "Go make the call. I'll wrap it here."

Silently, without any acknowledgment, Claire left the room. Alex sighed.

"What was that about?" Sandra asked.

"Long story."

"Alex, do you really trust Agent Brackett?" Sandra asked. She was not the only FBI agent that had heard tales of Agent Brackett's past alliances. Agent Sandra Eaves had known Alex Toles for years. She trusted Alex.

Alex looked at the door that Claire had just passed through. Did she trust Claire Brackett?

"Alex?"

Alex turned to her friend. "She's family, Agent Eaves. That's the best I can tell you."

Sandra smiled. Partners became family quickly. She nodded. "You think it's the same perp," she surmised.

Alex shrugged. "I think anything is possible—anything. My job is to separate the possible from the plausible and find the truth."

"I wish I could give you more."

"You've given me plenty," Alex assured her friend.

"Be careful, Alex."

Alex turned and smiled, understanding that Agent Eaves' warning was meant about more than the killer Alex was chasing. She nodded. Now, she had an additional concern—Claire's emotional state. She sighed. *Oh, Cass. I think I might need your help on this one.*

"Hello?"

"Sorry to bother you."

"No bother," the man answered his phone.

"I know you are probably anxious to get home," the voice on the other end of the phone replied.

"What do you need?"

"Seems there is an issue at Modicon. I can send someone else out, but…"

"No, no. I can take the call. Do you know the issue?"

"Sending you some information now. I've tested the system remotely. I'm not able to establish a video feed. No digital backup."

"I just need to wrap something up, and then I will be on my way," the man promised.

"Are you sure? We have a tech that's about two hours out. I can reroute him."

"No, it's fine. Send me what you have. I'll take care of it."

"I'm sorry. I know you were heading home."

"Goes with the territory. Besides, it adds to my bonus."

The caller laughed. "Hope you get a big one this year."

The man smiled and looked in the back of his van. "Oh, I wouldn't worry about that," he said as he disconnected the call. He lifted his arms over his head and stretched. "Well, another detour," he commented absently. He scratched his brow and shrugged. "Now, let's see what road we should take…"

"Hey," Cassidy answered her phone.

"Hi."

"Alex? Everything okay?"

Alex had told Claire that she needed to check on things at home. Claire had agreed to step into a coffee shop and grab them both some fuel while Alex made her call.

"Alex?"

Alex sighed. "Yeah… Well, I don't know. Cass, I was kind of hoping maybe Claire could stay tonight."

Cassidy sat down on the couch. "Uh-huh."

"I know. It's a weird request."

"From you; yes. Why don't I think this is about a late night?"

"It's not. In fact, I expect we'll be there in about an hour and a half."

"Uh-huh."

"Well, I want to see Speed before he leaves with Jane."

"Alex, what is going on?"

Alex glanced back toward the coffee shop and groaned. "I think maybe some things are triggering memories for Claire."

"What kind of things?"

"Cass…"

"Alex, I can't help you if you don't tell me what is going on."

"It looks like one of the women we found out there in the woods was strangled."

Cassidy closed her eyes. "Did Claire say something?"

"No. She walked away."

"I'll make tacos."

Alex chuckled. Tacos had long been Alex's choice for comfort food. She suspected that would always be the case. Cassidy had prepared tacos for dinner the first day that Alex had arrived on Cassidy's doorstep. Alex recalled that day often; more often than she had ever shared with her wife. Alex had been an FBI agent then too, assigned to investigate a series of threatening letters directed at Cassidy's ex-husband and his family. She had walked through Cassidy O'Brien's door expecting to be greeted by a snobbish woman of wealth and prestige. Instead, she met Cassidy, a down to earth school teacher who gently reprimanded her son, and delighted in the simplest things that life offers. In less than an instant, Alex Toles' life had changed. Every time her senses were greeted by the smell of tacos in the kitchen, Alex was reminded of the day she had met Cassidy. It had been the first time in many years that Alex had felt any sense of being part of a family.

"Alex? Are you still there?"

"Yeah. Tacos would be great."

"Well, at least you and Dylan will be happy," Cassidy laughed. "He'll be glad that you are here to see him off," she told Alex.

"Me too."

"I'll see you in a bit."

"You will," Alex promised, catching sight of Claire's approach.

"How's the missus?" Claire stepped into the car and handed Alex her coffee.

"She's good. She asked if you might want to join us for taco night."

"Depends."

"On what?"

"Is there wine or do I get saddled with that diet crap you're addicted to?"

"There's wine," Alex said. "I think that's how she survived the twins' terrible twos."

"Good. Been a while since Cass and I had a few glasses."

Alex smirked.

"What?"

"Might be a while longer."

"Why?"

Alex shrugged, but her smile broadened.

"Aw, fuck. You knocked her up again?"

"Classy, Brackett."

"Jesus, Toles. You're the most fertile lesbian I know."

Alex looked over at Claire and burst out laughing.

"What?" Claire asked.

Alex kept chuckling. *Bat shit crazy, Brackett—you are bat shit crazy.*

Why were they always so heavy? It seemed to him that they got heavier by the moment. Some people might think the weight had to do with his conscience. He laughed at the thought. Conscience? What was conscience? Right and wrong, black and white, up and down; did any of it really matter? Everyone was going out sooner or later. Someone would determine his fate; that much he knew. While he had time, he would determine the fate of others. Survival of the fittest, some called it. The hunter had the power over the gatherer. He laughed. His shoulder popped and he tossed the shovel in his hands aside for a moment.

"It'll do," he looked at the ground beneath his feet.

It wasn't an ideal situation. It was a detour. Detours were a pain in the ass as far as he was concerned. Even the most unexpected opportunity required order. There were rules to be followed—his rules. He shook his head. Perhaps this would serve his purpose—this detour. He picked up the small patch of earth he had set aside and placed it in the ground, stomping its edges with his boot. He knelt and smelled the single wildflower that sprang from it. "Mary, Mary, quite contrary; how does your garden grow?" he tipped his head. "With cockle-shells and silver bells, and pretty maids all in a row." He inhaled one final breath of the earth beneath him, stood upright, and closed his eyes. He grabbed the shovel, hopped to his feet and sighed. "Back to work," he mused. "Don't want to miss out on that bonus," he laughed.

Alex rolled her eyes as Mackenzie and her siblings scurried after Dylan and Maggie. The conversation at the dinner table had been animated. Mackenzie loved to hold court, and she had reveled in the attention everyone had directed her way over dinner. Alex had even caught Claire chuckling several times at Mackenzie's antics.

"Claire," Cassidy called to the younger woman.

"Yeah?"

"Do me a favor and go liberate a bottle of wine from the bar in the rec room?"

"I get a whole bottle?" Claire asked.

Cassidy laughed. "I'm sure Jane will give you a run for your money."

Claire shrugged and headed off to complete her appointed task.

"How do you do that?" Alex asked Cassidy.

"How do I do what?"

"Get her to follow directions."

Cassidy grinned. "Oh, I have a few secrets of my own."

"Ahh. This is about the sugar thing; isn't it?"

"Let's just say that we all have our secret weapons."

Alex wrapped her arms around Cassidy's waist. "Is that so?"

"It is."

Alex leaned in and kissed Cassidy tenderly.

"Oh, my God," Claire said. "Seriously, Toles, seducing a pregnant woman?"

Cassidy giggled and let her forehead fall onto Alex's chest.

"Sorry," Alex whispered to Cassidy.

Cassidy pulled back, smiled, and then winked at her wife.

"Come on, Toles, seriously; watching you two is creepy."

Cassidy shook her head with amusement.

"She's worse than Kenzie," Alex commented.

"Well, she'll certainly keep you on your toes," Cassidy whispered. "Go on. Go see Dylan. I will entertain Agent Nosy."

"I'm not nosy," Claire defended herself. "She just can't keep a secret."

"Open the wine," Cassidy raised her brow at Claire. Claire groaned but moved to follow Cassidy's direction.

"I'm going to find out that secret power, you know?" Alex kissed Cassidy's cheek.

"And, I'm going to hide all the sugar."

"You wouldn't dare," Alex challenged her wife. Cassidy shrugged. Alex groaned and headed out of the room. "Nah, she wouldn't."

"Watch me!" Cassidy called out.

Alex laughed. "Thank God none of the kids have inherited that superpower."

Cassidy chuckled. "She's going to freak out when she realizes Mackenzie hears everything she grumbles."

"What?" Claire asked.

"Never mind," Cassidy told her. She poured herself a glass of lemonade and sat across from Claire.

"Oh… I see what's going on," Claire said as she took a sip of her wine.

"What's that?" Cassidy asked.

"Big Brother, or rather the big-time agent out there thinks I'm going to fall apart."

Cassidy smiled. "Alex is concerned about you."

"Right. Concerned I'll fuck up."

"No," Cassidy said flatly. "She's concerned about you."

"That'd be a first."

Cassidy sighed heavily. Sometimes, Cassidy acted as everyone's mother, and sometimes that role was exhausting. "Claire, why do you think Alex hates you?"

"I don't think she hates me. She does hate me. She tolerates me because of you and Eleana."

"That's not true."

"Yes, it is, Cass. You just don't want to believe it."

"Claire, Alex doesn't hate you."

Claire shook her head and sipped her wine.

"She doesn't completely trust you," Cassidy admitted.

"Yeah, well, can't say I blame her there."

Cassidy grinned. "Want to talk about it?"

Claire huffed. "About what?"

"Whatever is bothering you. Claire?"

"What?" Claire bit.

Cassidy remained calm. She reached across the table and took Claire's hand. "Claire."

Claire shook her head. Cassidy tightened her grip on Claire's hand.

"You know, as strange as it is—even to me, I love you," Cassidy said. Claire looked at her. "I know it's insane to everyone else. I feel like you and I were meant to be part of each other's lives. Alex knows that. I trust you. She wants to trust you. You need to earn her trust. This is your chance to do that or at least, to start." Claire wiggled in her chair. It reminded Cassidy of one of her children when she had to reprimand them. "Talk to me."

Claire shuddered. "You didn't see her neck."

"You mean the woman you found?"

Claire shook her head, took a large swig of wine, and closed her eyes. "No."

Cassidy's heart plummeted in her chest. She took a deep

breath. "Your mother."

Claire nodded. "I remember it."

Cassidy squeezed Claire's hand in encouragement.

"It wasn't red. When I saw her on the floor? It wasn't red. It was almost black. That's how tightly he held her."

"I'm sorry."

"Fucking SOB. I hate him, Cassidy. I wish your father would've let me pull that trigger."

"No, you don't," Cassidy replied. She understood Claire's reaction.

William Brackett had been a sorry excuse for a father by Cassidy's standards. He'd choked the life from Claire's mother in front of his daughter, and then, he had spent his remaining years trying to convince Claire in every way he could that she had dreamt the entire scene. Admiral William Brackett's attempts to coerce, to control, and to alter his daughter's perceptions had all failed in the end. Claire's life had become a manufactured lie, first propelled by her father's actions, later by her own. All of it had been driven by one moment in a young girl's life; the moment she had witnessed her father kill her mother.

Cassidy had been the first to learn about Claire's past. It was a lesson that she related to easily—the betrayal of a father. When Cassidy was ten, her father had been the victim of a car accident. That's what Cassidy had always believed. That's what Cassidy's mother had been told. Cassidy had spent most of her life wondering about the father who had died in her youth. She'd missed him at the seminal moments in her life: graduation, marriage, the birth of her first two children. He had been her hero, and she his princess. He had turned her life upside down a second time when he reappeared more than twenty years after his supposed death.

Cassidy's life, much like Alex and Claire's, was anything but ordinary. The three women were part of a legacy; a legacy in which parents made casualties of their children. Sometimes it had been with the best of intentions. Sometimes it had been the result of recklessness and hubris. All their fathers had been embroiled in the espionage game. Cassidy and Claire had endured the brokenness that comes with childhood loss. That shared reality had formed a bond between the two women that Cassidy knew few would understand. And, it was the lessons of the past that gave Alex pause, both about Claire and her intentions and about rejoining the FBI.

The demons of their fathers' past actions had come back to haunt Claire and Cassidy in painful ways. For Claire, her father's deception and manipulation led to an unthinkable face-off. Cassidy's father, Jim McCollum had intervened before Claire had the opportunity to take her father's life. The two men had once been close friends—kindred spirits. They differed in one major way—Jim McCollum sought to atone for the betrayal of his family; William Brackett maintained his actions were necessary. If William Brackett had hoped that the end justified the means, Jim McCollum had given him a drastic lesson to the contrary.

"Claire," Cassidy called for the younger woman's attention. Claire looked up and met Cassidy's compassionate gaze. "No, you don't. For all my father's monumental faults, he would not have let you carry that on your conscience if he could prevent it—none of us would, not even Alex."

Claire shook her head. "You give me too much credit."

"I don't think so."

"He took the one person who loved me."

"Claire, there are a lot of people who love you." Claire's doubtful gaze made Cassidy's heart ache. When, she wondered, would Claire be able to accept that she was loved? When would she be able to let the past go, even just a little bit?

"I can't forgive him. I'm not like you."

Cassidy had forgiven her father. It had not been an easy road, and there were many days that Cassidy still struggled to keep her emotions in check when she recalled the past. There were moments when she would watch her father lift one of her children onto his lap and instead of gratefulness, she felt a pang of resentment. Forgiveness did not equate to forgetfulness. She loved her father. She couldn't change that fact even if she wanted to, and there were days that she wished she could. She looked at Claire and offered the younger woman a gentle smile. Cassidy could easily see the little girl that hid behind Claire's bravado. And, Cassidy understood what Claire needed most. She took a deep breath.

"Maybe it's not your father you need to forgive," Cassidy said. Claire shook her head. "Maybe it's yourself."

"I don't deserve that any more than he does."

"That's not true," Cassidy said.

"Really? And, what happened with Fisher?"

Cassidy closed her eyes and nodded. "That wasn't your fault."

"No? Cassidy, maybe you just see in me what you want to believe is there."

Cassidy opened her eyes and looked directly into Claire's. She felt a slight surge of anger. "Stop it."

"Stop what? Stop telling you the truth?"

"Stop feeling sorry for yourself. And, stop putting me on some Goddamned pedestal that I don't belong on," Cassidy said. Claire was stunned. Cassidy took another deep breath and continued. "You have some crazy idea about me in your head," Cassidy said. "I'm not perfect, Claire. There are still moments I hate my father. They are just moments, but I feel that some days. Sometimes," she paused and pushed back her tears. "Sometimes, I watch him with Dylan; I watch him reading to the twins, telling them those same tall tales he used to tell me, and I hate him for it. All I can think of is the years I cried myself to sleep; the times I heard my mother calling for him when she thought I was far away in dreamland."

"Cassidy, you are the best person I know."

"I'm not a hero, Claire. I just do the best I can every day. Some days are better than others. Some days? Some days I look in the mirror and I'm not very happy with who I see. I've made plenty of mistakes."

"Not the same. Do you think anyone has nightmares because of you?"

"You are not responsible for what Carl Fisher did to me."

"No, maybe not. I didn't help stop it," Claire said. "I knew what he was capable of. I knew because I know what I am capable of," Claire let out a disgusted chuckle. "I hurt the two people I love the most," she admitted. "Can you say that?"

Cassidy was beginning to see part of the picture in Claire's life that she often chose not to look at. Claire had spent most of her life in love with her best friend, Eleana Baros. Eleana's father had also been part of the alliance their fathers belonged to; an alliance that led their children unwittingly to follow in their footsteps. Claire had taken the life of Eleana's half-brother. Cassidy didn't know the details. She did know that part of Eleana would always love Claire. She was certain that Eleana had forgiven Claire.

The other ghost that Cassidy could see hovering in Claire's eyes was Carl Fisher. Claire and Fisher had been friends since youth as well. She had been instructed by her father to work with Fisher, to use Fisher as means to penetrate Cassidy's ex-husband's political campaign, and later to launch a different kind of campaign against the congressman. Claire had not caused Fisher's infatuation with Cassidy. That infatuation had been something of Carl Fisher's making. It had led Cassidy to the darkest experience of her life.

Alex had been an FBI agent then, assigned to investigate threats made against Cassidy, and to ensure her protection. She had been forced back to Washington DC. In her absence, Fisher had taken the opportunity to hold Cassidy against her will. Fortunately, Cassidy had been freed before Fisher had been able to do her any physical harm. That did not mean Cassidy escaped unscathed. The trauma of being held hostage, of being threatened, of fearing for her life remained with Cassidy years later. She would never forget that day.

She did her best to keep it in perspective. She had not only survived; her life had blossomed in the aftermath. Alex had become her partner in life. She felt love in ways she had never imagined possible. She had the family she had always dreamed about. Cassidy's life was anything but perfect. She would never be able to keep count of the mistakes she had made along the way, but she learned day by day to move forward. Regret was pointless. No one could change the past. The only thing anyone could do was take a step forward and try again.

Cassidy made her way around the table and sat beside Claire. For the first time since the two had engaged in their first earnest conversation, Cassidy realized who Claire was in her life. She wasn't the little sister Cassidy often wished she had. Claire was very much like another of Cassidy's children, strange as that might seem to her. That was the relationship they shared. Claire let Cassidy see parts of herself that no one else ever would. Cassidy understood that. She reached out and brushed a tear from Claire's cheek.

"Claire," Cassidy said. "You have to let this go. Let it go, please," Cassidy said.

Claire closed her eyes. "If I had known then…"

"No if," Cassidy said. She smiled. "How many times have I told you that there are no ifs and no maybes in life?"

Claire chuckled.

"Why is that funny?" Cassidy asked.

"It's not. I used that line this morning on Kaylee's brother."

Cassidy lifted her brow. "So, you mean sometimes you do listen to me?"

Claire chuckled again. She always listened to Cassidy. In fact, she listened to Cassidy more than she ever had anyone in her life.

Cassidy smiled. "Maybe it's time you took that advice."

"I don't want to disappoint you," Claire mumbled.

Cassidy's heart swelled and sank all at once. She pulled Claire into a hug, and was shocked when Claire's tears broke forth in a raging flood.

Alex stepped into the kitchen and stopped. She could hear Claire muttering something through her tears. She couldn't make out what it was. She heard Cassidy's words clearly.

"Claire," Cassidy tried to calm the younger woman. "No one can fill your mom's shoes," she said. "But, I can promise you, I will always be here for you. I promise. If I could take away that pain, I would in a heartbeat. But, if the past had been different, who's to say any of us would have found each other?" Cassidy asked. "And, maybe some things were hard, but I don't want to think about my life without the people I love in it. That includes you."

Alex took a step backward and silently left the room.

"Hey," Jane grabbed Alex's shoulder. "You okay?"

Alex nodded. "Just realizing something."

"Care to share?" Jane asked.

Alex led her back toward the family room. "I always kind of wondered how Cassidy could be so close to Claire."

"You don't say?" Jane teased.

"Thing is, I never took the time to really look."

Jane nodded. "And, now?"

"Cass is like her mom."

Jane smiled.

"You already had that pegged," Alex guessed.

"I did. I'm not sure they do."

"They do," Alex said. "I'm not sure they did. They do now."

"Does that bother you?" Jane asked.

Alex sighed. "I don't know how to answer that. Cassidy is the best judge of character I know. But, where Claire is concerned, I just…"

"You worry that she has a blind spot."

"Yeah."

"Maybe she does."

"Not instilling confidence here," Alex said.

"Alex, you and I both know that loving someone isn't rational. Those two have a bond that neither you or I will ever understand. God knows neither of our parents were perfect, but…"

"I know. It's more than that, though."

"I'm sure that's true."

"You like Claire," Alex observed.

"So, do you," Jane grinned. Alex groaned. "You know, Alex, you and Claire have more in common than you sometimes want to admit."

"Like what?"

"You mean other than the fact that you both love Cassidy?"

"Yeah, other than that."

"Neither of you is very good at letting the past go," Jane said. She saw Alex bristle and shook her head. "It's true. You both blame yourselves for every bad thing that's ever happened."

"Sometimes that's warranted."

"Maybe. Can you do anything about it?"

"You sound like Cass."

"I know you want to be able to fix everything, Alex. You want to be able to control what happens. You can't. You can only influence it. You can't control it. And, you can't change what's already happened no matter how much you wish you could. You and Claire both get yourselves in spin cycle, just in different ways."

Alex pinched the bridge of her nose. "Do you trust her?"

"Claire?"

"Yeah."

"Yes."

Alex groaned. It perplexed her how everyone seemed to trust Claire Brackett, and it made her feel guilty. What wasn't she seeing? "I hope you are right."

"Alex, Claire has been part of this crazy family for years. You can sit at the table with Jim and Edmond, with me and Jonathan, and you trust us. You might want to ask yourself why that is so hard for you where Claire is concerned."

Alex was about to answer when she felt a hand on her back. She turned to find a somber Cassidy behind her. Jane winked at Cassidy and made her way down the hallway to give her friends some privacy. "Is she okay?" Alex asked.

"No," Cassidy replied.

"If the case is too much…"

"She'll be all right," Cassidy said.

"You just said…"

"She needs a little time, Alex. She's going out for a drive."

"Do you think that's a good idea?" Alex asked.

"Worried about her?" Cassidy asked.

Am I? Alex nodded. "I'm a little worried about you too."

"I'm okay, love."

"I overheard you."

"I know."

Alex chuckled. "Of course, you did. She thinks of you like her mom."

Cassidy smiled. "I know."

Alex searched Cassidy's eyes and found exactly what she would have expected to see. She shook her head affectionately. "Mackenzie's not enough of a handful for you? You need a bigger challenge?"

Cassidy shrugged. "We don't decide who we love," she said. "Or how we love them."

"No, we don't," Alex agreed. "Are you sure she's okay?"

"She will be," Cassidy said confidently.

"You seem pretty sure."

"I know her."

Alex nodded.

Cassidy leaned in and kissed Alex sweetly. "Give her a chance, love. She might surprise you."

"She surprises me constantly."

"You know what I mean."

"I do," Alex admitted. "She's a good investigator."

"That's not what I meant."

"I know. I'm trying, Cass. I swear; I am."

"I know you are. Just try and remember that she cares what you think."

Alex's look of utter disbelief made Cassidy chuckle.

"I'll try."

Cassidy put her arm around Alex's waist. "Let's go see what the cavalry is up to."

Alex let Cassidy lead her away. Could my life get any stranger?

CHAPTER EIGHT

"More pictures?" Claire asked Alex.

"There is something here," Alex said more to herself than to Claire.

Claire looked over Alex's shoulder at the photos spread across the table. She moved a few aside, making Alex grumble. She pulled a few from underneath the pile. Her eyes focused on one. She reached out and pointed to it. Alex followed Claire's finger as it moved back and forth over several photos of the same area.

"Anyone could have moved that when they were hiking," Alex observed.

Claire shrugged and stepped back. "Pretty big pile of sticks to move. I mean, why not just go around it?"

Alex studied the photos again. She had been focused on the area where they had uncovered the two skeletons. The State Police and the FBI still had a team in the woods excavating several areas close to that location. So far, they had not uncovered anything. Alex felt certain that there were more victims, and she was confident that they were in the same forest where Kaylee Peters had disappeared. The question was where to look.

Alex looked back at the photos Claire had referenced. She shook her head. Claire was right. She picked up Claire's thought. "Why move it unless you were moving something?" Alex mused. She turned and looked at Claire who shrugged. Alex glanced back at the dates on the photos. "Not hunting season."

"Nope," Claire agreed.

Alex rubbed her temples. "I wonder where this is."

"I'll bet the kid knows."

Alex nodded. "Why don't you give Donovan a call?"

"Why me?"

Alex spun in her chair and looked at Claire. "He likes you."

Claire laughed. "No one likes me, Toles," she joked. "They just find me amusing. I'll call the kid."

Alex watched as Claire walked away. She sighed and turned back to the pictures. *Come out, come out, whoever you are.*

"Do you really think this is a good idea?"

"Why not? Don't you want to see what they find?"

"There are cops everywhere," Jared Gore told his friend.

Darren Black kept moving forward. "No one is up here. They're all down by the pond. Bill and I trekked in here yesterday. If we go around the red trail, we'll be able to see them from Flat Rock."

Jared followed reluctantly. Flat Rock was appropriately named. It was a giant flat rock that sat in a small clearing above a large pond in the state forest. It sometimes served as a make-out spot. Occasionally, Jared had hiked up to the area to find an artist sketching. It wasn't easy to find. A person had to veer off the path for nearly a quarter mile to reach the spot. Anyone unfamiliar with the area would never find it in spring with the tree coverage. In fact, Jared expected that he and Darren would leave this endeavor with a few scratches from low hanging branches. The rock offered a terrific view of the area below, but the surrounding tree coverage made it hard to see anyone sitting there.

"What do you hope to see from that far away?" Jared asked.

Darren shifted his backpack. "I brought eyes."

"Alex is working?" Rose asked Cassidy.

"No more weekends off," Cassidy replied. "At least, not when she's working a case."

"How are you doing with that?"

"Me?"

"Yeah, you," Rose replied. "Cassie, this is a big change for you too."

Cassidy shrugged off her mother's observation. "I'm happy for her."

"Really?"

"Yes, really. Well, not happy about what she has to do, but I am glad she's doing it. She missed it, Mom."

"And, you?"

"I'll miss her if that is what you are getting at."

"Do you think she will stay with the FBI?"

"After this case; you mean?" Cassidy asked. Rose nodded. "I think so. She doesn't," Cassidy laughed.

"What about you?"

"What about me?"

"Well, Alex is back at her old job, the twins will be in kindergarten in the fall. What are you planning to do?"

"Pretty sure I will be able to fill my time."

"Trust me, Cassie, when they are all out of the house, it can get a little lonely."

Cassidy grinned.

Rose looked at her suspiciously. "What aren't you telling me?"

Cassidy kissed her mother on the cheek. "I hope you and YaYa are up for a few more years of babysitting."

"You're pregnant?"

Cassidy tipped her head in acknowledgment.

"Seriously?"

Cassidy laughed. "Seriously."

Rose hugged Cassidy tightly. "You must be thrilled."

"I am. We didn't want to say anything right away."

"I understand."

"Seems like everyone is figuring it out anyway," Cassidy chuckled.

"Everyone?"

"YaYa, Dylan, even Claire."

"Huh. How did I miss this?" Rose asked.

"Too much wine?"

"Ha-ha," Rose goaded Cassidy. "You're just jealous that you have to give up the devil's juice again."

"Not really," Cassidy said. "From what I can tell, when I get to play grandma I will be swimming in the stuff."

Rose pursed her lips. "You might just be running to PTA meetings in the morning and changing your grandbaby in the afternoon," Rose said.

That thought had crossed Cassidy's mind. It wasn't only a possibility; it was a likelihood. By the time the newest addition to the Toles' clan arrived, Dylan would be approaching his eighteenth birthday. It wasn't a far stretch to imagine that he might have children in his twenties.

"You never know," Cassidy agreed.

"What did Dylan say about the baby?"

"Oh, I think he is mildly disappointed he won't be here to spend time with this one. But, he's excited about the academy."

"You don't say."

Cassidy smiled. "I'm happy for him."

"What do you think about him and Maggie?" Rose asked.

"What do you mean?"

"I mean, what do you think?"

"About teenagers in love?"

"About what teenagers in love do."

Cassidy shrugged. She had gently approached the subject of sex with Dylan. He had been far more uncomfortable with the discussion than she was. That led her to ask his Uncle Nick to step in and talk to Dylan. Alex's younger brother had two sons. He didn't share all the details of his conversation with Dylan with Cassidy. He did make her aware that he believed Dylan and his girlfriend would likely find themselves in an intimate situation sooner rather than later—if they hadn't already. It hadn't surprised Cassidy. It did give her pause.

"I think it's likely they already have," Cassidy said.

"Are you worried?"

"A little. You and I both know that things happen, no matter how careful anyone is."

"Yes, we do."

"But, things happen as they are meant to," Cassidy said. "I trust Dylan. He's got a good head on his shoulders. He's responsible, and he certainly knows what it is like to have babies around 24/7."

"True."

"I would hate for anything to change his trajectory. I also know that he has his own path. He loves Maggie. That much I do know."

"Young love doesn't always last," Rose reminded Cassidy.

"No. It doesn't make it any less real."

"Can't argue with that," Rose agreed.

"So? Are you still going away with Dad next week?" Cassidy changed the subject.

Rose smiled. "That's the plan."

Cassidy nodded. She often wondered when her parents would finally cross the bridge and get back together. That had yet to happen. Her mother and Alex's mother shared a three-bedroom ranch house on the other side of town. Cassidy's father had settled into a condominium a few towns over. The affection and love that existed between her parents were evident to everyone who saw them together. But, Rose had made no move to invite her husband back into her life full-time, and Cassidy was positive her father had never made any overture either. They spent time together; they even took trips together; they never discussed the context of their relationship, and they never sought to make it a formal commitment. Jim McCollum had been gone for over twenty years. He had broken Rose's heart. Broken hearts took time to mend. Broken trust was even harder to repair.

"Mom?"

"Hum?"

"Can I ask you something?"

"Sure."

"Do you love Dad?"

Rose smiled, but Cassidy could plainly see the sadness in her eyes. "With all my heart."

"But, you still don't trust him."

"I trust him," Rose said, surprising Cassidy. "Cassie, I've learned to live my life a certain way. I like it that way. I've made room for him; I am not going to give him the entire space."

Cassidy nodded.

"What brought this on?" Rose wondered.

"Claire."

"Claire?"

"Yeah," Cassidy said.

"Want to explain?"

"I worry about her."

"What's going on with her and Hawk?" Rose asked.

Cassidy sighed. Charlie Hawkins, Hawk as everyone called her, was Alex's former NSA partner. She was also Alex's former partner in life. It had been a brief romantic relationship, but Cassidy knew that it had meant something to both Alex and Hawk. Hawk and Claire had fallen for each other fast and hard. Their relationship, like everything in Claire's life, had been tumultuous—on again, off again. Cassidy was positive that Hawk desired a commitment from Claire. Commitment was a concept that Claire struggled with. She feared it. More than Claire feared Hawk would betray her; Claire worried that somehow, she would fail Hawk. Cassidy knew that.

"I'm not sure," Cassidy admitted. "I know that they couldn't both stay in DC. Hawk is an assistant director now."

"Can't one of them leave the FBI?"

"I'm sure they could. I don't think Hawk would do that without Claire making some kind of long-term commitment."

"You think Hawk wants to marry Claire?"

"I don't know. I think she wants more. That's hard for Claire. She carries a lot of guilt."

Rose nodded. "Some of that she earned," she reminded Cassidy.

Cassidy grimaced. "It's time to let it go, Mom."

"Honestly, Cassie. I know you have this affinity for Claire. You feel empathy for her…"

"It's not just empathy, Mom."

"I know," Rose confessed.

"I just wish she would let herself be herself."

"Well, if anyone is going to reach her, it'll be you."

"I'm not sure about that."

"I am," Rose said. "How is Alex doing with Claire?"

Cassidy laughed. Alex had an affinity, as Rose put it for Claire. Cassidy could see it clear as day. Alex was skeptical of Claire's motives, and she worried about Claire's potential reaction in situations. Cassidy couldn't blame Alex for that. But, Cassidy knew Alex better than anyone. Alex often would chuckle quietly at something Claire said, and Cassidy had observed that Alex listened attentively to Claire when she spoke.

"Better than she expected, I think," Cassidy replied.

"Worried about them too?"

Cassidy smiled and replied honestly. "Not at all."

"Shit," Jared tumbled and hit the ground.

Darren turned back to his friend. "What the hell did you step on?" he asked.

Jared grabbed his ankle. "I just sunk," he pointed to a small patch of earth.

"Right," Darren laughed. "The sinkhole swallowed you."

"It did!" Jared replied. "Look at my foot."

Darren groaned. Jared's sneaker was covered in mud. Worse, Jared was in pain. Darren threw his backpack on the ground and moved to help his friend up. "Can you stand?"

"Yeah. Walking might be a bitch, though."

Darren went to hold out his hand and his foot sank into the earth. He pulled his foot up and turned to look at the hole as it gave way. He jumped backward and fell into Jared.

"What the hell?" Jared pushed his friend aside.

Darren pointed to the hole his foot had left.

"What?" Jared asked. "You've been watching too many horror movies."

Darren shook his head. "Look."

Jared jostled himself forward and strained to see what Darren was pointing at. His face promptly drained of all color. He turned and lost the contents of his stomach. "Jesus."

Darren fought the urge to follow his friend's lead. "I think we'd better call someone."

"Agent Brackett," a young man's voice pulled Claire from her thoughts. She held up a finger.

"Are you sure?" she asked the person on the other end of the phone. "We'll pick you up," she said. She turned to the agent facing her. "Agent Jensen," she greeted him.

"A call just came in from Detective Siminski looking for you or Agent Toles. Says he couldn't reach either of you."

Claire guessed that Alex had stepped out to call Jane. "Did he say what he wanted?"

Agent Jensen nodded. "They found a body."

Claire nodded. "I'll call him. Thanks." *Shit.* Claire lifted her phone. "Siminski."

"Agent Brackett. Is Alex with you?"

"She stepped out for a minute. More skeletons, I understand?"

Siminski groaned. "I wish."

"What do you mean? Jensen just said you dug something up?"

"Not exactly. More like some kids tripped over it."

"Tripped over…"

"A body," Siminski explained. "And, she hasn't been there long."

"Where?"

"About ¾ of a mile from where we've been digging."

Claire sighed. "We're on our way." *Shit.* Claire started back toward the small conference room that Alex had taken over.

"Hey," Alex stopped her. "Did you get Donovan?" she asked. Claire nodded. "What?" Alex asked. "Did he give you a hard time?"

"No. Alex," Claire began, "Siminski just called. They found a body in the woods. This one has a little more meat on her bones."

Alex groaned. "Fuck. How long…"

"He didn't say. From what I gathered, she hasn't been there too long at all."

"He's changing the game," Alex observed.

"If it is him. He didn't say how she ended up there."

Alex stared blankly at Claire.

"Okay," Claire held up her hand in surrender. "I get it. Guess, we won't need those pictures now."

"I wouldn't count on that."

Alex squatted beside the huddled form in the dirt. She lifted the young woman's arm and grimaced at the bruises on her wrists. Her eyes traveled down the torso, noting the splotches of dried blood.

Fucking bastard. She could hear Claire's voice in the background, and she made a point to hone in on the discussion even as her eyes remained glued to the scene in front of her.

"Nothing else?" Claire asked.

"No," Siminski replied. "We might never have found her if those kids hadn't been so damned nosy."

Claire glanced over at Alex. "We'd have found her," Claire disagreed.

"Not any time soon," Siminski commented.

Alex made her way to her feet and exchanged a knowing glance with Claire.

"What aren't you two saying?" Siminski asked.

"What's to say?" Claire asked. "Dead girl. Stab wounds, clearly restrained against her will, naked in the dirt. That's the story here," she said. "Did I miss anything?"

For once, Alex was inclined to agree with the blunt assessment of her partner. Siminski was a great detective. He was a knowledgeable investigator. He was not a profiler. While profiler was not technically listed on Claire's resume, Claire was every bit as capable as Alex in designing a profile of a killer. Both Alex and Claire had been trained in a different world than the FBI. In the world of international spying, every agent needed to be a profiler. The spy world required skills beyond following facts, evidence, and clues. Survival demanded that an agent be superior at contemplating his or her adversaries' next move. The world that Alex and Claire had traversed for many years was not dictated by a game of cat and mouse. It was a ruthless world, where danger lurked not only in dark corners, but in the stark light of day. Claire's rebuttal was a flat assessment that this discovery gave them no more evidence than they already had, and at the same time, it changed the course of the investigation completely.

"What the hell does that mean?" Siminski looked at Alex.

"It means we won't know much new until we find out who she

is. The silver lining is that we have a good chance of finding that out and quickly. Someone is missing her."

"You hope," Siminski replied. "Come on, Alex. You know better than anyone that serial killers tend to target faceless people; the people no one pays attention to."

Alex nodded. "True."

Claire looked at the woman on the ground. "Problem is, everyone has a face," Claire said. She looked back at Siminski. "Everyone."

"You know what I meant," he said.

"Agent Brackett is right," Alex said. "No one is faceless in the end. And, someone is always paying attention. The question is always who that is." She looked at Claire. "He's making a turn," she surmised. Claire nodded her understanding.

"What the hell are you two talking about?" Siminski bit in frustration.

Claire met his gaze. "He dropped the Peters' girl in New York to throw you off—to throw us off this place."

"Yeah? So, why come back?" he asked.

"Because he's compelled to," Alex said. She squatted beside the victim again. "Look," Alex said. She pointed to the small red dots on the girl's eyelids.

Claire leaned in. "Fuck."

"She was strangled," Alex surmised.

"And?" Siminski said. "M.E. said Peters might've been dead before he finished stabbing her, and that other girl was strangled."

"Yeah, but there's no evidence of that in the third victim," Alex reminded him.

"Maybe they aren't all the same killer," Siminski offered.

"And maybe I can solve a problem like Maria," Claire rolled her eyes.

Alex bit back a laugh. "Maybe." She looked back at the body next to her and stood. "Let's hope you're wrong."

"Why?" Siminski asked.

Claire laughed. "Even I'm not that masochistic," she joked.

"What?" he asked.

"One sadistic psychopath is enough," Alex said. "Let's hope that's what we are dealing with." *Let's hope.*

"What's up with you?" Alex asked Claire.

"What?"

"You took that call earlier and you haven't said a word since."

Claire looked out the passenger window.

"Claire?"

"It was Hawk."

Alex looked back at the road. She wasn't expecting that answer, and she wasn't sure how to proceed with the conversation. She wasn't sure she should proceed at all. Hawk was Alex's friend and Alex's former lover. It was awkward. Made more awkward by the fact that Alex had also slept with Claire a few times before she'd met Cassidy. She'd regretted that for years; not for the reasons she knew most people would have guessed.

"She's getting in tonight."

"To New York?" Alex asked.

Claire nodded.

"Is that a bad thing?"

"I don't know," Claire answered. "I told her that things in the case had taken a turn."

Alex was curious, but she was reluctant to push.

"She has an offer back at the NSA," Claire offered.

Alex understood. "In the New York office?" she asked. Claire nodded. "And, that's why you are here now."

"Partly."

"She loves you," Alex said.

"I know."

Alex took a deep breath. Cassidy would want you to ask. "Do you love her?" Alex asked. Claire sighed. "Claire?"

"You know how I love," Claire tried to joke.

Alex groaned. "Why do you always do that?"

"What? Tell the truth?"

Alex shook her head. "I give up."

Claire looked back out the window. *Cassidy would want you to answer.* "I do love her."

Alex was taken by surprise by Claire's answer.

"What?" Claire chuckled. "You think I'm a monster."

"No," Alex replied. "I don't. I think the asshole who dumped those women in the woods is a monster. I think you're scared."

Claire's gaze retreated out the window yet again. "You're the profiler."

Alex decided to let Claire off the hook. "So? What do you think about this new development?" she asked Claire.

"You mean my girlfriend wanting a commitment or do you mean psycho stabber?"

Alex couldn't help but chuckle. "Either."

Claire smirked. "I think he got bored."

"I agree."

"Really?"

"Why does that surprise you?" Alex asked.

"That you agree with me?" Claire asked. She laughed. "I've never been one to believe in miracles."

Alex laughed. "Praise God," she said.

Claire laughed. "Alex," she turned serious. "He's going to up the ante."

"I know."

"I hope we can get that girl identified quickly," Claire said.

Alex detected the note of genuine concern in Claire's voice. She glanced across the seat briefly. Claire was looking out the window. Alex could make out the faint creases in the younger woman's forehead. Alex had long understood that Claire loved Eleana. She had accepted the truth that Claire cared deeply about Cassidy. She'd even allowed for the fact that Claire had feelings for Hawk. A stranger? Alex had never entertained the idea that Claire Brackett had the potential to feel empathy for a stranger. She looked back at the road. *I'll be damned.* Claire did care. A barrage of images passed through Alex's brain quickly. Claire had been affected by this case. It resonated with her on some level. Maybe it surfaced some of her latent guilt. Perhaps is conjured old memories. Alex felt sure both of those things were true. There was something more than that at work—empathy.

"I'm going to work on speeding up the process," Alex told her partner. "We need to know who these women are; where they came from."

Claire looked over at her, instinctively understanding her meaning. "Going outside the bureau?"

"Whatever it takes," Alex said.

"Hey," Cassidy answered her phone.

"Hi."

"Oh, no. What's wrong?"

"I'm not going to be home tonight," Alex said.

Cassidy took a deep breath. "Everything okay?"

"No. We found another girl in the woods."

"Oh, Alex…"

"I'm on my way to Natick."

"Pip?" Cassidy guessed.

"Yeah."

"He'll be glad to see you," Cassidy said. Cassidy had known Jonathan Krause since college; long before she had met Alex. She had nicknamed him Pip after the protagonist in Dickens' *Great Expectations.* Years later, the name still stuck. Alex had not had much of a chance to visit with her older brother for a few months. They spoke often, but Cassidy was certain that Alex missed time with him.

"I know," Alex replied. "I hate going to him with this," Alex confessed.

"Alex, he's your brother. You could go to him for anything; you know that."

"It's not that."

Cassidy took a deep breath. Jonathan Krause operated outside the overview of any government agency. "Is there another way?"

"Yes," Alex admitted. "We can wait for the system to do its job. Those wheels are already in motion, combing through missing person's reports, looking at photos, an autopsy, DNA, the whole drill."

"But…"

"But, that all takes time—a lot of time sometimes. I don't have time."

"Then you should do what you feel is best," Cassidy said.

"I'm not sure where it will lead."

Cassidy understood Alex's statement. She was also certain that the real reason Alex was headed to see her older brother had to do with her concerns about Dylan. Could Christopher O'Brien have toyed somehow with Dylan's mind? The possibilities and realities remained difficult for Cassidy to accept. Most people regarded mind control and conspiracy theories as the ramblings of nut jobs. Unfortunately, Cassidy had learned that even the craziest ideas were many times rooted in some nugget of truth. She also knew that Alex couldn't promise when she would be home. It had been years since Cassidy had confronted this reality—Alex leaving on a moment's notice. During those years, Alex's absences had been frequent. Cassidy seldom knew where Alex had gone or when she would return—if she would return. She felt a familiar wave of apprehension send shivers up her spine.

"Cass?"

"I'm here."

"I'm sorry."

Cassidy took a deep breath. "No need to be sorry, love. I told you; I will be here."

"I'd rather be there."

"I know," Cassidy said. "Someone else needs you more right now."

Alex closed her eyes. "Can you do me a favor?"

"Anything I can."

"Call Claire."

"Why?" Cassidy asked.

"I just dropped her off at the car rental place. Hawk's on her way here."

"Was she upset?"

"Worried, I think," Alex said.

"I'll call her."

"If she doesn't call you first," Alex chuckled.

"If she doesn't call me first," Cassidy agreed. "She's growing on you."

"Like a fungus."

Cassidy laughed.

"And, don't get any ideas. I'm not adopting her too," Alex said.

"I'll tell the lawyer to rip up the papers," Cassidy deadpanned.

"Funny."

"I know. I'll miss you."

"Me too," Alex said.

"I'm sorry for the reason, but I'm glad you are going to see Pip."

"Me too," Alex confessed. "I'll call you later."

"I hope so."

"I love you, Cass."

"I love you too, Alfred."

Alex laughed. "I get it. I have clean up duty when I get home."

"Just get home," Cassidy said.

"I will."

Cassidy put her phone on the table beside her and put her face in her hand. I'll never get used to it.

"Mommy?" Abby put her hand on Cassidy's knees.

Cassidy picked up her head and smiled at her daughter. "Hi, sweetie."

"Why ah you cwying?"

"I'm not," Cassidy promised. "Just a little sleepy, I think."

Abby considered her mother thoughtfully. "You sad?"

"No, honey; I'm not sad," Cassidy said, taking the opportunity to lift Abby onto her lap. Abby snuggled against her. "Where is Connor?" Cassidy asked.

"With Grandma."

"Oh, what are Grandma and Connor doing?"

"Readin'," Abby said.

"You didn't want to read?"

"Wif you."

Cassidy smiled and kissed Abby's head. "I love to read with you."

"Mommy?" Abby addressed Cassidy. Cassidy waited, knowing the question would follow. "D. went away."

"Dylan will be back, sweetheart."

"Not forevah."

Cassidy smiled. "No, honey; not forever. But, he will always come back to see you, even if he has to stay away for a while."

"How come?"

"How come, what?" Cassidy asked.

"How come he has to weave?"

Cassidy closed her eyes and held Abby close. "Well,

sometimes we all have to leave for a little while. Sometimes for a long time," Cassidy said.

"Why?"

"To meet new people," Cassidy said. "To try new things," she told her daughter. "Like Grandpa. He was away for a very long time."

"Did you miss him?"

"Very much. And, sometimes Mama has to go away for a few days too."

"She comes back."

"Yes, she does. And, Grandma and YaYa go away once in a while."

"We get presents."

Cassidy laughed. "Yes, you do."

"I want D. to stay."

Cassidy bit her lip gently. *So, do I.* "Well, in a way he will," Cassidy said. "Whenever you think about him, he will be right here with you. Like right now. Close your eyes," she told Abby. Abby shut her eyes tightly. "Now, think about Dylan. Can you see him?" Abby nodded. "Now, tell him something," Cassidy said. She watched as Abby began to smile. "What did he say?" Cassidy asked.

"He says I am silly."

"Now, tell him you love him. What did he say?"

"He misses me."

"Open your eyes," Cassidy said. Abby looked at her. "See? Dylan is right here," she pointed to Abby's heart. "So, even when he isn't sleeping upstairs, he will always be with you."

Abby sighed. She looked at Cassidy seriously. Cassidy raised a brow. "I don't want him to go," Abby said flatly.

Cassidy suppressed a chuckle. She pulled Abby close again. "I know, sweetheart," she said. "I know."

Alex walked down a corridor toward a door at its end. It was a walk she had made many times over the years. It was a walk she had hoped she would never have to make in any official capacity again. She concentrated on steadying her breathing, hoping to banish the memories this place conjured at times.

"Ms. Toles!" an excited woman hurried toward her.

Alex smiled genuinely at the animated woman. "Marta," she took her former secretary into a hug. "Keeping Jonathan in line, I hope."

Marta nodded. "I try. It's not the same without you, though."

"Ah, you just miss Cassidy's goodies," Alex joked. "And, maybe having weekends off."

Marta laughed. She had worked for Alex's father for years before his death, and had remained in her position when Alex took over at Carecom. Alex Toles had differed as a boss from her father in countless ways. Alex shared his dedication, his intelligence, and his thoroughness; she also possessed deep compassion and an ability to connect to people. Marta had marveled at Alex's ability to address complicated issues and reduce stress for the staff at Carecom. The company had been through multiple transitions over the last decade. Alex had made the decision to move operations closer to her home in Connecticut. Marta had followed. When Alex opted to leave Carecom, her older brother, Jonathan had stepped in and set up his office in the original space their father had once occupied. Marta had agreed to move again. She had come to adore her new boss. She had seen evidence of Jonathan's desire to connect with the man he had never known as his father, but she still missed Alex.

Marta's eyes twinkled. She put her arm around Alex. "How is Mrs. Toles?"

"Oh, for heaven's sake, Marta," Alex laughed. "After all these years, can't you just call us Alex and Cassidy?"

Marta winked. "In my eyes, you are still the boss," she said.

Alex shook her head. "Well, whatever you do, don't tell

Jonathan that."

"Don't tell me what?"

Alex looked up and met a similar pair of eyes to hers. She hadn't seen her older brother in a month. He had been traveling. She had been busy with work and the kids' activities. Looking at him now, Alex realized how much she'd missed him. "Marta and her formalities," Alex said.

"Ah. She is a bit of a—what is it the twins call it?"

"Stickler," Marta answered the question. "And, those kids are smart," she told him. "You should pay attention to what your sister and Mrs. Toles have taught them."

Alex snickered. "Is he misbehaving?" she teased Jonathan.

"I keep telling him to get used to leaving a little earlier," Marta said.

Alex nodded. Jonathan and his wife were expecting their first child. "Take my advice," Alex said. She looked at her brother, pointed to Marta and issued him a playful warning. "You'll take hers if you know what's good for you."

Marta gloated and headed back to her desk. Jonathan rolled his eyes and beckoned Alex into his office. "And, here I thought we were done with conspiracy theories," he joked.

Alex shrugged. "Little ones, big ones, one thing I know, there is always one."

"That was a mouthful."

Alex sighed.

"What's going on?" Jonathan wondered. "You know that I am glad you're here. I know you. You avoid this place like it's the plague. What gives?"

Alex flopped into a chair. Jonathan offered her a smile. She had been vague about the reason for her visit on the phone. He suspected that her reason for visiting had deeper roots than just the case she was working on.

"Should I get that bottle of scotch now?" he tried to pull Alex from her mood.

Alex chuckled. She had never been much of a drinker. Scotch? Just the smell made her nauseous. The truth was, given a chance just about anyone could drink her under the table including Cassidy. "No thanks," she replied.

"What do you need?" Jonathan asked more directly.

"I was hoping you could help speed things up on this case," she told him.

"What kind of things?"

"Red tape kind of things."

Jonathan nodded. "Hitting roadblocks already?"

"Not roadblocks, just slow-downs," Alex commented. "I don't have time for slow- downs—not now. This young woman we found," Alex closed her eyes and took a deep breath. She opened them and looked back at her brother. "He's not done," she said. "And, his taste buds are tingling."

Jonathan Krause understood. In the world of espionage, murderers were called assassins; as if that term somehow cleaned up the act itself, made it more palatable, even distinguished. He had taken life. He had been ordered to take life. He had never enjoyed that task. It was one of the reasons, Jonathan Krause had become an orchestrator rather than an interrogator or an assassin. He would live with the demons of his past for the rest of his life. His years in the underbelly of the spy game had acquainted him with the kind of person Alex was seeking. Assassin, murderer, henchman, serial killer—all words to describe a sadistic human being who enjoyed hunting human prey. He had little doubt that without the structure and expectation that existed in covert operations, many assassins would've become prolific serial killers. They craved the hunt. They relished the kill, and in more cases than he cared to recall, this kind of hunter enjoyed the taste of fear and pain of his prey.

"Alex," Jonathan began thoughtfully. "Look, you don't need me on this."

"Need? Maybe not. You and I both know that you have access to anything I might need without the red tape to cut through."

"How about we drop the bullshit and you tell me what is really going on?"

Alex rubbed her face for a minute and then looked back at her brother. "Cass is pregnant."

"Congratulations." He studied his sister closely. Alex's smile was dim. "Is that not a good thing?"

"It is."

"What gives, Alex? Are you worried something might happen?"

"It did once."

"Lots of things happen once," Jonathan replied. "What does Cassie think?"

Alex smiled. "You know her. She sees the best in everything."

"And, you don't?"

"I see reality."

Jonathan nodded. "Sometimes, maybe you project possibilities and not realities."

"Maybe I do."

"This isn't about Cassidy's pregnancy," Jonathan surmised. "Have you talked to him?"

"What?"

"Dylan. Have you talked to him since he left?"

Alex shook her head. "Why do I think you have?"

"He called this morning," Jonathan admitted. "He's just excited, Alex."

"I know."

"Let's have it," he said.

Alex sighed heavily. "Jonathan, what if… We both know there are risks."

"There's always risks."

"You know what I am talking about."

"I suppose, I do," he confessed. "Look, we don't even know if O'Brien managed to fulfill his objective."

"His objective? You mean planting something in my son's subconscious? That objective?" Alex snapped.

Jonathan remained steady. He understood Alex's concerns. They had spent several years working to uncover an international conspiracy. Neither of them could have predicted where the trail would lead them. It had led them home. Despite what they had uncovered, Jonathan remained grateful for the twists in the path. He had found Alex, and he had found family—so, had she. But, they had also discovered a web of secrets and lies that still confounded them both. The spy game and the political arena were both games of perception. In the end, every objective came down to controlling perception. Whoever mastered that ability was likely to be successful in their endeavors.

During their investigation, Krause had discovered a top-secret project called Lynx, given its name for the lynx's mystical ability to possess second sight. Lynx was the ultimate perception program. It went far beyond any of its sister initiatives. There had been many projects developed after World War II that delved into the area of mind control utilizing everything from hypnosis and subliminal programming to exploring electroshock therapy and sensory deprivation. Programs like MK-Ultra had utilized military personnel and unwitting citizens. Lynx took all the trappings of MK-Ultra a step further. The objective in Lynx had been to implant memory, belief, and directives in the minds of children to create sleeper agents. Lynx had begun as a program of the CIA. It had been co-opted early on, twisted, and used for undetermined purposes by a group known as The Collaborative.

The Collaborative was comprised of intelligence operatives, business and political leaders, and military personnel from The United States, Russia, France, The United Kingdom, and various other countries across the globe. Its initial purpose had been to prop up the Cold War narrative, ensuring economic growth for its partners, and stemming the possibility of another world war. As with all agencies, governments, and organizations, power had corrupted The Collaborative. Over time, individuals had begun to redefine objectives. The group had grown to epic proportions and competing ideas and initiatives had resulted in a splinter.

Alex and Jonathan's determination to infiltrate the organization and undermine its newest objectives had propelled them on a collision course with destiny. They had uncovered the secrets of their fathers. It had led them to learn of their relationship as brother and sister. It had uncovered the lie that Cassidy's father had built. He had been the father of Lynx, developing the program's foundations. The project he had developed had been his codename. Fearing its implications for his family, James McCollum had taken pains to fake a believable death and disappear for over twenty years. He was not the only father who possessed dark secrets.

The truth about Claire's mother's death had also been unearthed, shattering her father's vicious effort to control Claire's thinking for most of her life. And, another dark secret had been unearthed. Cassidy's former husband was one of the first products of Lynx. His loyalty lay not with his family nor the United States government that he had been elected to. It was not even to wealth nor power. Congressman Christopher O'Brien had sworn fealty to Russia. It had been ingrained in him since childhood. He had one objective: infiltrate The Collaborative via Lynx's family, and change the narrative. His marriage to Cassidy had been an order, not an act of love. His mission had been to produce a child with Lynx's daughter. Whether O'Brien had succeeded in implanting any latent directives in Dylan's mind was unknown. That possibility continued to haunt Alex.

"Alex," Jonathan reached across and placed his hands on Alex's knees. "Stop this."

"I can't. It's my responsibility to protect him."

"Have you talked to Jim?"

"You know what he will say—let it lie."

"He is the expert, Alex."

Alex closed her eyes. Cassidy's father, Jim McCollum was an expert on mind control. Lynx had not only been his project; it had also been his codename. Alex still struggled with the man. She'd managed to cultivate a friendship with him, although she would never deny that she kept a close eye on him. She hated to admit it, but Alex did know that Jim McCollum loved his family. That truth was written in his eyes whenever he looked at Rose, Cassidy, or any of his grandchildren. Alex was confident that he would never knowingly endanger Dylan. She had not approached the issue with her father-in-law in years.

"Talk to Jim," Jonathan suggested.

"Pip," Alex looked her brother. "If Dylan goes into the military it exposes him."

"And, if he doesn't? Alex, no matter what path Dylan takes that risk exists. Look at all of us. Cassidy's a teacher. That didn't prevent her from getting sucked into all our parents' insanity. Besides, it's in his blood."

Alex groaned.

"It is," Jonathan said.

"Don't remind me."

"Dylan is a smart kid," Jonathan said. "He's had a different beginning than any of us had."

"Oh? Look at what he had to go through with O'Brien."

"Yes, but he has had you and Cassidy. He's had an army behind him most of his life. He has all of us. That is something you and I did not have—none of us did."

Alex sighed. That was true. That is why she had come here, for the truth. Jonathan would always be frank with Alex. He would never seek to sugar-coat difficult or precarious situations. "I just want him to be safe."

"So, do I."

"I know you do," Alex replied.

"This is what he wants, Alex." Krause snickered.

"What?"

"I was just thinking about our father."

"What about him?"

"Well, Helen has always said that he would have walked through fire to keep you from going to West Point. We both know he pulled every string he could to keep me out of the game."

"Yeah, well…"

"Oh, come on," Jonathan looked at her. "It's what you had to do. It's where I wanted to go. For all the shit, Alex, I think it ended up working out pretty well for both of us."

"I suppose it did."

"Dylan will be okay," he told her. "He doesn't have to look to find his family. He has his family—all of us."

True again. Dylan knew who he was, where he came from, and Alex suspected that Dylan had garnered far more about their family than she or Cassidy had ever laid out specifically. "I just love him so much," she said.

Jonathan smiled. He understood. "I know exactly how you feel," he said. "I feel the same way about all of them."

"I know you do," Alex said.

She and Jonathan seldom discussed the biology of Alex's children. She had approached Jonathan Krause before either had any idea of their biological connection with a request. They shared two major things: both loved Cassidy, and both had considered John Merrow their best friend. Alex had not made her request lightly. She understood that Jonathan Krause would move heaven and earth to keep Cassidy and Dylan safe. If ever she had to be absent, if anything should ever happen to her; Alex knew he would do the same for her entire family. He had been reluctant at first. Family meant everything to Cassidy. He knew that. And, Jonathan Krause had never considered a family of his own. He'd never regretted the decision. After learning that Alex was his sister, his role in helping her create a family with Cassidy had taken on new meaning. He was their uncle. They were a part of both Alex and Cassidy; something anyone who saw Connor and Abby, or who spent any time with Mackenzie would find evident immediately.

"Alex, if it matters at all, I honestly believe Dylan will be okay. He's not only smart; he's strong."

"Yes, he is."

"Talk to Jim," he repeated his suggestion. "Now, what about this case?"

"What about it?"

"I'm not going to lie to you. I was a little surprised that you accepted Hawk's offer."

"So was I."

"Why did you?"

"I don't know," Alex admitted. "Something about that girl—seeing her in that pile of dirt, knowing someone dumped her there—I just feel there's something more to all of it."

"You do know; this is not him," Krause said.

Alex nodded. "I know it's not Fisher. It feels…"

"Similar. I get it," he said. "Any leads?"

"Not a one. The fact that some kids tripped over this latest victim is the best I've got."

"You want me to dig deeper about O'Brien," Jonathan guessed.

"Pip…"

"I'll see what I can find, Alex. There might not be anything to find. Maybe it's time I visit some of our old friends."

"Which old friends might those be?"

"Well, you know since Dmitri and the admiral have been gone, Viktor has been markedly quiet."

"You want to go to Moscow?"

"Been a while since I've visited," he smirked.

"Eleana will love that."

"She'll understand," Jonathan put the thought to rest. "She knows the drill. Besides, it's family. Put your mind at ease about Dylan, Alex. If you are that concerned, I promise; I will get to the bottom of it. How about dinner before you head home?"

"Actually, I need to hit the field office here. I was hoping you wouldn't mind if I spent the night."

Jonathan gauged his sister's demeanor thoughtfully. He took a deep breath and released it slowly. "I still haven't touched a thing in his old office," he told her.

Alex nodded. Jonathan had always been able to read her as if she were an open book. She wasn't sure what was compelling her to go back to her roots. It wasn't only agreeing to sign back on at the FBI; Alex felt drawn to the ghosts of the past. She'd thought she had put her questions to rest. Somehow, the questions she had about her father, about Cassidy's father—about Claire and Eleana's parents had begun to press in on her with a new weight. Whether that was the result of the investigation she found herself in, Dylan's plan for the future, Cassidy's pregnancy or some combination of things, Alex wasn't sure. She had come to believe that few things in life amounted to coincidence. Maybe there would come a time when she could allow the past to lie in its grave. That time wasn't now. She was certain of that much.

"Alex," Jonathan called for her attention. "You have been through that office a million times—so, have I. I don't know what you expect to find."

Alex smiled. The truth suddenly hit her. *Maybe I just hope he'll walk in.*

CHAPTER NINE

"Alex?"

"Hey, Dylan," Alex greeted her son over the phone. "I just wanted to see how your visit was going."

"Great!"

Alex tried not to laugh at Dylan's exuberance. "That's good."

"We've seen everything," he beamed through the phone.

"Well, if anyone can get you a behind the scenes look, it's Jane."

"Yeah. Steph and Jeremy are having lunch with us tomorrow before we fly back," he told Alex.

"That's an unexpected bonus," she said. Dylan's older half-sisters both adored him. Stephanie was the eldest. She and Dylan had developed a close bond, and Alex was grateful for that. In many ways, it reminded Alex of her and Jonathan. She would have missed a great deal had she not found Krause. She would never want Dylan to miss out on time with his siblings—any of them.

"Yeah. They're bringing the kids," he said.

"Aw, you get to play uncle. Missing the brood at home?" she teased her son.

"Maybe a little," he admitted. "But, I won't lie. I'm glad I will miss most of the diaper duty this time around."

Alex laughed. "The real reason you chose the academy."

"Maybe."

"I don't want to keep you," Alex said. "I just wanted to see how things were."

"Alex?"

"Yeah?"

"I love it here."

Alex closed her eyes. "I know you do, Speed. They'll be lucky to have you."

"Thanks, Mom," Dylan almost whispered.

Alex started to choke up and cleared her throat. “Just the truth,” she said. “I’ll see you soon.”

“Okay. Hey… Alex?”

“Yeah?” Alex asked.

“Thanks again.”

“Say hi to Steph for me. I’ll see you.”

“Who was that?” Jane asked Dylan.

“Alex.”

“Checking up on you already?” Jane joked.

“Probably,” he laughed.

“She just loves you.”

“I know. I can’t help but feel there is something she and Mom aren’t telling me.”

Jane patted his arm. “Dylan, be glad that there are things your parents want to protect you from.”

“I am. I’m just curious. They tell me everything.”

“No,” Jane shook her head. “Not everything, Dylan. And, trust me; you should thank them for that.”

“You know what it is.”

“I know a lot of things. One of them is that sometimes it’s better not to know everything. You know how people say that the truth will set you free? That the truth can’t hurt you?”

“Yeah?”

“Both lies. The truth can bind you up and break your heart.”

“So, it’s better to lie?”

“No, but sometimes it’s better to let sleeping dogs lie, better than getting bit on the ass.”

Dylan chuckled. “I think, I get it.”

“Trust your parents,” Jane said.

“I do.”

“Then trust me when I tell you, if there is anything at any time they think you need to know—something to keep you safe, to help you grow, or to ease your mind—they will tell you.” Jane grasped

Dylan's shoulder lightly and left the room.

Dylan looked at the phone in his hand. *I do trust you. I just wonder how many secrets there are.*

"Claire, talk to me," Hawk implored her lover.

"You don't want me to talk to you," Claire said. "You want me to say what you want to hear."

"What is it that I want to hear?"

"We both know you want me to say I'm ready."

"Ready for us, you mean?"

Claire huffed. "Damnit, Hawk! Why is this so important to you?"

"Maybe because I love you."

"You need to be married to love me or do you need that to believe that I love you?"

"Do you?"

"Do I what?"

"Do you love me?"

"Jesus, Hawk," Claire shook her head.

"You didn't answer me."

"Because you already know the answer."

"How can I know the answer when you won't even say the words?" Hawk asked.

"People say words all the time," Claire replied. "That doesn't give them any meaning."

"So, you just don't bother to say them at all; is that it?"

"Would you believe me if I said them? Would that change anything between us?" Claire challenged her lover.

"I don't know. If you can't; that might just change everything," Hawk said.

"Is that an ultimatum?"

"No. It's the truth."

Claire chuckled.

"That's funny?" Hawk asked.

"No, what's funny is that you think it's not an ultimatum. I tell you what you want to hear or you're gone; is that right?"

"Tell me the truth."

Claire shook her head.

"She's not coming back," Hawk said. Claire snapped to attention. "She's got a life with Jonathan."

"You think this is about El?"

"Isn't it?"

Claire shook her head again. "You are unbelievable."

"What do you expect me to think? You still love her. We both know that."

Claire walked to the window in the hotel room and looked out, considering how to reply. In the past, she would have either walked out or thrown down an argument. She was tired of avoiding the subject. She did love Eleana. She'd loved Eleana her entire life. A person didn't simply fall out of love. But, Claire had made her peace with Eleana's decision, with her marriage and life. And, Claire did love Hawk. The idea of marriage, however, terrified her. Any time Claire dared think about it, her chest would constrict as if someone were strangling her. That is what she feared most, being held down against her will.

"I do love her," Claire said. She took a deep breath. "What I can't understand is why you think that means I don't love you."

"Maybe because you've never said it," Hawk replied.

"I just did."

"No, you didn't."

Claire's frustration was growing. "I told you, words are just words."

"Not always."

"Why do you want to marry me?" Claire shifted the dialogue.

"Why? Because I love you."

"Okay, but will it make you love me less if we aren't married?"

"That's not the point."

"What is the point?" Claire asked.

"You are impossible!"

Claire softened her tone. She crossed the room and stepped in front of her lover. "I'm not trying to be difficult," she said. "I know you think that. I'm not."

"What do you want, Claire?"

Claire smiled. "I want to love you," she answered, her fingertip tracing a line from Hawk's throat to the swell of her breasts.

Hawk caught Claire's hand before it could descend any lower. "Stop. I mean it. What do you want?"

"I just told you."

"You want to love me? You want to fuck me; is that it?" Hawk's voice raised. She tore open her blouse. "Is that what love is to you?"

Claire pulled Hawk into her arms and held her close. Hawk struggled and then began to cry. "Stop," Claire whispered in Hawk's ear. "Stop," she said, kissing Hawk's head. "I do love you," Claire let the words out. "I don't understand how you can question that," she said sincerely. "I've never been faithful to anyone but you," Claire said.

Hawk pulled back and looked into Claire's eyes. "But?"

"What you're asking…"

"I'm asking you to share your life with me."

"I thought we were already doing that."

"Claire…"

Claire sighed. "I can't marry you, Hawk."

"Why?"

"Why can't we just leave things as they are?"

"Because I want all of you."

Claire kissed Hawk gently. "I'm not someone you want to

marry, Hawk. I'm not Alex."

"What the hell does that mean?"

"It means just what I said. I don't want to come home at six o'clock every night to a house of screaming kids."

"Who said anything about kids?" Hawk asked. "Wait a minute. Do you think I'm asking you because I want kids?"

"To tell you the truth, I'm still not clear on why this is so important to you."

"What's to be clear on?"

"Do you—want kids?" Claire asked.

"No. Lots of people get married without ever having kids."

"Lots of people aren't us," Claire said. "They're not me."

"What are you so afraid of?" Hawk asked.

"I can't," Claire said. "Even if part of me wants to."

"You keep running from everyone and you are bound to get what you want in the end," Hawk said.

"What's that?"

Hawk stepped away. "You'll end up alone."

Claire nodded and grabbed her jacket. "Maybe that's how it's supposed to be," she said.

"Claire?"

Claire put her hand on the door. "I know you don't believe me. I do love you, Hawk. If I didn't, I might have just said yes."

Hawk watched as Claire stepped through the door and closed it. She collapsed onto the bed and put her face in her hands. "What aren't you telling me, Claire?"

Alex sat at a large table at the FBI field office sifting through photos, reports, and occasionally searching on her laptop. "What is your game?" she muttered.

"Looking for Professor Plum?" a voice chimed from behind.

"He's in the dining room with the candlestick," Claire offered.

"What are you doing here? I thought you were with Hawk."

"I thought you were with Jonathan."

"I was," Alex replied. She passed Claire a file.

"Find anything?"

"Not yet," Alex replied. She handed Claire a file folder.

"What am I looking at?"

"Missing person reports for the last sixty days from New York to Connecticut."

Claire moved to sit beside Alex and looked over her shoulder. "And, you're looking at dirt."

"I can't help but think we are missing something out there. I just wish I knew where to look next."

"Yeah, I had that thought too."

"Really?"

"Am I speaking another language tonight? Seems like no matter what I say, no one understands me."

"Things didn't go so well with Hawk; I take it."

Claire shrugged. She sat down at the table and started looking at the pages Alex had printed out. "Why can't you scroll on the computer like a normal person?" Claire rolled her eyes. "You're old, not ancient."

"I process it faster on paper."

"Uh-huh. You mean you are less likely to get a headache," Claire guessed.

Alex's head snapped to attention.

"What? I've seen you at home with the kids. Hell, you get a headache when you play a video game for too long."

"It's the light."

"Right."

"What's that supposed to mean?" Alex asked.

"Nothing."

"No, it meant something," she said as she gently massaged her right temple with her thumb.

Claire shrugged. "Maybe you should think about some glasses."

"I don't need glasses."

"Hey, it happens as you age."

Alex glared at Claire.

Claire held up her hands defensively. "Just looking out for you."

"Thanks. I'm good. How about you look through what I handed you?"

Claire began studying the files that Alex had handed her. "You know that the victim could be from anywhere?" she commented absently.

"She could, but I doubt she is," Alex countered. "Kaylee went missing in Connecticut and turned up in New York. Let's just say, I am betting whoever those boys found out there in the woods was traveling somewhere along that path."

Claire's eyes zeroed in on the papers in front of her. "Alex."

"Huh?"

"Look."

Claire passed Alex the paper in her hand. Alex stared at it blankly. Strange how putting a name with a face could make a person feel numb in one second and violently ill the next. Alex pinched the bridge of her nose. "Damnit." She committed the page to memory. Deidre Slocum. Alex sighed. "Jesus, twenty-two."

Claire grabbed the laptop from the table and pulled it to her.

"What are you doing?"

"Checking out Deidre Slocum's Facebook page."

Claire sat at the keyboard typing.

"Claire?"

"Alex, if you wanted to find out where Dylan was headed what would you do?"

"I'd call him."

Claire laughed. "Okay, suppose it was Mackenzie at seventeen or twenty-two. Think she'd take your call at any time?" Claire asked. Alex groaned. "Uh-huh. So, let's see…"

Alex moved to stand over Claire's shoulder. "Wait," Alex stopped Claire's scrolling. "Go back." Claire complied. "Stop," Alex said.

Looking forward to backpacking my way to Jamie's! New adventures!

"Who is Jamie?" Alex mused.

Claire was already engaged in a search. "Jamie Matson," Claire said. "Portland, Maine. Looks like they were college roommates," she explained.

"See if you can get a number for Ms. Matson," Alex said.

"What are you going to do?"

"Well, I'm thinking we should start looking on that route from Schoharie to Connecticut, see how many women have been reported missing in the last twelve years."

"That's a mighty big hunting ground."

"It's a place to start."

Claire groaned. "Fuck, I hate milk cartons."

Alex laughed despite the gravity of the work ahead. "We'll divide the area," she told Claire. "I'll take New York. You take Connecticut and Massachusetts."

Claire sighed. "Fabulous. Can't we get some minions to do this?" she asked. Alex smiled. "This is my punishment for the Maria joke I made earlier; isn't it?"

Alex chuckled.

"I knew it. They should never have partnered me with the Von Trapps."

Alex shook her head. Claire's bit of levity was welcome. "I'll try not to break out into Edelweiss," she joked.

Claire looked at Alex in astonishment. "Holy shit, she has a sense of humor."

Alex winked and then focused on her computer screen. *Now, let's find out who you might be.*

"Long day?" the security guard greeted the man in the van.

"Long life, Brandon," the man replied. "I see you're back at the home office."

"For now."

"Two jobs must be exhausting," the man observed.

"You should know," Brandon said.

"Me?"

"Well, yeah. Seems like you're always on the run somewhere. I'll bet you're glad to be off the road."

The man smiled. "Oh, you know what they say; home is where the heart is," the man quipped.

"My wife tells me that all the time when she wants me to take out the garbage."

The man laughed. "Sounds familiar. You have a good night."

"You too, Mr. Duncan."

The man rolled up his window and yawned. "Home," he mused. "Well, let's hope they've already taken out the garbage."

Alex's temples were throbbing. Five hours of combing through missing persons reports and searching data bases had brought on a severe migraine.

Claire looked over and shook her head. *She needs those glasses.*

"Hey," Alex called to Claire.

"Find something?"

"I'm not sure. Look at this," Alex said. "These two girls went missing ten years ago, both from Middleburgh."

"New York?"

"Yeah, just south of Schoharie, not far from the area where they found Kaylee."

"Cold case?"

"Not even a case," Alex commented. "Just a missing person's report. One was eighteen, the other nineteen. Technically, they were both adults. No reason to suspect foul play—no substantial investigation."

Claire shook her head.

"What?"

"Two girls just up and disappear, and that doesn't warrant an investigation?"

Alex nodded. "I'm certain it warranted some phone calls, maybe even a few visits to distant friends. Over half a million people are reported missing every year, Claire. If every cop in America got assigned to work on a case, there would never be enough assets to run down every lead."

"Maybe. You and I both know nine times out of ten they didn't happily skip off to Wonderland."

Alex sighed. She looked at Claire. "Are you thinking what I'm thinking?"

"Worth a shot," Claire agreed. "Start at the beginning."

Alex nodded. Two girls missing from the area she and Claire had developed as this killer's likely hunting ground—two girls found buried where Kaylee had gone missing. Alex would love to have believed it was a coincidence. That seemed unlikely. She looked at the contact number on the original report filed by George Evans. What are the chances they are still there? She picked up her phone, took a deep breath, and dialed the number. "Hello?"

"Mom!" Mackenzie bellowed.

Cassidy threw her head back with exasperation. "I'm in the kitchen, Kenz."

"Mom," Mackenzie grabbed Cassidy's hand.

"What?"

"Abby fell off the swing in back."

Cassidy wiped her hands on a towel and followed her daughter outside. She sighed lightly and picked up her pace to reach her youngest child. "What happened?" Cassidy asked, pulling Abby into her arms.

"We went too high," Connor said, pointing to the tire swing.

Cassidy looked at her son. He was covered in dirt and grass, but he didn't look to have any injuries. She turned back to Abby, who clung to her. "What hurts?" she asked. Abby held up her hand. Cassidy kissed the little girl's head. "You're okay, sweetheart. Let's go inside and see what you did; okay?"

Abby continued to cry until Cassidy got her seated in the kitchen. Cassidy gently washed some dirt off Abby's hands and face. She grimaced at the dark bruise already apparent around Abby's wrist. *Of all the kids that could get hurt.* Cassidy smiled reassuringly at her daughter. "Abby, sweetheart; I think maybe we need someone to take a picture of your wrist."

Abby flinched and then wailed.

Cassidy picked her up and held her. "Shh," she tried to soothe her daughter. "You know, your big brother fell off that swing a few times. So, did Kenzie. Kenzie got to wear a pretty pink brace for a while."

Mackenzie stepped up and patted her little sister's knee. "Yep. And, see? I'm okay. I even got ice cream after," she tried to cajole her sister.

Cassidy smiled proudly at Mackenzie. She felt Connor tug at

her shirt and looked down at a pair of watery eyes. "It's all right, Connor," Cassidy assured him. "Abby will be okay; I promise," she assured him. "Kenz? Can you please go call Grandma and ask her if she could come by?"

Mackenzie nodded. "Don't worry, Abby," she told her sister. "Mom always knows how to make it better," she said and then skipped off to complete her assigned task.

"Mommy?" Abby called for Cassidy's attention. Cassidy turned back to her and smiled. "Do I get ice cream too?"

Cassidy chuckled, leaned in and kissed Abby's forehead. "I think when we get home later, we ought to have an ice cream party," she said.

"Party!" Connor yelled with delight.

Cassidy laughed. *Only in this family is a potential broken bone a reason to throw a party.*

"Hello. Mr. Evans? Mr. George Evans?" Alex inquired.

"Yes?"

Alex let out a deep breath. "My name is Agent Alex Toles. I'm with the FBI."

"FBI?"

"Yes, Sir. I'm sorry to call you out of the blue like this."

"Is this about Melissa?" the older man's voice caught.

Alex steadied her breathing. "I'm not sure," she replied honestly. "I'm investigating a homicide. The victim was from your area. I understand that you reported Melissa missing ten years ago." Alex heard a long sigh escape the man on the line.

"Is it her?" he asked.

"No, sir. But," Alex proceeded with caution. "We found two other victims close to where this young lady was discovered. Identification is proving difficult."

"And, you think one of them is my Melissa?"

"I don't know. I wish I could tell you more. I understand your daughter was last seen with a close friend."

"Yes," he replied somberly. "Darla."

Alex paused for a moment. "Sir, I know this is difficult. I would like to have an agent come out and collect a DNA sample if possible."

"What do you need?" he asked.

"If you have anything of hers still available—a brush perhaps, even a lock of hair from her youth—that would be ideal. If not, we can look to take a cheek swab from you."

George Evans closed his eyes.

"Mr. Evans?"

"Whatever you need, Agent Toles. How long will it take?"

"The faster we collect the sample, the sooner we will be able to make a determination."

"You know, you always hope…"

"I understand," Alex said gently.

"I'm just surprised that after so long anyone would even pay attention. Seems like no matter how many calls we've made or ways we've tried—well, it's never led anywhere."

Alex felt her heart drop. Finding out that someone you love had been murdered was shocking and painful. Not knowing what might have happened to someone you love? That was worse by far. She had witnessed that pain before. Families always clung to a glimmer of hope, even amid the darkest shadows of doubt. It was a way to survive the unknown. Never knowing the truth left a cavernous divide between hope and despair, one that families of missing persons were doomed to flounder in until there was a conclusion. Unfortunately, in Alex's experience, any conclusion that was ever reached rarely lifted their hope.

"I promise you," she said. "If this is not your daughter, I will do what I can to help you find some answers."

Claire's head snapped up. "Toles," she warned.

Alex ignored her partner. "I'll be in touch," Alex promised.

"What the hell was that?" Claire asked.

"What?"

"Alex, you and I both know the FBI is not about to waste resources on a case of two missing girls that was never even a case."

Alex shrugged.

"Toles…"

"What? It wouldn't be the first time you or I investigated something off the radar."

Claire shook her head.

"If it makes you feel any better," Alex said. "I don't think we will need to."

Claire nodded. "It doesn't—make me feel better that is," she said.

Alex sighed when her phone rang. "Toles."

"Hi."

"Cass?"

"I'm sorry to bother you."

"What's wrong?" Alex asked.

"Relax," Cassidy replied. "Everything is okay. Abby just had a little accident."

"What kind of little accident?" Alex wanted to know.

"She fell off the tire swing," Cassidy explained. She heard Alex groan. "She's okay. I called Dr. Brandeis. He suggested I take her to Yale; just in case."

"Just in case?"

"Alex," Cassidy softened her voice. "She's all right. I think she might have broken her wrist."

Alex's fingertips reached the bridge of her nose and pressed hard. "I'll be there as soon as I can."

"Alex, it's okay."

"No, it isn't," Alex disagreed.

"Alex…"

"I'm not that far, Cass. You'll be waiting a while. I can be there in a couple of hours."

"You're working."

"I'll be there."

"Alex," Cassidy's voice became firm. "Please, trust me. Abby is okay. You need to be where you are. She's more excited about the ice cream party I promised than worried about the emergency room right now."

Alex chuckled. "Bribing the kids?"

"Learned from the best," Cassidy deadpanned.

"I will never live that down."

"Not likely," Cassidy agreed. "Just do what you need to do. I'll call you when I know something."

Alex sighed. "Cass, if you need me…"

"Go on, Agent Toles."

"What are you doing?" Eleana asked Jonathan.

"Checking on some things for Alex."

"Things?"

"She's worried about Dylan."

"Find anything?"

"Maybe," Jonathan replied. "What are you doing here? I thought Helen was coming up today?"

Alex's mother had adopted Jonathan into her fold. It was a late in life relationship that Eleana could tell meant the world to her husband. He had never had a close relationship with the father who raised him, and had no idea that Nicolaus Toles was his biological father for most of his life. It was odd to him now. When Jonathan Krause looked in the mirror, he could see the resemblance he held to both his half-brother and half-sister. He and Alex shared many common traits from the color of their eyes to a tendency to pinch the bridge of their nose when stress began to build. Helen's acceptance of him into the Toles family had meant more than he had expressed to anyone. Alex's mother told him stories about the man who had tried to silently guide him from a distance. She held no bitterness toward Jonathan's mother nor her husband.

"Life is unpredictable," Helen told him before he married Eleana. "It twists on a dime. You can't yield to it, but you have to learn to bend if you hope to make it around those corners. Marriages are the same way."

Eleana smiled. "She was," she said. "She pulled YaYa duty this afternoon."

"Everything okay with Cassie? Is she sick or something?"

"No," Eleana said. "Abby took a tumble. Cassidy needed to take her to the ER."

Jonathan cringed.

"Why would Cassidy be sick?" Eleana inquired.

Jonathan offered his wife a sheepish grin. "She's pregnant."

"Seriously?"

Jonathan laughed. "I don't think Alex would joke about that."

"Huh."

"That surprises you?" he asked.

"Not really," Eleana replied. "She's just never mentioned that they wanted to try."

"Listen," Jonathan said. "I need to talk to some old acquaintances."

"Do I want to know?"

He smiled. "Believe me; it's much safer than dealing with Carecom business."

"Oh?"

"It's just Viktor."

"That's not funny."

"I'm not joking."

"Need my help?" Eleana grinned.

"No."

"Jonathan, I'm pregnant, not invalid."

"No," Jonathan said. "I still remember my Russian." Eleana had served as a translator for the US State Department A.K.A. The Central Intelligence Agency since her mid-twenties.

"Your Russian has never sounded much like Russian," she teased him.

"Very funny."

"Just curious, but why doesn't Alex just ask Jim if she's worried?"

"You know she's still cautious there."

"Uh-huh."

Jonathan groaned.

"Jonathan? What aren't you telling me?"

"She's back at the FBI."

"Yes, I know. What aren't you telling me?"

"I think she sort of has her hands full with her new partner?"

"Why? Did they assign her a rookie?"

"Not exactly—no," he said. Eleana looked at him curiously. Jonathan sighed. "Claire."

"Excuse me?"

"Alex's new partner," he tried to explain.

"Yes?"

"Is Claire."

"My Claire?"

Jonathan sighed.

"You know what I meant."

"Yeah, I do," he said. "Yes."

Eleana shook her head. "Claire and Alex are partners?" she asked again. He nodded. "Oh, boy."

Jonathan nodded.

"How is that going?"

"I'm not really sure," he admitted. "Alex said Claire is Claire light; whatever that means."

"Tell me how I can help."

"With Claire?"

Eleana laughed. "No, with whatever it is you think you are looking for."

"Oh." He opened his laptop. "Feel like digging through some old files?" he turned the computer toward her.

Eleana narrowed her gaze. "Digging up old skeletons?" she asked.

"Well, sometimes the past tells you a lot about the present."

"Jonathan…"

"I know," he said.

"Okay," Eleana replied. "Jonathan? What aren't you telling me?"

Jonathan groaned.

Eleana looked at the screen again. "Jonathan, Carl Fisher is dead."

"I know."

Eleana sighed. "She's worried about whether O'Brien fulfilled his objective," she surmised. "What does Fisher have to do with that?"

"Maybe nothing. He did know O'Brien." He saw Eleana's skepticism. "I know what you are thinking."

"Oh?"

"I'm sure that this case, working with Claire—all of it—I'm sure that it is bringing old demons back to the surface. The thing is, we never actually banished them. We just decided to let them lie; or, at least, Alex did."

"And, now?"

"The past has a way of coming back sometimes. You know that as well as I do."

Eleana nodded. "I'll look."

Jonathan leaned in and kissed her gently. "Thank you."

"You don't need to thank me," she told him. "Just be careful."

"I'll be okay."

"Jonathan…"

"I promise."

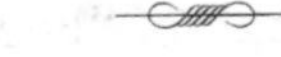

Cassidy ran her fingers through Abby's hair. Abby's head rested on her breast as she snuggled protectively against her mother.

"Hey."

Cassidy looked up to meet Alex's gaze. "What are you doing home?"

Alex made her way to the bed and sat on the edge. "How is she?"

"Tired."

Alex sighed.

"Alex, don't do this to yourself. She's okay. She was just hurting a little bit tonight."

Alex reached out and stroked Abby's back. "Why do we leave that swing up?"

Cassidy laughed. "Maybe because the kids love it."

"And, fall off it."

"I thought we agreed you were going to stay at Jonathan's and then head to New York?" Cassidy asked.

"Home is on the way," Alex said.

Cassidy smiled and patted the bed. Alex pulled off her shoes and laid down on the other side of their daughter.

"You okay?" Cassidy asked.

"Yeah."

"You are a horrible liar, Alex."

Alex chuckled. "Cass, I think we might be close to identifying those two women."

"Isn't that a good thing?"

"I don't know," Alex said. "I had to call this man today. His daughter went missing ten years ago with her friend. I could hear the way he lost his breath. Is this finally it? That's what he was wondering. People will say it gives you closure—to have the answer. I've always told myself that. Closure? Is closure better than hope, even if the hope is just a glimmer?"

"I don't know," Cassidy admitted. She covered Alex's hand with hers. "Loss is never easy. I don't know what's worse—never knowing, or knowing something horrific."

Alex sighed. "He's not done."

Cassidy watched as Alex's jaw became taut. Alex's eyes never left Abby. "Alex?"

Alex shook her head. "I'll never understand it."

"How could you?" Cassidy asked. "I don't know how anyone can understand that kind of violence," she said. She placed a kiss on Abby's head and started to move the sleeping toddler.

"What are you doing?" Alex asked.

"I'm going to put her down in her room."

"Cass, she can stay."

"She can, but she's okay. She'll be all right in her room."

"Cass…"

Cassidy smiled. "I have a feeling you might be on the road a bit," she said. "Call me selfish, I'd rather not have anyone between us tonight."

"I'll take her," Alex said. She lifted Abby and smiled at the toddler in her arms.

Cassidy loved to watch Alex with their children. Alex always looked at them in complete wonderment, as if she couldn't believe they were really hers. That had never changed, and Cassidy was confident that it never would. Alex moved slowly to the door, cooing to Abby when Abby wiggled in her arms.

Cassidy closed her eyes for a moment. The day had taken its toll on Alex. Fatigue was evident in both Alex's eyes and the slowness of her gait. "Oh, Alex."

Cassidy wasn't surprised at Alex's lengthy absence. She often found Alex sitting on the edge of one of their children's beds while they slept, particularly when they were ill or upset about something. Cassidy thought she had given Alex enough time. The last thing she wanted was for Alex to spend time beating herself up over Abby's mishap. She headed down the hall, and was surprised to find Alex sitting on the edge of Dylan's empty bed.

"Alex?"

Alex looked up and smiled. "How did this happen?"

Cassidy grinned. "Time flies, huh? He's not leaving tomorrow, love."

"No, but he will be leaving."

Cassidy moved to sit beside Alex. "I know. Sometimes, I can't believe it."

"He was so excited when I talked to him earlier."

"I know."

"He loves it there."

"He'll be all right, Alex."

"Jonathan thinks I should talk to your dad."

Cassidy sighed. "You're worried about what Chris might have done."

"I can't help it, Cass."

"I know."

Alex looked at Cassidy. "You too?"

"I'd be lying if I said I never thought about it."

"Do you think I should?"

"Talk to Dad?" Cassidy asked.

"Yeah."

"Couldn't hurt."

"I just wish there was some way to know what O'Brien did."

"He might not have done anything," Cassidy said.

"What do you think?" Alex asked.

Cassidy shook her head. "Where Chris is concerned, I'm not sure I'll ever know what I think," she admitted. "If anyone can help, it's Dad."

Alex nodded.

"Alex?"

"I just hate it."

"What?"

"That I can't protect them," Alex said.

Cassidy kissed Alex on the cheek. "Tell me," she said. She stood up and held out her hand. "Let's go, Agent Toles."

"Is that an invitation?" Alex smirked.

"Yep—to sleep."

"You mean to be your pillow."

Cassidy winked. "I think you might have that one backward."

"How do you figure?"

Cassidy snickered.

Alex laughed. Cassidy was right. She imagined it would surprise most people, but most nights, Alex fell asleep in the safety of Cassidy's arms. "Well, I can't help it if you are…"

"Squishy?" Cassidy teased. Alex shrugged. "Yeah, well, I will be squishier soon," Cassidy giggled.

Alex pulled Cassidy to her and kissed her tenderly.

"What was that for?" Cassidy asked.

"Do I need a reason?"

"Never."

Cassidy opened the front door and smiled at Claire. “Oh boy,” she said. “Coffee?” she asked.

“Where’s Alex?”

“Sleeping,” Cassidy said. “If you can believe that.”

“She sleeps?” Claire asked as she followed Cassidy to the kitchen.

Cassidy laughed. “Occasionally. You don’t look like you got much—sleep, that is. How is Hawk?”

“Not speaking to me, I would imagine.”

“What? Why not?”

Claire shrugged.

“Claire?”

“She proposed.”

Cassidy’s jaw fell open.

“Yeah, I know.”

“What did you say?” Cassidy asked.

“Not what she wanted to hear.”

Cassidy nodded and poured Claire a cup of coffee. “And, how are you doing with that?”

“Okay,” Claire replied honestly. Cassidy sat down and smiled at her. “I love her. I do.”

“I know.”

“I’m not ready for that, Cass. I’m not sure I will ever be ready for that.”

“I know that too. What I don’t know is why you are so afraid of it.”

“Marriage? Cassidy, come on.”

Cassidy sipped from a glass of juice. “Do you want to?”

“Get married?”

“Get married to Hawk,” Cassidy clarified.

“I want to be with Hawk.”

“But, not married to Hawk.”

“Why do we need to be married?” Claire asked with frustration.

Cassidy took another sip from the glass in her hand. "You think I should," Claire guessed.

"I didn't say that."

"But, you do."

"No," Cassidy set the glass on the table. "I think you should do what feels right to you."

"Really?"

"Why does that surprise you?"

"I don't know. I just don't see myself with a family."

Cassidy's brow furrowed in confusion. "Claire? Is that what Hawk said—that she wanted to get married and have a family?"

"Not exactly."

"Uh-huh. What did she say—exactly?"

"She said she wants to marry me because she loves me and she wants us to be committed."

Cassidy nodded.

"I thought we already were," Claire sighed.

"I know."

"You know? Cassidy… Could you maybe give me something more than, 'I know,' here?"

Cassidy chuckled. "I do know," she told Claire. "Can I ask you something without you getting angry?"

"If you have to ask that…"

Cassidy laughed. "Can I?" Cassidy repeated her question. Claire nodded. "How much of this is about Eleana?"

"Why does everyone think that?"

"Maybe because Eleana is the one person you have always trusted completely, and that is not easy to let go of."

"That's not true. I trust you."

Cassidy smiled. "Not the same, and you know it."

"I blew it with El. We all know that. I hurt her. Believe it or not, I'm glad that she found someone to give her what she deserves."

"Uh-huh. And, you think that you don't deserve that too?"

"Do I?"

"I think so," Cassidy replied.

"Cassidy, I don't," Claire shook her head and sighed.

"You're afraid you will fail Hawk," Cassidy said knowingly. Claire looked at her. "You are," Cassidy said. "Claire," Cassidy smiled at the younger woman. "You are not the same person you were then."

"But, I am."

"No," Cassidy disagreed. "You've grown. The fact that you understand that you hurt Eleana proves that. Your willingness to let her go, when part of her wanted you to hold on—your relationship with Hawk—all of it proves that."

"I know that she forgives me," Claire said.

"But, you can't forgive yourself," Cassidy interjected. Claire closed her eyes. "Maybe you should tell Hawk why you are reluctant to marry her."

"I did."

"Really? You said, 'Hawk, I love you, but I don't think I deserve you to love me. And, if I let you, I'm afraid I will ruin it.' You actually said that?"

"No."

"Maybe you should."

"Does it matter why?"

"I think so," Cassidy said.

"Easy for you to say."

"No, it isn't," Cassidy disagreed. "You can take my advice or not. We all look in the mirror some days and wonder who is looking back. We all see those shadows looking back—the things we wish we could have done differently. We all do."

"I'm not the marrying kind."

"I wasn't aware marriage applied to any certain kind of person."

"Cassidy, I can barely keep my refrigerator stocked."

Cassidy laughed. She patted Claire's hand in encouragement. "Talk to Hawk," she said.

"I'm not sure she wants to hear anything I have to say unless it is in the form of a one-word answer called yes."

"I wouldn't underestimate her," Cassidy said.

"Who are we underestimating?" Alex asked as she entered the room. "Hey," she greeted Claire. "You okay?"

"Yeah, some of us don't roll out of bed at nine in the morning," Claire offered.

Cassidy hopped up and poured Alex a cup of coffee. "So? Where are you two off to today?" Cassidy inquired.

"Looks like New York," Claire said. She turned her attention to Alex. "Think you might be onto something," she told her partner.

"Care to explain?" Alex asked.

Claire sighed.

"It's okay. I'm going to go check on Abby. See if she's starting to stir at all," Cassidy said.

"Oh, shit! How is she?" Claire asked.

"Sore," Alex replied.

"Alex was up with her a few times last night," Cassidy explained. She leaned in and kissed Alex's cheek. "Try not to overload on the caffeine," she advised her wife. "And, you," Cassidy looked at Claire. "Think about what I said."

"Yes, Mom," Claire teased.

Cassidy shook her head and started out of the room.

"What did she tell you?" Alex asked Claire.

"Oh, you know, to be less Claire-like."

"I did not," Cassidy called back. "Think about it."

Alex snickered at the expression on Claire's face. "She's part bat," Alex said.

Claire rolled her eyes and looked over her shoulder.

Alex took a sip from her coffee cup. "She's upstairs by now. What didn't you want Cass to hear?"

Claire groaned.

"Claire?"

"Eleana called me this morning."

"That's unusual?" Alex asked. Claire tugged at her lip with her bottom teeth. Alex wondered if that was a typical habit for her partner when she was worried. Cassidy did the same thing. "Claire?"

"No, it's not as unusual as you might think," Claire bit more harshly than she had intended. "Sorry."

Alex shook her head. "Why wouldn't you want Cass to know that?"

"She called about you."

"Me?"

"Well, yeah. She said she was worried about me and you being partnered," Claire explained. "I told her that I could handle you."

Alex snickered. "I've no doubt."

"That I can handle you?" Claire raised her brow.

"Ha-ha."

"Really, I think she called because Krause is on his way to Moscow."

Alex sipped her coffee.

"Want to tell me why Krause is off to Moscow to talk to Viktor Ivanov?"

"Not really."

"Look, Alex… I know that this case is probably…"

Alex held up a hand. "It's Dylan."

"Dylan?"

"Whatever O'Brien might have put in his head. Claire, if he goes into the military… In some ways as an officer he will be even more vulnerable."

Claire nodded. She doubted that Alex gave her much credit. Claire had known Alex longer than even Cassidy had. While she was confident that Alex doubted the sincerity of their original friendship/intimate engagements, the truth was that Claire had always admired Alex Toles. She'd never loved Alex. She liked Alex. And, Claire had regarded Alex as much more than the usual challenge she delighted in. She'd had years to study Alex from a myriad of vantage points. There was little doubt in Claire Brackett's mind that Alex Toles' return to the FBI, that working with Claire, that being back in the thick of her old life was conjuring old demons. Some old demons carried with them reason for concern.

"Do you really think O'Brien played with Dylan's head the way my father did with mine?"

"I don't know."

Claire nodded again. "Are you sure that the FBI is where you want to be?"

"What?"

"I'm just asking. Maybe you should go back to your true beginnings, Alex."

"I don't want to go back to that life," Alex said.

Claire accepted the answer at face value. "If there is anything to worry about, Krause will find it."

"I hope so."

"So?" Claire changed the subject. "New York?"

"New York."

CHAPTER TEN

"Do you know how many cases are on my desk right now?"

Alex made no reply. She respected Assistant Director Don Bower. She'd known him as a field agent during her time at FBI Headquarters. Right now, his caseload was not her concern.

"If I fast-tracked every request for DNA…"

"It's not every case," Alex replied evenly.

"No, it's your case," he said.

"Every minute that passes gives him a chance to get one more step ahead," Alex said.

Bower's jaw clenched. "What makes you believe these are related?"

Claire drummed her fingernails on her coffee cup.

"Agent Brackett?" Bower addressed her. "Something you'd like to add?"

The sarcasm laced grin Claire Brackett offered the assistant director almost sent Alex into a fit of laughter—almost.

"Well?" he prodded Claire.

Claire shrugged. "Maybe you should switch from using Schtick to Occam."

Alex chuckled.

"Find that funny, Agent Toles?" he asked Alex.

"Not really—just accurate," Alex replied. "No matter what we find—there is a connection."

Bower groaned. He met Alex's gaze. "Has it occurred to you that these might be unrelated?"

"It occurred to me; yes," Alex said.

"For about five seconds," Claire muttered.

Bower studied the pair before him. He was surprised to surmise that they had fallen into a unique rhythm. Any successful partnership required balance. He had balked at Hawk's suggestion to pair Brackett and Toles. Hawk had asked for his trust. As strange as it seemed to him, it appeared his colleague had been correct; Alex Toles and Claire Brackett complimented each other.

"You think it's the same guy," he surmised.

"I don't know. I'd bet my career that they are connected somehow," Alex replied.

"Not a very risky bet considering you haven't committed to more than this case," he reminded her.

"Okay, I'd bet her career on it," Alex pointed at Claire.

Claire smiled at their superior. "She's very generous."

Bower finally chuckled. "Well, you happen to be lucky on this one."

"How's that?" Alex wondered.

"Seems you still have some powerful allies."

Alex was genuinely curious.

Bower chuckled again. "A certain popular governor has raised concerns about the well-being of her citizens."

"I'll bet she has," Alex smiled. She knew immediately who Bower was referencing—the governor of New York.

Bower nodded. "So, fast-track it is. And, as a bonus, you get to brief the governor." He handed both agents a piece of paper. "If the results are what you suspect," he added. "And, these two women are the two who went missing ten years ago in New York, there will be a special task-force assigned. You'll be the agent in charge, Toles."

"And, me?" Claire asked.

Bower winked. "You keep her in line."

"Aww, shit," Claire groaned.

"Politicians," Claire muttered.

"This isn't just any politician," Alex replied. She took a deep breath and stood when the conference room door opened.

"Please, sit," the governor directed the group that had

assembled. Her eyes met immediately with Alex's. "Agent Toles, nice to see you again. I wish it were under different circumstances."

"Governor Reid," Alex nodded.

"Is there anyone you don't know?" Claire whispered.

Alex chuckled. Governor Candace Reid was a longtime friend of Cassidy's and of the Merrow family. The governor and Cassidy's ex-husband had both served as part of the congressional delegation from New York—Christopher O'Brien as a congressman and then Candace Fletcher as the senior senator. Alex admired the woman now seated at the end of the table. Candace Reid and Alex Toles shared more than a few things in common. They both had been close to President John Merrow, they both had a need to fix things, and they both were married to strong, intelligent women.

"So," the governor began. "I've got an entire corner of my state on edge over rumors and nothing I can give them as reassurance. Help me out," she looked at Alex. "Are we dealing with an active serial killer here or not?"

Alex took a deep breath. "That's what we are trying to determine."

The governor nodded.

"It's the FBI's belief, that yes, we are dealing with an active serial killer," Alex told her.

"Who is targeting upstate New York?"

"It would appear this is an area he frequents," Alex admitted. Candace waited. "I'm not convinced it's his only hunting ground."

Candace Reid felt a chill travel up her spine. "All right. Agent Toles, I assume that you know everyone present. I want to make certain that the FBI has the full partnership of our resources. Whatever we can provide, you only need to ask."

Alex nodded gratefully.

"You and Superintendent Foster are acquainted?" the governor directed her question to Alex.

Alex smiled. She had only recently met the State Police

Superintendent. The position was an appointee of the governor. She did not know Greg Foster well. She did have great faith in the governor. That told Alex everything she needed to know.

"We've been introduced," Alex said.

"Good. Now, give me the basics," the governor requested.

"As you know, several days ago a young woman named Kaylee Peters was found in the Conesville section of Ashland-Pinnacle State Forest. A day later, we uncovered the remains of two bodies where Kaylee Peters had last been seen—a state park in Connecticut."

"And, you believe these murders are related?" a voice asked.

Candace Reid looked at Alex for an answer.

"We believe that is a probability—yes," Alex replied.

"A probability?" another voice questioned.

Alex took a deep breath. "Two days ago, a young woman from this area was discovered with similar injuries to Kaylee's just a little over a mile from where Kaylee disappeared."

"And, the two other victims?" the governor asked.

"Awaiting identification," Claire interjected.

"That will tell us a great deal more," Alex explained.

"Any idea who they were?" Governor Reid inquired.

"We have leads. Until we have a positive ID, I can't comment."

"Do you have any profile at all yet?" Greg Foster asked.

"About as basic as it gets," Alex replied honestly. "Based on the two victims we do know, it is a male. He's likely someone who travels the New York to Connecticut corridor. Could be a truck driver or a salesperson of some kind. The identification of the other two victims will help us to determine if that is a narrow enough field."

"And?"

Alex sighed. She hated these types of meetings. As a profiler, everything Alex ascertained was an educated guess. Her assessments were almost always close to the mark. But, she had miscalculated before. The current circumstances demanded she hit a bullseye.

"His age could vary. My best estimate is someone in his mid-thirties to early forties. If these four victims are related; it appears that his pattern of violence has escalated over time. He likely has been at this a while," she explained.

"Go on," Candace Reid urged.

"He may have knowledge of or an interest in the military or law enforcement. I'd prefer not to examine those specifics in this setting."

Governor Reid nodded and let her eyes fall on each person in the room as she addressed them. "No egos. No assumptions. Agent Toles is running this investigation. All hands on deck," she told them. She looked at her Superintendent. "Anything pertinent, any new development, I want it before the press," she said. He nodded. The governor turned to a woman seated beside her. "Dana, you know the drill. Keep the press at bay as much as you can so that Agent Toles can stay focused."

"That's like trying to put a leash on a shark and take it for a walk," Claire mumbled. Alex jabbed her. "What?"

Candace Reid looked at the younger FBI agent impassively for a moment. She surprised the room with her laughter. "Accurate," she acknowledged Agent Brackett. "Keep me in the loop," she said with a nod. As the room began to empty, she held Alex's gaze. "Give me a minute with the good agent," she turned to the woman beside her.

"Now, why do I think there is a story here?" Claire whispered in Alex's ear.

Alex rolled her eyes. "Not the kind you read at bedtime," she grinned at Claire.

Claire shook her head. "I'm gonna talk to Foster."

Alex met the governor in the center of the room.

"Alex," Candace Reid softened her tone.

"Candace."

Candace sighed. "Not the way I'd hoped to catch up. Back in the saddle, I see?" she teased Alex.

"For now," Alex replied. "What about you? I hear you have

your eyes on a bigger house."

Candace laughed. "You've been talking to Jane."

Alex shrugged. "If it matters, I think you'd be great."

"It matters."

"Not sure you want that job, huh?" Alex guessed.

"The presidency isn't like anything else. We both know that," Candace said.

Alex nodded. "John would have loved to see you there."

"I know. I still miss that difficult son of a bitch," Candace laughed.

"Me too."

"How's Cassidy?"

Alex smirked. "Now, why is it I think you probably already know that answer?"

Candace winked. "I wish we had a chance to talk more often," she admitted.

"I'm sure Cass feels the same way. It's crazy with the kids."

"Tell me," Candace laughed. "If three's company, four is insanity."

Alex chuckled. "Imagine five."

"No, thank you," Candace said. "Oh, no! Really? Are you two expecting again?"

Alex nodded.

"Good for you. I'll tell you, being Nana and Mommy at the same time is not something I ever expected."

"I can imagine," Alex said.

Candace sobered. "Alex, this one—this is personal."

Alex was curious.

"Deirdre Slocum is the daughter of one of my high school friends," Candace explained.

Alex groaned. "I'm sorry."

"Me too," Candace said. "I don't want to meet again to review a body count."

Alex nodded. “Me neither.”

Candace led Alex to the door. “Do me a favor?” she asked Alex. “Let’s make sure we don’t keep being brought together by death?”

Alex smiled. She’d gotten to know the governor well after President John Merrow’s assassination and the death of Cassidy’s ex-husband. Senator Candace Fletcher had been one of the first people to call Cassidy and offer her support. Cassidy had never forgotten that, and neither had Alex. While they did not visit often, Alex knew that Cassidy kept in touch with the governor, and Alex considered Candace a trusted friend.

“When this is all over, you should come down and visit. Cass would love to see you.”

“Mm. Jameson would love to revisit that billiards table.”

Alex nodded. She and Candace’s wife, Jameson shared a few passions, not the least of which was a competitive game of billiards over some beer.

“You know, she keeps insisting we should get one,” Candace laughed. “I told her it’s already a full house.”

“Well, maybe that’s a good reason to upgrade,” Alex teased.

“Not you too,” Candace rolled her eyes. “A lesbian in the White House?”

Alex shrugged. “Hey, I landed Cass, that proves anything is possible.”

Candace laughed. She sobered when her hand reached the door. “Alex,” she said. “If you need anything at all…”

Alex smiled appreciatively. It wasn’t her policy to break protocol on a whim. But, Alex had traversed the mucky waters of politics and justice. The two collided more often than most wanted to admit. Any time that a serial killer was on the loose, public angst and public accusation swelled. That never had any good place to lead. Alex knew that too. “I’ll keep you in the loop,” she promised.

“You honestly think we have a serial killer on our hands?”

Candace asked.

Alex nodded. "I wish I didn't."

Candace clasped Alex's hand. "Me too. Be careful," Candace advised.

"We'll talk," Alex said. Candace nodded her thanks.

"What was that about?" Claire asked when Alex caught up to her.

"You mean Candace?"

"Yeah."

"She's just trying to figure out how to control things, I suspect."

"Control what? This guy isn't about to be controlled."

Alex nodded. "No," she agreed. "I meant keeping the public informed without causing panic."

"Good luck with that. He's not done yet."

Alex couldn't argue. If she was right, three dead women all from the area was not something likely to instill confidence in the community. She feared that there was more to come. "Let's hope we're both wrong."

"Where are we headed or should I not ask?" Claire wondered.

"I want to check out that spot where those kids were headed when they found Deidre Slocum."

Claire let her eyes track back to the scenery outside her window. A forensics team had processed that scene for more than three days. Claire wasn't sure what Alex hoped to find, but she understood the inclination. Four days of waiting for a positive identification of the two women they had found had seemed like a lifetime. There were plenty of clues as to the killer's motivation. There were painfully few that led to any leads regarding who he might be. It was frustrating. Four days of poring over backstories, photographs, scant physical evidence, autopsy reports, and psychological profiles had led them to exactly nothing new. The only thing Claire was certain about was that whoever had killed the women in the woods, he would kill again.

"You okay?" Alex asked.

Claire turned and looked at Alex in surprise.

"What? You're quiet."

Claire shook her head. "I was just thinking."

"That's not good."

"Funny, Toles. Does everyone else know what a comedienne you are?"

Alex shrugged. "Okay, I'll bite."

Claire smirked.

Alex rolled her eyes. "Do you ever stop?"

"Not really," Claire fluttered her eyelashes. Teasing Alex had become a game Claire enjoyed. She found it amusing how easily she could embarrass the older woman. "I was thinking," Claire turned back to the case. "What if he was sending us a message?"

Alex grimaced. "You mean with Deidre Slocum?"

"Yeah. I mean, think about it. No matter what anyone says, we both know that was too obvious for him. He didn't take any care with her at all."

"No, he didn't."

"Why would he change like that unless he was…"

"That's why I want to see where those boys were headed again."

"You think there is something we missed?" Claire asked.

"Not forensically. Sometimes, the clue that leads you home isn't something you can hold in your hand."

"Mr. Duncan?" a woman poked her head into the office.

"Oh, Janine," Bryce Duncan replied. "Come in."

"I know you're busy, what with being away so much lately and all."

Bryce Duncan smiled at his intern. "Nonsense. That just means business is good. What can I do for you?"

"Well, I fielded a call from Mr. Krause early this morning."

"Jonathan Krause?" he asked for clarification.

Janine nodded. "He said the Carecom warehouse in Stamford is ahead of schedule. He'd hoped we could move up our timetable."

"I'll give him a call."

Janine cringed.

"Is that a problem?"

"Well, he said he would be out of the country for the next week."

Duncan nodded. "Did he leave a contact?"

"He said his sister could review the specs if you sent them."

Duncan laughed. "My day just got longer."

"Sir?"

"Oh, nothing. Jonathan is a meticulous client," he explained. "His sister ran Carecom for years before he took over. If he's meticulous, she's next to impossible."

"You mean she's difficult?"

Bryce laughed harder. "You have no idea."

"I hate the woods," Claire complained. "I've got all these little tiny pricks everywhere."

"Sounds more like the résumé of your love life," Alex replied.

Claire stopped in her tracks. "Seriously, Toles; you have to stop making jokes. I'm beginning to think you have a personality."

Alex parted two large branches blocking her path and took a step forward onto a large rock.

Claire went to follow and was promptly hit in the face by the same branches. "Toles!"

Alex snickered as Claire stepped through and dusted herself off. She shook her head at Claire. "Be careful of all those little pricks," she wiggled her eyebrows.

"Ha-ha." Claire looked out at the view in front of them. "And, you didn't even bring a picnic basket."

"Nope. I wonder if anyone else has, though."

"You think he came here for this view?"

"I don't know," Alex admitted. She let her eyes fall over the landscape in front of her methodically. She shook her head.

"What are you thinking?" Claire asked.

Alex huffed. "We could have teams our here for months, all day, every day, and not find anything we are looking for."

"You mean anyone."

Alex turned to Claire. "I do," she said and turned her attention back to the horizon.

Claire's eyes tracked the distance, noting the area where they had discovered the two women buried some days ago. Slowly, her eyes moved to the ground at her feet. She nearly jumped out of her skin when something moved. "What the fuck?" Claire's feet left the ground.

Alex started laughing, "It's just a garter snake."

"A snake? Just a snake?"

Alex nearly doubled over with laughter.

"It's not funny, Toles."

"You can sneak into Russian SVR offices, steal cesium for a dirty bomb," Alex kept laughing. "I mean, I would have thought sleeping with O'Brien would have cured any fear of snakes."

"I'm not *afraid* of them," Claire scoffed at the notion. "I prefer they stay away from me is all."

Alex's laughter slowed to a dull roar. "I'll keep that in mind."

"Fuck you, Toles."

Alex laughed again.

Claire shivered slightly and looked out across the pond. Alex noted that her gaze had become pensive.

"What?" Alex asked.

Claire pointed off to an area on the left side of a large pond.

"What do you see?" Alex asked, following Claire's line of sight.

"Do you think Kaylee ever took pictures up here?"

"I haven't seen any, but there are thousands I haven't looked at yet."

Claire shook her head. "I wonder what it looks like after the leaves fall—how far you can see?"

Alex looked back across the pond. "Perfect spot to plan."

"And to watch."

Alex looked at Claire. Claire wasn't only smart; she was intuitive.

"What?" Claire asked.

"Let's go talk to Donovan."

Alex groaned as she walked back into the Peters' living room. She placed her phone back in her pocket.

"Everything okay?" Claire asked.

"Yeah."

"Cass…"

"It wasn't Cass. Just something Jonathan needs me to look at."

Claire nodded. "Donovan was just telling me that they didn't hike up there often."

"Any reason?" Alex asked.

Donovan shrugged. "It's not the easiest place to get to."

"No shit," Claire muttered, gently rubbing the red prickles on her skin.

Alex snickered.

"Used to be a party place," Donovan explained. "From what my dad said it used to get a little wild up there at times."

"Used to?" Alex asked.

"Yeah. They check that area a lot now. I mean, most of the forest you could walk for hours and never see another soul."

"And, Flat Rock is different?" Alex guessed.

"A while back, two kids got killed up there. The rangers make it a point to check that place out. For a long time, the police even hiked in at night."

The statement caught both Alex and Claire's attention immediately.

"What happened?" Alex asked.

"I don't really know the whole story," he admitted. "I was only seven. Kids partying—you know how that goes. It was night. From what I know, they were drinking beer and started wrestling. Somehow, two of them went over the edge. It was an accident. After that, they started watching that area more; you know?"

Alex nodded her understanding.

"Lots of ghost stories up there." Donovan shrugged. "Sometimes you'll find some beer cans or butts up there. Thing is, if you get caught up there drinking they don't go all that easy on you. Mostly, I think it's avid hikers that stop there now. They probably don't know the story. Kaylee never wanted to go up there. I think it creeped her out."

"What about you?" Claire asked. "Did you ever go up there?"

Donovan shook his head. "Not often," he told her. "It just feels…"

"Creepy?" Claire guessed.

Donovan replied with an embarrassed nod.

"Thanks," Alex said.

"Sorry, I couldn't help."

Alex shook her head. "You did help."

"How? I don't even have anything to show you. Maybe if I wasn't such a sissy—creeped out by an old story," he berated himself.

"Give yourself a break, kid," Claire chimed. "The asshole who did this? Well… Sometimes there's good reason to be creeped out."

Alex smiled at Claire and gripped Donovan's shoulder. "Yeah, you should have seen Agent Brackett up there earlier today."

Claire glared at Alex.

Donovan chuckled. "Sorry that I couldn't help more."

"Don't be," Alex said. "You've helped a lot. Call if you think of anything."

"Agent Toles… I mean, Alex?" he called to her before she could leave.

"Yeah?"

"Was it the same guy? I mean, those bodies you found—was it the same guy who killed Kaylee?"

"I don't know that yet, Donovan," Alex answered. "But, I promise you; Agent Brackett and I will figure that out."

Alex shook her head in frustration. "I wish we could get those IDs." She threw her coffee cup in the garbage." We need facts. I hate working on theory."

"Well, you'll hate this then."

"What?" Alex asked Claire as she opened the car door.

"He was up on that rock watching."

"You mean Kaylee," Alex surmised.

Claire slid into the passenger's seat. "Maybe not just Kaylee."

Alex pinched the bridge of her nose. She had been thinking the same thing. Whoever their killer was, he had spent time at Flat Rock. There was no question in her mind about it. That area would have provided the perfect vantage point throughout a good part of the year to see far in the distance without fear of being seen. That made her question the entire case. What if they were dealing with two killers? What if Kaylee's killer had been watching the man who had buried the first two victims?

"You think we have a copycat?"

"Whether Kaylee's killer killed those two women or not; whoever killed Kaylee had been on that rock. I guarantee it."

Alex groaned and rubbed her eyes. "Not a speck of physical evidence. Those kids were on their way up there. We both know that means that spot has gradually returned to a teenage hangout. How in the hell could there be *nothing* there—not a beer can, a cigarette butt, a gum wrapper—*nothing*?"

"Or maybe we weren't looking in the right place," Claire suggested.

Alex pulled her hand away from her face and looked at Claire.

Claire shrugged. "Donovan said two kids fell off the edge; right?"

"Yeah?"

"Must've hurt."

"What do you mean?"

"When the snake ran over my foot, and I jumped? You were standing on the rock. I was—what would you say? A foot from the edge?"

"Probably."

"Right. I looked down; it isn't a straight drop—not where I was standing."

Alex's brow furrowed.

"There's a tree growing out of the side of the hill. Wide enough to support someone."

"You think he might have been sitting there."

"I think we should test the theory," Claire replied.

"Beats looking at nothing," Alex turned the key in the ignition.

"Alex?"

"Yeah?"

"If there are two…"

"I know; Kaylee's killer might be the clue to the other."

"No, thanks for the offer. I need to take a look at this one myself," Bryce Duncan told his assistant.

"I know it's a big account."

"It's an account the secures many other accounts," Bryce replied. "It has to be right. And, trust me on this one—no one is more thorough than Alexis Toles."

"You mean you'd rather deal with Krause?"

Bryce laughed. He had been at the helm of Gestalt Industrial Security's Special Accounts Division for ten years. Gestalt enjoyed a reputation nearly beyond reproach in the security business. The company provided systems and service for everyone from the Department of State to some of the largest prisons in the United States. Gestalt employed experts on both the technical and human side of security. Bryce's grandfather had started the company with a handful of security guards back in the 1950s. By the 1980s, Gestalt had grown into a national force, breaking barriers with new technology and safeguarding some of the nation's most prized documents and most secretive facilities. Carecom, like many of its CIA counterparts was one more feather in the cap of the security giant. The endorsement of people like Jonathan Krause and Alex Toles bolstered Gestalt's already shiny credibility, and ensure that the behemoth would only continue to grow. One thing that Bryce Duncan understood was that one slip up, one breach in trust or integrity, and it could all go to hell in an instant. Safeguarding the powerful left no room for mistakes. He'd known Alex Toles for nearly ten years. He respected her attention to detail. There would be no T's left uncrossed or I's left without dots in her presence.

"Let's just say that she checks everything and forgets nothing," Bryce said.

"Should I wish you luck?"

"Luck never got anyone anywhere, David. Planning and execution—that is what you need. If you want to graduate from assistant to leader, stop looking for luck."

Cassidy threw her head back against the couch and closed her eyes. It had been a long day already and it wasn't even dinner time. Abby had come down with a nasty cold, Connor was already sneezing, Mackenzie needed to get to soccer practice, Dylan had a track meet, and all she wanted was a glass of wine—something she would be foregoing in the foreseeable future. "Well, at least I'm not throwing up," Cassidy giggled. She sighed when her phone rang and answered it without looking. "Hello?"

"Hey," Alex's replied.

"Uh-oh," Cassidy detected the fatigue in Alex's voice.

"Going to be a late night."

Cassidy sighed.

"I'm sorry, Cass."

"It's okay," Cassidy promised. "I hope that means you've made some progress."

"I'm not sure I'd define it as progress, but we are definitely moving."

"Do me a favor?"

"Sure."

"Eat."

Alex laughed.

"I'm serious," Cassidy said.

"I know."

"That doesn't mean coffee, Agent." Cassidy heard Alex's faint chuckling. “Alex, I mean it. I know you. By the time you get home, you’ll have a raging headache—eat.”

“I promise. How’s Abby?”

“Not complaining about her wrist, if that’s what you mean.”

“Something wrong?” Alex asked.

“No,” Cassidy replied. “Just an average day.”

“Cass?”

“Alex, honestly, it’s a typical day.”

“Are you feeling okay? I mean, are you…”

“So far, I have not had the need to count the tiles on the bathroom floor.”

Alex laughed. “That’s good.”

“Be careful.”

“I’ll see you later.” Alex disconnected the call and looked ahead at the forest in front of her. “Here we go again.” Her phone buzzed again and she lifted it without thinking. “I promise; I will eat.”

“All that hiking worked up an appetite?” the voice answered.

Alex groaned. “Assistant Director.”

“Sorry, I’m not calling to deliver you a pizza.”

“I didn’t think so.”

“They were able to get a match,” Bower said.

Let me put you on speaker. “Go ahead.”

“Your suspicion was correct. Melissa Evans and Darla Maynard were the victims you found.”

Alex closed her eyes. “I wish I could say thanks.”

“I happened to be in a meeting with Agent Eaves when she got the call,” he explained.

“Well, it certainly gives us some direction to follow,” Alex replied.

“Alex,” he lowered his voice. “This could get big faster than we’d like.”

Claire spoke up. “Why is that?”

"It's not just that Slocum's father is a friend of Governor Reid. Darla Maynard's mother is Jed Ritchie's sister."

"As in the CEO of Interstellar?" Alex asked.

"That would be the one—yes. Seems he's spent a considerable amount on private investigators over the years trying to locate his niece. I put a call into Hawk. She's talking to the director."

"You think Ritchie might make waves for the FBI?" Alex asked.

"I don't know. Ritchie is anti-establishment. He doesn't have much positive light to throw on anything he views as part of that establishment. That includes the FBI. With you in Connecticut, I thought it best to send Agent Morales and Agent Carver to make the notification to the families—waiting is too much of a gamble."

Alex reached for her temple. Investigating any homicide was daunting; investigating multiple murders that might be the work of two separate killers with two distinct motives was new territory even for Alex. The possibility that the case could become politicized added another dimension to an already complicated case. "I agree."

"I'll move on the establishment of the task force," he said. "Alex?"

"Yeah?"

"Any leads at all," he began.

"You'll be the first to know," Alex promised and placed the phone back into her pocket.

"Well, look at the bright side," Claire commented.

"There's a bright side?"

Claire lifted her cell phone to Alex. "Yeah, you get to have dinner with me."

Alex shook her head and laughed at the text message displayed on Claire's phone:

Make her eat something. And, that goes for you too.

"Always something to be grateful for," Alex laughed.

The road seemed to stretch on forever. No matter how many years he traveled this long expanse of farms and fields, he never tired of it. It was quiet, and it allowed him time to think. He reached beside him and lifted a cooling cup of coffee to his lips. He groaned with dissatisfaction but sipped greedily anyway. The sun was just beginning to set in front of him, making the road ahead difficult to see. He lowered the visor to throw a small amount of shade. Off in the distance, a growing figure caught his attention and he smiled. How he loved this mundane stretch of road. As familiar as it seemed, he had learned long ago that it could offer the unexpected.
"Always something to be grateful for."

CHAPTER ELEVEN

Alex began to lower herself onto a large tree branch that sat just below the edge of the hillside overlooking a pond.

"What the hell do you think you're doing?" Claire grabbed hold of Alex's arm.

"What does it look like?"

"I'll go."

"Why you?"

"I don't have a pregnant wife."

Alex rolled her eyes. "And, somehow that makes you more athletic?"

"No, but it makes me more expendable."

Alex shook her head. "I think you're forgetting something."

"What's that?"

"You promised Cass you'd feed me."

Claire groaned.

"Listen, if either one of us comes home broken or bruised, we're both going to land in time-out," Alex joked. "I'll go first. I'd like to think I can still keep up with partying teenagers."

"Fine, but if you fall, I'm going to kick your ass."

Alex chuckled at Claire's empty threat. She made her way back to the edge of the hillside, grabbed hold of a massive rock, and gently lowered herself onto the branch below.

"See anything?" Claire called down.

Alex was engaged in an exploration of the small ledge that sat just below the branch. It was wider than it had appeared from above. She was certain this would be a place that partying teenagers would find enticing. It provided just enough risk to make it alluring without being so dangerous that it would deter a person from making the climb. She shimmied herself across the log until she could gain a footing on the dirt beneath. At first glance, there appeared to be nothing of interest—dirt and rocks. She looked underneath the tree branch and shook her head at the tangle of weeds and roots. Nothing jumped out at her. There were no cans, no evidence of anyone smoking anything. That did not add up in Alex's mind. She doubted anyone, even their potential killer would have taken the time to clean the entire area of garbage. And, Alex was positive that people had been here recently. There were marks in the tree that she immediately recognized as crude carvings of initials, probably with a key—that was her best guess. That might prove valuable. Nothing else was there. She shook her head.

"Not possible," Alex muttered. "There has to be some footprint left behind." She turned carefully to look down from her vantage point.

"Toles?!"

Alex startled, grabbed onto a large root growing near the branch to steady herself, and glared up at Claire. "Could you maybe not scare the shit out of me when I'm standing on a six-inch ledge?"

"Told you I would go down there. What'd you find?"

Alex did not answer immediately.

"Well?"

Alex hoisted herself back onto the branch and accepted Claire's hand.

"Nothing there?" Claire asked.

"No," Alex said. "But below?" She pointed the ledge.

"Yeah?"

"Go down and take a look yourself."

Claire eased herself off the large flat rock and down the side of the hill onto the branch. She looked out across the pond and then followed the same steps Alex had taken to gauge the height of the location. She let her eyes fall directly below. "Son of a bitch," she said.

"Right?"

Claire looked up at Alex. "You know, it'd be hard to see anyone here unless they were standing right where I am."

"Sure would," Alex agreed.

Claire accepted Alex's hand and hopped back up onto the rock. "The water isn't very deep below." She had been able to make out what she guessed were a few cans toward the edge of the pond.

"No, it isn't, and we've had a lot of rain in the last month. I'm betting that when there isn't much rain, there's little to no water at all below us."

Claire tugged at her bottom lip with her teeth as she contemplated Alex's train of thought. The pond water was murky. She had been able to discern the outline of a fallen tree branch beneath the water's surface. If she and Alex had been able to note that from their considerable distance, the water had to be shallow. If she and Alex were following the same line of thinking, the question they were both asking was if there might be evidence beneath the water—evidence of who might have been sitting in this place. Alex had suggested dragging the pond days earlier and had been rebuffed. Assistant Director Bower had deemed it unlikely to produce any evidence and therefore an unnecessary expenditure.

"You want to drag the pond," Claire said.

Alex grinned. "Well, how about we start with what's below us," Alex said. "See what we get."

"You're the boss."

Alex's brow shot up into her hairline.

"Aw, don't get all cocky," Claire waved off her partner.

Alex laughed and then sobered almost immediately.

"We'll figure it out," Claire said.

"Yeah. I just wish we didn't have to follow a trail of bodies to do that."

"Maybe we won't."

Alex raised her brow again.

"I said maybe," Claire rolled her eyes. "Come on. I promised to feed you." She walked ahead of Alex.

Alex smiled as she watched Claire go. She had the fleeting

thought that Claire was growing on her. *Nah.*

"Mmm," the man groaned with satisfaction. He looked down at the innocent face below him. She had regaled him with colorful stories for hours before he brought her here. For a breath, he had considered sparing her this time as a reward for his amusement. No. She was like all the others. Fairy tales were not meant to have happy endings. She was as pure as the driven snow. Perhaps, purer than Snow White herself. A smile tugged at his lips as he considered the dark head of hair that stood in contrast to her milky white skin. So many lessons he had to teach. He cocked his head curiously. Would they ever learn? No matter. He cherished a deep breath as he admired the red splash across her cheek. He bent down and nuzzled her neck with his nose.

A maniacal laugh escaped his throat when she pulled against her restraints. "Tsk. Tsk. Don't you remember?" he asked her. "Ring around the rosy," he cooed in her ear. She pulled away as far as she could. He nipped at the flesh of her neck and grabbed her right wrist. His fingertip traced her bindings gently. He smiled down at her as if to offer comfort. In an instant, his smile transformed into a sneer. "Ring around the rosy," he repeated. He sat back on his haunches above her. "And you know what comes next; don't you?" His hand came back and he reached for the knife in his pants. "Ashes, ashes," he sang to her. "Oh, we all fall down."

Alex took a sip from her can of Diet Coke, set it aside and lifted the piece of pizza in front of her into her mouth, never removing her gaze from her computer. She caught Claire's reflection in the screen. "What the hell are you doing?" Alex asked.

"Proof," Claire explained. She typed a few words into the phone and moved to show Alex the text message she had just sent to Cassidy.

"Clever," Alex replied.

Claire shrugged, admittedly pleased with herself. "What are you looking for?"

"I don't know," Alex said. "I'll know it when I see it."

Claire loomed over Alex's shoulder.

Alex stilled her temper. *Yeah, she's growing on me—like a fungus.*

"Hey," Claire's arm draped over Alex's shoulder, and Alex moved to bat it away. "Hey!" Claire scolded Alex and then grabbed a picture from the table, placing in front of Alex. "Look," she said.

Alex's gaze narrowed in on the photograph. She studied every detail. Kaylee might not have spent time at Flat Rock. She had spent time photographing it from a distance. Alex massaged her temples. "We need to get someone on these—yesterday."

"It's your task force."

"Right, which we will not have completely in place until tomorrow."

"And, tomorrow is not yesterday. I got it," Claire replied.

"You have an idea?" Alex asked.

Claire shrugged. "Depends."

"On what?"

"Whether you really are Agent By the Book," Claire answered.

Alex sighed, immediately understanding Claire's idea. "You do know if Hawk finds out you called someone outside the bureau..."

"Hawk's not speaking to me," Claire said. "And, anyway—you and I both know she would do the same thing."

Alex let her face fall into her hands.

"You don't agree," Claire surmised. "Still just think I'm a fuck up, huh?"

Alex pulled her hands away from her face and smiled at Claire.

"No," Alex said emphatically. "I think you're a good agent who wants to get answers as quickly as she can."

"Right."

Alex sighed. "Claire, we can't. Trust me; I'm tempted to call Jonathan right now. But," Alex groaned in frustration. "When I saw him the other day, he told me I didn't need his help. We can't. How do we explain to the team that we have information before they've even seen the cursory evidence? Claire," Alex shook her head. "That team needs to trust…"

"Everyone trusts you," Claire said. "Hell, most of them want to be you."

"This isn't about me. They need to trust *us*. They need to trust you."

Claire nodded. "Do you? Trust me?"

Alex looked Claire directly in the eye. She took a deep breath and released it slowly. "As much as I hate to admit it; yes, Claire; I do. In fact, I trust you with my life."

"Because of Cass."

Alex decided that it was time to lay all her cards on the table. "Partly," she confessed. "Cass is the best judge of character of anyone I know. I'm not going to bullshit you. If we're going to be partners, honesty is something you should expect from me."

Claire listened without comment as Alex continued.

"I'm not going to pretend that I understand you. And, I'm not going to tell you that I forgive you for everything. I don't."

Claire nodded.

Alex looked at the ceiling and sighed before looking back at Claire. "I do trust you. Cass loves you, Claire. Weird as it is to me—to her? Well…"

"It's cool," Claire held up her hand.

"No, you need to hear this, and I need to say it."

Claire nodded.

"For a long time, I didn't get it; you and Cass, I mean. Thing is, it's a lot like me and Dylan." Alex saw Claire's eyes begin to water. "Everybody probably thinks I love Dylan because of Cass. That's partly true. I would've loved Dylan even if Cass and I had never been together. I can't explain it. I never wanted to. He's just... He's my son. I know he feels the same way. I'm his mom just as much as Cass. It's not the same, but it means just as much to us both."

Claire swallowed hard.

"That's you and Cass. She's the mom you lost in a lot of ways. The thing is, Claire, she loves you just as much as she does our kids. I've tried to get it," Alex chuckled. "Some things just are. So, yes—I trust you. Maybe that's the first step in forgiving us both."

"What do you need forgiveness for?" Claire asked.

Alex's smile was tainted by regret. "Plenty," she said. "You need to believe that you can do this job without going outside the lines again. You need to learn to trust yourself, to trust me."

Claire stared at Alex silently for a moment. "Okay."

"Okay?"

"I told you; you're the boss."

"Call Agent Remke," Alex said. "See if he can start working on these photos. Who knows what Kaylee might have captured without knowing it? And, Claire?"

"Yeah?"

"For what it's worth, I'm sorry."

Claire nodded. There were many things for which she felt a need to atone. She and Alex had a sordid past. They had been lovers. They had been adversaries. Ultimately, they had become allies. They had never managed to bridge the divide and become friends. Then again, friendship remained a struggle for Claire. Eleana had been her only true friend for most of her life. Now, she had Cassidy. She'd never seriously considered Alex Toles as a potential friend. Claire had never loved Alex. She had admired Alex. Despite what many people believed, Claire hadn't seen Alex as a conquest. She had been surprised by Alex's advances when they had first met, and she'd been flattered. While she never intended to admit it, more than her ego had been bruised when Alex had brushed her aside casually. Claire did not respond kindly to feeling injured or betrayed. The resentment she had harbored toward Alex had caused pain in people's lives that she now cared for deeply. It had caused Alex pain too. She looked at Alex. "So am I."

"I hate the media," Alex grumbled.

Claire snickered.

"Laugh it up, Brackett."

"Yeah, well, for once I am glad you *are* the boss."

Alex couldn't help but chuckle at Claire's admission. She waited for Agent Aaron Lapper to finish his explanation and introduction of her as the leader of the FBI-led task force. This was not her forte; speaking to the press. But, it was her job. Alex stepped up to the microphone and looked out at the sea of reporters, attempting to avoid eye contact with anyone for too long.

"Good afternoon. As Agent Lapper explained, my name is Alexis Toles, and I will be heading this investigation with the assistance of the Connecticut and New York State Police, local law enforcement, and the FBI. Late last evening, The Federal Bureau of Investigation was able to make a positive identification on two sets of human remains found last week in the State Forest on the Glastonbury, Connecticut town line. The remains were identified as those of Melissa Anna Evans and Darla Marie Maynard, both age nineteen. Ms. Evans and Ms. Maynard were reported missing ten years ago on October 3, 2008. They had last been seen in each other's company near Middleburgh, New York where both kept residence." Alex looked down at her notes and back at the reporters in front of her. "As you know, over the last two weeks, two other women have been found. Kaylee Peters was discovered in the Ashland-Pinnacle

State Forest here in New York after being reported missing from Connecticut the previous afternoon. Two days later, another young woman, Deidre Slocum was discovered in the same State Park where Ms. Peters had been reported last seen. It is the FBI's belief that two or more of these deaths may be connected. We are asking that anyone with any information regarding the movements of these young women contact the task force at 1-888-234-8869. Again, that number is 1-888-234-8869. We want to thank you for your cooperation and assure you that law enforcement is committed to resolving these cases as quickly as possible."

"Agent Toles?"

"Yes?"

"Is this a serial killer?"

"We don't know that yet. That is a possibility; yes."

"Agent! Three of these women were from the same area. Maybe, it's a serial killer? How can you ensure the safety of the local community?"

Alex offered the reporter a strained smile. "As I said, we are working every lead, and we will draw our conclusions as we press forward. As for safety; you will find in the press release that Agent Lapper provided, we suggest caution when traveling. Should you require roadside assistance; call the local police and notify them. Do not accept the help of strangers, and do not accept rides from anyone you do not know. That is honestly your best defense."

"Do you have any leads—at all?" a woman's voice demanded.

Alex met the women's gaze with harsh stoicism. "As I said, we are working every lead we receive. If anyone has any information, no matter how innocuous it may seem, we are asking that they contact the task force at the number provided. Thank you." Alex stepped away from the podium and allowed Agent Lapper to step back into her place. "I hate the media."

"So, you said," Claire commented. "What now?"

"Back to the pond."

"You do know that anything under the water isn't likely to give us much to go on."

Alex nodded. "Depends on what we find."

"Don't take this personally, but you look like hell."

Cassidy laughed. "Thanks, Mom."

"Are you feeling all right?"

"Oh, I'm fine. Abby and Connor just decided to share their cold with me."

"Beats worshiping the porcelain God," Rose offered.

"That it does," Cassidy agreed.

"So? No morning sickness yet?"

"Nope. No afternoon or evening sickness either. Keeping my fingers crossed. Maybe fourth time is the charm in my case."

"Leave it to you to set a new trend."

Cassidy winked at her mother. "How was your weekend with Dad?"

Rose's eyes twinkled with amusement. "Cassie, for once why don't you just ask me what you want to ask me."

"What do you mean?"

"Oh, please. How many nights have I taken this brood of yours so that you can ride the wild pony?"

Cassidy nearly choked on her iced tea. "Ride the wild pony?" She laughed.

"Call it what you like. I've seen her handcuffs."

Cassidy rolled her eyes. "Jealousy doesn't become you, Mom."

"Ha! See, I knew it."

"Yes, you caught me. That's the whole reason I married Alex; you know?"

"I could think of worse reasons."

"Stop," Cassidy choked again.

Rose grinned.

"I just want you to be happy," Cassidy told her mother.

"I've told you a million times, Cassie; I was happy long before your father came back."

"Um-hum, you have. But, are you *happier* now?"

"You mean now that I have a wild pony of my own to ride?"

"Mom!" Cassidy sprayed iced tea through her nose.

Rose laughed. "I just made it easy for you," she said.

"I really didn't need to know."

"Maybe not, but you sure as hell have been curious. You've been throwing hints for five years now."

"I told you; I want you to be happy, and not so alone."

"Good Lord, Cassie. You can't be serious? You do realize that you have four children and Alex living in this house?"

Cassidy chuckled.

"All of whom frequently require Helen or me to babysit. Adding your father to the equation was not a cure for loneliness, it was another reason for wine."

"Okay, point taken," Cassidy sipped her iced tea. "How is Dad?"

"You know, you could call him and ask him yourself."

Cassidy sighed.

"Want to tell me why you've been avoiding him?" Rose asked.

"I'm not avoiding him."

"Okay. Want to tell me why you aren't making a point to call him and tell him you are expecting again?"

"I figured you would."

"Well, you figured wrong. Now, what's going on?"

Cassidy shook her head. "I don't know if I can answer that."

"Why don't you try?"

"It's… Mom, sometimes I just… It hurts. I don't know how else to explain it. Watching him with Dylan and Kenzie… Watching him with the twins—I know that I should be grateful. I know that.

Sometimes, it makes me so angry I want to scream."

Rose clasped Cassidy's hand. "Because you missed so many things with him."

Cassidy nodded.

"Maybe you should tell him that."

"I've told him plenty."

"Yes, you have. As I recall, most of that was about how he hurt me. Maybe it's time you told him just how much he's hurt you."

"Why? What good would it do? That would only hurt him and…"

Rose smiled. "And, you love him. Yes, I know. You have every reason and every right to feel the way you do."

"That doesn't make me feel any better about it."

"I know that too."

"What about you?" Cassidy wondered.

"What about me?"

"Do you ever feel that way with him?"

"You mean resentful and angry?"

"I guess I do."

"Sometimes. It's one of the reasons I can't live with him. God knows I love him. I don't think I could ever love anyone else—not even after everything he put me through. I can forgive him. I can't forget it. He knows that. He loves you, Cassie. You know that. I know that it doesn't make sense to either of us, but I know he honestly believed he was doing the right thing when he left."

"I know," Cassidy admitted. "That doesn't make it hurt less. You would think I could let it go now."

"Who would think that?"

"Mom, that was a long time ago."

"And, some days it still feels like yesterday that he left and yesterday he came back."

Cassidy closed her eyes. "Alex is worried about Dylan."

"You mean about him choosing the military."

Cassidy nodded.

"And, that's why you're avoiding your father."

"I'm not sure that I want to know any more than I already do."

Rose understood. She had never attempted to wade into these waters with her daughter. Since Jim McCollum's return, Rose had demanded complete honesty from Cassidy's father. She'd gotten far more than she had bargained for. She'd never told Cassidy how much she had come to know about Jim McCollum's past career, nor about what Alex had been engaged in for years. Now, it seemed to her it was time to put her cards on the table.

"You're worried that Christopher might have used Dylan somehow."

Cassidy was shocked.

"Oh, I know. I might just know more than you do about some things," Rose said.

"How…"

"I had a few conditions when your father came back into my life. Honesty was the first."

"He told you?"

"He told me more than I ever wanted to know," Rose said. "But I needed to know. So, yes; he told me about the experiments he led. He told me about Christopher—that Alex had concerns about whether Dylan might have been exposed to anything when he was with his father."

"I want to protect him," Cassidy said. "Selfishly, part of me is afraid to find out if Chris did anything to him. My God, Mom… He was Dylan's father. At least, he acted in that role for the first seven years of Dylan's life. How could he do anything to hurt his son?"

"And, that makes you angry with your father."

"It does. Rationally, I know that everyone makes his or her choice. Believe me; I know that. I know that in some way the chaos that Dad and Alex's father were engaged in, Claire's father, Chris… I know somehow it brought us all together. For that? For that, I am grateful. But that doesn't change the fact that things he did might have compromised Dylan's well-being. It compromised mine, Alex's—Claire's. Some days I still can't believe it—everything we've all been though, everything I've learned. It seems like a spy novel; you know? The government altering people's thoughts, families colliding because of their parents' choices and past. It's insane to me," Cassidy said. "Then I remember that all fiction has some foundation in truth—even stories that seem wild and outrageous. This isn't fiction. It's not a dream. And, in some way I blame him for it—for all of it—even if I know it's not his fault."

"I understand," Rose said. "He will understand too. Talk to him, Cassie. Not for him—for you."

Cassidy nodded.

"How's Alex?" Rose shifted gears.

"Stressed," Cassidy answered.

"I saw the press conference."

"She didn't sleep last night," Cassidy said. "I'm not sure what had her more anxious—the case or a case of having to face the press. She hates dealing with the media."

"How are you?"

Cassidy shrugged. "Worried about her."

"Do you regret encouraging her to go back?"

"No," Cassidy answered assuredly. "I always knew she would someday."

"But?"

"I also know that there is danger."

"Cassie, Alex is excellent at what she does."

"Yes, she is. But, Mom not every danger comes from the outside."

Rose patted Cassidy's hand. "Cassie, we all have demons. Putting them on shelves to avoid facing them down never works. One way or another they always come back to haunt you until you stand up and face them."

Cassidy closed her eyes again. That was the truth if ever she'd heard it. "I just hope she gets this case solved sooner rather than later."

"So that she can quit?"

"No," Cassidy said. "So that she realizes she can continue."

"What do you think?" Claire asked.

Alex grabbed the bridge of her nose and pinched forcefully. "Think? I think we need something to go on. Three sites, Claire—three that we've excavated out here that bear resemblance to where we found Melissa Evans and her friend—nothing. Nothing to go on from Deidre Slocum's murder. All we really have is a bunch of nothing, except for the piling up of dead girls."

Claire was not accustomed to seeing Alex genuinely frustrated. She watched as a team of forensics experts retrieved items from the pond and looked up at Flat Rock above. "We're just not looking in the right place," she said. "Why here? He knows it," Claire mused more to herself than to Alex. The team had found several partially crushed beer cans in a tangle of vines and weeds underneath the branch that she and Alex had found below Flat Rock. Somehow, they had not made it into the pond. "Those cans will have DNA," she said.

"Let's hope that leads to someone—anyone."

"Do you honestly believe there are two killers?" Claire asked.

"I don't know. All we have are theories, and that one is as plausible as any other. Either we have one sadistic son-of-a-bitch, or we have one SOB and his fan."

"I wonder what one would say about the other?" Claire mused.

Alex kept her eyes fixed on the work a few feet away. *Good question, Claire. That is a very good question.*

Governor Candace Reid listened carefully to her staff as they ran down a list of issues that were likely to land on her plate. Some days the list seemed endless. The beep of her phone's intercom stifled the conversation in her office.

"Yes, Susan?"

"Sorry to disturb you, Governor. You have a call from Agent Toles."

Candace wasn't sure whether she should be grateful for the reprieve or apprehensive about the reason. She looked at her staff. "We'll continue this after lunch," she told them, leaving no room for debate. She watched as her press secretary nodded and closed the door. "Put her through, Susan…. Alex."

"Governor."

"Why do I have the feeling this call is not an invitation for dinner?"

"Probably because in that case, it would be Cass calling."

Candace chuckled. "Something I need to know?"

"Actually, no—something I need your help with."

"I'm listening."

"I'm not sure you are going to like it."

Candace laughed. "Alex, I don't like ninety percent of the things I get told. You wouldn't be calling me unless it mattered. I told you; whatever you needed to let me know. So? Let's have it."

"Okay. Here it is…."

Cassidy sat glued to the television. It had been years since she had seen images of Alex on the screen. She listened attentively.

According to a source close to the case, the FBI's working theory is that there are two killers at large. At least one of the murders they are investigating was committed by a different person.

Cassidy's jaw dropped as a female anchor asked the next question. "So, the FBI believes these are unrelated?" Cassidy waited to hear the response.

That's the interesting part. The source would not go as far as to say the murders are unrelated; only that they were committed by different people. Tandem killers? We just don't know. What we do know is that there are four dead women and according to that same source, the FBI suspects there are more victims.

"Oh, my God," Cassidy shook her head as the anchor levied another question.

You've covered these kinds of cases for years, Mark. How unusual is this? Two killers? That must make the situation far more difficult for the investigators.

It does. To answer your first question, I've not seen a case quite like this in my career. If there are two killers working in such close proximity, the FBI has to consider the possibility that they are working together. That scenario would be preferable from an investigator's standpoint. The possibility of unique serial murderers operating so closely at the same time will present enormous challenges.

Alex hadn't shared any of the specifics of the case she was working with Cassidy. They'd been like ships passing in the night for two weeks. When they had time together, conversations had centered on family, not on Alex's day at work. Cassidy was ready to turn the television off when the anchor's next statement stopped her.

This investigation has some history attached to it. The agent in charge as I understand it is a bit of a celebrity. Does that give you any more confidence in a timely resolution?

You are right, of course. Many people will recognize Agent Alexis Toles from her connection with President John Merrow and the high-profile case that introduced her to her wife.

Cassidy felt her mouth go dry as footage from her abduction ten years earlier rolled across the screen.

"That's enough," Alex's voice echoed from the door way. Alex moved to the bed, picked up the remote and switched off the television. "You don't need to watch that."

Cassidy shook her head. "Is it true? Do you think there are two killers out there?"

"It's a possibility—yes."

"How much will this hurt you? The press getting hold of this?"

"Might not hurt at all," Alex commented. She shed her clothes and slid into the bed beside Cassidy. "I don't want to talk about any of that."

Cassidy sighed. "I wish you would talk to me."

"How do I explain this to you?"

"Just say what you feel."

"Cass, when I come home after a day like today? You're the place where I can banish those images. I don't want to see that ugliness. I don't want to visit that when I'm here—not here. I know there is ugliness in the world. I don't want you to see it. I don't…"

"Alex, I have seen it. We both have. But I understand. At least, I think I do."

"I'm sorry that you had to see those pictures again."

Cassidy closed her eyes as Alex cuddled up beside her. "It's all right. It's part of the past."

"I'd rather think about the future." Alex moved to place a

loving kiss on Cassidy's lips. "I hate being away from you so much," she confessed as her kisses drifted lower.

Cassidy looked down at Alex. Alex was placing light kisses across Cassidy's stomach while her left hand traced a delicate pattern in their wake. Cassidy's eyes fluttered shut in contentment. This would be a frequent exercise for months. Cassidy would treasure every moment while she could. Alex had done this with each of Cassidy's pregnancies. When Cassidy had miscarried, she'd awakened the next night to Alex in this same position. She often pondered that many people would be surprised by the tenderness Alex possessed.

"Alex," Cassidy called softly. Alex lifted her face to look in Cassidy's eyes. Cassidy wiped a tear from the corner of Alex's eye with her thumb.

"Cass?" Alex asked.

Cassidy smiled. Alex's hand sat protectively over Cassidy's middle. She combed her fingers through Alex's hair, and lifted her brow in reply.

"If it's a boy," Alex began. "I was wondering... I mean, I know we always talk about this, and I know it's a long way off still, and who knows? It could be another girl..."

"Alex," Cassidy chuckled at the familiar rambling

"Just... How would you feel about the name Brian?"

Cassidy caressed Alex's cheek. She had loved Alex's former FBI partner as much as Alex had. Just as the images Cassidy had witnessed on the television had conjured memories, Cassidy was sure that the case Alex was working had taken Alex back in time more than once. That would inevitably lead to thoughts of Brian Fallon. Fallon had been more than Alex's partner; he'd been part of their family. In fact, his children and his widow remained close to Alex and Cassidy's family. Fallon's death had dealt an emotional blow to them both. Cassidy had thought that Alex would want to name Connor after their friend. When Alex didn't suggest it, Cassidy assumed the loss of their friend had still been too fresh.

"I think it's perfect," Cassidy replied honestly.

"Are you sure?"

"Positive."

Cassidy felt Alex's breathing even out. She kissed the top of Alex's head. She felt Alex move in her embrace and mumble.

"Alex?" Cassidy laughed when she realized Alex was asleep. The only words she made out were tacos and Batman. She laughed. "I love you, Alfred."

CHAPTER TWELVE

"No offense, Toles, but you look like shit."

Alex lifted her coffee cup from the holder beside her and took a sip. Her eyes remained focused on the road ahead. She was exhausted. The night had taken an unexpected turn when Alex had been awakened by Cassidy screaming in her sleep. The notion that the past couldn't hurt you was a crock of shit from Alex's perspective. She hated the reality she found herself in.

"Maybe we could just hook you up to that," Claire pointed to the coffee cup in Alex's hand.

"I didn't get much sleep."

"I thought married couples gave that shit up."

Alex sighed. "Cassidy had a rough night."

"She sick?" Claire asked with concern.

"No."

Claire thought for a moment. It was unusual for Cassidy not to come down and greet her in the morning. "What's wrong with Cass?" she asked Alex.

"She had a flashback. To tell you the truth, I thought maybe those were a thing of the past for her."

"Fisher," Claire guessed. It was understandable. The serial killer case had made the national news for the past two nights. Alex's face was everywhere, and that inevitably meant the media felt the need to revisit the past. Someone had leaked details of the investigation—details and theories to the press. "Fucking news. I swear, it wasn't me that leaked that shit."

"I know."

"You know?" Claire had expected Alex to suspect her immediately. "How do you know it wasn't me?"

"Couldn't have been you if it was me."

"What? You leaked that information to the press? Why?"

Alex took a deep breath and exhaled forcefully. Reality. She would deploy every asset she needed to if she thought it might help her catch their killer or killers. Claire's musings over what one killer might think of the other had sparked an idea. Alex was fortunate that she had people she could trust to implement that idea. Having powerful friends sometimes proved beneficial. Alex never reached out to the friends she had in public office unless she deemed it necessary. She had no doubt that whether one or two killers, the victims would continue to pile up until she and Claire put a stop to it. She'd lost her temper two days earlier when one of the agents assigned to the task force had said, "Time is on our side, not his." Technically, that was true. Eventually, the truth would come out as long as they persisted in a dogged investigation. Some tiny piece of evidence would turn up, some witness; either that or the killer would make a mistake. Time was on the side of the investigator, not the criminal. Time was not on the side of the next innocent woman who fell prey while investigators combed through tin cans in ponds. Alex needed something to tip time in that girl's favor. She'd approached the one person she knew could help without discovery. If there was any small ray of light in this case, it was the fact that she had Governor Candace Reid in her corner.

"Sometimes, Claire if you want to catch the devil you have to go to hell."

"Yeah? So, that means Cass has to go too?"

Alex set her coffee cup back in the holder and massaged her temple. She hated it when Cassidy revisited the ordeal with Carl Fisher. She remembered the fear she had felt, the anger that seethed in her veins when she saw Cassidy's wrists, and the relief she had felt when Cassidy had collapsed into her arms. And, now? Now, it conjured animosity toward the woman beside her; an emotion Alex could afford. Claire had manipulated Fisher, toyed with him, perhaps even encouraged him. Alex did know that Claire Brackett had done nothing to stop him from harming Cassidy. That was the past. That's what Cassidy would say. That's what Cassidy had reminded Alex earlier that morning. Stop chasing ghosts. It wasn't the first time someone had given Alex that advice.

"I'm all right," Cassidy told Alex.

"Cass, I know how..."

Cassidy smiled gently at her wife. "You know," she said. "When I was a kid, not long after my father disappeared, I went through this period where I was afraid of ghosts—terrified, actually. My grandmother sat at the side of my bed one night. I've never forgotten what she told me. She said, 'Cassidy, you have far more to fear from the living than you do from the dead. Ghosts can't hurt you.' She was right, Alex. That's all this is—a ghost."

Alex pulled Cassidy into her arms. Ghosts might not have the ability to inflict physical harm; memories could torture a soul. Alex knew that as well as anyone. She had battled demons from the past for years, memories that at times were so vivid she could feel the heat of the explosion that had injured her, and the blood that pooled down her back. But, it was just a memory of a moment. Cassidy was right. The living had the ability to create that scenario for each other. It was Alex's job to put an end to that as often as she could.

"Just find him," Cassidy whispered in Alex's ear. "Stop him," she said. "No one deserves that nightmare, Alex."

"Why?" Claire asked Alex.

Alex pulled the car over to the side of the road, cut the engine, and looked at Claire.

"Well?" Claire urged.

Alex contemplated her answer for a moment. Claire Brackett was a talented agent. Alex couldn't deny that. But, Claire had spent most of her career playing both sides of a convoluted game. Being an FBI agent in earnest differed. Alex had spent years before immersing herself in the spy game as an FBI profiler and investigator. She'd worked cases like this before. Her job was to immerse herself in the mind of the killer so that she could catch him. That sometimes meant taking a journey to hell that Alex hoped she'd come back from. She sighed.

"Claire," Alex said. "Do you know the difference between a serial killer and an assassin?"

"One is on the payroll."

"Right. One gets paid for his pleasure. The other's pay is his pleasure."

"So?"

"It's a game," Alex said. "There's a reason serial killers escalate their violence over time. At first, they don't even kill. They hunt. They watch. They might even indulge. They get that first taste of power, of controlling life and death and they can't stop. After a while? After a while, it's not enough. They've mastered that. Their violence becomes more sadistic. Their predatory inclination goes into overdrive."

"What does that have to do with you leaking shit to the media?"

"No serial killer likes to share the spotlight."

"You think if there is only one killer, he'll want the credit."

"Exactly. He still thinks he's the cat chasing the mouse. He's about to face the wolf chasing the cat."

"Sounds like one of my father's nursery rhymes. His way of giving me lessons."

"Might be a good analogy. We're about to become the teacher," Alex said. "He's no longer just the hunter. He's being hunted. It's a new game."

"So, you thought you'd lay a trap for him?"

"Not a trap, just a breadcrumb."

Claire nodded. "You think he'll follow the breadcrumbs home?"

"I'm counting on it."

"Horrible news," a woman's voice commented.

Bryce Duncan sat back in his comfortable recliner and sipped his beer. "It is."

"Do you think they'll catch him before he kills anyone else?" his wife asked.

"Hard to say," Bryce replied.

"I'll bet you'll be getting a lot of calls from that area for security systems."

"Not my division," he said. "But, I suppose that's probably true."

"Don't you know that detective?" she asked.

Bryce smiled. His wife sometimes amused him. He often forgot that just because he lived in the land of law enforcement, security, and intelligence agencies; she did not. FBI, CIA, police, NSA—he doubted May knew the difference between any of them. "You mean, Agent Toles?" he asked. She nodded. "We've met a few times," he told her. "Funny thing—she's actually supposed to meet with me tomorrow."

"Why?" May wondered.

Bryce Duncan had spent years in the military before signing on to work at Gestalt. Twenty years as a Navy Seal had taught Bryce a good deal about security systems. He was the ideal person to design impenetrable systems. After all, he's been cracking them for years. "Oh, she's just filling in for her brother, I suspect," he explained. "Their family holds controlling interest in Carecom. It's one of our largest accounts."

May looked at the television and back at her husband. "Who would do such a thing?" she shook her head.

Bryce sipped his beer and shrugged. *Oh, you'd be surprised.*

Alex walked through the door after another long day of dead-ends. She set down her bag and stretched her back until it popped.

"Mom!"

Alex looked up the stairs and chuckled. "Hold your horses, Kenz!" Alex called up.

"Oh, God," Cassidy walked into view. "Please, no visuals with horses," she shuddered.

Alex looked at her curiously.

"Don't ask," Cassidy said, holding up her hand. "Let's just say I don't think anyone in this house will be going on a pony ride for a while."

Alex knew better than to ask.

"Mom!" Mackenzie's voice grew demanding.

Cassidy's jaw tightened.

"What's her 911?" Alex asked.

"Who knows?" Cassidy replied dryly. "She has an awards banquet at school tomorrow. I imagine she is rehearsing acceptance speeches or something."

That wouldn't surprise Alex at all. "You want me to go?"

Cassidy shook her head. "No. You could do me a favor and attempt to pry the twins away from the television for dinner."

"Oh? What's in it for me?"

"Paper plates," Cassidy said.

Alex laughed. "You mean, I get to avoid dish duty?"

Cassidy grinned.

"Mom!"

"I'm coming!" Cassidy yelled back and headed up the stairs.

Alex shook her head. She honestly believed that what Cassidy dealt with far eclipsed the challenges she faced at work. "I have no idea how she does it."

"Used to be with wine," Cassidy called back.

Alex chuckled at Cassidy's good-natured sense of humor. She imagined that there were days Cassidy would love to drink an entire bottle of wine. She wandered the short way down the hall and around the corner to the family room.

"No, Abby," Connor scolded his sister. "You stay down."

"Why do you get to be on top?"

"Cause, I'm the boy."

Uh-oh. Alex stood just outside the door to the family room. She was almost afraid to look inside and see what her children were doing. She edged carefully closer and peeked into the room.

"So?" Abby replied indignantly.

"Boys are bigger," Connor explained.

"You're not taller than me."

"Am so."

"Not."

"Am too."

"Not."

"Boys are taller."

"Are not!"

Alex felt herself beginning to get dizzy. *I can't believe Cass wanted another one.* She thought for certain she would reveal herself with laughter when Abby stepped up onto the couch to stand beside Connor.

Abby placed her hands on her hips and glared at her twin brother. "I'm bigger," she said assuredly.

Alex covered her mouth to stifle a laugh. Abby was by far the most sensitive and reserved of her children, except when in the presence of her twin brother. Abby seldom backed down when it came to Connor. Thankfully, the two were generally the best of friends. Occasionally, like all siblings, the pair could become competitive. Today's contest appeared to be about who got to stand on the couch in whatever game they had concocted. Alex was tempted to hover in the doorframe and let the scene play out. Unfortunately, Abby still had a cast on her wrist. Alex was confident if either of her children somehow left this scenario damaged, she would be the one in time-out the longest when Cassidy got hold of them.

Alex swooped in and tucked a child under each arm. “Now, what is this about boys being bigger?” she teased.

“Momma!” they cried out in tandem.

Alex set them both on the floor. “Now, who says boys are bigger?”

“D. is bigger than you,” Connor pointed out.

“Oh, he’s got you there,” Cassidy’s voice whispered from behind.

Alex huffed dramatically.

Connor and Abby giggled. “And, Uncle Pip is taller than you too, Momma.”

“Whose side are you on?” Alex playfully teased her daughter.

“Mommy’s!” Abby laughed and pointed at Cassidy.

“Yeah, well, I’m bigger than Mommy,” Alex defended herself.

Cassidy snickered, moved beside Alex, and patted her on the stomach. “Yes, you are, honey.”

Alex’s jaw dropped. Cassidy kissed her on the cheek. “Come on you two, time for tacos.”

“Momma loves tacos,” Connor said.

“Yes, I know,” Cassidy smirked and patted Alex’s stomach again.

Alex pouted.

Cassidy leaned into Alex’s ear. “Oh, honey, don’t worry. I’ll have you beat in a couple of months,” she teased as she offered a hand to each of the twins.

Alex’s jaw fell slack. “I’m not fat.”

“Not at all, love,” Cassidy called back.

“Am I fat?” Alex looked down at her middle. She heard Cassidy and the twins laughing in the distance.

“What are you doing?” Mackenzie asked.

Alex turned to the sound. “Do I look fat, Kenz?”

"Nope, just old," Mackenzie shrugged and walked out of the room.

"What is this; pick on Momma day?" Alex groaned.

"Alex!" Cassidy called out. "Hurry up or Connor said he's eating your tacos."

Alex headed toward the kitchen. "Maybe, I should let him," she grumbled.

Cassidy looked over at Alex as she entered the kitchen and smiled. She shook her head affectionately. Alex wasn't only the most beautiful woman Cassidy had ever seen; she was the most beautiful person Cassidy had ever known. Cassidy loved teasing her wife. At times, a little teasing could cajole Alex out of a sour mood. And, while Alex had not been outwardly irritable, Cassidy did recognize the circles under her wife's eyes and the slight slow in her gait. Alex needed a diversion. This was the first night she'd managed to make it home for dinner in over a week. A little playful banter seemed appropriate. She'd make it up to Alex later if given the chance. She sidled up to Alex and whispered in her ear. "Eat as much as you want. I'm sure we can work it off later."

Alex swallowed the sudden lump in her throat. She sat down at her place, looked at her kids and then at Cassidy. "Load me up," she grinned.

Alex was finishing cleaning the table when Cassidy walked back into the kitchen.

"I almost forgot," Cassidy handed Alex an envelope. "This was in the mail today."

Alex looked at it curiously. Cassidy handled paying the bills. Actually, when Alex stopped to think about it, she seldom opened a piece of mail. She chuckled.

"What?" Cassidy asked as she poured herself some iced tea.

"I was just wondering if anyone knows I live here."

"What?"

"Nothing. It's just rare that I get mail."

Cassidy smirked. "You get plenty of mail. It's just that you prefer not to look at the bills, so I open them."

"Well, you are better with numbers."

"Says the woman with eidetic memory," Cassidy teased as she took a seat back at the kitchen table.

Alex looked at the envelope and shrugged. Now and again, something arrived with Alex's name that Cassidy didn't recognize. Whenever that happened, Cassidy passed it to Alex. Normally, it ended up in the circular file. Alex peeled the envelope open and slid out the contents. She stared at it for a moment before sinking into one of the kitchen chairs.

"Alex?"

Alex made no reply. Her eyes were riveted to the paper in her hand. Her face had gone pale.

"Alex?" Cassidy called again.

Alex looked up and took a shaky breath. "I need to call Claire and Bower."

Cassidy's brow furrowed in confusion for a moment. She felt her heart drop rapidly. "No…"

Alex's body had erupted in a wave of unpleasant tingles. They were the tingles of fear. She looked at the letter in her hand and shook her head. "I need to call Claire."

Cassidy looked at Alex for any sign of reassurance that she was gauging the situation incorrectly.

"I don't know," Alex answered her unspoken question. "I don't know if it's from him or if it's a prank," Alex said. "I need to preserve it. I might have already contaminated evidence."

"Alex, are you saying this person might know where we live?"

Alex caught the panic is Cassidy's voice and immediately moved to kneel in front of her. "Cass, listen to me; it could be anyone.

It could be a prank. After all the press coverage, that wouldn't be surprising."

"But, you don't think so," Cassidy observed. "I saw your face, Alex. You don't think it's a prank."

"I never dismiss anything. You of all people know that."

"Alex…"

"You listen to me; this is not Fisher, Cass. This is not the past. It's not about you or about us. It's not the same. You know that I will never let anyone hurt this family. I would die before…"

Cassidy pressed her fingers to Alex's lips to silence her. "I know," she admitted. "I just…"

Alex leaned in and kissed Cassidy's lips softly. "Go upstairs," she suggested. "Let me handle this."

Cassidy closed her eyes and released a nervous sigh. She'd thought she was prepared for Alex's return to this life. A letter at their home was reminiscent of the past—of Carl Fisher and his obsession with her.

"Cass," Alex cupped Cassidy's cheek. "Please, trust me."

"I do trust you, Alex."

"Then trust that you're safe."

Cassidy nodded. "You'll tell me if you have to leave?"

"I promise." Alex watched Cassidy head out of the kitchen. She sat back in the chair Cassidy had just occupied and rubbed her face vigorously. "Shit." She placed the call she needed to make.

"Missed me, huh?" Claire answered.

"Seems the breadcrumbs I left worked."

"What? They find another girl?"

"No," Alex said. "I guess he was busy with something else."

"What the hell are you talking about?" Claire asked.

"You need to come here, and we need forensics."

"What?"

"I got some mail today," Alex said.

"Fuck…."

—⊸⊸—

Alex felt sick. She could hear Claire's voice speaking behind her to the forensics team. Her mind was preoccupied with the words on the letter she'd received:

She went a wandering in the forest deep, looking for a few little lost sheep.
Shall we go hunting, Agent Toles?
Very well. A hunting we will go.
Where do we start?
Let's see:

Mary, Mary, Quite Contrary,
How does your garden grow?
With silver bells and cockle shells
You will find all the pretty maidens in a row.

"Toles," Claire called for Alex's attention.

Alex looked at the words she had copied down. "Cockle shells…"

"Alex," Claire grabbed Alex's shoulder. Alex finally looked up at Claire. "The team is leaving. We need to talk to Cass."

Alex shook her head.

"I don't want to either," Claire said. "We have to. You know that."

Alex sighed. "She doesn't need this now."

"Let me talk to her."

"Why you?"

Claire smiled. "Because your need to protect her is going to get in the way."

"Oh? And, yours isn't?"

Cassidy had heard the front door close and had made her way downstairs. "Protect me from what?" she asked.

Claire and Alex both turned.

"Well?"

Alex stood up and made her way to Cassidy. "Cass, it's just routine."

Claire rolled her eyes. Cassidy caught the expression over Alex's shoulder.

"Nothing about that letter you got is routine," Cassidy said. "We both know that. So, let's have it. Is it from him or not?"

"We don't know," Claire said.

"What do you *think*?" Cassidy asked the pair. "Alex?"

"I think it's a strong possibility, but," Alex rushed to clarify. "I don't think it has anything to do with you or this family."

"Then why send it here and not to the FBI?" Cassidy asked.

Claire crossed her arms and smiled at Alex as she waited.

"Because he knew I would open it—me, probably alone without a team of agents here. That's why."

"Why?" Cassidy asked.

Alex led Cassidy to sit at the table and directed Claire to join them. "Look, Cass, this is a game to him. It is. I've seen it before. He knows we're chasing him."

"So, he wants you to find him?" Cassidy asked.

"No, he wants to prove we can't. At the same time, he doesn't want anyone else to get credit for his work—for his hunt."

"I didn't see anything, Alex. I just picked up the mail like I do every day."

"No, you wouldn't have seen anything," Claire said. "The letter was postmarked from New Haven yesterday. He mailed it."

"So, then what do you need to ask me?"

"You just need to keep watch," Claire said. Cassidy's alarm was immediate and evident. Claire smiled at her. "Cassidy, Alex isn't a target and neither are you. She's right. Neither of us will take any chances, though. Not when it comes to your family."

Alex smiled gratefully at Claire. "Trust me; please. Just be aware, not afraid."

Cassidy wanted to tell Alex that she could comply with the request. This might be the one instance when she could not, and she had no intention of lying to her wife or to Claire. "I can't promise you that—either of you. I want to. I can't."

Alex sighed. "Claire, can I have a minute with Cass?"

Claire nodded and left the room.

Cassidy took one look in Alex's eyes and shook her head. "Don't even think about quitting."

"I won't put you through this. If you don't feel safe—I'm out."

"Alex, you cannot quit because of my demons."

"What I can't do is allow you or anyone in this house to be afraid. I won't do it, Cass. Don't ask me to."

"I love you, Alex. You can't walk away from this. I'm not going to lie to you; the idea that this psychopath knows where we are and who we are scares me. I can't help that. It feels like that night we came home and the picture was taped to the front door. I remember you walking around that house… Alex, I think that was the only time I was more frightened than when Carl Fisher had me. If you…"

"That's why I can't continue."

"No, that's why you need to. Alex, someone else will get hurt and…"

"And, someone else can solve this case."

"No. Find another way."

Alex was growing frustrated. She groaned. "What other way?" she raised her voice. "What am I supposed to do?"

"So, my telling you the truth means you quit? That's not fair, Alex."

"Damnit, Cassidy! I won't do that again."

"I'm not going to be the reason you quit again."

"Why do we have to keep fighting about this?"

"We're not—you are."

Alex threw her hands up. "I need some air."

“Where are you going?” Claire asked when Alex passed her in the hallway.

“I need to clear my head.”

Claire made her way back to the kitchen and found Cassidy sitting silently, face in her hands.

“Cass?”

Cassidy sighed. “I can’t lie to her about this. She can’t quit again. She can’t make me the reason she quits.”

Claire leaned against the counter. “She’s scared.”

Cassidy looked up.

“Not that you’re in danger; that she’ll fail you somehow.”

“What are you talking about?” Cassidy asked.

“Alex,” Claire said. “I get it. She blames herself, you know? I mean, for everything that you’ve been through. Hell, I think she blames herself a little bit for me. She wants to make everything better. That’s Alex. Sometimes, you can’t. That’s hard for her to accept.”

Cassidy smiled. “Sounds like you two have done some talking.”

“Some. Thing is, we have one big thing in common.”

“What’s that?”

“You,” Claire said. “I get why she wants to walk away. She loves you, Cassidy. Even when we’re out on the road, she’s always thinking about you—always. It always comes back to you. I don’t know if you really get that.”

“I know that,” Cassidy said. “But this is part of her, Claire.”

“Yeah; it is. Cass... The thing is, Fisher—he haunts all of us because he hurt you. I see it. I feel it working this case. It’s not him. It could’ve been him,” Claire’s voice dropped to a whisper.

“Claire,” Cassidy spoke. “I said that I was afraid. I can’t help that. I am. Some days… There are still days when I come home and no one is here and I feel a chill go up my spine as I head to this kitchen. It’s not the same place. It was ten years ago. I can’t help it.

A letter here—to our home?" Cassidy looked upward. "My children are here. This is… It just feels…"

"I know," Claire said.

"I know you do. I can't lie to Alex, not about this. She'd see through it in a minute. I also know that safety is an illusion. We're as safe, maybe safer than anyone. Things happen. Alex can stop some of those things from happening, and she needs to."

Claire nodded.

"Would I feel safer with her here all the time? Yes, I would," Cassidy confessed. "But I wouldn't feel happier and neither would she. And one day? One day, something will happen even if she is here around the clock. I know that too. Part of loving someone is letting them be who they are, even when that scares the hell out of you."

"I have an idea."

Cassidy was curious.

"Any idea where your missus went?"

Cassidy grinned. "She didn't change, so chances are she's down by the pond."

Claire nodded. "Are you going to be okay?"

"Promise," Cassidy replied. "Where are you going?"

Claire winked. "Hopefully, not for a swim."

"Did Cass send you out to look for me?"

"Nope," Claire said. She sat down on the log Alex occupied. "Looking to kiss some frogs?"

Alex chuckled.

"You need to talk to Cass."

Alex groaned. "We've been arguing about this since I left Carecom."

"Do you want to quit?"

"It's not about what I want, Brackett."

"What about what Cass wants?"

Alex turned and glared at Claire through the darkness.

"Just asking. You don't want her to lie, but you want to use the truth as an excuse to quit."

"It's not an excuse."

"Really?"

"You know what, Brackett? Just mind your own business."

"It is my business."

"Fuck you."

"Didn't work for us," Claire deadpanned.

Alex chuckled again.

Claire cast a stone at her feet into the pond. "That was from him."

"I know."

"And, you know as well as I do that he might just target Cass or anyone else if it gets his rocks off."

Alex sighed.

"And, we both know that he's going to get off on playing with us."

"You're making my case for me," Alex pointed out.

"Am I?" Claire challenged. She threw another stone into the water. "Fuck it. You're the best agent I know, Toles. Hell, that's why my father wanted me to keep an eye on you all those years ago."

Alex shook her head ruefully. "That's not true."

"Which part? The part about you being the best agent I know or the part about my father?" Claire replied. "It is true," she disagreed. "Cass knows that. She knows you. It's like you're asking her to be responsible for changing you."

"I have changed."

"Not really."

"Suddenly, you're an expert?" Alex replied harshly.

"You were always a sap," Claire picked up a rock.

Alex laughed. "Fuck you."

"And, again with the fucking." Claire sighed. "Look, I don't know anything about relationships. We both know that's true. I don't know the first thing about families. I do know Cass. And, I do know you. Better than you think. The only way you will ever let her down is by not being yourself and being honest. That's it. Stop trying to be who you think she needs." Claire chuckled.

"What's so funny?"

"Just realizing how much you and Hawk are alike."

"What are you talking about?" Alex asked.

"Hawk wanting to marry me. That's all about being what she thinks I need. It's about proving she really loves me. I already know that," Claire said. "I don't need her to be anyone but Hawk. No matter what, I'd still love her. I'm not going to be the reason she leaves behind what she loves—no way."

Alex looked at Claire. It wasn't the first time that Claire had surprised her. She heard a compassionate wisdom in Claire's words. She recognized that wisdom long ago in Cassidy. "What have you been reading—Tony Robbins or Dr. Ruth?"

"Neither. Think they could help?"

Alex laughed.

"Look, Alex, I know you don't like me all that much, even if you do trust me as your partner. Cass is right on this one. This is who you are, part of it anyway."

"She doesn't feel safe," Alex sighed.

"Well, about that—I think I have an idea."

"I'm listening."

"Pretty sure the doorway will stay up without you holding it," Cassidy's voice echoed in the darkened room.

Alex plopped down onto the bed. "I'm sorry."

Cassidy pulled Alex into her arms. "Me too."

"Cass, what would you think about your Dad coming to stay here for a while?"

"You mean having my father live here?"

"I guess you could call it that. Just for a while."

Cassidy stiffened beside Alex.

"Bad idea?" Alex guessed.

"No," Cassidy replied.

Alex sat up, clicked on the light and looked at Cassidy. "Talk to me."

"I know why you're suggesting it."

"Actually, it was Claire's idea."

Cassidy's surprise was evident.

"I know! Who knew she had a brain and a heart?"

"Stop," Cassidy laughed. "She's growing on you."

"She made some good points."

"Not the least of which is that my father should stay here while you work this case."

"That was one of them."

"And, that would let him spend more time with Dylan. Maybe he would be able to put your mind at ease about Dylan joining the Navy somehow," Cassidy guessed.

"Tell me that you wouldn't feel a little safer with him here."

"Physically? Yes."

"Talk to me," Alex repeated.

"Oh, Alex… I don't know what to say. I love my father. Sometimes, it's hard to be around him—to watch him with the kids. I…"

"I know. I know you missed so many things. I know. Maybe this is a chance for you too, Cass."

"If I agree, do you promise you aren't going to quit again?"

"I'm not going to quit either way."

Cassidy raised her brow.

"I never want to see you hurt, Cass. I'm sorry."

"It's all right."

"No, it isn't. You've given up so many things to take care of all of us."

"I've given up nothing," Cassidy said. She took Alex's face in her hands. "This is who I am, Alex. You're talking about teaching. Someday, I'll go back. I didn't quit. I chose something that means more to me. It's not the same, love. You have this crazy idea that everything I do is for you. I've told you a million times, it's every bit as much for me. This is where I want to be. And, I know that if what I *wanted* was to work in a classroom again, you would move heaven and earth so that I could. You have to trust that I would do the same for you."

Alex nodded. "I know. The thing is, sometimes I feel like all I can give you is protection."

"Alex, you give all of us so much more than you realize. All these years, I should think you would know by now that no one can make me laugh the way you do. It's the same with the kids. That's the best protection; you know?"

"What do you mean?"

"Well, when the bad things happen it's all the laughter and all the memories of the good stuff that carries you through."

Alex kissed Cassidy's forehead. Cassidy had been repeating that mantra for years. "So, you've said a few thousand times."

"Mmm. Maybe by the time I reach a million, you will listen."

Alex shed her clothes and flipped off the light. She pulled Cassidy into her arms. "Still want to work off dinner?"

"If that entails you holding me while I snore us both to sleep—yes."

Alex laughed. "Je t'aime."

"Je t'adore, love."

Alex walked into the kitchen to find Claire sipping a cup of coffee.

"At this rate, I will need to put on an addition," Alex commented as she poured herself a cup from the coffee pot.

"Hey, you're the one competing with the Waltons. I'm just a couch crasher. You might need a mountain with all these kids you keep having."

Alex rolled her eyes.

"So? Where are we off to today?" Claire inquired.

Alex sipped her coffee. "I think we'll take a little hike."

"More woods? Does Cass have any bug spray?"

"Are you sure you don't mean snake repellent?" Alex teased.

"Do they make that?"

Alex laughed.

"You think that letter was a clue, don't you?" Claire guessed.

"I do, and if I'm right, we need to look for some place with flowers."

"You mean like a garden?"

"Maybe."

Claire gulped the last bit of her coffee and placed her mug in the dishwasher. "Well, let's go."

Alex looked at the mug in her hand.

"I'll buy on the way."

"You'll buy?"

"Listen, Wonderland ain't easy to find, Toles. You want to catch the rabbit we'd better find his hole soon."

Alex blinked rapidly. "What was in your coffee?"

"I'm not the one writing nursery rhymes."

"Alice in Wonderland is a book, not a nursery rhyme."

"Yeah? Well, it's still creepy," Claire said as she and Alex made their way toward the door.

"Alice in Wonderland is creepy?"

"Smoking caterpillars and shrinking girls? Yeah, Toles—it's creepy."

Alex watched as Claire climbed into the car.

"Well? Come on, Alice! You want to catch the rabbit or what?"

Alex shook her head. *If we meet a smoking caterpillar, I quit. I don't care what Cass says.*

CHAPTER THIRTEEN

"What are you doing?" Alex asked Claire.

Claire flopped down onto a large rock beside the trail they had been walking. "We've been walking through these woods for three hours."

"And?"

"We've checked out seven places that Kaylee photographed and I've yet to see any cockle anything."

Alex groaned. "There has to be something."

"Yeah, but what and where?"

Alex sat down under a tree and pulled a binder out of her backpack. She began flipping through the pages. She massaged her right temple with her thumb while her left hand leafed through the pages.

"What are you looking for?" Claire asked. She sipped from her bottle of water. "God, I wish this was wine," she muttered.

Alex stopped turning the pages and leaned closer to the binder in her lap.

"What is it?" Claire wondered.

"Shit. We've been looking in the wrong places."

"No shit, Toles."

"What if the only time there are flowers is in the fall, not the spring or summer?"

"Come again?"

Alex moved to sit beside Claire. "We've been looking at places that show buds in spring and summer."

"Yeah?"

"What if what we're looking for isn't there until autumn?"

Claire groaned, stuffed her water bottle back in her backpack and dusted off her pants. "You owe me wine. I suppose you have an idea where we're headed?"

Alex placed the binder back in her pack and shrugged. "One of about a hundred places."

"A lot of wine, Toles. And, shoes. You definitely owe me shoes."

Cassidy opened the door and greeted her father with a smile.

James McCollum leaned in and kissed his daughter on the cheek. "Cassie."

"Hi, Dad."

"Are you sure you are okay with this?" he asked.

Cassidy nodded and rubbed her father's arm. "I am. Come in."

"How are you doing?" he asked Cassidy as he followed her to the living room.

"I'm okay, Dad."

"Your mother tells me you have some news."

"Is that right?"

"Yes, but she wouldn't tell me what it was."

Cassidy chuckled. Her mother amused her. "Any guesses?"

"Well, after Alex called me, I guessed you might be headed back to work."

"And, you thought we needed you to babysit?"

Jim laughed. "Guess I wouldn't be the first choice, huh?"

"I wouldn't say that exactly."

"Mm. So? You and Alex are moving? You're already married so it can't be that."

"We're expecting."

Jim's eyes widened. "As in a baby?"

"Well, as much as I enjoy Alex's love of X-files, I certainly hope it isn't an alien."

"That's terrific, Cassie."

"Really?"

"Of course."

Cassidy sighed.

"I can't imagine it was unexpected," Jim winked at his daughter.

"Not in the typical way—no. We'd hoped. I'd hoped. I wasn't sure it would happen again."

Jim smiled.

"You think we're crazy, don't you? I mean, one on the way to college and one just arriving at the same time."

"No."

"Really?"

"Not at all," Jim replied. "Your mother and I tried like hell to give you a brother or sister. It just wasn't in the cards."

Cassidy noted the sadness in her father's voice. "Mom never mentioned that."

"No? Well, I supposed it's probably still hard for her to talk about. She would say that we struck gold on the first try. Does that surprise you?"

"That you struck gold on the first try? No," Cassidy teased.

Jim chuckled. "Well, we get to live vicariously through you—with time off, I might add."

"Ahh, the advantages of being a grandparent," Cassidy said. Jim smiled, but Cassidy immediately felt the sadness from her father. "Dad?"

"I just wish we hadn't missed so much time."

Cassidy nodded. "Me too."

"Are you sure you are all right with this arrangement?"

"Yes," Cassidy patted her father's knee. "On one condition."

"What's that?"

"Do not, under any circumstances put sugar on the kids' cereal."

"Why do I think I am missing something?"

Cassidy winked. "Top secret, Dad. You understand."

Jim laughed. "Whatever you say, Cassie."

"Well, good. Then I say we go get you settled before the twins discover you."

"Cassie?"

"Yeah?"

"Thanks."

Cassidy smiled. "Don't thank me yet. Wait 'til you see the dishes after dinner."

"Alex?"

"Shit."

"What is it?" Claire asked as she came even with Alex.

Alex pointed in the distance.

"I don't see anything."

"Look over there about fifty yards."

Claire strained to focus on what Alex was pointing at. "Yeah? There are old stones everywhere out here. I thought we were looking for flowers, not rocks."

"We are." Alex pulled the binder out of the backpack again and flipped through a few pages. "Look."

Claire glanced at the photos on the page. She looked down at the pictures and then up at the line of bushes ahead. "I don't see what you are seeing."

Alex rolled her eyes. She pointed to one of the pictures. "Look over the bushes, past that foundation.".

Claire looked down at the picture again and back to the field just beyond the stone wall in front of them. It was the same place—no question. In the picture, small white flowers were blooming in a long, straight line. Just as Alex had suggested, the picture was dated September. Claire shook her head and pointed to a sign nailed to a tree. *No Trespassing. Private Property.*

"Aww, shit, Toles. It's not state property."

Alex grinned.

"No one's gonna give us a warrant based on this."

"Maybe we won't need one."

"What are you talking about? You can't have a team start digging in someone's backyard without a warrant. Even I know that."

"Don't need one if they give us permission."

"So, you're just going to walk up to whoever owns that land's door and say, 'hi, sorry to bother you, but I think there might be dead girls buried in your backyard. Mind if we borrow a shovel?' That's your plan?"

"Sort of," Alex replied.

"Sort of?"

"Yeah. I'll knock; you ask." Alex put the binder away, heaved her pack over her shoulder and started forward.

"There's not enough wine on the planet for this."

"Told you," Alex whispered in Claire's ear.

"Keep gloating," Claire replied. "You'll owe me a vineyard by the time this is over." Claire let her eyes travel slowly across the scene a few feet away. "I hope you're wrong."

Alex sighed. Part of her hoped that this would prove fruitful. She needed clues. She needed more to go on if she hoped to flush out this killer and end his reign of terror. But, she understood Claire's feelings. The woman who had opened the door when they finally had reached the edge of the property had been more than agreeable. Ellen Moriarty had told Alex and Claire that she and her husband had owned the property for more than forty years. He had passed away two years earlier. It explained the overgrowth where the team now began to dig. Alex had almost missed the spot. In Kaylee's pictures, the property had been well cared for. Telling the gentle older woman that the edge of her property had been used as a graveyard was not something Alex would enjoy.

"Maybe there's nothing," Alex commented.

Claire couldn't explain it, but she felt something tugging at her gut. "There is," she said.

"Agent Toles!" a voice boomed.

Alex looked at Claire.

"You'd better take a look at this!" the man called out.

Claire shook her head. "For once? I really wish I was wrong."

Alex groaned. "Me too," she commented.

"What do you have?" Alex asked.

The young agent pointed to the ground beneath him.

Alex closed her eyes for a moment.

"It's a femur," he explained.

"I know," Alex said.

Claire looked over Alex's shoulder. "I asked the lady. This one is all on you," she told Alex.

Alex took a deep breath. "Keep on it. As carefully as you can. Don't remove or touch anything. Stop if you need to. You treat this like it was family," she ordered the agents in front of her. "You coming?" she asked Claire.

Claire was ready to make a clever retort. She stopped herself. Ellen Moriarty was a kind, innocent woman. No one deserved to learn what she was about to. No one should have to deliver that news. "I'm right behind you," Claire promised.

Alex walked back toward the dig site. She'd stepped away to give Cassidy a head's up before she turned on the news. She stopped and regarded Claire in the distance. Claire was kneeling beside one of the forensic agents. What caught Alex's attention was the expression on her partner's face. Claire was deep in thought, attempting to put the pieces of the scene together. Alex also detected disgust, disbelief, and a hint of anger in Claire's eyes.

"Hey," Alex warned Claire of her approach.

Claire stood up and offered Alex a solemn grin. "Six," she said. "That's what it looks like."

Alex nodded.

"They've been here a while," Claire said. "Not all the same amount of time."

Alex nodded again.

"You're not surprised."

"I wish I could say I'm surprised," Alex replied. She edged closer to the scene and let her eyes commit it to memory.

"You don't think Mrs. Moriarty knows something?" Claire asked.

"I do, actually."

"Come on, Alex. She's a sweet old lady."

"I didn't say she knew they were here. She knows something. This property was kept up for years. She said her husband died after a long battle with cancer; right?"

"Yeah?"

"Well, I doubt he was the one tending this property. It's three acres, Claire. Someone had to have helped."

Claire looked back at the remains in the ground. "Landscaper?"

"Maybe. I think we'll have a better idea when we know how long he used this place."

"Agent Brackett? Agent Toles?"

Claire and Alex turned around and headed toward the sound of the voice calling them.

"What do you have?"

The agent pointed to the ground beneath his feet. It was about eight feet away from the other bodies.

"Son of a bitch," Alex commented.

"Alex? What the hell is going on?" Claire asked.

"I don't know," Alex confessed. "Something tells me it all

started with her."

Alex was stunned when Cassidy opened the door to greet her at three in the morning.

"Cass? Are you okay?"

Cassidy smiled. "I'm fine. Connor was up with the sniffles. I couldn't go back to sleep. How are you?"

Alex shook her head. "I've had more pleasant days."

Cassidy took Alex's hand. "Come on."

"Where are we going?" Alex lifted her brow.

"You are going to take a shower."

"That bad, huh?"

"I've experience more pleasant smells."

Alex laughed. "Thanks."

Cassidy winked. "Did you eat? Never mind, I already know that answer. I'll get you something."

"Cass, it's three in the morning. You don't need to…"

"Yes, I do."

"I don't have much of an appetite," Alex said honestly. Scenes from the day were burned into her mind. It hadn't left her with much want of food.

Cassidy sighed. "What about a glass of wine? It'll help you sleep."

Alex nodded.

"Do I want to guess when you're leaving tomorrow?"

"You'll be glad to know, not until a little later. I have a meeting in New York at one. I have to leave here by eleven."

"Good. Go on. I'll be up in a few minutes."

Alex climbed the stairs gingerly. Cassidy watched her and sighed. She heard Alex's back pop in the distance and winced. *I wish she would take care of herself.*

Alex peeled off her clothes and climbed into the shower. The feel of the hot water cascading over her skin instantly began to relieve the tension in her body. She closed her eyes as the steady stream washed over her. She wiped some droplets from her face and startled slightly when the shower door opened.

Cassidy stepped in behind Alex. She wrapped her arms around Alex's waist and pressed against her.

"Cass?"

"Just relax, Alex." Cassidy reached for the shampoo and poured some in her hand. She began to massage it through Alex's hair, working it into a lather. She heard Alex sigh. Cassidy directed Alex back under the water and rinsed the suds out. She could see the fine lines at the sides of Alex's eyes that indicated stress. "Relax, love."

Alex tried to comply with Cassidy's request. She was enjoying the feel of Cassidy's hands as they traversed her body and the warm spray that slowly began to ease her aching muscles. She opened her eyes and looked at Cassidy.

"Yes?" Cassidy asked.

Alex captured Cassidy's lips with a searing kiss.

"Alex," Cassidy gasped. "I wasn't trying to seduce you."

Alex knew that. Cassidy's intent had been to calm Alex. Alex couldn't prevent her body's reaction. Truth be told, she had no desire to. The strange thing about death was that it sometimes reminded a person about life. As Claire had driven Alex home, Alex had found herself wondering who the women they had found had been. Finding out who had taken their lives seemed secondary at that time. Who had they been? Had they loved? Had they been loved? Did they know love before someone had thought to show them evil? All those questions disappeared the moment Cassidy had opened the front door. Alex was home. All that mattered to her now was that Cassidy loved her.

Alex brushed Cassidy's hair out of her eyes. She turned them in the small space so that Cassidy stood under the flow of water. Alex's licked the stream of water off Cassidy's neck until their lips met again.

Cassidy's hands gripped Alex's shoulders. She understood Alex. Alex's touch was not lustful; it was loving. Cassidy relished the feel of Alex's lips as they wandered over her shoulder to her breast.

"Alex…"

Alex's lips began to explore Cassidy's breasts. She felt Cassidy quiver in her arms. Slowly, Alex knelt before Cassidy. She held Cassidy securely as her kisses rained down with the hot water. Cassidy's hands held onto Alex's shoulders in anticipation. Alex felt no need to contain her desire. She looked up briefly just as Cassidy's lips parted and a soft moan escaped the back of Cassidy's throat. Alex answered the unspoken request gently as Cassidy's fingertips dug into her flesh.

"I've got you," Alex promised, sensing Cassidy's need to feel grounded. Her kisses descended to Cassidy's center. Cassidy's pleading moan nearly sent Alex over the edge. She fought to keep her touch gentle, circling Cassidy's need repeatedly, tenderly but firmly.

"Alex, please… Please," Cassidy begged Alex for release.

Alex had taken her by surprise. It was a surprise she welcomed. She'd missed Alex's touch—missed making love with Alex. Life had been more chaotic than normal. Cassidy had been feeling bottled up emotionally, tending the needs of everyone in the family, and desperately wanting an escape. Perhaps, they both needed that now—an escape into each other.

Alex wrapped one arm around Cassidy protectively, and dropped the other so her fingers could gently move inside her wife.

"Oh, God, Alex…"

Alex felt Cassidy's quivering shift almost immediately to violent shaking. Cassidy's cry of pleasure was Alex's undoing. She felt a series of soft tremors erupt in her core. She pulled away slowly, whispering Cassidy's name. Alex's arms wrapped around Cassidy's waist and her head fell against Cassidy's stomach. "Cass," Alex choked on the name as she began to cry.

Cassidy ran her fingers through Alex's wet hair. She managed to turn off the shower without breaking their connection. She carefully guided Alex to her feet, reached outside the door, and wrapped Alex in a towel. "Come on, love."

Cassidy helped Alex get dry and dressed before doing the same. She led Alex to their bed and pulled Alex into her embrace. "Let it out," Cassidy encouraged.

Alex continued to cry. She was sure that people would be surprised by the strength of Cassidy's arms as Cassidy rocked her gently.

"I'm sorry, Cass."

"Sorry? For feeling? Alex, never be sorry for that. You don't have to pretend to feel anything here. You know that."

"Sometimes, Cass I find it hard to understand the world."

"Sometimes the world is hard to understand," Cassidy pointed out.

"There is evil in the world," Alex whispered.

Cassidy pulled Alex a little closer.

"People don't want to believe that—there is. Not everyone is broken," Alex continued. "Sometimes they're just evil."

Cassidy made no reply. She kissed Alex on the head and held her.

"You don't believe that," Alex guessed.

"That there is evil?"

"Yeah."

Cassidy took a deep breath. "That would make life a bit easier; wouldn't it?"

"What do you mean?" Alex wondered.

"I mean that if something is just evil, there isn't much you can do to change it."

"You have to stop it," Alex said.

"But can you, Alex? If it's evil, can you stop it? You can stop an action. You can't kill evil. You can't make it something else."

"You *can* kill it," Alex said tacitly.

"No, you can only kill its hand," Cassidy disagreed.

"You think I'm wrong."

"No. I think there is evil."

"You do?"

"Yes, I do. I just don't think people are inherently evil."

"That doesn't make sense."

"Doesn't it? What can a person do if they are born evil? Do they have any choice in that, Alex? Do we have any chance to change that?"

Alex sighed.

"I'm just saying that maybe people can do evil without being evil."

"Because they are broken."

"Maybe," Cassidy said. "I don't know. I don't have the answers, Alex. It seems like I have more questions each day that passes. About the only thing I do know is that people are responsible for all the good things and all the horrors in the world. I don't know that I believe anyone is a saint or anyone a is demon. I have to believe that we can change things—that people can change. Without that? I'm not sure what's left."

"I wish I could see it that way. What I saw today goes so far beyond broken. It's just…. Evil."

Cassidy ran her fingers over Alex's back. She wished she could banish the visions Alex wrestled with. "Go to sleep," Cassidy kissed Alex's temple. "No more talk about evil. Think about the good stuff."

Alex grinned.

"What's that about?"

"Showers," Alex yawned.

Cassidy chuckled. *Oh, Alex. I love you so much.*

"You all right?" Alex looked at Claire.

Claire kept her eyes focused on the door at the end of the corridor. "Yeah."

Alex stopped abruptly, grabbed Claire's arm and pulled her into a smaller room.

"What the hell?" Claire asked.

"You need a clear head for this meeting."

"I told you; I'm fine."

"Bullshit," Alex disagreed. "You know that Hawk will be in that room and it's playing with your head."

Claire stared at Alex without comment.

"Claire?"

"Let's just get through this meeting."

"No."

"No?"

"No. I need you on point in there."

"You think I'm incapable of being professional?" Claire bit.

"No, I think you love Hawk, and I think you're afraid to face her."

"Work is work."

Alex shook her head. "Not always."

"Are we still talking about me?"

"Yes," Alex replied. "But, I'd be the first to admit that keeping a professional distance isn't always possible."

Claire nodded. Alex had met Cassidy while assigned to investigate a case involving the former school teacher, and as an added layer of protection. "Not the same."

"I think it is in a lot of ways."

"I can handle it."

"I know you can handle it," Alex said.

"Then why are we standing here?"

"Because I need you to be focused on this case, and you can't focus if you are worried about running into Hawk constantly. You need to settle things."

"I think they were pretty well settled when I refused her proposal."

Alex sighed. "I think you underestimate Hawk."

"Since when do you care about my personal life? You can relax, Toles. I promise; I won't let my personal life fuck up this case."

Alex took a second to consider her response. "I care because you're my partner."

"And, I might just slip and hurt our chances of…"

"No," Alex interrupted Claire. "Jesus, Claire, come on. Give me a break, here."

"Hawk's your friend, I get it."

"Yeah, she is. You're my partner. You don't think I care about you? We have got to move past this."

"This?"

"Just talk to Hawk."

"I don't think this is the time or place."

"I agree. So, pull her aside, make a time and pick the place. Face it. For once, Claire give yourself a chance."

Claire scoffed at the idea. "You think I should marry Hawk?"

"I think you should tell Hawk the truth—all of it, no matter how much you don't want to. That's what I think. I think you need to stop running."

Claire shook her head and opened the door. "Noted. Now, can we go, please?"

Alex sighed and nodded. *Impossible. She's impossible.*

"Agent Toles, you have the floor," Assistant Director Bower introduced Alex.

"Here's what we know: As of yesterday, we have eleven victims. We now believe that all eleven were murdered by the same person. All but two victims were found buried naked. As you can imagine, the lack of evidence available has made this case challenging. Last week, some pertinent information regarding two theories we were working leaked to the press. Two days later, I received a letter at my home from someone posing as the killer."

"Posing?" Agent Eaves asked. "You don't believe it was?"

"After our discovery yesterday, yes; we do believe the letter was from the killer."

"And, what did the letter say?"

"It was a rhyme," Alex replied. "A rhyme with a clue. You each have a basic profile in front of you. Agent Brackett and I spent several hours with the owner of the property where the latest victims were found. As of now, her recollection of people and companies employed to care for the property is our best hope of developing a solid lead."

"Nothing on the letter?" another agent asked.

"The letter was tested for DNA and was negative. He must have sealed it with a sponge. Prints have been lifted, but my best guess is that we will find the postal service, myself and my wife's prints—nothing from our killer. He's too smart for that. Agent Brackett…"

Claire nodded to the group. "The prose in the letter is being analyzed by psych. The best lead from the letter Agent Toles received is the postmark. And, that's daunting to run down. Where it was picked up might hold the key. There is a team working that as we speak. It was postmarked from New Haven, Connecticut. The question is whether it was retrieved at a residence, business, dropped in a box or at one of the local offices. That will take time to uncover. Best case scenario; someone saw something. That's a longshot, though."

"Your brief mentions something about the victims found yesterday," another voice commented.

Alex nodded. "Identifications are underway," she said. "As I said, only two victims were found with any clothing. Kaylee Peters and one of the seven we discovered yesterday. She was buried some distance from the other six. There are traces of fabric still with the remains. Hopefully, those will hold some clues. The identities will either confirm the theory Agent Brackett and I have been working that this killer is on the prowl from New York State down through Connecticut or it will upend that. For now, we will continue to concentrate on that area and will expand that circle as needed."

"And, you believe he is still active?"

"We do. That's why I believe we need to refocus our efforts in Ashland–Pinnacle. The presence and focus here in Connecticut will force him to find another place to bury his victims," Alex explained.

"What makes you think he will bury them?"

Claire spoke up. "It's a compulsion," she said. "We have reason to think he may visit."

"Are we surveying those areas?"

Alex shook her head. "The areas are broad, we're talking hundreds of acres."

"We have one other potential piece of evidence," Claire said.

"Care to share?"

"Some soda cans," Claire said.

"Soda cans?"

"Yeah," Claire replied abruptly. "You know, cans that you drink soda from."

Alex couldn't help but chuckle. In this case, Claire's frustration was well-placed. She stepped in. "We recovered some potential evidence from a pond about three quarters of a mile from where Melissa Evans and Darla Maynard were found. DNA was compromised in almost every case, save a few cans. That could be good news."

A young agent spoke. "Could be?"

Claire's frustration was growing. In her view, this was time wasted—apprising desk wonks and rookies about facts in a case they should be out actively investigating and supervising. "Right. Could be," Claire said. "Unless there is a match to the DNA in the database, it doesn't provide a lead."

"How is that good?" the agent pushed back.

Alex noted the vein in Claire's neck popping out. She had no intention of reigning in her partner. Whoever this young agent was, he reminded Alex of a young Claire Brackett—brash, cocky, and annoying. She would enjoy watching Claire eviscerate him. Claire's smug smile made Alex laugh inwardly.

"Agent," Claire leaned over the table. "What was your name again?"

"Robbins," he said.

"Right, Robbins," Claire sat back. "Well, Agent Robbins, let me explain how it works."

Alex exchanged a smirk with Hawk in the distance. Things changed sometimes. At the moment, Alex was immensely proud and pleased with her partner. Educating a snot-nosed rookie was filling time that could be far better served.

"At the FBI, we get assigned a case because either a crime has been committed or someone suspects a crime is being, has been or will be committed."

"I'm aware of what we do," Robbins replied flatly.

"Are you? Apparently not," Claire continued. "The way we investigate a case is to collect evidence." She saw the rookie begin to speak and held up her hand. "That might be as boring as listening to an old lady talk about her lawn service. It might be something as mundane as a soda can. We collect it and hope it does one of two things: leads us toward a conclusion or leads us to the criminal. That's what we do."

"Thanks for the handbook. I don't see what that has to do with your statement," he countered.

Claire looked at Alex and raised her brow. Alex offered the rookie a sickly, sweet smile. "The can might not lead us to the killer. When we do find our suspect; it may confirm who he is."

"Long shot," Robbins replied with a chuckle.

"Long shots are sometimes the best shot we have," Alex replied dryly.

"Not much to go on," he muttered. He turned to the agent next to him. "She's been outta' the circus a little too long," he whispered.

Despite Robbins' attempt to whisper, Claire heard his comment clearly. She leaned over the table menacingly. "Something to say, Agent Robbins?" she challenged him. He smirked. "Let me tell you something," Claire lowered her voice. "If you have any inclination that you will ever be half the agent or investigator my partner is, you will learn to shut your arrogant mouth and listen to what she says. And, if you have a prayer of surviving the next five seconds in my presence, you'll heed that advice."

Assistant Director Bower cleared his throat and stood. "All right. We know where we are at. You each have your assignment," he told the group.

Alex put her hand on Claire's shoulder. "Go talk to Hawk."

"I don't…"

"Go," Alex repeated. "I want to have a word with Agent Robbins."

"Yeah? I'd like to kick his…"

Alex laughed. "I got that," she said. "Go talk to Hawk. Agent Robbins," Alex called. "A word."

Claire made a point to brush against the rookie. She whispered to him. "Fuck with my partner, Robbins, and you are fucking with me. You don't want to do that," she warned him.

Robbins made his way to Alex. "Your partner there is pretty protective."

Alex looked over his shoulder as Claire walked up to Hawk. She slowly returned her attention to him. "We've been through a lot together."

"Really? I thought you just came back?"

Alex nodded. "Let me make something clear to you," Alex said. "You're on this team because someone recommended you. That's why you're here. I can only assume that recommendation came from either Bower or Hawkins—both whom I respect."

Robbins gloated.

"What you should know is that you serve on this task force at *my* pleasure. Neither AD Hawkins nor AD Bower will question my decision to release you. If you can't work under my direction or under Agent Brackett's, I suggest you do yourself a favor and recuse yourself now."

"It's not an issue."

"See that it isn't," Alex said. "You might think this is a circus. You might be right. You're no ringmaster, Robbins. You're just a clown in the car. You want to command the ring? Learn your place." Alex walked away leaving the rookie with a lump in his throat.

"So?" Bower caught up to Alex.

"Not an easy one," Alex said.

"Are we talking about the case, the rookie, or your partner?"

"Yes."

Bower laughed. "You need more resources locally."

"I agree," Alex said.

"You know who can help with that."

"I do."

"You want me to have Hawk give her a call?"

Alex shook her head. "No. I have her number."

Claire chewed on her thumbnail as she listened to Agent Eaves tick off observations of the remains that were lying on the long, silver table.

"Agent Brackett?"

"Huh?"

"Did you hear me?"

"Sorry," Claire apologized. "Go on."

Eaves pointed to the skeletal remains. "If I'm right? Whatever she was wearing had a logo or an imprint on it."

Claire was curious. "How can you tell?"

"Well, the fabric is almost glued to the remains. It happens sometimes. Depends on what the body was exposed to."

"Any idea how long?"

"A long time. At least, the same amount of time as Evans and Maynard. I would guess longer. That's not my specialty."

Claire nodded. "Can you remove it without damaging it?"

"I think so. We've gotten pretty adept at this kind of thing, unfortunately."

Claire sighed. "He's like a ghost. Leaves nothing," she said. She chuckled caustically. "My father used to say never be afraid of a shadow, but a ghost? Those you have reason to fear."

Eaves listened intently. Claire Brackett's demeanor surprised her. The agent seemed genuinely worried about the case. It was clear that something was competing for Claire Brackett's attention. Eaves wasn't sure if it had anything to do with the exchange in the conference room earlier.

"Robbins is a pain in the ass," Eaves commented.

Claire smiled. "Reminds me of someone I knew once."

"Really? Who?"

"Me," Claire replied. She sighed heavily. "Eaves?"

"Yeah?"

"They were strangled?"

"Hard to say. Hard to say what caused their deaths in most cases. Nothing evident."

“What about her?” Claire gestured to the table.

Eaves took a deep breath. “The hyoid bone is fractured. I can’t say that strangulation killed her. I can tell you something or someone was bearing down on her neck. That much I can say.”

“Asshole,” Claire muttered. “Any idea of her age?”

“Guesstimate?”

“Yeah.”

“Younger than the others.”

“Really?”

Eaves nodded. “I’m not an anthropologist, Agent Brackett.”

“I got it. Between us. We’re running a clock here.”

“She’s not over twenty if I am seeing things correctly. Look, the team will be able to give you a better picture. As best I can tell, there’s still some fusion left to occur.”

“Fusion?”

“Bone fusion. After twenty we look for decline. She’s young, Agent Brackett. Past puberty, but….”

“But?”

“Barely adult. Sixteen? That’s a guess.”

Claire hopped down from the desk she was sitting on and looked down at the remains. “We’ll find him. I promise you; we’ll find him.”

“I wish I could say it’s a pleasure,” Candace Reid wrapped Alex in a hug.

“I won’t take it personally,” Alex promised.

“Sit down,” Candace offered Alex a seat. “Let’s have it.”

“He’s out there, Candace. He’s not looking to stop—not now. He wants to play.”

“You mean with these girls?”

“And with me.”

Candace sucked in a deep breath and let it out slowly. "And, you think he's here—in New York?"

"I think he travels through here."

"And?"

"I think it's likely there are a lot more than eleven victims."

"You mean before he's through?" Candace asked. Alex shook her head. Candace groaned. "I was afraid you would say that."

"We might never know unless we catch him," Alex said.

"What do you need?"

"Bodies. Cops on patrol. He's picking them up somehow, Candace. Whether it's at a bar, a truck stop or on the road—that I can't say for sure. What we do know is that three of the four victims we've identified were from New York, not far from your home. We're certain Deidre Slocum was hitchhiking her way to Maine. Claire talked to her friend. It was raining like a bitch for two days around the time Deidre disappeared. My bet is the road. God knows, there are long stretches up there with nothing—no one to see but an occasional farm, house or car driving past."

Candace nodded.

"I'm sorry. I know this comes at a shitty time for you—politically, I mean."

Candace smiled. "Is there a good time? Politically, I mean?" she winked. "Don't worry about that. We'll get you the resources you need. You speak with Superintendent Foster. He's better with the particulars. I'll see to it that it happens."

"Candace?"

"Yes?"

"Just…Tell the girls to be careful."

Candace's jaw tightened. She had two daughters and a daughter-in-law.

"I don't think you're a target," Alex continued. She sighed. "But, in the interest of caution, I'd be… Well, cautious. He sent a letter to the house—our house."

"Oh, no. How's Cassidy?"

"Spooked," Alex admitted. "Her dad's staying. The thing is, this guy, whoever he is, he wants to think he's more powerful than anyone—smarter. With you in the spotlight now that you've announced your candidacy…"

"Say no more."

"Sorry," Alex apologized. "I don't mean to make it personal, but…"

"I understand," Candace promised. "Any leads?"

"Between us?"

"Of course."

"Yes. Running through the rolls of two separate landscaping companies."

"You think he's a landscaper?"

"I don't know. I think he was at some point."

"Keep me posted."

"I will. By the way."

"What?" Candace asked.

"I'm glad you decided to do it. We could use you in that house."

"And, here I thought you hated politics."

Alex shrugged. "I do. It's just some politicians I like."

Candace laughed. "I'll take that as a compliment."

"You should."

CHAPTER FOURTEEN

Claire inhaled a breath for courage and opened the door to her apartment. "Hi."

Hawk stepped inside. "Hi."

Claire closed the door, took another deep breath and looked at Hawk. "I know we need to talk."

"I agree."

"Wine?"

"No, I'd prefer to be sober for this," Hawk said sadly.

Claire nodded and gestured for Hawk to have a seat on the sofa. "I'm not sure I know where to start."

"How about with why you walked out on me?"

Claire's surprise was genuine. "Is that what you think?"

"What else would I think, Claire?"

"I said no. I didn't think you'd want to hear much else from me."

"You think that turning down my proposal made me stop loving you?"

"No. I didn't say that. But, you were clear that you wanted more."

"I do," Hawk said.

"Why do you want to go back to the NSA?" Claire asked.

"What does that have to do with this?"

"Can you please just answer me?"

Hawk sighed. "Claire, I want to be with you. We can't both stay at the FBI and be in the same place. You know that."

"And, so you think that if you marry me, that will guarantee us? That way you can leave?"

"What? No!"

"Really?" Claire challenged. "Hawk, I'm not marriage material. I'm damaged goods. Everyone will tell you that."

"Who would tell me that?" Hawk asked.

"You want the list? Start with my partner and your ex."

"Alex doesn't think that."

"It doesn't matter," Claire said.

"I think it does," Hawk disagreed. "We're all damaged goods, Claire."

"Maybe. Not all of us have my past."

Hawk nodded. "Do you want to know what I want? Does that matter?"

Claire smiled. It did matter. "It matters."

"I want you. I don't mean that I want you for a minute, and I don't mean in my bed. I mean I want you—all of you. That's what I want."

"And, that means we need to walk down some aisle and sign some paper?"

"Jesus, Claire! Most women would be thrilled to have their partner propose."

"I'm not most women, Hawk." Claire got up and began to pace.

"What are you so afraid of?" Hawk asked.

Claire closed her eyes. For some reason, she could hear Alex's voice telling her to be honest. "I don't want anyone to end up like her."

"Who? What are you talking about?"

Claire shook her head, unable to face her lover.

Realization hit Hawk. *Your mother*. "Dear God, Claire," she whispered. Hawk made her way across the room and turned Claire to face her. "You are not your father."

Claire would not meet Hawk's eyes. "You don't know that."

"I do know that."

"How can you? I let him, Hawk. I stood there and I watched him."

"You were a child," Hawk took Claire's face in her hands. "He knew that. He took advantage of your innocence."

"I didn't stop him. What does that make me? I followed him

all those years."

Hawk pulled Claire into her arms. "Claire, stop this. You are not your father. You're not."

"I've done it, Hawk."

"Done what?"

"Killed people."

Hawk closed her eyes. "So have I," she reminded Claire.

"Not the same. I could have walked away from Elliot. I didn't have to follow my father's orders. After what he did to my mother? Why did I? Why did I follow him at all? I should have killed him, not Elliot. What does that make me?"

Hawk stepped back a pace and held onto Claire's arms. How could she have missed this? Claire was convinced that no matter how much time passed, no matter how much she had grown and changed, somewhere deep within her lurked a monster—the likeness of her father. "Look at me."

"I can't."

"Claire, please… Please look at me."

Claire reluctantly met Hawk's gaze. "I can't, Hawk."

"You can't marry me or you can't love me?"

"I do love you," Claire replied as a tear slipped over her cheek. "I don't want to."

"Why not?"

"Love leads…"

"Love leads here," Hawk said. "Stop this. Stop blaming yourself for who your father was. You are not him, Claire. No one believes that except you."

"What if I am and then one day who I am turns on you."

Hawk wiped Claire's tears away with her thumbs. Few people ever saw the little girl hidden beneath Claire's commanding exterior. Eleana, Cassidy, and Hawk—those were the only people who had ever seen the real Claire. After seeing Claire's response to Agent Robbins that afternoon, Hawk was sure that Alex had begun to see pieces showing through. More and more, Claire was shedding her past; learning to open herself to people and to trust others. Now, Claire needed to learn to trust herself.

Hawk placed a tender kiss on Claire's lips. "All I want is you," she promised. "Don't you understand that? I'm not afraid to love you. Stop being so afraid to let me."

Claire opened her eyes. "Hawk…"

"You're afraid of hurting me one day," Hawk said. "You think you can just push me away by refusing my proposal? You don't know me that well," she smiled. "You underestimate me, Claire."

Claire chuckled nervously.

"That's funny?" Hawk asked.

"No. That's what Alex said."

Hawk nodded. "She knows me pretty well."

"Did you? Did you love her?" Claire asked.

"Yes, I did," Hawk answered. "Not the way I love you. Did you? Love her?"

"No," Claire replied honestly.

"But?"

"I admire her."

Hawk nodded. "And?"

Claire sighed.

"Claire?"

"I care about her, okay?"

Hawk smiled. "That was painful; wasn't it?"

"You have no idea."

"You're not your father," Hawk repeated. "I'm not your mother."

"No, but we are a lot like them in some ways. Hawk, I still don't remember everything. How can you be so sure I'm not like him?"

"Because you don't want to be."

"That's not…"

"That's why," Hawk continued. "We all have choices, Claire—all of us. Your father chose his path and he put you on yours. You were a girl. You lost your mother. You needed your father. He took advantage of that. That was his choice. You're not that little girl anymore. You're not the same Claire you were ten or fifteen years ago because you've made different choices."

"You sound like Cass."

"Cassidy's a smart woman. She loves you. That should tell you something."

"Cassidy loves everybody."

Hawk shook her head. "Cassidy cares about people. You're part of her family, Claire. She doesn't let everyone that close, and you know it. And, trust me, if Alex didn't think you'd changed; she wouldn't have let you that close no matter what Cassidy said."

"That's why you partnered us?"

"No. You're partnered with Alex because you are the best pairing. Alex needs someone who's not afraid to challenge her and so do you. And, you care about each other. Maybe that's mostly because of Cassidy, or maybe it started that way—I don't know. I do know this much; you are not William Brackett any more than Alex is Nicolaus Toles or Cassidy is James McCollum. Don't you think Alex and Cassidy fight those same demons? Let it go, Claire—please."

"I don't know how."

"Let me help."

"How?" Claire asked.

"You can start by not walking out."

"Hawk, I don't know if I'll ever be ready to get married."

"How about living together?"

"You just said that we can't both be…"

"I took the job at NSA."

"What?"

Hawk shrugged. "No matter what your answer had been, I was

going to take it. I don't belong at the bureau. You do. You're a talented agent, Claire. You are. Me? I need to go home."

Claire nodded. "And us?"

"Home for my work is NSA. Home for me is you. At least, that's where I would like it to be."

"I…"

"You don't have to give me an answer now," Hawk said. "Promise me you will think about it."

Claire brought their lips together. "I don't need to think about it."

"No?"

Claire shook her head. "No," she answered. Her hand began to unbutton Hawk's blouse. "I'm tired, Hawk."

"Tired?"

Claire kissed Hawk tenderly. "Tired of missing you."

Hawk closed her eyes. "I'm not going anywhere."

"Not tonight," Claire commented before leading Hawk toward the bedroom.

Alex took a sip from the cold cup of coffee beside her. "Gross," she shuddered. Her eyes returned to the computer screen in front of her. "Who are you?" she mused.

"Momma?"

"Abby?"

Abby looked up at Alex. "Mommy's sick."

Alex smiled reassuringly at her daughter. "She is, huh?"

Abby nodded. "She's in the bathroom."

Alex closed her computer and pulled Abby onto her lap. "Mommy's tummy is a little upset is all."

"How come?"

Alex and Cassidy had not told their younger children about

Cassidy's pregnancy yet. It seemed clear that the time had come. "Where's your brother?" Alex asked.

"Playing in the bedroom."

"What do you say, you go find Connor and Kenzie and I'll go check on Mommy? Maybe we can all sit down here and have a talk."

"But Mommy's sick."

Alex kissed Abby's cheek. "I promise; Mommy is okay. You go find your brother and sister and I'll take care of Mommy."

Abby's reluctance was obvious. "Momma?"

"Yes?"

"Mommy doesn't get sick."

Alex forced herself not to laugh. Cassidy had suffered through more than a few cases of the flu or a nasty cold. She had four children to deal with. Seldom did Cassidy let her children know how sick she was. Abby clearly thought her Mommy was Wonder Woman. "She'll be okay, sweetie. Now, go find Connor and Kenzie."

"What about D.?"

Alex smiled. "Dylan is at Maggie's. He'll be home later."

"I can call him?"

Alex smiled. Abby was so serious she couldn't refuse. She pulled her phone out of her pocket. "Now, when he answers you tell him who it is and what you want."

Abby nodded and Alex handed her the phone.

"D., it's me!"

"Abby?"

"Yep. Come home."

Alex covered her face to keep from laughing.

"Abby? Why do you have Momma's phone?" Dylan asked.

"Cause Mommy's sick."

"Mom is sick? Abby, is Momma there?"

"Yep."

"Could I please talk to her?"

"Nope."

"No?"

"Nope. You come home, D," Abby said firmly.

Alex had to bite her lip to keep her laughter in check. "Abby, let me talk to Dylan, okay? You go find your brother and sister." Abby huffed but handed Alex the phone. "Dylan?"

"Alex, is mom okay?"

"She's not dying if that's what you mean. Although, I suspect there are some moments she wishes she would right now."

"Oh, no."

"I'm about to go check on her. She was fine when she went upstairs. I think it might be time we told your brother and sisters what's going on."

"I'll be home in about twenty minutes."

"Maggie is welcome," Alex said.

"Thanks. We were wrapping up anyway."

"Okay. I'll see you in a few," Alex said. She looked back at her laptop and took a deep breath. Work would have to wait.

Alex stepped into the bedroom just as Cassidy was emerging from the bathroom. "How many speckles did you count?"

Cassidy shook her head. "I was too busy gripping the toilet bowl."

"I'm sorry, Cass."

"I'm all right. Doesn't seem to last too long. I thought you were working downstairs?"

"I was."

"Did something happen?" Cassidy asked, expecting that Alex came up to tell her that she was leaving.

"Abby happened."

"Abby happened?"

"Yep. She must've gone looking for you."

"Oh, no."

Alex nodded. "I think it's time, Cass. She was a little freaked out by the Exorcist impression you had going on in there."

Cassidy chuckled. "I think my head might actually have spun around a few times on that one."

"I asked her to get the kids."

"I wish Dylan was here."

"He's on his way home now."

"You called him?" Cassidy was shocked.

"Not exactly. Abby did. Well, Abby had me call so she could talk to him."

Cassidy laughed. "What did you tell him?"

"The truth."

Cassidy exhaled forcefully. "Do me a favor?"

"Sure."

"Give me a few minutes to put myself back together?" Cassidy requested. Alex nodded. "And, Alex?"

"Yeah?"

"I'm sorry if this interrupted you. I know…"

Alex waved off Cassidy's concern. "It was going to be a long night no matter what."

Cassidy watched Alex leave and took a deep breath to stave off a wave of nausea. She looked down at her belly. "Behave, kiddo."

"Long day, Mr. Duncan?"

"You could say that, Brandon."

"Seems like it's busier than normal around here," the security guard observed. "Everybody's on overtime."

"It's that time of year."

"I'll bet all those girls they keep finding are good for your business."

Bryce flinched. "That's a bit callous, don't you think?"

Brandon shrugged. "I know my wife wants a security system. She says you can't trust anybody anymore."

"You live nearby, don't you?" Bryce asked.

"Stratford."

"I think you can reassure your wife that she's as safe as she was before all this craziness."

"Really? They found all those girls."

Bryce smiled. "I don't think Stratford's in this guy's path."

"Well, you'd know better than me, Mr. Duncan."

"Just going on what they've said on the news."

"My mother always said not to trust what the news says."

"Have a good night, Brandon," Bryce laughed.

Brandon watched Bryce Duncan pull past the guard gate. "I wonder where he's headed now?"

"What are you thinking about?" Hawk asked Claire.

Claire's fingertips traced faint circles over Hawk's chest. "I wonder who they were."

"Who?"

"Those girls," Claire said so softly that Hawk almost didn't hear her.

Hawk pulled Claire closer.

"He strangled them," Claire said.

"I thought most of the deaths were undetermined?"

"Technically," Claire said. "I don't know about the stabbing. I mean Kaylee and Deidre. I think that's some sadistic turn on or something. The strangling? That's his power."

"Claire…"

Claire closed her eyes and nestled closer to her lover. "Ever see someone choked to death?"

"Claire…"

"First it's gasping. You can hear it until the pressure increases. Then? Then it's silence and flailing, and fear. You can feel it—the fear."

Hawk held Claire securely. "I wish you had never had to see that."

"What could they have done to deserve that?" Claire sighed. "Eaves thinks one of them was about sixteen. That's even younger than Kaylee."

"Claire, if this case is too much…"

Claire shook her head. "No. We need to find him. I need to find him."

With a deep breath, Hawk shifted to look at Claire. She brushed a strand of red hair out of Claire's eyes. "You will."

"I couldn't save her," Claire said. "I couldn't stop him."

Hawk kissed Claire on the forehead gently. Claire's memory of watching her father strangle her mother with his bare hands would haunt her for the rest of her life. Hawk understood that some things could never be forgotten, perhaps not even shelved. Claire's mother had been Claire's light. She would forever mourn that loss. In some way, Hawk understood that solving this case would both torment and help Claire to heal.

"I love you, Claire."

Claire smiled. Hawk had accepted her without conditions. Claire had never thought she could love anyone but Eleana. Part of her would always love Eleana. Nothing could change that. Charlie Hawkins held Claire's heart in a completely different way—she held it knowing all of Claire's demons and all of Claire's questions. Claire had struggled to say the words to Eleana, "I love you." There remained moments when the sound of the words as they escaped her lips sounded foreign to her ears, as if she were speaking another language. She would not make that mistake again. Choice. It all came down to her choices, that's what Hawk had said.

"What?" Hawk asked as silence lingered.

Claire placed a gentle kiss on Hawk's lips. "I love you too."

Hawk smiled. "There's hope for you yet."

Alex took Cassidy's hand. "Are you up to this?"

Cassidy winked.

"Is somebody else moving in?" Mackenzie looked at her parents expectantly.

"What?" Alex asked.

"Well, Grandpa moved in," Mackenzie explained her logic. "You made us all sit down when you told us that."

Cassidy grinned. "She's got you there," she whispered in Alex's ear. She looked at the three children sitting in front of her. "Well, Kenz you're on the right track."

"YaYa?" Mackenzie asked.

"No," Alex laughed. "YaYa and Grandma are happy where they are, I think."

"Who?" Mackenzie asked.

Connor pulled on Mackenzie's shirt and she turned to him. "Somebody's coming to live here with us," she told her little brother.

"Maggie?" Connor bounced.

Dylan coughed. "Umm, no. Sorry, buddy," he shook his head.

Cassidy chuckled. "Not Maggie," she said. "This person will be quite a bit smaller."

Three sets of eyes looked at Cassidy with confusion then tracked to Alex.

"You're all going to have a new brother or sister," Alex told them.

"Who?" Abby asked.

Dylan laughed. "We have to wait to find that out," Dylan spoke up.

"Why?" Connor wanted to know.

Alex looked to Dylan, indicating he should run with his explanation.

"Mom is having a baby," Dylan said. "And that takes time."

Mackenzie looked directly at Cassidy. "Just one?"

Cassidy lost all hope of maintaining composure and erupted in laughter. "I hope so."

Alex rolled her eyes.

"When do we meet him?" Connor asked.

"Always a him in this family," Cassidy commented.

"Around Christmas," Alex said.

"But Mommy is sick," Abby said.

Cassidy smiled at Abby. "I know it seems like that," she said. "That's just because I have to get used to carrying the baby. I'm not sick, sweetie. It just takes a little time. In a couple of weeks, I will feel much better—honest."

"Where is he?" Connor asked.

Mackenzie rolled her eyes and pointed to Cassidy's stomach. "In there, like in Auntie El's."

Connor wrinkled his nose. "In there?" he asked.

Alex nodded. "Just like you were," she said.

Connor shrugged. "Can I talk to him?"

Cassidy lifted her brow. She suddenly had visions of Connor and Alex building tin can telephones to speak with the baby. *Oh, boy.* "I suppose you could," she said.

Connor walked up to Cassidy and put his mouth directly on front of her stomach. "Hi!"

Cassidy looked at him and felt her heart swell. Alex met her gaze and smiled.

"He's not listening anyway," Mackenzie said. "You have to wait a while. Then you can make him somersault." All eyes turned to Mackenzie to explain. "It's true! Momma used to make me somersault. She told me."

Cassidy looked at Alex with a raised brow. Alex shrugged. "Well, that is interesting, Kenz," Cassidy said. "Your Momma talked to all of you," she said. Dylan looked down. Cassidy sighed. "Maybe Momma can tell you all about it over some cookies in the kitchen,"

Cassidy suggested.

Mackenzie sprung to her feet. "I'm in!"

Alex watched their three youngest children sprint toward the kitchen. She turned to Cassidy and noticed Dylan was gazing at his feet. Cassidy's silent arched eyebrow told Alex to give her a minute with their son. Alex nodded. "I'll save you a cookie," she promised.

Cassidy regarded Dylan thoughtfully for a moment before speaking. "She talked to you all the time too when you didn't know it."

Dylan looked up.

Cassidy smiled. "I used to catch her in your bedroom talking to you when you were asleep," she explained. "You know, she still goes in there when you are away."

"It's stupid, I know," Dylan said.

"No, it's not," Cassidy disagreed. "I understand. You feel you missed something with Alex."

"That's no one's fault," he offered.

"Doesn't mean it doesn't hurt," Cassidy said. "I understand more than you think."

Dylan sighed.

"Sometimes, I see you sitting with Grandpa—you might just be talking with him and I feel so alone."

Dylan cocked his head curiously. "Mom?"

"It's true. I'm grateful that you have him in your life. I'm glad that he's in mine, but I missed so much with him," she explained. "He missed my first boyfriend. He missed my prom, my wedding—both of them. He missed seeing you be born. Seeing Kenzie be born—so many things, Dylan. As happy as it makes me that you and your sisters and brother get to have those things with him; sometimes? Sometimes, it makes me a little sad. Maybe even a little jealous."

"I'm sorry."

"Don't be," Cassidy said. "He loves me. I know that. I know

that if he could get that time back, he would be here for all of it. Just remember the same is true with Alex." Cassidy shook her head. She felt tears building in her eyes.

"Mom?"

"She loves you so much, Dylan. Do you know that she made me tell her everything I could remember about being pregnant with you? She wanted to know when you took your first step—everything. Every time Kenzie did something, Alex would get so excited. Later, she would get quiet. It took me a while to realize why. She was thinking about you, wondering when you did those things. The truth is, most of us forget more details than we'd like. Alex? She remembers them all," Cassidy laughed.

"I know. I wish it didn't make me feel like…"

"Like you missed something?"

Dylan nodded.

"You both did," Cassidy said honestly. "Surprised I'd say that? It's the truth. But, Dylan we all miss certain things. I missed Connor's first step. I missed Kenzie's first word. It's what you do share that matters."

Dylan nodded. "Mom?"

"Hum?"

"Maybe you should take your own advice."

Cassidy grinned. "Maybe."

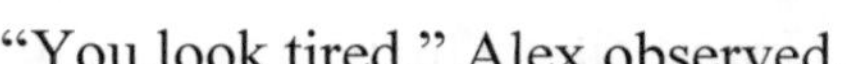

"You look tired," Alex observed.

Claire shrugged. "Spent the night with Hawk."

"Uh-huh. Is that a good tired or an I don't want to talk about it tired?" Alex asked.

"Both. You look a little worn yourself."

"I was up all night looking through the landscapers' personnel files."

"Find anything?" Claire wondered.

"Lots of things. I just don't know if any matter," Alex replied. "Three names kept popping out at me."

"They worked on Mrs. Moriarty's property?"

"That's the thing," Alex said. "I can't find any details of who worked at what property."

"So, what made them stand out?"

"Timing," Alex said. "All were employed between 2004 and 2008."

"Let me guess; we're on our way to check them out."

"Well, we *are* on our way to talk to one of them."

"Do tell."

Alex focused on the road in front of her. "Look in that file on the backseat."

Claire retrieved the folder and opened it.

Mark Jacobs
315 Sunnymade Drive
Agawam, Massachusetts

"Based on this he doesn't fit our profile," Claire commented as she continued to read. "Says he's a pharmacist in Agawam. Not exactly someone who's on the road frequently."

"That's why I want to talk to him first. I want to see what he remembers about who was working at Greenscape during that time."

"What aren't you saying?"

Alex shrugged. "When I was talking to the owner yesterday, he got skittish when I started asking about how many people they employ."

"You think he's hiding something?" Claire asked.

"About the killer? No. He's not the original owner. I suspect he might be engaged in similar hiring practices. I'd bet Greenscape has a long history of hiring off the books help. Certainly, would have helped if the same family owned it now."

"I wonder why they don't. Think Jacobs knows something?"

"Well, based on everything I read about Mr. Jacobs, I'm convinced he is not the person we are looking for. That doesn't mean he doesn't know the person we are looking for. I suspect he has nothing to hide. That means he's apt to be forthcoming with everything and anything he recalls. That might just give us a starting point."

Claire nodded and then looked out the window beside her.

"How did you make out with Agent Eaves yesterday?" Alex asked.

"It'll be slow," Claire replied. "Identifying them. Two interesting things."

"Care to share?"

"Well, the girl who was buried apart from the rest?"

"Yeah?"

"Eaves thinks she was younger, probably around sixteen."

Alex's jaw tensed.

"And, that fabric that was stuck to the top of her ribcage?"

"Yeah?"

"Eaves is pretty sure it had some writing or a logo on it. With the light on the table you could see the white outline."

"Interesting."

Claire sighed.

"You okay?" Alex asked.

"Not really."

Alex was taken aback by the honest response. "Want to talk about it?"

Claire turned and looked at Alex. Alex felt her gaze and glanced at her with a smile.

"I woke up thinking that the best chance we might have for a lead is a new victim. How fucked up is that?"

Alex nodded. "I know how you feel."

"What?"

"I hate it, but you aren't wrong. I want to stop this bastard before he kills anyone else—I do. The lack of evidence is frustrating."

"Maybe this landscaper thing will pan out."

"I hope so."

"How did you make out with the governor?"

"She'll make sure there are more feet on the ground where we need them."

"You don't sound happy about that," Claire observed. "Worried she'll bag us when the political pressure starts?"

"Candace?" Alex asked. "No. I just worry that as this investigation becomes more focused, he'll become more unhinged."

"You think he might target someone?"

"I don't know. He already made it personal by sending that letter to my house."

Claire looked back out her window. She needed to process all the information before responding. "We won't let it get that far." *I won't let it get that far.*

"Mr. Jacobs," Alex extended her hand.

"Mark, please."

Alex nodded. "This is my partner, Agent Claire Brackett. We appreciate you taking the time."

"I'm not sure how I can help you," he said.

"You worked as a landscaper for a time; is that right?" Alex asked.

"Yeah, I worked my way through college that way. Started mowing lawns when I was fourteen. Took a job in college working all summer with a company back home."

"Greenscape?" Alex asked.

"Yeah. Why?"

Alex offered the man before her a reassuring smile. Even innocent people tended to become unnerved when the FBI knocked on the door. She needed to put him at ease if she hoped to get accurate information from him. "Greenscape has come up as a vendor for someone close to our investigation. You know how it goes sometimes. Not everyone is a great record keeper," she said. "We just wanted to talk to some of the people who worked for them back when you did."

Mark Jacobs nodded. "Well, I worked a lot when I was in college. Most weeks fifty or sixty hours."

"And, did you mainly work in the same places?"

"Not always. Lots of people came and went; you know? Kids would take a job and think it was all fun and games. Lots of times you were alone on a property. You got dropped off and picked up later. It wasn't always social. It was hot and dirty. People suddenly didn't show up. That meant you went wherever they needed you."

Alex nodded. "So, a lot of people came and went?"

"Yeah. I'd say every week there was someone new."

Claire listened intently. "How many people stayed?" she asked.

Jacobs shrugged. He thought for a moment. "I worked for them for five years. In all that time, there were only four people that were there for more than two summers when I worked."

"Do you remember them?" Alex asked.

"I think so. Umm… There was Don; I'm sorry; I don't know his last name," he apologized.

Alex smiled. "That's okay. Go on."

Jacobs brow furrowed as he attempted to recall the names. "Gordon Daniels. He worked for the first three summers with me. Then he went into the military, I think. Never saw him again. I remember because that next summer was hell. Gordon worked his ass off. It made the time go; you know?"

"So, you worked with Gordon a lot?" Claire wondered.

"Yeah. Almost every day for the last two summers he was there. They sent us to the bigger properties. Places that needed more than a mow," he explained. "Gordon was pretty artistic. I mean, he could do anything. His grandfather had owned a nursery. At least, I think it was a nursery. He knew all about plants. So, we did a lot more than mow and trim those two summers."

Alex filed away the information. "And, the other two?"

Jacobs combed his thoughts for a minute. Ralph. Sorry, I can't say I ever paid much attention to him. He was kind of quiet. Didn't work with him much."

"Doesn't sound like you spent much time with the people you worked with," Claire observed.

"Not really. Like I said, people came and went. Just Gordon. I mean, and BJ. He was there on and off. I think he had another job too. Never really asked. He just appeared when he appeared. Sometimes, he worked with us. Sometimes, he was off on his own."

"Not a friend, I take it," Alex said.

"Nah, Gordon was the only one I ever went out with after work. I know that he and BJ were friends. They used to drink together on weekends. My last summer he was there a few times and then he just stopped showing up at all."

Alex nodded. "Any idea what BJ's last name was?"

"Nah, sorry," he said. "Gordon might know."

"One more question," Alex said.

"Sure."

"Do you remember any of the properties you worked at?"

He nodded.

Alex pulled out a few pictures that Mrs. Moriarty had given her. "Do you remember this place?"

"Sure. That's the Moriarty's house."

"Did you ever work there?" Alex asked.

"My last summer there. A few times. Mr. Moriarty was sick that year. They'd had flower beds put in a few years earlier. I remember because it was such a mess. No one had tended them. Really, they were just weeds. We weeded and it just became grass again. Kind of sad. I remember seeing them the year they were put in. Rows of orchids. It was beautiful."

Claire looked at Alex. *Mary, Mary, Quite Contrary, how does your garden grow?*

"You don't know who worked on the flower beds by any chance?" Alex asked.

Jacobs shook his head. "That was my first year there. I do remember that Gordon was bummed out that we didn't get to work there. He said everybody loved Mrs. Moriarty."

Alex smiled. Mrs. Moriarty reminded her a bit of her mother. It was easy for her to imagine the woman doting on anyone who came to the house whether they were being paid or not. Helen Toles had always been the same way, if you stepped onto her property you were fed. "Listen, I'm sorry that we interrupted your day," Alex said.

"I'm sorry if I wasn't any help," Jacobs said.

"You were. Anything and everything we learn helps," she told him. "If we should need to…"

"Any time," Jacobs replied.

"We appreciate that."

Alex gestured to Claire to follow her.

"Thanks," Claire looked at the pharmacist. "I'm sure it was a little freaky having the FBI show up at your job."

"I almost pissed my pants if you want to know truth," Jacobs said.

Claire laughed. "Well, I think I saw some Depends on the shelf over there. So, at least you're in the right place. Thanks again."

Alex looked at Claire and chuckled. "Depends?"

"Just trying to help out."

Alex laughed. *Shit, I think she's growing on me.*

CHAPTER FIFTEEN

Alex listened as three names were read to her. Christina Johnson, Michaela Brown, and Jessica Glendale—three more names to add to the list of victims, three more families to learn the fate of a loved one. That still left four women to be positively identified—four more families waiting and wondering. "What information do we have on them?" she asked her team. She was surprised when Agent Robbins spoke up.

"Johnson was from Watertown, New York. Glendale and Brown were both from the west coast," he told her.

"Go on," Alex said.

"Glendale was a student at Syracuse University when she went missing. Here's where it gets interesting; Brown was last seen in Taunton, Massachusetts. She was a nurse at a local hospital there," he explained.

Alex remained expressionless. "Find out more," she said. "Just because Taunton is where she was last seen; that doesn't mean it was the place she last visited. I want every detail you can get about these women—all of them. I mean boyfriends, friends, where they worked, where they ate…"

"When they took a shit," Claire interjected. Alex looked at her. "What? I'm serious. Women have routines. That's my point." She was surprised by Alex's response.

"What Agent Brackett is so eloquently trying to tell you is that nothing is unimportant. We need to know their habits and we need to know if they broke those habits when they went missing."

"Agent Toles," Agent Robbins called for Alex's attention. "Brown and Johnson were reported missing eleven years ago. Glendale was last seen in 2006. That's a long time for people to remember details."

Alex was ready to dress down the young agent when Claire spoke.

"That's your job, Robbins," Claire said. "To help them remember. Talk to their friends and family, their professors, classmates, lovers; hell, talk to their dogs if you think it'll help. Finding out their names is the easy part. Finding out who they were and why they ended up here is your job."

Alex smirked. "You heard Agent Brackett; get to it." She turned to Claire. "First Depends, now dogs? You definitely have an interesting way with people."

Claire shrugged. "He's overconfident. If he's not careful, it'll get him fired or worse."

Alex nodded. "Reminds me of another rookie I once knew."

"Me too," Claire replied. "So? What now?"

"Now? Now we go talk to Gordon Daniels."

"You found him?"

"It's what I do," Alex said.

"And, where might we find Mr. Daniels?"

"He's stationed at Quantico."

"You're shitting me."

"Nope. So, that gives us an excuse to peek in on the forensics team."

"When do we leave?" Claire asked.

"6:00 p.m. from Albany."

"Albany?"

"Brief local law enforcement and the governor. Then? Press briefing. Bower's orders."

"Shit," Claire muttered.

"Couldn't have summed it up better myself."

"Mr. Ritchie!" a reporter called out.

"Yes?"

"Do you have a comment about the FBI's investigation into

your niece's death?"

Jed Ritchie stopped and looked at the reporter. "Apparently, it takes a dozen or more bodies before the FBI cares to investigate at all. That's my comment."

"The governor said this afternoon that there will be an added patrol presence on the state roads. She was emphasizing caution. Do you think if people had taken your pleas seriously, that lives could have been saved?"

"I'm sure Governor Reid finds it important now that you are asking questions. Let me ask you one. If she can't keep the state of New York safe, how do you imagine she'll protect the country?"

"Asshole," Claire muttered. She clicked off the television. "Clueless asshole."

"We agree on more than you think," Alex said.

"Do you think he'll cause problems?"

"For us? Distractions, maybe," Alex replied.

"What about for the governor?"

Alex grinned. "Candace can handle Jed Ritchie."

"You trust her."

"You don't?"

"I don't have a great track record with politicians," Claire reminded Alex.

Alex laughed. "Well, maybe this one will surprise you."

"Why? Think she'd sleep with me too?" Claire asked.

Alex sprayed the sip of coffee she'd just taken across the room. "Not a chance in hell."

Claire grinned triumphantly.

"You did that on purpose."

Claire shrugged. "You're so easy, Toles."

"I'm not *that* easy."

"Don't go there," Claire laughed. "So? What do we know about Gordon Daniels?"

"He's a Gunnery Sergeant. Specializes in ordinance."

"Huh. Not our guy."

"No. I check on a few things. No way could he have been the one to kill Kaylee or Deidre; that's not a question. I have a feeling he's met our guy."

"Safe bet," Claire agreed. "I just hope he can offer us something to go on."

"Me too," Alex agreed.

"Is Sergeant Daniels expecting us?" Claire asked.

Alex nodded. "I spoke with his superior earlier. Wanted to make sure he would be available. We'll meet him at 8:00 a.m."

Claire paced the hotel room.

"Why are you pacing?" Alex asked.

"I just don't feel like sitting still."

"Okay? What do you want to do?"

Claire stopped her movement and looked at Alex. "I want to know about that girl's shirt."

Alex sighed. "Claire, I hope they get something—I do, but we both know that could take a considerable amount of time."

"Well, we have a timeline. Why don't we just do some research? Come on, Toles, she had on a blue T-shirt with white lettering."

"Claire," Alex addressed her partner cautiously. "That T-shirt could have been from a concert, a restaurant, a movie, a team—until the lab digs into it…There are millions of possibilities."

"Do you think Robbins and his crew will take that seriously in trying to make an identification?"

Alex's gaze narrowed.

"Come on, Alex—that T-shirt is the best chance we have of identifying the girl quickly. If she was wearing that the last time she was seen…"

"That's a big if."

"Maybe it is. It's better than anything else we have, at least until we talk to Daniels tomorrow. She's under twenty. Eaves is almost positive she was about sixteen. She wasn't a college student, so chances are she was local. It's a shot."

Alex reached across her bed and grabbed her badge and keys. "Well, pacing this room isn't going to help us. Let's go somewhere that can."

"Where are we going?" Claire followed Alex to the door.

"To see about a girl in a blue T-shirt."

Cassidy was enjoying a few moments of silence when she sensed a presence in the doorway to her bedroom. "Come in, Kenz," she told her daughter without prying her eyes from the pages of the book she was holding.

"Mom?"

Cassidy set the book down and looked at her daughter. "What is it Kenz?"

"Where'd Mom go?"

Cassidy patted the bed for Mackenzie to join her. "She had to make a trip to Virginia."

"To see Aunt Jane?"

"No, for work. She's with Claire."

Mackenzie bit her lip. "Mom?"

"Yeah?"

"Is Mom gonna catch that guy?"

Cassidy smiled. "She will."

Mackenzie frowned.

"Kenz? Is something bothering you?"

"Mom was on the TV again."

Cassidy nodded. She had tried to shield her younger children from the news. The serial killer case had gained momentum. She'd been around the media enough over the years to know how it worked. There was a fine line between news and entertainment, informing and inciting people to some belief or action. It was nearly impossible to turn on the television now and not have some mention of the case Alex was working. Many times, it came in the form of a short snippet advertising the evening news. Now, Alex's case had taken on a political tone. It still amazed Cassidy that anyone sought political gain through tragedy. She'd survived that too.

"Well, I think your mom will be on the TV a lot until this is over," Cassidy said honestly.

"People are scared," Mackenzie said.

"They are," Cassidy agreed. "That happens sometimes. You know, Mom and Claire will figure out who this is and they'll stop him."

"What if something happens to them?"

"Your mom and Claire are both very good at what they do, Kenz—very good—the best, in fact."

"But, Mom teaches."

"Well, that's true. She did that for a while. That's mostly what you remember her doing. You do know that when I met your mom she worked for the FBI."

"Yeah, but she wasn't on TV and stuff."

Cassidy's eyes sparkled with amusement. Mackenzie thought of herself as a conqueror. In reality, she was a seven-year-old that still possessed incredible innocence. *Oh, if you only knew, Kenz.* "That's not actually true," Cassidy corrected her daughter.

"Mom was on TV?"

"A few times," Cassidy winked. "She knows what she's doing, Kenz; I promise you."

Mackenzie sighed.

"Something else you wanted to talk about?" Cassidy asked.

"Why is Grandpa here?"

"I thought that we explained that. Mom is going to be working late for a while, and sometimes she might be traveling. Grandpa is here to help me with all of you."

"Why not Grandma?"

"I thought you liked it when Grandpa was here?"

"Yeah, but Grandma and YaYa take care of us when you can't," Mackenzie reminded her mother.

Cassidy considered how to reply. Mackenzie, while innocent, was both intelligent and intuitive. Alex was on the TV and people were talking about being afraid, and now her grandfather had temporarily moved into the house. One plus one was not a hard equation to solve. "What if I told you that I needed to have Grandpa here for a little bit?"

"How come?"

"Well, I spent a long time away from my father. Having him here is a chance for me to spend more time with him before we have a baby in the house again."

Mackenzie thought for a moment. "I have a dad; don't I?"

Cassidy took a deep breath. "You do have someone who helped Mom and I have you—yes."

Mackenzie wrinkled her nose. "Think he's like me?"

"Oh, I think you are a bit like all of us," Cassidy replied. "Kenz? Are you curious about your father?"

Mackenzie tapped her forehead for a minute and then shrugged. "I don't know him," she said as a matter of fact.

Cassidy nodded. This was a subject that she and Alex had discussed at length. When would the day come that one of their children would ask how they came to be? They had both agreed that honesty would rule the day. Cassidy had hoped that her children would be older before she and Alex needed to dive into these waters. "Kenzie? Does that bother you?"

Mackenzie shook her head. "Dylan says that we are all lucky to have two moms. Most people only get one. He didn't really get to know his dad either."

Cassidy felt as though the wind had been knocked out of her.

"Mom?" Kenzie put a hand on Cassidy's arm. "Are you sick?"

"No," Cassidy said. "I hope you know how much Mom and I love you."

Mackenzie's nose wrinkled. "You're gonna get gushy now, huh?"

Cassidy snickered. Mackenzie was not looking for answers. She was being naturally inquisitive. "You know, if you ever want to know who your dad is, Mom and I will tell you."

Mackenzie shrugged noncommittally and then grinned.

"Kenzie?"

"Uncle Pip didn't know his dad either."

"Well, not the way he could have—no."

Mackenzie shrugged again.

So much shrugging. "Mackenzie?" Cassidy urged.

"YaYa says we get what we get."

"She does, huh?"

"Yep, but she says it's who we choose that matters."

Cassidy brushed Mackenzie's bangs aside and smiled. Alex's mother was an amazing woman. Cassidy thought she was perhaps the wisest person she'd ever met. "And, what else does YaYa say?"

"I dunno."

"It's okay if you talked to YaYa about this."

"She says she had two babies but she ended with a brood. And, Grandma says that's cause you and Mom are like rabbits. I don't know what that means."

Cassidy covered her face and shook her head. *Leave it to Mom.* "Well, if it had been up to your mom the brood would be more like be a football team."

Mackenzie giggled. "YaYa says that me having two moms is like her having four daughters. She says she gave birth to Mom and Uncle Nicky but then she got you and Aunt Barb. She thought she was done. But then she got Uncle Pip and Auntie El too."

"Yaya is a smart lady," Cassidy said.

"Yeah."

"Grandma says she's glad she got to have so many kids and only had to count the tile once. What does that mean?"

Cassidy laughed. "That's just Grandma's way of saying she only gave birth to me, but she ended up with her 'brood' as she calls it. I want you to know that you can talk to your mom or me about anything, Kenz."

"Okay. Mom?"

"Yes?"

"What if that guy finds Mom?"

Cassidy smiled. "Mom will be okay."

"But, what if he does?"

"Claire will make sure Mom is okay."

"But, what if he finds Claire?"

"Mom will make sure Claire is okay."

"But…"

"Mackenzie, trust me," Cassidy said.

"Mom thinks Claire is crazy," Mackenzie said. She flopped into Cassidy.

Cassidy closed her eyes and kissed Mackenzie's head. She couldn't remember the last time Mackenzie had wanted to cuddle. Mackenzie was proud. Right now, it appeared Mackenzie was seven.

"Claire is funny," Mackenzie offered.

"She is," Cassidy agreed.

"Not as funny as Grandma."

"Probably not."

"Are you tired, Mom?"

Cassidy closed her eyes and pulled Mackenzie a little closer. "I am a little tired. I'm also a little lonely. How about you fill in and keep me company tonight?"

"Okay," Mackenzie replied. "Mom told me to take care of you."

Cassidy smiled. *I'll bet she did, Kenz. I'll bet she did.*

"There has to be something," Claire rubbed her eyes.

"There is; we just haven't found it yet. Take a break," Alex suggested.

Claire shook her head and looked at the computer screen. "How can this many people go missing and no one is out looking for them?"

Alex had been watching frustration build in Claire for hours. "Claire," Alex put her hand on Claire's shoulder.

"They're kids for Christ's sake."

"Claire," Alex spun the chair Claire was sitting in. "Take a break."

"A break? Seems like everybody's been on break for years. Look at all those names! Who the hell helps them?"

Alex sighed. There were realities in the world that Alex detested. The fact that not every case got solved, that not every victim was found, that not every family got answers was one of those realities. It had taken her time to put it all into perspective. This case had struck a deep personal chord with Claire. If Alex were to be honest, it had with her too. More times than Alex cared to count, she'd found herself thinking back to the day Cassidy had been held against her will. Alex was positive that Claire continued to recall the death of her mother. They both had demons and ghosts to confront, and they both needed the past to propel them forward rather than hold them back. Alex pulled up a chair, took a deep breath and looked directly into Claire's eyes.

"*We* help them."

"Great job we're doing."

"Claire, if we weren't working this case who is to say anyone would have ever found those graves on the Moriarty's property?"

"Yeah? We don't even know who they all are yet."

"No, but we will. And, as painful as it is; we've been able to give closure to three families. That's largely because of you."

"How do you figure that?"

"You're the reason we went back to that rock."

"And?"

"Claire, every place we've gone has led us here—right here. We're closer to this son of a bitch than anyone has ever been. Can we save everybody? Can we find everyone? No. We do the best we can for as many people as we can. That's all we can do."

"It's not enough."

"It has to be."

Claire's eyes fell to the floor. "What if it's not?"

"Claire, what your father did—that was not your fault."

"You don't know that."

"Yes; I do."

"How can you know that when I'm not sure of it?"

"I know you," Alex replied. "I understand more than you think I do."

Claire shook her head. "Maybe if I had…"

Alex took a deep breath and let it out slowly. "Do you know why John and I were so close?"

"You saved his ass in Iraq," Claire replied.

"No. He said that. The truth is if I'd seen things sooner none of us would have gotten hurt that day. I trusted the wrong people, Claire and people got killed—people I cared about."

"Somehow, I doubt that's the whole story."

"Maybe it is and maybe it isn't. I guess that depends on who you talk to. I can't go back. Even if I did; who knows? That's one thing I do know. You can't change the past and you don't know what would happen if you did. All you can do is try—try to make a difference for as many people as you can. That's what you're doing."

"Not well enough, apparently."

"I told you; it is enough."

"You think like Hawk does; that I can just let it go."

Alex shook her head. "No, I don't." Alex saw the surprise in

Claire's eyes. "You can't ever let it go completely. They don't understand that, not Cassidy and not Hawk. They've both been through a lot, Claire. They've both been hurt. Neither has ever had to watch as someone they loved died in front of them—not violently anyway. They don't know what that's like—wanting to scream, wanting to stop it and being paralyzed. I hope they never do understand it. That experience isn't something you can ever let go. It's part of you."

"Then what?"

"You learn to make it fuel," Alex said. "It can either be the thing that holds you back or the thing that spurs you ahead. That's your choice. And, I'm not going to bullshit you; it's a choice you make every, single day on some level. No matter how good things get? That one day? That one moment? It's always there in the back of your mind."

"Alex…"

"Yeah?"

"If I find him? I'll let him know what it's like."

"No; you won't."

"You don't think so?"

"No. That would keep you from helping the next person. But for the record?"

"Yeah?"

"I wouldn't mind giving him a lesson myself."

"It appears that the FBI may be closing in on the killer dubbed The Woodsman. Sources close to the investigation say that the taskforce is currently interviewing several people of interest, all of whom worked for a local Connecticut landscaping company. So far, eleven victims have been found. According to some close to the case, the identities seem to confirm the theory that The Woodsman has

chosen his victims by locale rather than any other determining factor."

"Think you know, do you?" he glared at the television screen. "Found the pretty maidens all in a row."

The sound of his maniacal laughter sent a chill up the spin of the young woman tied to a chair. "Please," she choked through a strained voice.

He turned, cocked his head and considered her. "Please?" he asked. He watched as her eyes grew wider with fear. He moved to stand over her. Silently, he circled her. He stopped over her shoulder and whispered in her ear. "Looking for all the little lost sheep over the hill," he whispered in her ear. "Oh, well. Whatever shall we do?" he breathed.

"Please," she whimpered.

"Mm. Riddles and rhymes. All in good time."

"Alex?" Cassidy answered her phone.

"Mom?" Mackenzie tossed in the bed.

"It's okay, Kenz," Cassidy whispered as she pulled herself from the bed. "Alex? Is everything okay?"

"We're both safe if that's what you mean," Alex replied.

"It isn't."

"Then no, everything is not okay."

Cassidy walked into the bathroom for some privacy and closed the door. "What happened?"

"I think we might have identified another victim."

"I'm sorry," Cassidy said. "Isn't that a good thing for you, though?"

Silence hovered.

"Alex?"

"For the case? It might be."

"What is it?"

"She was fifteen, Cass. If Claire is right, she was just fifteen."

Cassidy leaned against the sink. "Oh, Alex."

"Monica Leibowitz. She was reported missing thirteen years ago."

"From New York?"

"That's the thing Cass, she was from Pennsylvania."

"That's not that far."

"No, but something about it feels different."

"Alex, have you slept at all?" Cassidy asked.

"Just got back to my room."

"Just now? Alex, it's four-thirty in the morning."

"Yeah, well, serial killers don't work banker's hours, neither do we," Alex snapped. She heard Cassidy sigh. "I'm sorry, Cass. That didn't come out the way I wanted it to."

"It's all right."

"She was on her way to a high school baseball game when she went missing," Alex explained.

"Alex…"

"I need to find him."

"You will."

"I'm glad you're so confident."

"How are things with Claire?" Cassidy waited several beats for Alex to reply. "Alex?"

"Claire's okay."

"That's not what I asked you."

"Claire and I are okay too."

Cassidy smiled. "It really is painful for you, isn't it?"

Alex chuckled, appreciative of Cassidy's levity. "Claire is the one who figured it out, Cass. She's relentless. How are things there? Were you talking to Kenzie?"

"Everything is fine. Yeah, Kenzie crashed in our room."

"Is she okay?"

"She's Kenzie," Cassidy said. "She's missing you."

"I miss you."

"I miss *you*."

"How are you feeling?"

"I've only counted about half the tiles on the floor since you left," Cassidy promised. "I'm okay, love. Just take care of you."

"I'm not sure…"

"It's okay, Alex. There are people who need you more right now than we do. We'll be here. Go get a little sleep."

"I'll try. I love you, Cass."

"I love you too."

"Sergeant Daniels." Alex extended her hand. Daniels accepted her grip firmly. "I appreciate you coming over here to our side of Quantico."

"My pleasure, Captain," Daniels nodded respectfully.

"It's Agent Toles now, but you can call me Alex."

"No, ma'am. You're a superior officer."

Alex wondered when her past would stop haunting her. "I'm retired, Sergeant. Just a regular old FBI agent now."

"Old being the key word," Claire muttered.

"I'm sorry, I don't believe you've met my partner, Agent Bullshit."

Claire batted her eyelashes dramatically. "Bullshit at your service," she said with a mock salute.

Daniels laughed. "What can I help you with?" he asked.

"You worked for Greenscape Landscaping; right?" Alex began.

"Yeah, for four years until I enlisted."

"Do you remember a house owned by Mr. and Mrs. Moriarty?"

Alex asked.

"Sure. Everybody loved Mrs. Moriarty. When I left for the Marines, she sent my mom a card."

Alex smiled. "So, you worked on her property?"

"Not as much as I would have liked. Mostly, I was there the summer before I left. For some reason, BJ always seemed to get that assignment—for the first couple of years I was there. He seemed to get most of the great jobs."

"BJ?" Claire asked.

"Yeah."

"Do you know what BJ's last name was by any chance?" Alex asked.

Daniels shook his head. "Nah. He never talked all that much to me. We had a couple of beers a few times, but he was kind of a loner. He had his own car so he didn't get dropped off like most of us did."

"Excuse me; Agent Toles?"

Alex turned to find a young FBI agent standing behind her.

"Yes?" Alex asked.

"Sorry to interrupt. There's something you need to see."

Alex looked at Claire.

"I got this," Claire promised.

Alex nodded her thanks. "I'll be back." Alex made her way down the hallway to another room. She was surprised to see an old friend waiting for her. "Hawk? What are you doing here?"

"I could ask you the same thing. I had a meeting. What's your excuse? Missing the classroom?" Hawk teased.

"More than you know," Alex sighed. "You had a meeting here? For what?"

"Sewing up some loose ends on a few things. Looks like the FBI would like to entice me to stay."

Alex nodded. "Are you leaving?"

"Claire didn't tell you?"

"Just that she saw you."

"I've accepted a role back at NSA," Hawk explained. "Seems the FBI would like me to consider changing my plans and coming here."

"To Quantico?"

Hawk nodded. "Story for another day, Alex. Bower called me a few minutes ago. He thought you should get this from someone in person. Seems a message came in for you on the tip line."

"What kind of message?" Alex asked.

Hawk moved to a computer terminal and sat down. "Put these on," she told Alex.

Alex accepted a pair of headphones from Hawk and placed them over her ears.

"I see you found all the pretty maidens in a row. Still looking for the little lost sheep?"

Alex steadied her breathing as a sickening chuckle erupted from the voice on the line.

"Ah. You know that rhyme? Ding, dong, bell, Pussy's in the well?" He laughed again. "The question, Agent Toles isn't who'll pull her out, but who put her in. Poor thing, she never did him any harm. He lured her with his charm. A hunting we will go, Agent Toles."

Alex threw the headphones on the desk. "Son of a bitch!"

Hawk nodded. "Alex…"

Alex shook her head with disgust. "I need to talk to Claire."

"Alex, wait."

"What?" Alex turned. "No trace; right?"

"No, but…"

"He's killed again, Hawk. He followed my breadcrumbs; now he's laying some of his own."

"I know. Do me a favor?"

"What?"

"Don't tell Claire I was here."

"What? Why not?"

"I didn't know you two were going to be here until Bower called me and asked me to give this to you personally."

Alex pressed on her temple with her thumb and took a deep breath. "I'm not going to lie to Claire."

"I'm just asking you to…"

"No," Alex said. "I'm not keeping anything from her. She's my partner, Hawk. You want to come with me? Feel free."

"I don't want her to think that I was trying to check in on her."

Alex groaned. "You don't give her a whole lot of credit."

"Did I just hear you correctly? Are you sticking up for Claire?"

"You heard me as clearly as I spoke. You and Cass have been trying to convince me for years to trust Claire. I still have my issues. Claire is my partner, Hawk. She's also part of my family. I'm not going to undermine how much work we've both put into this bizarre partnership you dreamed up because you two have things to sort out."

Hawk grinned. "Never thought I'd see the day."

"Me neither. Are you coming or not?"

"On your heels."

"BJ was older than you?" Claire asked.

Daniels nodded. "A few years—at least."

"What can you tell me about him?"

"That would be helpful? I don't know. Not much. Like I said, he didn't talk much—not to me anyway."

"Do you remember what he looked like?"

"Sure," Daniels replied without missing a beat. "That was over ten years ago, though."

Claire nodded. "Sergeant Daniels, would you be willing to work with a sketch artist?"

"Sure. I might be able to do you one better, though."

Claire's curiosity was piqued. "I'm listening."

"I think my mom probably still has it. Mr. Lawson, he owned the company my first year there—he took a picture of all of us that year before he handed the business over to his son, Brad. I think BJ was in it—pretty sure. Brad would know BJ's name. Might even know where he is. They were friends, I think."

Claire nodded. Unfortunately, Brad Lawson was off the grid completely. They had managed to run down his last address but there was no sign of Brad Lawson. Neighbors had told the FBI agents who went to make contact that the property had been vacant for over a year, although a local lawn service still maintained the property. Claire and Alex hoped that they'd manage to track down the former Greenscape owner through payment records. So far, efforts had proved unsuccessful. Claire's mind was spinning with possibilities. The more pieces of the puzzle that came into view, the less she liked the picture she was seeing.

"Hey," Alex walked through the door with Hawk a step behind her. "Sorry, to interrupt."

Claire looked up, ready to speak when her eyes met Hawk's. "Hawk?"

"That would be me," Hawk replied.

Claire shook off her thought and turned her attention to Alex. "Sergeant Daniels might have a picture of the work crew from 2005."

Alex's ears perked. She nodded. "Interesting," she commented. "Hawk just shared something with me. I think you should check it out; give me a few minutes with Sergeant Daniels."

Claire looked at Alex for any sign that this was personal. Alex's smile told her it was not. "Sure," Claire agreed. "After you," she gestured to Hawk.

"Like I told your partner; I'm not sure how much I can help," Daniels told Alex.

Alex nodded. Life on a military base could be somewhat insulated. "News down here isn't always the same as it is at home," she said. "Did Agent Brackett explain what led us here?"

"No, not really."

"Well, it isn't a secret. We discovered a number of women buried at the edge of Mrs. Moriarty's property line."

Alex watched Daniels' reaction with interest. He stared at her blankly for a second as her words sunk in. She noted that his gaze diverted from hers once the words had taken root. Alex pulled up a chair and sat across for the sergeant. He shook his head.

"Sergeant Daniels," Alex spoke calmly. "Someone put those women there—someone with access to that property.

"We worked in the light of day. I can't see how…"

Alex nodded. "I understand. If you remember, that property abuts the state forest. It's not a well-traveled area."

"Yeah, I remember."

"How well do you remember most of the places you worked for Greenscape?"

"Some like I was there yesterday, some I only was there once or twice."

"Out of curiosity, do you recall if any of the places you worked had a well?" she asked.

Daniels combed his thoughts, his tongue snaking across his lip as he concentrated on old memories. He rubbed his forehead and shook his head. "No. I mean, not that I saw."

Alex sighed. *It was worth a shot.*

"Wait," Daniels looked at Alex. "Not on any property that I worked at. But…"

"But?"

"In the back of the Greenscape office? A long time before I worked there, they had greenhouses. Greenscape started as a nursery. By the time I started there, they were all rundown. Me and Mark used to go have a few beers after work behind them. It was overgrown out there. You could disappear," he said. "Always thought that was crazy for a landscaping company. Not the best advertisement; you know? Anyway, there's an old well out there. We found it by accident one day."

Alex bit the inside of her lip gently. *Son of a bitch.* "Thanks," she said. "I assume Agent Brackett has the information about that photo?"

"Well, you'd have to see my mom to get it. All my stuff is still in her attic. It should be there in a box with my pictures from high school. I never tossed it. I doubt she would have."

Alex slid her chair back and stood. "Thanks again. If we need anything else, we'll be in touch."

"Agent Toles?"

"Yes?"

Daniels sighed and shifted his weight.

"Sergeant Daniels if there is anything you think we should know, I need to know it."

"Me and Mark saw BJ out there once."

"Out where?"

"Out behind the greenhouses."

"What was he doing?" Alex asked.

Daniels swallowed hard. "He wasn't alone."

Alex nodded. "Thank you."

"I wish I could help more.

"You've helped more than you know."

"Claire," Hawk caught hold of Claire's arm.

"What? Don't you have something to show me?"

"I didn't know you and Alex were going to be here."

Claire stopped walking and looked at Hawk. She took a deep breath. "I'm sorry."

Hawk wasn't sure she had heard her girlfriend correctly.

"Well, I am," Claire chuckled. "How could you know we'd be here when we didn't know until after I'd called you?"

"Alex is good for you."

Claire rolled her eyes.

"And, maybe you're good for her too."

"God, that sounds eerily like you're trying to hook us up."

"Never. I'm not into sharing," Hawk said.

"What is it that you showed Alex?"

Hawk led Claire to the room she and Alex had vacated a few minutes earlier. "You're not going to like it."

"Since when does my liking anything stop you?" Claire teased.

Hawk handed Claire the same pair of headphones she'd given Alex.

"I thought we were past phone sex," Claire raised an eyebrow.

"Just listen."

Claire fell silent and listened to the same message. Unlike Alex, she did not remove the headphones. "Play it again," she directed Hawk. Hawk complied. Claire concentrated.

"I see you found all the pretty maidens in a row. Still looking for the little lost sheep? Ah. You know that rhyme? Ding, dong, bell, Pussy's in the well?"

"Stop," Claire held up her hand. "Go back a bit."

"Claire?"

"Just go back a bit."

"Ah. You know that rhyme? Ding, dong, bell, Pussy's in the well?"

"Play it again."

Hawk complied. She watched as Claire's temple twitched with concentration. Claire began stroking her bottom lip with a fingertip and shook her head.

"One more time," Claire requested.

"Ah. You know that rhyme? Ding, dong, bell, Pussy's in the well?"

"He's near an airport."

"What?" Hawk asked.

Claire removed the headphones. "I'm sure there's already a team analyzing this."

"I'm certain Bower put them on it immediately," Hawk replied.

"He can't be more than twenty miles from an airport. I would guess closer," Claire said. She handed Hawk the headphones. "Listen. Wait for him to say the word ding."

Hawk followed Claire's direction. She listened attentively. She stopped and played the recording again, and then a third time. Slowly, she put the headphones down beside her. "Not many people would have heard that," she said.

Claire shrugged. "They're too busy listening to the words," she said. "We have a time stamp on that, I assume? I mean, exactly when that call came in."

"To the second; I'm certain," Hawk said.

"Guess we have some more work to do," Claire said. "I need to talk to Alex."

"That's good," Alex replied as she entered the room. "I think I might have something interesting to share too. You first."

"He's within twenty miles of an airport," Claire gave Alex her assessment. "Since we can gather he's somewhere on the east coast; I would think checking landing times against that tape might be a good idea."

Alex nodded. "Good catch," she offered.

"You?" Claire asked.

"Well, it seems Sergeant Daniels and his old friend Mark Jacobs used to enjoy some cold brews out on the far end of Greenscape's property."

"And?"

"And, the good sergeant remembers seeing BJ out there with a woman."

"And?" Claire urged.

"And, there is a well nearby."

"Son of a…"

"Ready to head home?" Alex asked.

"Depends."

"On what?"

"Do I get to crash in a bed or do I have to sleep on that damn couch again?" Claire asked.

Alex laughed. "I think we can figure something out. Hawk," she winked at her friend. "I'll meet you outside," Alex told Claire.

"Right behind you."

Hawk waited for the door to close. "You do; you know?"

"I do what?" Claire wondered.

"You and Alex—you make a good team."

Claire looked back at the door Alex had just closed. She nodded and turned back to her lover. "Yeah, I guess maybe we do."

CHAPTER SIXTEEN

"Jesus. This is worse than those damn woods. You would think a lawn care company would mow its property," Claire grumbled.

Alex had to agree. It puzzled her. Granted, this part of the property was out of public view. Even so, it didn't completely add up to Alex. She looked behind her at the team that followed. A month of pursuing this case seemed like an eternity. Silently, she was praying they would find an empty well. Realistically, she expected she would find another victim. She looked ahead and saw the top of the well hovering just above the tall weeds.

Claire noticed Alex's gait slow. She grabbed hold of Alex's wrist. "I'll go down," she offered.

Alex smiled at her partner. Claire had seen enough for a lifetime. Alex shook her head. "I got this one," she replied.

"Uh, Alex, maybe you should let me go."

"Why? Think I'm too old?" Alex joked.

"Well…"

"With age comes experience," Alex winked.

Claire rolled her eyes. "Yeah, and arthritis."

Alex chuckled. "I got this one."

Claire and Alex both stepped up to the well and peered into the darkness below.

"Maybe there's nothing down there," Claire offered.

Alex stared into the abyss. Her stomach turned over and rose into her chest. *Maybe*.

"Agent Brackett," another FBI agent called for Claire's attention.

"Not now," Claire dismissed him.

"But…"

Claire kept her eyes on Alex as she descended the well.

"But, Agent…"

Claire turned abruptly. "You see that hole in the ground?" she asked the agent. He nodded sheepishly. "My partner is down there on a rope. Whatever it is you want to tell me, it will hold until she is back up here on solid ground. Questions?" she dismissed him again. He shook his head and walked away. "Fucking rookies. Alex?" she called down the hole.

"Still here," Alex's voice echoed back up the tunnel.

"See anything yet?" Claire asked.

"Yeah, a lot more of nothing."

Claire groaned. "I don't like this," she muttered.

"She knows what she's doing," a voice offered.

Claire's eyes remained riveted to Alex's figure as it shrunk in the distance. "Don't we have some better light?" she asked harshly.

"Working on it," someone answered.

"Work faster," Claire demanded.

"Shit!" Alex's voice carried in the distance.

"What is it?" Claire called down. "Alex?"

A crackling sound in Claire's ear told her that Alex had gone to com. "What is it?"

"I can't see the bottom," Alex said.

"You've gotta be close," Claire replied.

"I need more slack, Claire."

Claire was liking the current situation less and less. *I wish she would have let me go.* "All right." Claire turned her attention to the team beside her. "It's deeper than we thought. Let it out," she directed them. "Alex?"

"Yeah, I'm moving again," Alex replied.

Alex gently let her feet glide over the side of the well, looking up briefly and then back to the seemingly endless pit below. She tugged on the line as a signal to stop and shined her flashlight. How deep was this hole? Alex tugged the line again and continued to descend. She noted the jagged rock just ahead. She swung her feet with gentle force to keep the line out of its path. Without warning, she heard a snap. "Shit!"

"Alex?" Claire called for her partner over the com line. "What the hell just happened?" She turned to the team behind her. Two agents shook their heads. "Alex?" Claire called again. No reply. Claire's hands went to her face and she ran them through her hair. "God Damnit!"

"Agent Brackett, we can…"

"Get me set up now," Claire ordered.

"But…"

"Do it."

Alex opened her eyes and groaned. *That's gonna leave a mark.* She felt the muscles in her back spasm and winced. *Shit.* Alex tapped on the hard hat she was wearing. "Must've hit the light on my way down. Damnit. "Claire?" She tried her com line. "You out there?" No answer. *Oh, just great. No light, no line, and no damn way to talk to anyone. Well, at least I'm alive—I think.* She closed her eyes to stave off a wave of sudden pain through her lower back. "Okay, Toles, gently." Alex maneuvered herself carefully onto her side. "Well, if you're down here, so is your flashlight," she surmised. She began to feel around for it. The ground beneath her was damp, and she could hear the faint trickling of water. The space she found herself in was wider than she would have imagined. "Where is that damn light?" she complained. Her hand met something cold and solid. Alex shivered and closed her eyes. She suppressed the urge to vomit. "On second thought, maybe I'd prefer the darkness."

"Alex!" a voice called.

Alex breathed a sigh of relief. *Claire*. "Claire?!"

Claire released the breath she hadn't realized she'd been holding. *Maybe Cass will only maim me if she's broken but alive.* "Are you okay?"

"Yeah, I think so?" Alex shouted back.

"Thank God," Claire whispered.

"But, I don't think I'm alone," Alex called back.

Claire was surprised by the queasiness that immediately made its presence known in her stomach. Lying in a dark, dank well with a corpse was not her idea of fun. "I'm coming!" she called out.

"I'm blind down here!" Alex called.

"Just stay put!"

Alex smiled. *Always the comedienne.*

The light from Claire's hard hat came into view and Alex sighed. "Took you long enough," Alex called to her. She was relieved to know Claire was close. She could hear Claire chuckling.

"Alex," Claire called when she could see Alex a short way in the distance. Alex's eyes were closed. "Are you okay?" Claire asked. Alex nodded. "If you're lying, you won't have to worry about Cassidy kicking your ass, 'cause I'll do it for her."

Alex laughed. "I'm okay."

"I'm going to shine the light," Claire warned her partner. She saw Alex's nod of recognition. Claire reached back, grabbed her flashlight and shined it in the distance. She closed her eyes and shook her head. "Damnit."

Alex reluctantly opened her eyes. She took in the broken form beside her and fought the urge to vomit again. In less than a breath, Claire was above her.

"I've got her," Claire told the team and then clicked off the com. "Well, when you fall, you sure do it hard," Claire commented.

Alex smiled gratefully.

"Can't say I ever saw myself in this position again," Claire said.

"What position is that?" Alex asked.

"Carrying you over any threshold."

Alex rolled her eyes. "Just get me the hell out of here, will you?"

"Oh, I don't know. What's it worth to you?" Claire teased. She felt a thousand pounds lighter knowing that Alex was all right.

"Wine. Lots of wine. I know where Cass keeps her secret stash."

Claire lowered herself another inch. She managed to get a solid footing, unclipped her line and clipped it to Alex. "Not the best offer I've ever had," she told her partner. "Cass can't drink it anyway."

Alex laughed. "Thanks," she told Claire.

"You scared the shit out of me," Claire admitted. "Are you gonna' be okay going back up?" she asked.

Alex nodded.

"Alex, don't bullshit me right now. Can you make it up on your own or not?"

Alex nodded again. "Just sore. I'll be okay."

"You'd better hope so for both our sakes," she said as she tugged on the line. She clicked the com back on. "One *senior* agent coming up," she said.

Alex shook her head. "Are you okay down here?" she asked.

Claire smiled. "I've got company."

"Claire…"

"See ya' topside, Toles."

Claire watched as Alex slowly faded away in the distance. She shined the light on the body next to her feet. Claire's eyes tracked up and down the huddled form. Even with the aid of her light, it was difficult to make out the woman's features. She was covered in dirt and Claire was sure she'd been there at least a couple of days. It was ghoulish. Claire had seen more disturbing things in her life than she cared to count. This topped them. She looked up the hole above them. Her eyes tracked back to the body beside her. Claire crouched as best she could. Whoever this was, The Woodsman had left her clothed.

Claire moved the light to the woman's shirt. It was dirty and torn. Claire could discern the picture of a cat on the grey T-shirt. "Pussy's in the well," she mused. "Nursery rhymes and fairy tales," she scoffed. "He wants us to go hunting." Claire looked back toward the pinhole of light above. "He has no idea who he's baiting."

Claire walked up to Alex who was sitting in the back of an ambulance. "Is she broken?" she asked.

Alex smiled. "I'm sitting right here. I didn't go deaf in the last few hours."

"She'll survive," the EMT commented. "Maybe a few broke ribs, but she doesn't want to get checked so…"

Claire folded her arms across her chest.

"What?" Alex asked. "I'm fine."

"Uh-huh. Then why not go with them?" Claire challenged.

Alex looked ahead in the distance as a team lifted the lifeless body out of the well.

"I don't think there's anything they can do for her," Claire said.

"Claire…"

"What?" Claire barked. "You know if Bower were here, he'd make you go."

"He's not."

"No, so that puts me in charge."

"You?"

"Right. You're out of commission. That makes me the lead."

"I'm not out of commission!" Alex argued. She moved too quickly and her face contorted in pain.

"Pack her up," Claire told the EMT. Alex's jaw fell open. "Don't bother, Agent Toles," Claire told her partner.

"Claire! This scene needs to be processed!"

"Yep, and there are at least a dozen capable agents here to do it with an army behind them."

"I'm not leaving."

Claire looked at the EMT. "Could you give us a minute?"

"Brackett…."

Claire stared at Alex. "I thought you trusted me."

"I do."

"Really?" Claire asked. "Then prove it."

"What?"

"I can handle this, Alex."

"It's not about you handling it."

"It is. I always thought that Batman thing was a joke between you and Dylan."

"What the hell are you talking about?" Alex bit.

"You—you think you're the caped crusader or something. Newsflash, Toles, you aren't wearing armor. It's not a fucking comic. You can break, just like Humpty Dumpty. You want to put this whacko out of business? Then you need to be running on all cylinders. And, you need to trust that I have your back. And, not just when you fall down a hole."

Alex sighed and let her face fall into her hands. She nodded.

"Good. I'll meet you at the hospital."

Alex's head snapped to attention. "I thought you were going to process the scene?"

"I thought you were going to trust me?"

Alex huffed. She hated to admit it, but Claire was right. "I want to know everything."

Claire chuckled. "Yeah, I got it, Agent. See you in a bit." Claire turned and made her way to the EMTs. "Pack her up," she said. She looked back at Alex who had resumed the pose of holding her face in her hands. She sucked in a ragged breath. "And, take care of her or you'll deal with me."

"Agent Brackett," Agent Robbins greet Claire smugly.

"Agent Robbins."

"What can I do for you?" he asked.

Claire grinned. "I think you missed the memo, Agent," she told him. She pulled him aside. "You're here because I know you want to prove yourself." She saw him begin to speak and lifted her brow. "What was that? Did you want to go back into the office and compare files and run through databases?" she asked. "I didn't think so."

"So?" he asked.

Claire gestured to the greenhouses in the distance.

"What about them?" he asked.

"That's my question," she replied. "You and Agent Reaves are going to take this team and comb through every nook and cranny in those places. I mean every, single, solitary inch."

"I'm in charge?" he asked.

Claire's raucous laugh turned everyone's attention. "Right," she said. She pointed across the field to where a car was pulling up.

"Who is that?" Robbins asked as a woman stepped out of the car.

Claire smiled. "That is Deputy Assistant Director Corrigan."

"Why would a desk jockey," he began.

Claire shrugged. "It's a high-profile case, Robbins. Here's your chance," she said. "They say she's headed for the top."

"And?" he asked.

"I'm gonna give you some advice, Robbins. I've been at this a while. I've seen people come and seen people go—in ways you don't want to imagine," Claire told the rookie. "Corrigan was a special agent when I started. She worked under former NSA Director Tate when he was at the FBI."

"So?"

"So, she's connected, Robbins. Just like Agent Toles. You seem to want to piss off the wrong people. Trust me; you don't have the connections to survive that. You think the FBI is A-political?" Claire chuckled. "You're more of a rookie than I thought. This case is bigger than these girls. Get that? It's become political. Watch your ass, Robbins. I'm giving you a chance to make a case for yourself. It's a chance Agent Toles would think twice about giving you—for good reason. You really want to be somebody? Don't piss me off. Don't disappoint me. And, Robbins? Whatever you do, don't make a fool of me."

"Is that a threat?"

"It's a friendly piece of advice. Agent Toles has more power in the bureau than the classification on her badge suggests."

"Because of that charade with her wife? Come on, Agent Brackett. She gets hero status for screwing the person she's…"

Claire grabbed Robbins' shirt, pulled him close and whispered in his ear. "You either take my advice, Robbins or I swear, I will finish you myself."

"That was a threat."

Claire stepped back, smiled, and brushed the wrinkles from Robbins' shirt. "No, Agent Robbins, that was just a fact." She nodded to Jill Corrigan as the Deputy Assistant Director approached.

"Agent Brackett," Corrigan shook Claire's hand.

"Thanks for agreeing to help," Claire replied.

"AD Bower didn't give me much choice," Corrigan winked. "Who is this?" she asked.

"This is Agent Robbins. I was just explaining how working on this case is a good way to learn the ropes."

Corrigan gauged the rookie silently. *Cocky, brash, obnoxious, know-it-all; no wonder Claire wants to help him.* "Agent Robbins," she shook his hand and turned back to Claire. "Tell Toles that I expect her back pronto."

"Oh, I wouldn't worry about that," Claire said. *Not unless Cass puts her in timeout.* She watched as the Assistant Deputy Director nodded again and walked away to take command. Claire looked at

Robbins and addressed him a final time. "You think you know Agent Toles. I thought that once. You don't," she said. "I knew a rookie once who got the same advice I've given you and chose to ignore it."

"Yeah? What happened to him?" Robbins asked.

Claire offered him a regretful smile. "She went to hell."

"You mean Toles buried her career?"

Claire shook her head. "No. In a way, she's the one who saved it."

Cassidy opened the front door and smiled at Claire.

"How is she?" Claire asked.

"Stubborn," Cassidy replied.

"I'm sorry, Cass."

Cassidy smiled. "Don't be," she guided Claire through the door. "She's on the couch."

"If this is…"

"She'll be glad to see you."

"I'll try not to get her…"

"Claire," Cassidy took hold of Claire's hand. "She needs to work right now. Don't hold back. She's okay."

"You're not mad?"

Cassidy sighed. Mad? She was scared to death when Alex called from the hospital. Cassidy had been through enough injuries and illnesses in the Toles' family that she'd learned not to overreact. "Worried," Cassidy said. "Not mad."

"Is she…"

Cassidy could plainly see the concern in Claire's eyes. "A couple of broken ribs," she said. "Banged up. It won't keep her down," she said knowingly.

"How are you?" Claire asked.

"I'm good."

"Cassidy…"

"Claire, stop worrying," Cassidy laughed.

Claire shifted uncomfortably. She often felt like a child in Cassidy's presence. No one's opinion mattered more to her, and she still found that difficult to understand.

Cassidy led Claire to the living room. "Hey," she called to Alex. "Look who I found?"

Alex looked up from the paper in her hand. "Hey," she greeted Claire. "You look worse than I feel."

Claire shrugged. "Long day at the office."

"Tell me," Alex replied.

"Did you eat?" Cassidy asked Claire. Claire shook her head. Cassidy rolled her eyes. "Peas in a pod," she muttered. "I'll get you two something."

"I'm good," Alex said. Cassidy lifted her brow. "On second thought, food sounds good."

"Cass, you don't have to," Claire began.

"Don't get too excited. I'm ordering pizza," Cassidy said as she left the room.

"I swear, she gets to be more like my mother by the day. She feeds everyone who walks through the door."

"I heard that!" Cassidy called back.

"Well, it's true!" Alex replied loudly.

"Keep it up, Alex, and I'll use the good China."

Alex laughed.

"I don't get it," Claire said.

"China gets washed by hand. You called me Batman? Maybe Dylan thinks so," Alex shook her head. "As far as Cass is concerned, I'm more like Alfred."

"You guys are weird," Claire said.

"So? Did you find anything?"

"I don't know. Depends on what you mean. They'll be out there for at least another day going through everything."

"And you?" Alex asked.

"The woman in the well was a twenty-one-year-old bartender from Albany. Her name was Donna Reardon."

Alex sighed heavily.

"No one even reported her missing."

"How did you get the ID so fast?" Alex asked.

"Easy when her license was in her back pocket."

"You're kidding?"

"Nope."

"Holy shit."

"There's more."

"What?" Alex asked.

"This nursery rhyme thing of his," Claire started.

"Yeah, I was thinking about that. Kind of strange, right? The well at the nursery. Seems like a pretty big coincidence."

Claire nodded. "We need to find this BJ person." Claire reached into her laptop bag and pulled out a picture.

Alex accepted it and looked at it closely. "You saw Mrs. Daniels."

"Yeah."

"When?" Alex asked.

"I asked Corrigan to come out and supervise the scene."

"You're not kidding."

Claire shook her head. "It wasn't hard, Alex. This is getting big in the public sphere. That asshole Ritchie gave an interview saying if it were Governor Reid's kids missing, the case would already be solved."

"That's total bullshit."

"Yeah, well, we both know how this works. No one wants to admit the FBI is political. Everything is political. People are paying attention more than ever now."

"Do we know which one is BJ?" Alex asked

"One of these two," Claire pointed to two faces.

"This is a copy; I take it?"

Claire nodded. "Yeah. They're working the original now."

"What are you thinking?" Alex asked.

"I think he's living out some sadistic nursery rhyme."

"Which rhyme?"

"One of his own making," Claire said. "The ID on Monica Leibowitz was confirmed this afternoon."

"Damn."

"There's more."

Alex looked up.

"The lab we sent that piece of fiber to from her shirt?" Claire began.

"Yeah?"

"You won't believe it."

"Try me."

"That dye was only used by two manufacturing companies."

"And?"

"They found a long list of purchases for shirts," Claire said.

"Not surprised."

Claire nodded. "I did some digging." She took a deep breath. "I thought maybe some local screen printer might still have records of orders for that T-shirt to be imprinted. So, I checked New York, Pennsylvania, and Connecticut. Well, actually, El checked half for me."

Alex smiled. "How is my sister-in-law?"

"Okay, I think. Really pregnant," Claire commented.

"Claire?"

"Don't sweat it, Alex," Claire said. "I love El. I always will. We've both moved on."

Alex accepted Claire's declaration. Eleana and Claire had a long history. While Alex felt sure that Eleana loved Jonathan, she also knew that Claire and Eleana would always have feelings for each other. She wasn't surprised that Claire reached out to Eleana.

Jonathan was off pursuing leads on Christopher O'Brien's past. That was one of the only reasons she had not sought her brother's help to expedite research. The CIA operated outside of normal parameters. Eleana and Jonathan would be able to fast track things that often took the FBI weeks.

"Did you find anything?" Alex wondered.

"I was right. El found one for a mechanic shop in Philly. One was for a local college in New Haven."

"And?" Alex inquired.

"You ready for this?"

Alex nodded.

"I found a couple of printers in Connecticut. Get this; one order was for none other than Greenscape Nursery."

"But, Leibowitz wasn't from Connecticut," Alex pointed out.

"Nope."

Alex pinched the bridge of her nose. Something had nagged her from the moment they had found Monica Leibowitz buried apart from the others. It was a gut instinct. Now, her suspicions had been confirmed. "He knew her."

"Yeah," Claire agreed.

"Claire," Alex slowed her speech.

"I told them to hold the ID until we talked."

Alex contemplated the options. If their killer knew this victim, notifying her family might tip him off to their leads. Alex feared that he would either take his show on a different road or simply up the body count. "Her family deserves to know."

"I agree. But…"

"I agree," Alex was sure Claire shared her concerns. "Let's follow up on the photo. Hold off another day or two on the notification. I hate it. I think…"

"It's the right call," Claire said.

"Whoever BJ is…"

"He's our guy," Claire said.

Alex felt certain that BJ's identity would reveal their killer. "Let's hope they get some DNA off Ms. Reardon's person or possessions."

"Let's hope."

Cassidy watched Alex try to remove her T-shirt. "Let me help."

"I feel like a toddler."

Cassidy smirked. "Sometimes you act like a toddler," she teased.

"Yeah, yeah. Thanks, Cass."

"You're welcome. Do you need any pain medication?"

"No," Alex answered. "I could use a shower," she wiggled her eyebrows.

"Nice try, Agent Toles," Cassidy pulled the covers back on their bed.

Alex followed Cassidy to the bed and gingerly slipped between the sheets. "Ugh."

"Hurts, huh?"

"A little," Alex confessed.

"The last time you came home with broken ribs, you'd been fighting with Claire," Cassidy recalled.

Alex started to laugh and winced. "Don't make me laugh."

"I wasn't trying to," Cassidy said as she placed her head on Alex's chest.

"That seems like a lifetime ago," Alex said.

"Sometimes, it does," Cassidy agreed. "Do you want to talk about today?"

"No," Alex answered. "I want to talk about the doctor's appointment I missed this morning."

"You didn't miss much," Cassidy promised. "Everything is fine, Alex."

"Are you sure?"

Cassidy propped herself up to look at Alex. "We are both fine. December 10th if he decides to arrive on time."

"You think it's a boy?" Alex's eyes lit up.

"Maybe."

"Do you?"

Cassidy laughed. She kissed Alex's lips tenderly. "Does it matter?"

"Not at all," Alex replied. "But, you haven't been wrong yet."

"Yes, I think it's a boy."

"I don't care; you know? Not at all."

"I know."

"How are things going with your dad?"

"Okay," Cassidy replied.

"Cass?"

"They are," Cassidy said. "The kids love having him here, especially Dylan. I swear Dylan's been home more over the last couple of weeks than he has in the last two years."

Alex heard the slight hurt in Cassidy's voice. "You do know that there is no one Dylan loves more than you?"

"That's not true," Cassidy disagreed. "And, don't look at me like that. I don't need that to be true."

"I know. But, Cass, it's true. You can see so much when it comes to everyone else, but when it comes to Dylan, you have this blind spot."

"I don't think…"

"I know you don't think so, but you do. You have to let go of this guilt you have about you and John."

"How am I supposed to do that? I lied to my son."

"Yes, but you did it because you love him. And, Cass? You're the only person who is beating you up over it. Before you start arguing with me, please hear me out. I know that Speed loves me. He loves your mom and my mom. God knows, he loves Nicky and Pip.

But, Cassidy, *you* are the most important person in the world to him. You always have been. Maybe he does want to impress me. I know that. You don't think I do, but I do. You? You're the person he trusts completely. He always has. He still does."

Cassidy sighed. "Sometimes it hurts, Alex. I know that's wrong of me. It just hurts. It hurts to know that I betrayed that trust. It hurts to see him laughing with my father. I just…"

"It's not wrong. I just wish you could let it go, just a little bit."

Cassidy put her head back onto Alex's chest. "How are things with Claire?"

Alex sighed.

"Alex? You two seem to be getting along. Did I miss something?"

"She saved my ass today, Cassidy."

Cassidy sat up. "You mean when you fell?"

Alex nodded. "Don't get me wrong, someone would have come down, but…"

"But…"

Alex looked at the ceiling to gather her thoughts. "She was as relieved to see me alive as I was to see her hovering there."

Cassidy smiled and snuggled into Alex. It gave her comfort to know that Claire was watching out for Alex, and that Alex was watching out for Claire. "I'm just glad you're safe."

"Me too," Alex confessed.

"Want to talk about it?"

"I don't know where to begin. Lying there… Knowing that young woman was beside me. Jesus, Cass, I fell a short way. It sounds awful, but I hope she was already gone when he threw her in that hole."

Cassidy felt Alex shudder against her and tightened her hold on Alex's waist. "I'm sorry you had to go through that."

"We're close, Cass—close to finding him."

"Isn't that a good thing?"

Alex sighed.

"Alex, what is it?" Cassidy moved again so she could look in Alex's eyes.

"I don't know for sure…"

"Know what?"

"I think he knew the first victim—intimately."

Cassidy struggled to take a full breath. "Like a girlfriend?"

"Maybe. I don't think so, though. I have a feeling they had history. She was fifteen, Cassidy. There's only so many options."

"How close are you?"

"Close. I just worry that when we find him…"

"You think Claire will go off the rails."

Alex shook her head. "I wouldn't blame her, and that scares me."

Cassidy kissed Alex's cheek. "I don't blame either of you for wanting to give him his due."

"You don't?"

"No, but I know that you won't."

"I have to get him before he…"

"I know."

Alex pulled Cassidy back into her arms. "I don't want to talk about it anymore."

"Okay."

"Just like that?" Alex asked.

"Just like that. Have you heard from Pip?"

"Only to give me work to do," Alex chuckled. "In fact, I need to get up early in the morning."

"Alex…"

"Don't worry, it's not strenuous. Claire and I are headed to Pennsylvania in the afternoon. I need to stop at the Stamford warehouse on the way to the airport."

"You're going to Carecom?"

"Just to check the new security system. Won't take long with

Claire there to help me."

"About the girl?"

Alex swallowed hard. "It's not something you need to worry about right now."

Cassidy sighed.

Alex stroked Cassidy's back. "When this is all over?"

"Yeah?"

"What do you think about a weekend away with me?"

"Depends."

"Really? On what?"

"Do I have to cook?"

Alex laughed. "No cooking for you. No cleaning for me. Now that you've stopped counting the bathroom tile, I think we can find other things to occupy our time."

Cassidy giggled. "Are you propositioning me, Agent Toles?"

"Completely."

Cassidy laughed. "Proving my mother's point about rabbits."

"Do I want to ask what that means?"

"Kenzie was curious about her father," Cassidy explained.

"What?"

"Relax," Cassidy soothed Alex. "Just Kenzie being curious. When I tried to dive a little deeper, she was uninterested.

"I didn't think they'd be asking about that for a while."

Cassidy kissed Alex's chest. "Does that bother you?"

"I don't know. It's normal; I know. I kind of hoped it'd be when they were all older."

"I think it will be," Cassidy said. "And, Alex? It won't change how they see you or Pip."

"I hope not," Alex said.

"Maybe you should talk to Dylan about it," Cassidy suggested.

"Dylan?"

"I can't think of a better person to allay your fear," Cassidy explained. "He lived with Chris as his father for seven years. He found out about his biological father and after all of it? You are the one he sees as his parent. I don't know why you would think it would be any different with Kenzie and the twins or this baby for that matter."

"I just love them so much," Alex said.

"I know you do. They love you. You're their mom, Alex; every bit as much as I am. And, you know that Pip feels that way."

"I do. I just wonder what they'll want from him."

Cassidy looked at Alex. "They already have anything they could want from him. Uncle Pip loves all of them equally, including Dylan just like you and I do. The fact that he was our donor won't change our family. We've talked about this a million times. You have to trust that."

"I do trust it," Alex said. "Doesn't mean I don't think about it sometimes. Kenzie is a lot like him."

Cassidy nodded. "Mackenzie is a lot like *you*. Everyone comments on that, Alex."

Alex's lips curled into a smile. Mackenzie looked like Cassidy, but her personality resembled Alex a great deal.

Cassidy grinned. "And, you love that fact," she teased.

"Maybe a little," Alex confessed.

"Um-hum."

"I wonder who this one will be like?" Alex mused.

"He'll be like Brian."

"You really think it's a boy?"

Cassidy shrugged. "Don't know why. I just do."

"Maybe it'll be twins again," Alex offered.

Cassidy's gaze hardened. "If you hope to participate in the rabbit show, you will take that back."

Alex laughed. "Tell me about this rabbit show."

Cassidy kissed Alex passionately. "Get some rest, pray for one healthy baby and I will give you the show on this weekend getaway you've promised."

"Praying as we speak," Alex promised.

Cassidy resumed her position in Alex's arms. "Get some sleep, love."

Alex closed her eyes. "Will there be hopping?"

"Go to sleep, Alex."

"How about carrots? Do I need to bring carrots?"

Cassidy giggled. "Not this trip, love."

Alex sighed with contentment. "I love you, Cass."

"Love you too, Alfred."

"Humpty Dumpty sat on a wall," he recited the familiar rhyme as he drove. "Humpty Dumpty had a great fall. And, all the king's horses and all the king's men couldn't put Humpty together again." He looked at his phone mounted to the dashboard, smiled, and pressed the necessary button. He waited for a connection. "Make it fast," he reminded himself.

"A hunting we will go, Agent Toles
Heigh ho, where will I go?
Find the chair who's oh so fair,
Just grab that girl and give her a twirl
And then I'll send her home."

He disconnected the call and closed his eyes. "Let's go hunting, Agent Toles."

CHAPTER SEVENTEEN

"This place is like Fort Knox," Claire commented.

"Jonathan thrives on overkill," Alex said.

"I guess so."

Alex paced nervously.

"Jesus, Alex, you'd think Cassidy was giving birth or something. What's wrong with you?"

"I just want to get this done and get to the Leibowitz's."

"Yeah, I get that. Do you think they'll cooperate?"

"You mean with keeping things under wraps for a day or two?"

"Yeah."

"I hope so," Alex said. "That's why I wanted us to make the visit. I can't help but think BJ has some connection to Monica Leibowitz." She sighed with relief when she saw the Gestalt van pull up. "Good, he's here." Alex opened the door. "Bryce."

"If it isn't my favorite Toles," Bryce Duncan made his way to the door.

"I'm the only Toles you know."

"Technically," he agreed. "You must be Alex's partner."

"Or she must be mine," Claire replied.

"Got a comedienne on your hands, huh?" Bryce asked Alex.

"Oh, she's a regular one-woman show."

Claire rolled her eyes. "Do you need me for this?"

"Nope," Alex said.

"Good. I'm gonna make a call."

"Say hi to Hawk!" Alex called after Claire.

"Thinks she knows me so well," Claire mumbled as she walked outside.

"I take it you looked at everything before I got here," Bryce said.

"Looks good. Anything I need to know?" Alex asked.

"Seems like your brother wanted the full treatment. Nobody is getting in here without approved access."

Alex smirked. *Somebody always gets in without approved access.* "If only that were true, Bryce. I'm afraid all the security cameras and protocols that exist are never enough."

"You're talking cyber."

Alex shrugged. "Someone always wants a challenge," she said.

"Speaking from experience?" he asked.

"Maybe." Alex was about to ask Bryce a question when her cell phone rang. "Toles," she answered. "I'm sorry? What did you just say? What? When?" Alex pinched the bridge of her nose forcefully.

"Came in ten minutes ago," Assistant Director Bower told Alex.

"Specifically for me?" Alex asked.

"Yes."

"I need to hear it."

"I'll put it on speaker. You ready?"

"Go ahead," Alex directed. She listened attentively.

"A hunting we will go, Agent Toles
Heigh ho, where will I go?
Find the chair who's oh so fair,
Just grab that girl and give her a twirl,
And then I'll send her home."

Alex's hand trembled slightly as she waited for AD Bower's voice to return to the line. "Toles?" he said.

"Yeah, I heard it. Can you send the transcript over?"

"Of course. What do you need?"

"I need you to call Governor Reid."

"Why?" Bower asked.

"Increase her security detail now," Alex ordered.

"You think he's going after the governor? That's not his M.O."

"I'm not sure what he's doing," Alex said. "He's grabbing the spotlight. Typical. He likes the attention. What better way to get attention? Better safe than sorry."

"Toles, how worried do we need to be?" Bower asked.

"Worried."

"I'll make the arrangements," Bower promised.

"Thanks. I'll follow up. Agent Brackett and I need to get to Philly ASAP." She hung up the call. "Shit."

"Everything okay? Bryce asked Alex.

"Okay is not the word I'd use. Listen, I hate to cut this short," Alex apologized. "I thought I'd have a little more time, but…"

Bryce held up his hand. "Not to worry," he assured her.

Alex nodded her thanks and briskly headed for the door. She opened it for Bryce. "Jonathan's overseas again. He'll be back next week," she said. "I trust your work. I'll make sure he knows to follow up with you."

"I appreciate that," he replied. "Next time, maybe we can catch up over coffee. I'll buy."

"You should buy with what you charge," Alex chuckled.

"Ah, Agent Toles," he said. "You get what you pay for in life."

Alex waved him off and headed for Claire.

"I just heard," Claire said. "I take it we're driving instead?"

"It will be faster."

"Okay, get in," Claire said.

"You're driving?"

"Don't make a thing out of it," Claire said. "Just get in the car."

"You okay over there?" Claire asked. "We're only an hour out."

"Just stiff," Alex replied. "I just keep thinking."

"About?"

"Lawson."

Claire sighed.

"You too?" Alex guessed.

"I just don't get it," Claire said. "Where the hell is Brad Lawson? No one just disappears. No one knows that better than us."

Alex chuckled despite the gravity of the conversation. Claire was correct. No one vanished without a trace. There was always a trace; it was a matter of someone finding the trail. There could be a million reasons that Brad Lawson was missing. She was confident he hadn't left the country. There was no passport registered to a Bradley Lawson with the same birthdate. Alex had been able to amass a wealth of information on the missing man. He possessed a valid Connecticut driver's license that was set to renew in six months. They had moved to track his bank accounts, but that would take time. He had no criminal history. He had served four years in the Army and had been honorably discharged. He'd never been married. His parents were deceased. There were more than enough circumstantial factors to give her pause. The problem was, the FBI and the courts did not function on circumstantial factors. For Alex to obtain a warrant to trace Brad Lawson's bank accounts, she needed evidence that he might be a viable suspect. Right now, she had none.

"Alex?"

"We need access to his bank accounts to see where he is—what he is spending."

"We could get that; you know?"

Alex sighed. "Going to our contacts in intelligence is not a good idea. How do we explain it?"

"I'm betting he knows something," Claire said.

"I agree," Alex said.

"You think he's our guy?"

"I think one of them is. Whoever we find first, we either find the killer or the person who knows where we can find the killer. That's what I think."

"Why would Monica Leibowitz be wearing a Greenscape shirt?" Claire wondered aloud. "I mean, our guy likes to leave them naked; right? He wouldn't dress her after the fact."

Alex nodded. "Not likely. Like I said, that would mean she knew him. I wish they'd get something from that photo."

"It's old, Alex."

"I know. Lawson disappears and no one knows BJ? It doesn't make sense."

"Guess that's why we have jobs," Claire said.

Alex couldn't help but chuckle. "True."

"You really think he'll make a play for the governor?"

"Who knows?" Alex said. "You heard that message. *Find the chair who's oh so fair?* He's talking about someone of prominence. It's one of two people," Alex surmised.

"One of two?"

"Yeah; Candace or me. I can take care of myself."

"Let's just hope there are no holes in the ground where we're headed," Claire said dryly.

"Thanks," Alex laughed.

"Any time, partner."

"No," Bryce spoke into his phone. "I'm in Stamford right now. Is it that important?" He sighed heavily. "I can make the detour if you need me to. Yeah, I'm sure." He hung up the call and slapped the steering wheel. "Another damn detour. I hate detours."

Claire pulled the car in front of a small coffee shop. "I'll get us some coffee before we head down the street to the Leibowitz's."

"Thanks," Alex replied. She needed to make a follow-up call, and she was sure Claire was giving her privacy to make it.

"Don't thank me. Trust me; you need it," Claire said.

Alex chuckled. She watched Claire move toward the coffee shop and took a deep breath. She waited for a voice to answer.

"Alex."

"I'm sure you are thrilled to be getting my call."

Candace Reid laughed. "That depends on whether it's to tell me I need to head to a bunker or not."

Alex smiled. There was little doubt in her mind that Bower's call would have unsettled the governor. But, Alex had known Candace for many years. She was a seasoned politician who was often in the spotlight. Threats were a reality someone of Candace's notoriety had to deal with. "If it makes you feel any better, I think you are safe."

"But?"

"I'm not one to take chances. You know that."

"I suppose; I do."

"Have there been any unusual threats lately?" Alex asked.

"Not that have been brought to my attention," Candace said. "Which means, if there have been, they were not deemed credible."

"No letters or anything?"

"There are always letters, Alex. I get thousands of letters," Candace replied. "It takes time for staff to pour through them."

"I'd like our team to take a look," Alex said. "Just to be certain."

"Out of an abundance of caution?" Candace asked.

"Something like that," Alex said.

Candace laughed. "We both know this is a courtesy request."

Alex sighed. It was true. The FBI wouldn't meet with resistance if they asked to see Candace's "fan" mail. "It is," she admitted. "As an FBI agent, I want you to know that coming after you does not fit his profile."

"And, as a friend?"

"I won't take any chances."

"Whatever you need, Alex. I told you that at the beginning."

"Candace, if you see anyone new around that doesn't fit, I want you to call me."

"Alex, there are new faces around me hourly."

"Everyday contractors, press, new security guards at the Capitol, volunteers at the campaign—those kinds of people."

"Alex, that's a daily occurrence."

"I know. You make a living reading people, just like I do. If someone doesn't *fit*, I want to know—me, not Bower, not anyone else—call me."

Candace closed her eyes and nodded on the other end of the phone.

"Candace?"

"I'll keep my eyes open."

Alex debated with herself for less than a second before clarifying her reasons. "I don't think he's coming for you. I think he might want us to think that. He's delighting in the spotlight. Someone close, a campaign or staff member—that might be enough for him. Don't over think it, just pay attention."

Candace sighed. "You'll be the first to know."

"Good."

"Do me a favor?" Candace asked.

"Yeah?"

"Catch this son of a bitch?"

"Working on it."

He watched as the garage door rolled up and pulled the van inside. A quick break, a cup of coffee, and then he would need to run some errands. His phone buzzed. "Hello? Sorry I missed you earlier. You know how it is. I go where they tell me they need me. No," he cut the engine and stepped out of the van, and ran his hand over the car parked beside it. "At least, they put me up," he told the caller. "I'll be home as soon as I can. Overtime is good. I promise." He opened the door and stepped into the small kitchen. "It's nothing like home," he said. He smiled as he took in the familiar scenery. "You too." He savored a deep breath and released it slowly. "No, nothing like home," he spoke. "This is the house that Jack built."

"Mrs. Leibowitz," Alex softened her tone.

"I'm sorry," the woman apologized. "You must think I'm ridiculous. It isn't as if we didn't expect this news."

"No one expects news like this," Claire interjected.

Not for the first time, Alex found herself impressed with Claire's compassion. "Agent Brackett is right," she offered. "I know this is difficult, but we need to ask you a few questions."

"I'm not sure I can help you," Beth Leibowitz replied.

"Well, you let us be the judge of that; okay?" Alex said gently. Beth Leibowitz nodded. "I know this will sound like a strange question, but I have a reason for asking. Do you know if Monica had any friends by the name of BJ?"

"BJ?" Beth Leibowitz asked. "I don't know about friends; my ex-husband's nephew, Jack—some people called him BJ."

Alex forced herself to remain stoic. "Why BJ?"

"Well, his name was actually John, but everyone called him Jack growing up. For some reason, he hated it, said he wanted to be called Brandon."

"Brandon?"

"As I recall he was obsessed with Brandon Lee."

Alex nodded. "How old was Jack?"

"Oh, he was four years older than Monica. We saw them infrequently when the kids hit their teens. His parents had moved to their summer home in Connecticut full-time by the time Monica was in junior high school."

Alex looked at Claire.

"What does Jack have to do with Monica?" the woman asked.

"Other than the fact that they knew each other, maybe nothing," Claire said.

Beth Leibowitz looked at Claire skeptically.

"We've been looking for a man who went by the name BJ," Alex explained. "He happened to work for a company that has come up in our investigation, but no one seems to know his last name."

"Well, if it's Jack his last name is Carter," Beth Leibowitz offered.

"And, his family moved to Connecticut?" Alex sought to clarify.

"Yeah. That had to be sometime around 2003. Monica was in eighth grade. I remember that much."

Alex nodded at Claire. Claire understood the direction. She reached into her pocket and retrieved a copy of the photo Gordon Daniels' mother had given her and handed it to Alex.

"Can I ask you," Alex began. "Would you take a look at this picture and tell me if you see Jack in it?"

Beth Leibowitz nodded. Alex placed the picture in her hands.

"That's Jack—right there in the back," Beth Leibowitz pointed to a face in the photo.

"Are you sure?" Alex asked.

"I'm positive. One of the last times we saw Jack, he had that same haircut. Said he was going to open his own landscaping company or something."

"Landscaping?" Alex questioned.

"Yeah. He'd spent a few years working for his friend, I guess. Even brought him to one of our barbecues."

"Do you remember the friend's name?" Claire asked.

"No, I'm sorry; I don't. He was older than Jack. I do remember that. Jack was about to turn nineteen. I remember that because his birthday is a month after Monica's. She had just turned fifteen. Do you think he knows something about what happened to her because you found her in Connecticut?"

Alex sighed. "I don't know for sure," she replied honestly. "Your ex-husband—is there any chance he might know where Jack is now?"

Beth Leibowitz shook her head. "I doubt it. Aaron has been in London for over three years now. After Monica… Well, it took its toll on both of us. He drifted apart from everyone, not just me," she explained.

Alex's chest tightened. Losing a child was an unthinkable pain to endure. She nodded sympathetically. "One last question. Do you have any idea where Jack's family might be?"

"As far as I know, they settled in Connecticut. After Aaron and I divorced, I never had any interactions with them. I can't tell you for certain that they are still there."

"Do you remember where in Connecticut they lived?" Claire inquired.

"Hebron. That much I do recall."

"Thank you," Alex squeezed Beth Leibowitz's hand. "I'm so sorry for your loss."

"I appreciate that. I just hate the thought that she could have suffered."

"I promise you," Alex said. "Agent Brackett and I will find the person who took Monica from you."

"Do you think it's the same person who killed all those other girls?"

"We don't know for certain," Claire said. "Either way, we will find him."

Beth Leibowitz nodded. "I hope you do," she said.

Chills went up Alex's spine at the cold venom in Beth Leibowitz's voice.

"And, I hope he rots in a tiny little space the rest of his life."

Alex swallowed the lump in her throat. "If you think of anything at all…"

"If I remember anything else, I'll call you."

Alex nodded again. Claire offered the grieving mother a hand. "I'm sorry," she said. "From everything you told us; Monica sounds like she was a great kid."

"She was."

Claire offered the woman a final smile and followed Alex out of the house. She shook her head with disgust.

"Claire?"

"There's a special place in hell for people who hurt kids," Claire said.

Alex agreed. "Not even a question," she said.

"Brackett," Claire answered her phone. "Yeah? What did you get?" Claire listened as the caller answered her question. "You're positive? Okay. Interesting. No, don't make any house calls. Let me talk to Toles." Claire took a deep breath and walked back into the diner that she and Alex had stopped at.

"Everything okay?" Alex asked when Claire slid back into the booth.

"There's a lot of John Carters in Connecticut."

Alex sighed. "I figured as much."

"Corrigan's team found something in one of the abandoned greenhouses."

"What?" Alex asked.

"A business card for Crow Electrical Services."

"I hope there's more to this."

"There is. Crow Electrical Services' address is listed as Dunmore, Pennsylvania."

Alex's ears perked.

"They service parts of Pennsylvania, New York, New Jersey, and Connecticut. Ready for this? The company is registered as owned by a Brad Lawson."

"Our Brad Lawson?"

"What would you say if I told you that of all the John Carters in Connecticut there is only one who is employed as an electrician."

"Let me guess; he works at Crow."

Claire nodded. "No, but Brandon J. Carter does."

"And?"

"Well, the interesting thing is, the address Crow has for Brandon J. Carter is John Carter's parents' home in Hebron."

"So, he's living at his parents'?"

"No. His parents have been dead for years."

"For Christ's sake, Brackett! Just tell me what you found out."

Claire grinned. "Corrigan took Robbins to the Carters'."

"Robbins? Are you…"

"Not the hot issue here," Claire reminded Alex. Alex groaned. "Seems Jack Carter lives in Stratford with his wife and daughter, not in Hebron. No one was home at the parents' house. Kind of overgrown, but Corrigan says the neighbor down the road told her the son still stops by to mow the lawn."

Alex was already pushing her plate aside.

Claire snickered. "Not hungry anymore?"

"I'll pay the bill," Alex said.

"Get us coffees to go. I have a feeling it's going to be a long night."

"Hi," he peeked in through the door.

"Welcome," an attractive blonde woman greeted him.

"I heard you were looking for some help," he said.

"That, we are," she ushered him in. "Have you ever worked on a campaign before?"

"No. Is that a problem?"

"Not at all. I used to be a teacher," she said with a wink.

"You're the governor's daughter," he observed.

"Guilty as charged," Michelle Fletcher held out her hand. "Shell," she introduced herself.

"Brad," he said.

"Nice to meet you, Brad."

"I hope I can help with something," he said.

"Well, can you man a phone?"

"Sure."

"Can you use a computer?" Michelle asked.

"I think so," he answered lightly.

"You're hired. Starting wage—unlimited coffee and the pleasure of my company from time to time," she joked.

"I'll take it."

"Let me grab you a cup and a seat."

Alex looked over at Claire. "Ready?"

"Think he's here?" Claire asked.

"We're about to find out," Alex said. She lifted her hand and rapped on the door. A couple of moments passed. Alex rapped again and she heard a woman's voice muffled in the distance. She was about to knock a third time when the door to the small white, Cape Cod home opened.

"Can I help you?"

Alex smiled at the woman. Over the woman's shoulder she could see a young girl running in a circle. "Sorry to disturb you," Alex said. She lifted her FBI badge. "My name is Alex Toles. I'm a special agent with The Federal Bureau of Investigation."

The woman was puzzled. "The FBI?"

Alex nodded. "I'm sorry," she apologized. "Is this the home of Jack Carter?"

The woman nodded hesitantly. "Yes, it is. Jack's not here right now. He's working."

"That's all right. You must be Mrs. Carter," Alex surmised. She extended her hand. "Would you mind if my partner and I asked you a couple of questions?"

The woman fumbled slightly. Alex smiled to reassure her. "It's just part of the routine of an investigation we're working on.

Jack Carter's wife stared at Alex for a minute and her jaw fell slack. "You're that agent from the TV."

Alex smiled again. *Damn press. I hate the press.* "Unfortunately, yes, I am."

"Is Jack okay?"

"I've no reason to think otherwise," Alex told her. "Please? Would you mind if we came in?"

The woman shook her head and opened the door for Alex and Claire to enter. "Can I get you something? Some…"

"No, that won't be necessary," Alex replied. "We won't take up too much of your time." She glanced at the little girl who was now doing some form of somersault and chuckled.

"Oh. That's my daughter, Janelle. She thinks she's a monkey most days. I'm sorry, I'm Jenny, Jack's wife."

"Nice to meet you, Mrs. Carter. How old is she?" Alex gestured to the little girl. She could tell that their arrival had unsettled the woman. She hoped that finding a little common ground would put Jenny Carter at ease.

"Four," Jenny Carter smiled. "Going on fourteen some days, still a baby others."

"Sounds like your house, Toles," Claire commented.

"You have children?" Jenny asked Alex.

"Four," Alex said. "Another one on the way."

Jenny Carter looked at Alex's midsection.

Claire laughed. "Yeah, right; Alex pregggers? I'd love to see *that*."

Alex shot Claire a stern gaze before turning her attention back to Jack Carter's wife. "Not me," she said. "My wife is expecting."

Jenny nodded.

Alex spoke calmly. "I'm sure having the FBI show up is a little unnerving."

"You could say that," Jenny agreed.

"We've been trying to track down some people who worked for a company called Greenscape Landscaping. Your husband's name popped up."

Jenny nodded. "I know that Jack did some yard work and mowed lawns when he was a teenager. He worked with a friend of his."

"Do you remember his friend's name?" Alex asked.

"Brad Lawson. I've never met him," Jenny said. "He helped Jack get the job he has now."

"At Crow Electrical?" Alex asked.

"What?" Jenny's confusion was evident. "No, Jack's a security guard. He works second shift for a private company."

Alex looked at Claire.

"Do you know the name of the company?" Claire asked.

"Dryer Security. They provide guards for all kinds of places. Jack's been working at Gestalt mostly. He's been hoping to get on their payroll for years, but nothing there has opened up."

"Gestalt Security?" Alex asked.

"Yeah."

Alex processed the information. While she knew that Gestalt hired outside security for its facilities, getting assigned to Gestalt would be no easy feat. "So, your husband isn't an electrician?"

Jenny laughed. "God, no! I barely let Jack change a lightbulb."

Claire paced around the small living room while Alex directed the conversation. She let her eyes explore the various decorations and pictures. Most of the pictures were of the little girl who was now standing at Claire's feet.

"Hi," the little girl looked up at Claire.

"Hello."

"You is tall."

Claire smiled. "Taller than you."

"You has wed hair."

"Huh?" Claire asked.

"She loves red hair," Jenny Carter explained.

"You's bwave!" the little girl exclaimed. "Mommy! Mewida! Bwave!"

Alex chuckled at the perplexed expression on Claire's face. "She thinks you're the princess from the movie *Brave*."

Claire gloated. "A princess, huh?"

Alex rolled her eyes.

"Your husband likes to fish?" Claire asked curiously. She gestured to a picture on a small table.

Jenny smiled. "He does. He doesn't have much time now for it with work. He still tries to get out when he can. His parents lived out in the country. He likes to go hiking and fishing there. I think it makes him feel closer to them. That's where that was taken," she offered. "Not long after we met."

Alex paid close attention to Jenny Carter's demeanor. She was open and willing to share. She smiled when she spoke about her husband, but Alex detected an underlying sadness in the woman sitting before her. If Jack Carter was their killer, Alex would not be surprised to learn that he had a temper nor that he often sought distance. She was curious about the contradictions in the information Jenny had shared. Who exactly was BJ? She still was not sure she had a clear picture.

"Well, we won't take up any more of your time. Do you by any chance know where your husband is right now?"

"He called earlier. He said that he's working in Albany for a few days. Someone is out, I guess."

"Albany?" Alex asked.

"Yeah. Gestalt has an office there. When they are short-handed, they usually offer Jack the overtime. They even put him up in a hotel," Jenny explained.

"Sounds like he's on the road a lot," Claire commented. Jenny sighed. "Long distance relationships suck sometimes," Claire said.

Alex shook her head. She was relieved to see that Jenny Carter was smiling.

"Certainly, feels like one sometimes," Jenny told Claire.

"I feel you," Claire said. "And, I don't have any of those," Claire pointed to the little girl who was now lying on the couch beside her mother.

"No kids?" Jenny asked.

"Nope. Toles here is enough for me to deal with."

Jenny laughed. "I'm sorry if I didn't help you at all."

"That's all right," Alex said. "We really were just trying to get with people who worked for that landscaping company to ask them about a couple of the places they might have worked."

"Do you want his number?" Jenny offered.

"That would be great," Alex said.

"I don't expect him to call again tonight, but I can tell him…"

"Don't worry too much about it," Alex played off the conversation.

Alex felt confident that, at least for the moment, Jenny Carter and her daughter were safe. She did have every intention of putting them under surveillance—not just in the hopes of finding the elusive BJ, but for their protection. If Brandon Jack Carter or whatever he called himself was who Alex suspected he was, once he learned she was this close, anything was possible.

"Thanks again," Alex said. "One thing," she said. "If you hear from Brad Lawson by chance, I'd love to talk to him. He used to be the owner at Greenscape."

"Sure. Like I said, I've never met him, only heard of him."

"In any case," Alex said. "Take care. Nice meeting you. Sorry to barge in."

"Hey, it was company," Jenny replied good-naturedly.

Alex took a deep breath when she heard Jenny Carter close the door. "Set up surveillance on Jenny Carter," she told Claire.

"I was thinking the same thing. Should I guess? We're heading to Albany?"

"You should charge for that psychic ability of yours," Alex deadpanned.

"Pretty close to your friend the governor."

"Too close," Alex said. *Much too close.*

"Bryce?"

"This is Bryce."

"This is Alex Toles."

"Alex? Don't tell me there's an issue with the system?"

"No, I'm afraid I'm not moonlighting for my brother this time. I was hoping you might be able to help me with something."

"If I can."

"You travel a lot with Gestalt; right?"

"That's an understatement. Donna's ready to divorce me. Why?"

"How difficult is it for security guards to get assigned to your facilities?"

Bryce pulled his van over. The tone of Alex's voice told him this conversation required his undivided attention. "We use three agencies," he said. "All three have the highest credentials. You know what I mean—top notch security clearances. Anyone assigned has to also pass muster with Gestalt."

"Who does that?" Alex asked. "Is that on paper or interview?"

"It depends," Bryce said. "Someone in senior management makes that call."

"Have you ever been that person?"

"A couple of times. Alex, what is this about?"

"Bryce, I am going to go out on a limb here; you don't know a Jack Carter do you?"

"Jack Carter? No, I don't think so."

"No Jack Carter works as a security guard that you've encountered?"

"I don't pay much attention, Alex."

"Bullshit," Alex said. Bryce was a retired Navy Seal Captain; he recalled everything. He was the senior person in the most lucrative and scrutinized department at Gestalt. It was his job to pay attention to the smallest detail. "You notice everything."

Bryce chuckled. "There is a Brandon Carter who works the gate occasionally." He heard Alex sigh. "Alex?"

"Did you see him today by any chance?"

"Not today. He's a part-timer that's usually on second shift, though."

"In Albany?"

"No," Bryce replied. "I've never seen him at the Albany office. He's always in New Haven."

"Thanks."

"Alex, is Brandon in some kind of trouble?"

"Just trying to hunt down some leads."

"If you say so. You know, if he's a risk to our security…"

"I can't tell you that," Alex said. "He's someone I need to track down."

"Do I get a bonus for helping?" he joked.

"Call my brother."

"So?" Claire asked.

"Bryce knows him."

"Is that a good thing?"

"Well, Bryce is a retired Navy Seal. He's been where you and I have been; if you get my meaning."

"You mean he was one of those secret squirrels chasing other people's tails too?"

Alex laughed at Claire's assessment. "He's trained to remember everything he sees. He says he's never seen Jack Carter or Brandon or BJ, whatever he goes by in Albany."

"So, he lied to his wife. Doesn't make him a serial killer."

"Not by itself, no," Alex agreed. "It does mean he has something to hide."

"What about Lawson?" Claire asked.

"I don't know."

"Think he's covering somehow for Carter? Maybe Carter is covering for him."

"We need to find one of them if we hope to find that out."

"Well, we know what BJ looks like now. I saw that fishing photo."

"That's something."

"Let me guess; we're taking a detour to visit to Crow Electrical."

"No, you are."

"Me?" Claire asked.

"Yeah, and not with your FBI badge."

"Ooo. Sneaky," Claire said. "I like it."

"Just do me a favor?"

"What?"

"Be careful."

"I can be very charming," Claire said.

"I know. That's what worries me."

Michelle Fletcher held the door open for the volunteers at her mother's campaign headquarters.

"Any place good to eat around here?"

Michelle smiled. "It's Albany, Brad. You should just ask if there's any place good."

He laughed. "Come on, I don't spend much time in this area."

"Try *The Merry Monk* down the street," she said.

"Get a little God with my beer?" he joked.

"My mother would say a little prayer and a little wine are good for the soul."

"Care to join me?" he asked.

Michelle looked off in the distance. "I would," she said. "But I have a standing date with my step-mother on Wednesdays."

"Really?" he asked

"I swear. It's painful, but someone has to do it."

He followed Michelle's line of sight to the attractive brunette coming toward them. "That's the governor's wife; right?"

"Yep. My evil step-mother," she laughed.

"Hey, Shell. Ready?" Jameson Reid greeted the pair.

"Only if you're buying," Michelle replied. "JD meet Brad. He's our newest recruit."

Jameson offered her hand. "Thanks for helping out on Candace's campaign."

"Who wouldn't want a beautiful woman in the White House?" he said.

"You'd be surprised," Jameson replied.

"Thanks for your help today," Michelle smiled at Brad.

"Not sure I helped all that much, but you're welcome."

"I hope we'll see you again," Michelle said.

"I have a little time between jobs. I'll stop by sometime tomorrow to see if you need any help."

"Great," Michelle said. "Come on, old lady," she grabbed Jameson's hand.

"Nice meeting you," Jameson said to the man. "Sorry, I need

to get this one home before her bedtime."

"Yeah, she's got Bible Study at eleven and she needs to concentrate," Michelle said.

Brad shrugged, not understanding the inside joke between the two women. "See you tomorrow then," he said his goodbye.

"Bible study? Really, Shell?" Jameson laughed.

"Well, Mom certainly calls God enough after eleven."

"Just rent a billboard," Jameson laughed. "Let's go before I get a ticket for you violating curfew."

"Can't sleep?" Jim McCollum asked his daughter.

Cassidy set down the book in her hands and smiled. "Just enjoying a little quiet."

"Alex is still on the road, I take it?"

"She's in Albany. Looks like she'll be working from that office for the next few days, maybe longer."

Jim sat down on the end of the couch where Cassidy had been sprawled out. "How are you doing with that?"

"It's what she needs to do."

"That's not what I asked you."

Cassidy smiled. "It's not the first time that Alex and I have been apart, Dad."

"I suppose not. It's been a long time, though," he pointed out.

"I guess it has," Cassidy agreed. "But this comes with the territory."

"Worried about her?"

"I always worry about her when she's working a case. I don't have any illusions about the danger she sometimes faces."

Jim nodded. "How do you deal with it?"

Cassidy looked at her father curiously. He had worked for the Central Intelligence Agency for years. He had been far more than an analyst or an office worker. She didn't know all the details of his past and she had no desire to. Cassidy was confident that her father had been exposed to violence, danger, and uncertainty many times. She wondered what was prompting his questions. "How do I deal with the reality that Alex might get hurt?" She took a deep breath. "There isn't any choice," she said. "When I met Alex, she was with the FBI. I know about her past. I don't know every detail and I don't need to. I've seen her lying in a hospital bed after taking a bullet. I've watched her hobble up the stairs after an altercation. I know the kind of people she sometimes pursues and what they're capable of. I've experienced it."

"Cassie, I'm sorry that you had to see any of that. I wish I'd been able to protect you from the likes of Fisher."

Cassidy sighed. "Things happen for a reason," she told him. "Maybe that happened to me so that I could understand why Alex feels compelled to do what she does. Maybe it helped me to understand why it matters so much that she is able to do it."

"So, you support her being back in the FBI?"

"I've always supported her going back to her roots, Dad. It was her decision to leave Carecom and the CIA. It was her choice not to take a job back at the FBI or NSA, not mine."

"It almost sounds like you wanted her to go back."

"Does it?" Cassidy chuckled. "No, I don't think that I would say that. I love Alex because of who she is. I accepted that I would always worry when I agreed to marry her. If I thought that teaching or coaching fulfilled her; I would encourage her to do that too. She loves those things. I know she does. But what she's doing now is her passion. Things happen, Dad. Look at you."

"Me?"

"Well, I didn't know the truth for years. So, let's talk about the lie."

"Cassie…"

Cassidy shrugged. "I wish you would just hear me out."

"I'm listening."

"I spent most of my life believing you were dead, not from a firefight or some villainous plot—from a car accident. Things happen to people. That's just part of life. I'm not suggesting there aren't more risks for Alex, but she could work twenty years as an agent without injury and get killed driving down the street. Am I supposed to stop her from driving?"

"Interesting perspective."

"I love Alex. I trust that she will do everything she can to be here for as long as she can be. That's all I can do."

"You didn't want me to stay here; did you?" Jim asked.

Cassidy could see the hurt in her father's eyes. "I'm not sure how to answer that."

"Honestly?"

"Part of me is glad that you're here."

"Because you and Alex hope I can find out if there is anything to worry about with Dylan?"

"No," Cassidy replied flatly. "Alex is more concerned about whether Chris subjected Dylan to any psychological experiments than I am."

"You don't think that he did."

"I don't know what to think where my ex-husband is concerned. Just like I don't always know what to think where you are concerned. You both lied to me. You both pretended to be someone else."

"Cassie, I…"

"But I also know that he loved Dylan just like I know that you love me. He may have been an absentee father. He may have been a self-absorbed liar, but I saw his face when Dylan was placed in his arms. So, while nothing would shock me, the answer is no; I don't think he deliberately tried to harm Dylan."

"Then why agree to have me stay here?"

"Because the kids love you, because it will ease Alex's

mind…"

"I see."

"And, because I want you here." Cassidy smiled at the evident surprise in her father's eyes. "It's not easy for me sometimes—seeing you celebrate milestones with my children; milestones that you missed with me."

"I didn't want to miss them."

"That's not the point," Cassidy said. "Whether you wanted to, you chose to. Neither of us can change that."

"I know that sorry will never cover it."

"No; it won't," she replied. "I will always have to confront the hurt, Dad. That's not something I can change."

"I know," he confessed. "Every time I see one of your children cross a threshold, I find myself wondering what that was like for you. I love being with them, but it doesn't replace that time."

Cassidy reached over and took her father's hand. "I know that."

"You do?"

"I see that with Dylan and Alex all the time. It's different because the circumstance is different, but the emotion is the same. Alex missed the first six years of Dylan's life. When she sees Mackenzie or one of the twins do something new, as excited as she gets, there always comes a time later when I find her quietly reflecting. She thinks about Dylan. It's the same for him."

"Never thought about that," Jim said.

"It's part of loving someone. You can't be there for everything, even if you wish that you could."

"Alex is lucky."

"It's not about luck," Cassidy said. "It's about love. If it hadn't been for her job, if it hadn't been for some of the darkness in life, we might never have found each other. Things happen the way they are meant to, I think. Maybe I just need to believe that."

"Well, you make sure you tell me if I overstay my welcome."

"I don't think that's possible, Dad."

"Alex will be okay."

"I know she will," Cassidy said.

"What do you think of her and Claire working together?"

Cassidy smiled. "I think it's exactly what they both need. Neither will let a thing happen to the other."

"Because of you," he guessed.

"No," Cassidy said. "They're a lot alike."

"You think they're alike—Alexis and Claire?" he nearly laughed.

"You don't? They both spent their life trying to win their father's approval. They both feel they failed in that endeavor. They're the two most intelligent people I know, and they both need a challenge."

"And they both love you," he reminded her.

"They do," she agreed. "Alex and Claire both want to feel part of a family more than they want anything else. They're more alike than most people realize."

"More than they realize," he chuckled.

Cassidy grinned. "I wouldn't be so sure of that," she said. "Though, I doubt either will ever admit it."

"Safe bet," Jim laughed.

Cassidy sighed. "If any two people can find this psychopath; it's them."

Jim nodded. "Probably so."

"So?" Cassidy stood up. "I'm awake. You're awake. How about some ice cream?"

"At midnight?"

"Why not? Don't have to share with any kids. I'd offer you wine, but I'm afraid my best substitute is in the freezer."

Jim helped Cassidy off the couch. "Got any whipped cream?"

"Never go without it," she laughed.

"Then you're on."

Cassidy walked hand in hand with her father to the kitchen. For a moment, she felt like the little girl he'd left behind. Her heart swelled. Alex's suggestion to have Jim McCollum stay at their home for a while had little to do with safety or Dylan. Cassidy hadn't seen it clearly until now. *Alex wanted him here for me. How did I not see that?* She giggled.

"What's so funny?" Jim wondered.

"Nothing. Just realizing how lucky I really am." *I really am.*

CHAPTER EIGHTEEN

Alex closed her eyes and rubbed her temples. She was not looking forward to the conversation she was about to have with the governor of New York, not even a little bit.

"You look like hell," Candace observed as she entered the room.

"Thanks," Alex opened her eyes.

Candace took a seat across from Alex and smiled. "Let's have it."

"I think our guy is close. By that, I mean close to you."

Candace nodded. "You actually think I'm in danger? We haven't had any threats that have been viewed as credible. And, trust me; with Jed Ritchie and Lawson Klein out doing the two-step together about my ineptness, there have been plenty of promises to show me the light."

Alex sighed. "He won't come directly to you," she said. "It's not about you."

"You lost me, Alex."

"The press has been all over my story."

"Yes, I know," Candace said.

"It's not a secret that we have been friends over the years."

Candace began to follow Alex's reasoning. "He's taunting you."

"I think so. Cass is too far. He is close to you. Maybe not you personally, but someone that you might value. You're convenient—no offense."

Candace grinned. "None taken."

"He's here, Candace—in Albany."

"Are you sure?"

Alex nodded. "He's within twenty miles of the airport. It's just a matter of where. We're searching hotels, but so far? Nothing. Which means he is likely renting or purchased something. That could be harder to pin down."

"Do you know who he is?"

"Yes and no." Alex handed Candace a photo of Jack Carter.

"John (Jack) Carter? Is this the killer?"

"I'm not sure."

"Explain."

"We have three names to run down."

Candace narrowed her gaze. "You have three potential suspects?"

"No."

"He has three aliases?"

"Maybe," Alex said. She watched as Candace's eyebrow arched in challenge. "He could be working with someone. We're working on some Pennsylvania databases now." Alex handed Candace another photo. "That's Brad Lawson. This is the most recent photo the DMV had on file."

"You think they are both involved?" Candace tried to understand.

"That's a possibility. I think one person might be giving cover to another. They've been friends since their teens. Listen," Alex said. "He doesn't have to go after you to get the notoriety you bring. It could be anyone close to you, even someone working on your campaign, a member of your staff."

"We don't have the resources to watch everyone who might be considered close to me. I asked Shell to stick close to campaign headquarters and keep her eye open. I'll pass this along to the paid staff. But you need to know, we already have a tribe of people coming and going. That's the nature of a campaign. It's the nature of an open society."

"I know. I want to put some eyes closer," Alex said.

"Someone to pose as campaign staff?"

Alex nodded. "It can't be me or Claire."

"No, I wouldn't imagine so. FBI agents?"

"Yes. I have two agents that will be there in the morning. It's important that no one knows who they are, not even Shell."

Candace considered Alex's direction for a moment. Michelle was running her campaign office. Michelle was her daughter. That put her in the crosshairs, and that was not something Candace felt comfortable with. "No."

"Candace, if she knows she might inadvertently give someone away. Shell is great. She's not trained for this."

"No," Candace repeated. "If what you suspect is true, Shell is the person in the most danger."

"You have to trust my judgment," Alex argued. "I'm trying to protect anyone who might end up in his line of sight."

Candace nodded. "No," she repeated. "If you want to place agents in that campaign office then we tell Shell. She needs to know who she can go to. I'm not going to hand her this picture and let her think she's by herself in there."

Alex understood her friend's concerns. Michelle needed someone to go to should she see or suspect anything was amiss. "I figured you'd say that."

"Let me guess; you have a solution."

"We have a powerful mutual friend who knows what to look for, and who we both trust. Someone who has a direct line to me, and someone Shell will trust."

Candace immediately understood. Alex wanted to bring Jane Merrow into the equation. "Alex, I don't think Jane wants to spend time in Albany. It's Albany, for heaven's sake."

Alex chuckled. "She wants you to win this election. That means you need to stay safe first and foremost. She'll do it if I ask her. I need you to give me the green light to do that. I'm not a politician, Candace. I do know that sometimes a high-profile figure can hinder a campaign more than help it too early in the game. I don't want to hurt your campaign. Jane," Alex hesitated. "She's familiar with both our worlds."

"I'm aware that Jane is more than the picture painted for the people, Alex."

Alex smiled. Candace Reid had been around politics her entire life. She'd also served on the Senate Intelligence Committee for years. That committee had held inquiries into President John Merrow's assassination and into the possible obstruction of justice by his successor Lawrence Strickland, who had left office disgraced by innuendo and ineffectiveness. She doubted that Candace knew the full scope of who Jane Merrow was or that something called The Collaborative worked under the cover of the CIA. It was clear that Candace Reid had surmised there was more to Jane Merrow than a former Hollywood actress who became a fairy tale First Lady.

"But?" Alex asked.

"There's no but. You're right. She could be an asset to both of us right now. I'm guessing that you ran this idea by Cassidy?"

"She knows the drill," Alex said. Cassidy had been married to a congressman for years—a congressman who had once been thought to be headed for the top. She knew the ins and outs of campaign life and the political arena. "She lived it for years."

"Yes, she did. So, what was her thought on this idea of yours?"

"She thinks that with the media feeding on Ritchie's drama, having Jane take up a presence might help you with the press."

Candace smiled. "I agree. The former First Lady would be an asset."

"But?"

"I should make that request of her, not you."

"No," Alex disagreed. "Candace, she needs to know all the reasons she's there."

"I think we both know she's ahead of the curve," Candace grinned. "You can fill her in on all the details after I speak with her."

"Candace…"

"Alex, this isn't up for debate. I've heard your case, and I agree with your assessment. Nonetheless, you need to understand that I put myself in a vulnerable position when I decided to run for the White House. I can't appear vulnerable. Do you understand? This kind of thing goes with the territory."

"What kind of thing? A serial killer wanting to exploit you?"

"Anyone wanting to exploit me," Candace said. "The reason isn't important. I entered this race on a promise to see it through to the end. I knew the risks. We both know that the road to hell is paved with good intentions and the road to the White House is the road to hell."

"You sound like John."

"President Merrow wasn't just our friend, Alex. He was the leader of the free world. That's not something you seek unless you are prepared to sacrifice yourself when the time comes; whether that's your reputation or your person."

Alex shook her head. *If only that were true.* John Merrow and Candace Reid were cut from the same cloth. They both believed in serving something greater than themselves. She also knew that many people who sought higher office only sought to serve their private interest. In Alex's view, that put people like Candace at greater risk. She cared. Like it or not, that made her more vulnerable.

"All right," Alex agreed. "But, you have Jane call me after you speak to her."

"You have my word. Alex?"

"Yes?"

"You find this son of a bitch and put him where he belongs," Candace said.

"You have my word, Governor."

Claire noted the cars and license plates as she walked through the small parking lot toward Crow Electrical Services. It was curious to her. She would have expected a company that serviced four states to have a fleet of trucks and vans. There was only one in the parking lot. *Either business is great or something is rotten in Dunmore.* She reached the door to the small cement building and took a step inside.

"Can I help you?" a woman's voice inquired.

Claire nodded. "Sorry, I was looking for a friend of mine that works here," she said. "I got back into town and I thought maybe I could catch him."

The woman behind the steel desk gauged Claire cautiously.

Claire turned on the Brackett charm. She smiled. "You probably think I'm a nut case," she laughed. "I'm not; I swear." She pulled out a picture and handed it to her friend. "That's us when we were younger," she said.

The woman looked at the picture and smiled. She looked back at Claire.

"I wanted to surprise him," Claire said shyly. "I haven't seen BJ in a while."

The woman looked puzzled. "I'm sorry?" she said.

Claire studied the woman's puzzled gaze with interest. "We went to school together in Connecticut. That was his nickname back then."

The woman nodded as if beginning to understand. "Well, he's not here right now. I'm not sure when he'll be here. He took a few days off."

Claire sighed. *Let's go out on the limb.* "That's a bummer. I'll bet he headed to some lake," she said. "Brandon always did like to fish."

"Brandon?" the woman asked.

"Brandon," Claire replied. "BJ? That's my friend in the picture," she said.

The woman shook her head in disagreement. "No, that's Brad."

Claire narrowed her gaze at the woman.

"I don't know who Brandon is," the woman said "But, this picture you gave me is of my boss. There's no Brandon that works here."

"Are you sure? Brad and BJ were friends years ago, but that's BJ in that picture. They always looked alike," Claire offered a reason for the misunderstanding. "But, I promise; that's me and Brandon."

The woman shook her head again. "Then they must be twins," she said. "I guess Brad could have someone doing some side work. He only has himself and one tech to work client calls these days. If he did hire anyone; he didn't tell me."

Claire shrugged. "Like I said, they always were weird," she played it off. "Practical jokers."

The woman laughed.

Thank God, she bought it. "Well, I guess I struck out," Claire replied.

"Here," the woman scribbled something on a business card and handed it to Claire. "If he gets mad, you didn't get it from me. That's Brad's private number."

Claire smiled gratefully. "Thanks. I promise; your secret if safe with me."

"If Brad calls, I can tell him…"

Claire refrained from offering the woman a sly grin. "Tell him Alex stopped by."

"Sure," she said. "Sorry, I couldn't help more."

"Like I said, they were always weird," Claire joked. "Thanks again."

"Good luck!"

Claire waved and made her way out of the office. *What the hell is going on here?"*

"Hi."

"Oh, that doesn't sound good," Cassidy replied over the line.

"What? All I said was hi," Alex responded.

"It's not the word; it's the way you said it. What's wrong? Did you talk to Candace?"

"Yes."

"And?"

"She agrees with you," Alex said.

"What's wrong?"

"I just want this over so that I can come home."

"How's it going?" Cassidy asked.

"That depends on what you mean," Alex said. "Every time I think we're close, something changes and I'm not sure what direction we are headed. And, every minute I lose puts someone else's life in danger."

"What does Claire think?" Cassidy wondered.

"I don't know. She's not here."

"What do you mean she's not there? Where is she?"

"She's fine, Cass. She was following up on something. I talked to her a couple of hours ago. She should be here within the hour."

"Where are you staying?" Cassidy asked.

"Jameson's old condo," Alex said. "Lucky for me the kids all abandoned it," she laughed. "Candace insisted."

"So, no hotel?"

"Nope."

"Does it have a kitchen?" Cassidy teased.

"Why? Worried I'll forget how to do dishes?"

"No, just thinking maybe you will remember to eat."

"I did find the coffee pot."

"Alex…"

Alex laughed. "When Claire gets here, we'll order something. What's going on there?"

"Not much."

Alex laughed harder. With four children in the house, there was always something going on. "Are you trying to tell me that you're bored?"

Cassidy chuckled. "Hardly, just nothing out of the ordinary. Abby gets her cast off tomorrow—thank God."

"Is it bothering her?"

"No, but it bothered Connor last night."

"What?"

"They had a little squabble. Apparently, Abby thought playing Rocky with her cast against Connor's face was a good idea."

"Oh no, is he okay?"

"He's fine, just a bruise—a good sized bruise. Just be glad Mom is staying here with my father while I take Abby tomorrow. With that bruise on Connor's cheek, you might be bailing me out."

"Nah. They're used to the kids' war wounds."

"That doesn't make me feel better."

Alex sighed. "I'm sorry I'm not there."

"I was kidding," Cassidy reassured Alex. "I wish you were here too, but we're all okay."

"I'm not sure how that makes me feel," Alex confessed.

"I said we're okay. I never said we didn't miss you."

"How's Kenz?"

"She's at Maggie's with Dylan. Apparently, she is interviewing them for some project."

"A project for school? The year's almost over."

Cassidy snickered. "I'm sure that's what she's led them to believe."

"Oh no."

"She found Dylan's old tape recorder," Cassidy explained.

"Oh boy."

"I think we have a little spy on our hands."

Alex groaned.

Cassidy laughed. "Alex, relax. She's just playing. You know Mackenzie; she's curious about everything. She's just like you."

"That is not necessarily a good thing, Cass."

"I think it is."

"You're biased."

"Completely," Cassidy confessed.

"I'll be home as soon as I can."

"I know you will."

"How are you feeling?" Alex asked.

"Good, except for one thing."

"What is it?" Alex grew concerned.

"My father has turned me into an ice cream junkie."

Alex chuckled.

"It's not funny, Alex. If I don't slow down, I'll be the size of our SUV before this baby comes."

Alex erupted in laughter.

"Alex! I'm serious."

"I love you, Cass."

"Good thing for you, there will probably be a lot more of me to love soon."

"Thanks," Alex said.

"You're welcome."

"Call me after Abby's doctor appointment tomorrow."

"I promise. Eat something."

"I'll have Claire pick up some ice cream."

"Alex!"

"Goodnight, Cass."

"Goodnight, love."

Alex laid back on the couch and stretched. *I love ice cream.*

"Thanks for helping out again this afternoon," Michelle said.

"Happy to. Sorry, it's so late in the day. I had a few things to take care of this morning. What can I do?" Brad asked.

"Strange request."

"Strange doesn't scare me."

Michelle pointed up at the ceiling. "Three lights blew this morning. I called the management company but they don't have anyone available for that until tomorrow. JD said she'd take care of it tonight. I'd prefer not to have Mom kick my ass. She hates it when JD climbs ladders."

"Why is that?"

"Oh, the cat knocked JD off one once and Mom found her in the emergency room with a concussion."

"Ouch. Well, you're in luck. Shedding a little light is my specialty."

Michelle laughed. "What are you a pastor in your spare time?"

"Not exactly, but I have been known to recite a passage or two."

"Really?"

He smiled. "I do a little handiwork on the side."

"Huh."

"What?" he asked.

"Oh, nothing. Just, sometimes JD looks for people to help out with her projects."

"Your stepmother?"

"Yeah," Michelle said.

"I thought I read somewhere that she was an architect?"

"She is. She'd rather play with wood, though."

He tilted his head.

"Oh, that did *not* come out the way I meant it," Michelle sighed. "She likes building things is all."

He nodded.

"Hey, you know; if you need some extra work, she might need some help."

"That would be great."

"I'll ask her. Besides, it might help keep JD out of trouble with my mom," she joked.

"Aw, you know what they say? Needles and pins, when a man

marries, his trouble begins."

"Can't say I ever heard that one. Does it apply to women too?"

He grinned. "I'm sure."

"You know," Claire said as she set a pizza box down onto a coffee table, "I'm not Dial a Delivery, Toles."

"You're not?"

"Ha-ha."

Alex chuckled. "I promised Cass we'd order something."

"Yeah? Heard of Dominos?"

"Sure, but why eat that crap when I have Dial a Delivery at my disposal? Look, I just press three…"

Claire threw a can of Diet Coke at Alex. "Wait to open that…."

Before Claire could finish her thought, Alex opened the can in her direction. Diet Coke sprayed across the short distance all over Claire's white blouse.

"You really are a pain in the ass," Claire said.

"Shouldn't have thrown the can."

"How does Cass deal with you?" Claire asked.

Alex shrugged. "That's a question I ask myself every day. So? Whatever it is you need to tell me, it must be good if you didn't want to talk about it over the phone. Did you find anything out about Brandon Carter?"

"Nope. I did find out about Brad Lawson."

"You found Lawson and you didn't think it was important to tell me that?"

"I didn't say I found Lawson. I said I found out *about* him."

"Brackett!"

Claire grinned. "Paybacks, Toles. You want to know my story? Hand me a piece of pizza—gently."

Alex rolled her eyes and opened the box. "What did you find

out?"

"I went in like we planned. Only one person works in the office. I told her I was looking for my friend BJ and then I showed her the picture we had made."

"Did she know him? Alex asked.

"Oh, yeah; she knew him."

"Did she give you any idea where he is?"

"No."

"Why not?"

"When I showed her the picture, she told me she didn't know any BJ or Brandon."

"I thought you said she recognized him?" Alex questioned.

"She did—as Brad Lawson."

Alex's jaw dropped and a piece of cheese drizzled out.

"Sexy, Toles," Claire took a bite of her slice of pizza.

"You're telling me that the guy who is in that picture is Brad Lawson?"

"Nope. But, she sure as hell thinks that's who it is."

Alex set down her pizza and began to pace the room. She pinched the bridge of her nose and shook her head. "That doesn't make sense. There's a record of him…"

"Yeah, their payroll company has a record of Brandon Carter. That doesn't mean she knows him."

"Claire," Alex started and then stopped. "Who are we chasing?"

Claire shrugged and took another bite of her pizza. "Who knows?" she said. "Jenny Carter thinks we're looking for Jack. Your buddy Bryce seems to know him as Brandon, and this woman at Crow Electrical is convinced he's Brad Lawson. He can't be both. Who he started out as? Who the hell knows?"

Alex continued to pace. "What if he is both?"

"What? You mean like a split personality of something?"

"No. We know that there was both a Brad Lawson and a Jack

Carter at one time who called himself BJ. What if he's using both identities?"

"Neat trick."

Alex nodded. "He's got to be close," Alex said. "Corrigan found Carter's parents' house empty; right?"

"No one is living there."

"They didn't make entry," Alex groaned.

"No. No warrant."

"Time to change that. Pack up your pizza."

"Alex, it's seven o'clock at night and we're in Albany. How the hell are you gonna get a warrant to go into that property?"

"Who said anything about warrants?" Alex replied.

Claire smiled. She started unbuttoning her blouse.

"What the hell are you doing?" Alex asked.

"Not like you never saw it," Claire rolled her eyes. "I'm grabbing something dry and less Cokey, if you must know."

"Hurry up."

Claire grabbed a T-shirt from her bag and pulled it over her head. "What makes you think there's something there?"

"Might not be," Alex admitted. "You want to knock door to door all through this city?"

"You're really not going to get a warrant?" Claire asked.

"Are you coming or not?"

"Just packing up the pizza like I was told."

"Pack faster."

"Thanks again, Brad," Michelle said. She took a sip from her coffee.

"I'm not afraid of heights."

"Good thing for me."

"I learned to get over that," he said.

"Why? Did you used to be afraid?" Michelle asked.

"Yeah; for a long time. I fell down a well when I was a kid."

"Shit. That must've hurt!"

"Broke a leg and my left wrist," he told her.

"I don't think I'd ever get over that."

He smiled. "The fall wasn't the worst part. I was stuck down there for two days before anyone found me."

"Oh, my God. How did you get out?"

"This older kid heard me down there. He got help, kinda' took me under his wing after that. So, it didn't turn out so bad," he said.

"I hate falling and I don't like the dark. I would probably be scarred for life," Michelle said.

"Well, you either master your fears or they'll master you," he said.

"Interesting perspective," she said as she tossed her paper cup into the trash. "Well, thanks for helping me clean up."

"My pleasure. Do you need a lift?" he asked.

"Thanks, but my ride should be here any minute."

"Another standing date?"

Michelle laughed. "You could say that; it's my wife."

He nodded. "Lucky lady."

"Yes," Michelle grinned. "She is," she joked. "I'm kidding. Trust me on this; Mel is probably the only person alive who could put up with me full-time."

"I find that hard to believe," he said.

"You've seen my housekeeping skills," Michelle pointed to her disheveled desk. She turned to the sound of the door opening. "Speak of the devil."

"Hey," Melanie McKenna greeted the pair. "Am I late?"

"No," Michelle answered. "Brad, this is my wife, Melanie."

"Nice to meet you," he said.

"You too. You ready?" Melanie asked Michelle.

"Beyond."

"Home?"

"Actually," Michelle cringed. "Mom asked me to stop by."

"Okay."

"Okay?" Michelle sounded surprised.

"Yeah, I need to ask JD something anyway. Might as well do it in person."

"Hey, by the way," Michelle said. "Has JD mentioned getting into any projects back at home?"

"JD always had projects," Melanie laughed. "She'd rather be on a roof than at a drafting table. She hasn't mentioned anything that I remember, though. I know she said that the Governor's Mansion needs a chimney cleaning. But, you know she won't get to do that one herself."

"Safe bet there," Michelle agreed.

"Why do you ask?" Melanie wondered.

"Oh, just Brad here is between jobs right now. I thought she might have something she needed someone to look at back home."

Melanie shrugged. "Don't know. I think she's preoccupied with other stuff these days. All I do know is someone better clean out that chimney. I heard her tell Jonah she thinks something died up there."

Michelle laughed. "Sorry, Brad. If something comes up, I'll let you know."

"No problem," he said. He nodded his farewell and stepped out the front door.

"New recruit?" Melanie asked.

"Yeah."

"Something wrong?" Melanie wondered.

"No," Michelle said. "He's a nice guy."

"But?"

Michelle shook her head. "I don't know. I can't put my finger on it. I feel like there's more to his story; you know?"

"I'm sure there is."

He closed the car door and sighed. “Chimney needs cleaning, eh?” He laughed. “Watch out for Eeper Weeper. Had a wife, but couldn’t keep her. Had another, didn’t love her. Up the chimney he did shove her,” he recited the rhyme. “Chimney sweeps,” he chuckled.

CHAPTER NINETEEN

"Boonies," Claire muttered.

"What?" Alex looked over her shoulder at Claire.

"I thought my house was in the boonies. This is ridiculous. Did we really need to hike through the woods? No one is going to see us anyway."

"I'm not taking any chances," Alex said.

"Yeah, well, you better hope you don't end up with poison ivy after that trek."

"Are you going to keep bitching or are you going to help me?"

"What? You know how to pick a lock."

Alex groaned and went back to her appointed task. She moved her fingers deftly until she heard a click. "We're in."

Claire stepped through the door behind Alex. Her eyes followed the line of Alex's flashlight. "You take this room," she told Alex. "I'll move ahead."

"Be careful."

"I don't think the Boogie Man is here," Claire replied as she made her way toward the kitchen.

"I'll bet he *was* here," Alex muttered. She took a seat on an old sofa and began to sift through some magazines that sat on a coffee table. "Old," she commented. She made her way to a line of bookshelves and noted that there was no dust on any of the book bindings. "Someone reads *Good Housekeeping*." Alex's eyes scanned the titles. The second bookshelf caught her attention. One shelf was filled with colored bindings. Alex began to read the titles aloud. "*A Treasure of Rhyme, Classic Nursery Rhymes and Fairy Tales, The Nursery Rhyme Book, Poetry for Children…*"

"Alex!" Claire's voice pulled Alex from her private thoughts.

Alex made her way toward the sound. "What is it?" she asked.

Claire was standing beside a door. She pointed her flashlight down the stairs.

Alex moved hesitantly until she was standing beside Claire. In the distance, she could see a wall full of pictures. Her stomach lurched violently in her chest. “Shit.” She descended the stairs cautiously with Claire on her heels.

“What the hell is this?” Claire asked. She reached up and pulled a string attached to a light fixture.

Alex forced herself to take a breath when the room came into full view. She’d seen this type of display before. Deliberately, she moved to stand in front of it, willing her stomach to behave.

“Jesus Christ,” Claire mumbled. “They’re all here,” she said.

Alex steadied her breathing. Her eyes wandered to a picture of Kaylee Peters bound and gagged. “Fucking son of a bitch,” she muttered. Her eyes scanned the display methodically, finding the faces of several more victims they’d identified spread among faces she did not recognize. “There have to be at least thirty women here,” she mused.

Claire moved to investigate a large shelving unit. Anger boiled in her veins when she realized this was his trophy case. She reached out and picked up a small journal. “Alex, I think you’d better look at this. More rhymes.”

Alex’s eyes swept over the collage a final time. She turned to Claire and accepted the journal. She read each page. It became immediately apparent that every woman came with a story. She wondered if he had recited the rhymes to his victims. The possibility sent shivers over her skin. She searched to find the last few passages. “Lucy Locket,” she read the words. Her eyes moved to the shelving until. “Son of a…” Alex pointed at the camera on the shelf. “Kaylee,” she whispered. With a deep breath, her eyes returned to the journal in her hands. She turned a few more pages to reach the end and stopped. Silently, she processed the words:

Little boy blue,
Come blow your horn.

Your friend's in the well,
His arm is torn.
Now, where is that boy,
Who set him free?
He's under the barn,
Right where he left me.

Alex looked at Claire.

"What?" Claire asked. "I don't like that look on your face."

"There's a barn out back."

"Yeah? It's the boonies."

"I have a feeling we might find someone we've been looking for there."

"Who?" Claire asked.

"Brad Lawson."

"You think Lawson is hiding in Carter's barn?"

"No, but I think someone might have put him under it."

"Fuck."

Cassidy hung up the phone and sighed.

"You okay, Mom?" Dylan asked.

Cassidy offered him a reassuring smile. "You're still up?"

"Finals."

"Ah," Cassidy said. She patted the cushion beside her. "How was your afternoon with Kenzie?"

Dylan laughed. "Don't be surprised if she becomes a reporter or something."

"Why is that?"

"She is nosy!" he said

"As long as she doesn't become a spy, we're safe."

"Yeah, I doubt Alex would like that," he said.

"Understatement."

"Mom? Can I ask you something?"

"You can ask me anything, just remember that I'm not allowed wine."

Dylan chuckled. "That's what Alex was—a spy?"

Cassidy smiled. "Alex worked in Intelligence."

"So, she was a spy."

"I'm not sure I would say that," Cassidy said.

"What would you say?"

"I would say that Alex needed some answers and she accepted a role that she thought she needed to."

"That's cryptic, Mom."

"I'm not trying to avoid your question. I am curious why you are asking me and not her. What brought this on?"

Dylan sighed.

"Dylan?"

"I don't want you to get mad."

Cassidy took a deep breath. "Something put you into this line of thinking."

"It's not like I didn't know she and Uncle Pip were doing something. I mean, come on, Mom; CEOs don't carry guns."

Cassidy nodded. She decided to let Dylan lead the conversation.

"I heard Grandma and YaYa talking about Grandpa and Alex's dad."

"Why would I get mad about that?"

"I sort of eavesdropped when I heard what they were talking about."

Cassidy smiled. "I see. Maybe you have a little spy in you," she teased.

"You're not mad?"

"Well, I don't condone you listening in on your grandmothers, but I think I can understand why you wanted to hear what they were saying."

"Did you know?" he asked her.

"About my father?" Cassidy asked. He nodded. "No, not until he came back—no."

"Is that the real reason he left?"

Cassidy took a deep breath and let it out slowly. "What do you say to some ice cream?"

"Ice cream?" he asked.

"Yeah. If I can't have caffeine or alcohol, I'll take sugar."

"Mom?"

"Come on," Cassidy grabbed his hand. "This is going to take a while."

"You don't have to…"

"I'll be honest," she interrupted his thought. "I'd hoped that we could have this conversation with Alex before you left for the academy."

"We don't even know if I'll get in."

Cassidy raised her brow. "Dylan, you are in the top 3% of your class. You'll get in."

"Because I have people to help me."

"Everyone needs people to help them," Cassidy said. She pulled the ice cream out of the freezer and grabbed two spoons. Cassidy set it on the table and took her seat, immediately dipping in for a bite.

Dylan's brow raised just as his mother's had moments before. "No bowls?"

"Why? You think there'll be any left?"

Dylan laughed and dug his spoon in. "I want to do it on my own."

"No one does anything on their own, Dylan. They just think they do."

"You know what I mean."

"I do. You don't want Jane or Candace or anyone else pulling any strings."

"Exactly."

"What makes you think they will need to?" she asked him before taking another bite of ice cream.

"See? Just by you asking that, you think they will try to help."

"Jane loves you," Cassidy said. "Candace is my friend. Why wouldn't they want to help you? They care about you."

"Is that how Alex got into West Point? Her dad?"

Cassidy nearly choked on the ice cream in her mouth. "No," she said. "Just like you, she didn't need help."

"But, did she have it?"

"I don't know that answer, Dylan. It's possible that someone might have helped push Alex along. I can tell you this much; it was not her father."

"But, YaYa said he…"

"I'm not sure what you heard. Your grandfather and Alex's father both worked for the CIA for years. What I do know is that Nicolaus wanted to keep all three of his children as far from that life as he could. Obviously, Alex and Pip had different ideas."

"So, why is she so opposed to me going in?"

"She's not," Cassidy said. "She's told you why she has concerns."

"Somehow, I think she left something out," Dylan said.

Cassidy set her spoon down. "This family has a unique legacy, Dylan."

"Spies."

"If that's what you want to call it. I think your idea of what that might be and what it has been are likely different. If you want to know the truth, I think Alex would like to keep you from being recruited into that world."

"And, me going into the military makes me a target."

Cassidy nodded. "It's not 007," she said soberly. "This family has suffered because of it, more than I am prepared to share with you right now."

"Why not? You think I can't handle it?"

"It's not a matter of handling it. It's not all my story to tell. Your grandfather led a project for years that put me and Alex, Claire, Jonathan, Pip, and your father in jeopardy. It's why he left."

"Because he was guilty?" Dylan asked.

"Because he thought his absence might shield us."

"Shield you from what?"

Cassidy sighed. "From becoming part of that program," she said.

"Sounds like 007."

"It's not," Cassidy said. "It's much deeper, much darker, and it's real. People get hurt."

"Like when Alex got shot?"

"That's one way," Cassidy said. "There is worse pain than a bullet wound," she told him. "Alex would tell you that."

Dylan looked at his mother curiously. Cassidy had grown reflective in an instant. She looked sad to him. That was not an emotion he saw from his mother often. "Mom?" Cassidy's strained smile nearly broke his heart.

"I know that you have suffered because of my choices," she said.

"No…"

"Yes, you have, Dylan. I know you love Alex. God knows, she loves you. But, you missed out on getting to know your biological father. You are more like him than you realize. And, I know that Jane has told you this, but he did love you."

"I know," Dylan said. "But, you think I miss him more than I do. I don't think about it as much as you all do."

"I know that," she replied. She chuckled at the look of skepticism in her son's eyes. "I do know that. I also know that your relationship with your father was sometimes painful. I also know that you loved him."

Dylan looked at the table. "Maybe. That doesn't mean he ever cared all that much about me."

Cassidy reached for Dylan's hand. "Not true," she said.

"Mom, you and Dad…"

"At one time, Dylan, I did love him. I was never in love with him," she confessed. "And, I don't think he was ever in love with me. One thing I do know, we both loved you; even if he struggled to show you that at times."

"What does he have to do with this?"

"Everything," Cassidy said. "Every wound leaves a scar. Some leave lasting pain in their wake. I lost my father to that life, to what people like to call 'Intelligence.' Alex lost hers. Claire lost both her parents because of it. Eleana lost her brother. You lost both the men who would be fathers in your life. Jane lost her husband. You lost out on years of knowing your grandfather, and ever having the chance to know Alex's father. Those wounds never completely heal, Dylan. You learn to live with the pain. You learn to love despite it. It never goes away—never. It shapes you."

"What if I did decide to…"

Cassidy smiled. "Oh, Dylan, Alex and I will support you no matter what you decide to do if it is what you truly feel is best for you. Don't ask either of us not to worry or not to express concern. Like it or not, we've both lived a little longer."

"Is that why Grandpa is really here? To talk me out of going to the Naval Academy?"

"No," she said flatly. "He's here for me."

"For you?"

Cassidy picked up her spoon and dipped into the ice cream again. "Yep, for me," she said. She swallowed her bite and grinned. "He is trying to get me fat, I think."

"What?" Dylan laughed.

"Never mind," she waved him off. She smiled but grew serious. "I have a lot of anger toward him.," she confessed.

"I get that," Dylan said thoughtfully.

"I'm sure you do," Cassidy said.

Dylan looked at his mother. "I wish I could remember more of the good things about him."

"You were small," she said. "Your father was in Washington most of the time."

"It feels strange, you calling him my father."

"Would you prefer I call him Chris?"

"No," Dylan said. "I just always think of Alex as…"

Cassidy smiled. "I know you do."

"I wish she was," he said. "That hurts."

"I understand."

"How do you deal with it?" he asked.

"You mean how do I deal with what I know or how do I handle the loss?"

"Both."

"Well, for all the pain and all the craziness that has happened in my life, it brought me you," she said with a smile. "I can tell you that I was never happier than the day you were born."

"I'm sure that's not true."

"No? It is true. Don't misunderstand me. I love your sisters and your brother every bit as much. I love Alex more than I could ever express. You were always my light, Dylan. You were first," she told him. "I could never regret my time with your father. In a strange way, it did bring about you. And, if it hadn't been for your biological father, and for all the things I didn't know about back then, I would never have met Alex. That's how I deal with it. I focus on all the people I love."

"And, if I decide to go to college instead? Would you think it was a cop-out?"

"I think you need to make the decision that calls to you," she said.

"What did they do?" he asked. "Grandpa and Alex's father?"

"That's not my story to tell, Dylan. If you want to know that answer, you need to ask your grandfather."

"He won't tell me."

"Not everything," she agreed. "Don't underestimate him. Just be sure you are prepared for the truth. Because one thing I do know; he will not lie to you."

Dylan nodded.

Cassidy spooned some more ice cream into her mouth. "Eat," she handed him his spoon.

"Can I ask you something else?"

"I don't know," Cassidy said. "This is the last half gallon of ice cream I have."

Dylan laughed. "Who were you on the phone with when I came in?"

Cassidy licked her spoon. "Candace."

"You kind of seemed upset."

"And, you thought that it would be a good time to talk about spies?" Cassidy teased him.

"No, I just…"

She laughed. "I wasn't upset—just thinking."

"About what?" he asked.

"Candace wants me to work on the campaign as a speech writer."

"Seriously?"

Cassidy had a mouthful of ice cream. "Why's dat suwrwising?"

Dylan laughed. "Oh, my God, you sounded just like Abby."

"Why is that surprising? Cassidy asked.

"It's not, I guess. Are you going to do it?"

"I don't know. Think I should?"

"Yeah!" Dylan said.

"I don't know," Cassidy shook her head. "I already have my hands full."

"What did Candace say?"

"She said she thought I could find her voice better than most."

"You two are kind of alike," Dylan said.

"You think so?"

"Seriously, Mom? Aunt Jane always says you should have been the one in Congress."

"No, thank you," Cassidy replied.

"I think you should do it."

"We'll see."

Dylan smiled and dug into the ice cream.

"What are you smiling about?" Cassidy asked.

"Nofin," he replied with his mouth full.

"Now, who sounds like Abby?"

"You know, you could write a book," Dylan said.

"You think so?"

"Yeah. You have experience with presidents. Call it *The Spy Wife at The White House*."

Cassidy choked on the ice cream in her mouth she laughed so hard.

"What?" he chuckled. "Sell it as fiction, no one would believe it was true anyway."

Cassidy kept laughing. *That's the truth.*

"I don't like this," Claire said.

"I don't like it either," Alex replied.

Claire moved her flashlight side to side. "Under the barn? What do you want to do? Dig the barn up to see if Brad Lawson is under it?" she asked. Alex made no reply. "Alex?"

"I don't think that will be necessary," Alex said.

Claire turned around and followed the light from Alex's flashlight. "Ugh."

"I think we found our missing landscaper."

"That's under hay, not under the barn."

Alex nodded. "Well, the original rhyme has Little Boy Blue asleep under the hay."

"I remember. What's with the rhymes anyway? You're the profiler."

Alex crouched down beside the body. She cringed. "He's been dead a while."

"Smells like it."

"Claire!"

"What?"

Alex stood back up and took out her phone.

"Who are you calling?"

"Bower. We need a team out here. He needs to know what we found."

"And, how exactly are you going to explain that we were in that house without a warrant?"

"I'll blame you."

Claire chuckled. "That's what I'd do."

"Mom? What's going on?" Michelle Fletcher asked her mother.

Candace smiled. "Relax, Shell. Just sit down."

"Oh, this can't be good. Please tell me you're not quitting the campaign."

"Hardly."

"Then why are you telling me to sit down? Oh, God! You and Jameson decided to have another kid!"

"You have a vivid imagination, Shell."

"Well, what? Someone's sick?"

"Shell!" Candace sniggered. "Take a breath."

"Sorry, too much coffee."

Candace nodded. "Jane's flying in tomorrow."

"Jane Merrow?"

"Yes."

"Are you planning to campaign together?"

"Eventually," Candace said. "She's going to spend a few days at headquarters taking the lead with the press."

"Why? Did I do something that…"

"No," Candace held up her hand. "Hopefully, it's only for a few days. Jed Ritchie is out making the rounds on the morning shows. Having a serial killer on the loose is not helping bolster confidence in me. And, Lawson Klein is happy to help fund Ritchie's crusade."

"You're not the FBI," Michelle pointed out.

"Facts are sometimes less important than optics, Shell. You know that better than most."

"I hate those assholes."

Candace laughed.

"What else?" Michelle wanted to know.

Candace sobered. "Remember when I told you to keep your eye out for anyone that seemed to be lurking?"

"Yeah?"

"No concerns?"

"No lurkers," Michelle replied. "Some new volunteers. No one that has made me suspect anything."

Candace nodded. She made her way over to her desk and retrieved the pictures that Alex had given her. "I need you to let me know immediately if you see either of these men."

Michelle looked at the picture of Brad Lawson first. "Nope." She put it behind the second photo and froze.

"Shell?"

"This is Brad."

"What?" Candace asked.

"This—this picture is of our new volunteer, Brad Lawson."

Candace looked over Michelle's shoulder. "Shell? That's a picture Alex gave me of some man named Jack Carter."

Michelle shook her head. "No, that is Brad Lawson."

Candace grabbed her cell phone.

"Mom? What are you doing?"

"Alex?" Candace began.

"I'm surprised Bower didn't hand you your ass," Claire said.

Alex shrugged. "Bigger fish to fry."

"Think it's him?" Claire asked as they looked on.

"Yeah. Don't you?"

"Yeah, but I wonder what the deal is with that rhyme. You never answered me. What do you think?"

Alex shook her head. "If I were to place a bet, I would say he has some childhood attachment to them. Maybe he had an abuser that used to read them to him. I don't know. It's like a sadistic fantasy."

"But, why Lawson?"

"Good question. Maybe he just needed cover. Maybe Lawson was onto him. The rhyme… It's like his justification."

"Mm."

"What do you think?" Alex asked.

"Me? I'm not the legendary profiler."

"You're every bit as proficient at profiling. Let's hear it," Alex said.

"I just keep thinking about that line he wrote, 'where is that boy who set him free?' That's gotta' mean something."

Alex sighed. *She's right on point.* "The question is what." Alex's cell phone began to ring. She looked at the caller. "Candace?"

"Alex…"

"What's wrong?" Alex asked.

"Shell recognized the photo of Jack Carter as someone who

started volunteering a couple of days ago."

Alex held her breath.

"But, she knows him by the other man's name—Brad Lawson. What's going on?"

Shit. "I'm not totally sure. Is Shell with you?"

"Yes."

"Keep her there."

"What?"

"Candace, if he knows Shell, he might know where she lives. She's secure with you. No one's coming after any of you there."

Candace sighed. "I can't keep her in the dark."

Alex groaned. "I know. I can't get there right now. I'm in the middle of something."

"Alex…"

"Listen, I am going to send someone to you. Don't let Shell or Jameson leave alone."

"Jameson isn't here. She worked late."

Alex groaned. "At her office?"

"Yes. Do you think Jameson is in danger?"

Alex took a deep breath. "Jameson can handle herself," she said. "Just call her and tell her to stay put until someone gets there."

"Someone? Alex…"

"Candace, please—trust me on this one."

"What do you want me to tell Shell?"

"Tell her I will fill her in when I get there."

"You're coming here?"

"As soon as I can. I need to deal with some things where I am first."

"All right. I don't know why, but I feel like I need to tell you to be careful."

"I always am," Alex said. "Shit."

"What's up in Governor land?"

"He's been to Candace's campaign office. Shell recognized

him. We need to look through that house again."

"What do you hope to find?"

"Some idea of where he might be. What he might be driving. I don't like the idea of using anyone as bait."

Claire nodded. "What are we waiting for? Nothing we can do to help him," she gestured to the body.

Alex grimaced. *No, nothing at all.*

"Damnit!" Alex yelled in frustration.

Claire appeared in the small bedroom a moment later. "You okay?"

"There has to be something here. Something of Lawson's—something."

"There's a lot here, Alex," Claire said. "Maybe you need a break."

"I don't have time for a break."

Claire nodded. "They're your friends; I get it."

"What are you talking about?"

"The governor, her family—they're your friends."

"That's not…"

"It's gotten close," Claire said. She shook her head. "It always gets close sooner or later."

"They'll be okay."

"I agree. We know where he is."

"Approximately."

"Alex, unless he knows we are onto him, he's gonna' show up to that campaign office again."

"Maybe."

"You think he knows we're onto him?"

"He will when this hits the news," Alex said.

"What about the governor's daughter?"

Alex snapped to attention. "No way. We are not using Shell as bait."

"You have a better idea?"

Alex shook her head. "Even if I did agree, Candace would never allow it."

"Is she a minor?"

"What?"

"The governor's daughter. Is she a minor?"

"No."

Claire shrugged. "Seems to me it's her call then."

Alex pinched the bridge of her nose.

"Can't you use the governor's spin machine?"

"What?" Alex asked.

"She offered; right? Spin the fact that we don't know who we found out here."

Alex stared at Claire. "He'll want to make a move before we figure it out."

Claire nodded.

"She'll never go for it," Alex said.

"Alex, it's our best chance to end this."

Alex sighed nervously. "Yeah. That doesn't mean I have to like it."

Claire nodded. "If things were the way we liked, we wouldn't have jobs."

Alex looked at Claire for a moment. *Right again.* "I wish there was another way." She groaned. "He left just enough breadcrumbs. Just enough to put us on his scent. Not enough to lead us home."

"But he has," Claire said.

Alex nodded.

"You want me to drive?" Claire asked.

Alex shook her head. "Keep looking here. I'll talk to the governor."

"Good luck with that."

"I think I'm going to need a lot more than luck."

"Absolutely not!" Candace raised her voice.

"Candace, just listen," Alex implored the governor.

"Mom," Michelle pleaded for her mother's attention.

"You want to use Shell to lure this sadistic son of a bitch? You've lost your mind."

Alex shook her head. "We have a window."

"You know what he looks like. Arrest him!"

"We have a warrant out. We've notified law enforcement of the Crow Electrical vans and their plate numbers. Nothing. There's been nothing, Candace."

"You said he's close to the airport," Candace said.

"I did—within twenty miles. There's no record of Brad Lawson or Jack Carter owning or renting property here. We tried pinging the phone. He's not using the numbers that either Jack Carter's wife or Brad Lawson's receptionist gave us—nothing, Candace. He's a serial killer. Serial killers are sadistic. They are not stupid."

"I don't need a lesson," Candace bit. "I'm well-aware of the intellect he likely possesses. That in no way engenders confidence in this idea you have."

"Let me do it," Jameson chimed. All eyes turned to her.

"What?" Candace asked her wife. "Let you do what?"

"Shell said she told this guy I might have some work for him. Let me offer him something."

"Are you insane?" Candace asked.

Jameson shook her head. "It would get him away, Candace. Marianne is leaving for Scott's tomorrow morning. I can come up with some project to do at the house."

Candace stared at her wife in disbelief. "I'm not risking you either."

Jameson nodded. "Can we have a moment please?"

Alex looked at Shell.

"That means get out now," Shell said. "Coffee?" she asked Alex. Alex nodded.

Jameson waited for the door to close.

"No," Candace said. "It's too risky."

"Alex is not going to let anything happen to me. Besides, I can take care of myself."

"Jameson…"

"Candace, you know that I'm right. You heard Alex. There are at least thirty victims if she's right. If I can help; I have to."

Candace sucked in a shaky breath.

"I know that house like I know you," Jameson said. "I've been in every nook and cranny. Alex will be able to put people close without him knowing. It's their best chance to end this without anyone else getting hurt."

Candace closed her eyes. "I don't have to like it."

Jameson moved to her wife. She pulled Candace close. "I'll be fine. Just think how much it'll piss off Jed Ritchie."

Candace chuckled nervously. "Promise me that you will do whatever Alex says."

"I promise."

"I mean it, Jameson."

"I promise. Now, let's go talk to Alex. And, Candace?"

"What?"

"This is not her fault. Don't put this on her. Alex is just…"

"I know."

"Alex? You sound out of breath. Are you okay?"

"Just tired."

"Did you just finish your morning run?"

"No."

"What happened?"

Alex closed her eyes. "If all goes as planned, I'll be home tomorrow."

Cassidy shivered. "Alex, what aren't you telling me?"

"A lot," she said. "But I promise I will tell you everything when I get home."

"Are you still at Jameson's condo?"

"Just got back here a few minutes ago."

"Are you telling me that you haven't slept? It's seven-thirty in the morning."

"No. Some things came up."

Cassidy sat down in a chair at the kitchen table. "Did you find him?"

"We found him. We just haven't apprehended him yet."

"I don't understand."

"I know. I'll fill you in when I get home. I just wanted to hear your voice."

Cassidy closed her eyes. She didn't need any details. Whatever had transpired since they had last spoken, whatever Alex suspected was about to unfold, it was weighing on Alex's mind. "Just be careful."

"Always."

"Let me know when you'll be home. I'll make tacos."

"Yeah? Do I get ice cream for dessert?"

Cassidy laughed even as a few tears rolled over her cheeks. "Vanilla," she replied.

"Perfect. I'll see you tomorrow."

"I'll be here."

"I love you, Cassidy."

Cassidy felt a weight on her chest she had not experienced in years. "Je t'adore," she promised.

"French," Alex commented. "See you tomorrow."

Cassidy set her phone down and put her face in her hands. *Whoever is listening, please keep her safe.*

CHAPTER TWENTY

"Overnight, Connecticut State Police made a grisly discovery—not far from where the bodies of seven women were found buried just over a week ago. Sources say the remains of an unidentified male was found in the barn of a vacant property nearby. Investigators are working to piece together the puzzle of how the man ended up there," a reporter said.

The morning news anchor threw him a question. "Is this related to the other victims?" she said

"Difficult to say. We have seen an FBI presence here, but that doesn't necessarily mean they suspect the two are related. My sources say that until they determine the identity and cause of death; it's unclear if this individual met with foul play at all."

"So, it could be an accident?" the anchor inquired.

"At this point, they are not ruling any possibilities out."

Candace looked at her press secretary. "I hope that works."

Dana nodded. "It's the truth," she said. "All I did was make certain it filtered down that way."

Candace shook her head. "I wish to God it *was* the truth."

Dana regarded her boss thoughtfully for a moment. Candace prided herself on honesty, even when it was uncomfortable. There were times when politics required artful spin. Reality existed in perception. It was Dana's job to shift perception in Candace's favor. "Candy, you heard Alex. She suspects it's this Brad Lawson person. They don't know anything yet. It was the truth."

"Truth is a funny thing sometimes, Dana. They say it sets you free. Sometimes, it just bites you on the ass. Let's hope we don't have to deal with the latter on this one."

He sipped his cup of coffee as he listened to the local morning news. He hummed a note and began his verse. "Badly Bradley, with the girls he tried, I told him to wait until they cried; But when the girls screamed his name, Badly Bradley ran away." He sighed and then laughed. "Oh well." He stood and placed his coffee cup in the sink, flipped off the small television and made his way to the bathroom. "Well, Bradley," he looked at his reflection. He turned on the water and splashed his face. He reached for the towel draped over a nearby bar and dried his face before looking back in the mirror. "Hickory dickory dock, the cops are on the clock," he said. "Before the clock strikes one, you'd better finish what you've begun." He grinned. "Hickory dickory dock."

"Are you sure that you're ready for this?" Alex asked Michelle.

"I think so."

"All you have to do when he shows up is smile and tell him that Jameson is looking for some last-minute help. Jane will be here in less than an hour. She'll give you cover if you need it; okay?"

"What if he doesn't show up?" Michelle asked.

Alex forced herself to smile. "Then we go to plan B."

"Is there a Plan B?"

"There's always a Plan B. Listen, Shell… Agent Robbins and Agent Johnson are here. They know how to blend in, just like Jane knows how to work this."

"What about you and JD?" Michelle asked. "If he goes to the house…"

"I can take care of myself," Alex assured her. "Jameson can handle this. Claire will be close to her the whole time without him knowing. There'll be a small invisible army ready to take him down.

Trust me; I have no intention of pissing off your mom."

Michelle chuckled nervously. "Did you try the address he listed?"

"It doesn't exist," Alex said. "Sorry, Shell. That would've been the easy way."

"And, Plan B?"

"Not for you to worry about," Alex said. "I'll see you later." Alex made her way to Agent Robbins. "Claire gave you the green light," she said.

"But you have your doubts."

"This isn't a chance for you to make a name for yourself," Alex said. "It's your responsibility to give me ears, and to keep Michelle steady if needed. That's it."

"I got it."

"Make sure you do, Robbins. You and Johnson aren't the only eyes I have in this office," she warned him. With a deep breath, Alex turned and walked out the door. *Please let this work.*

Cassidy shook her head and laughed at Abby and Connor as they ran through the backyard.

"They certainly have a lot of energy," Helen Toles observed.

"That, they do."

"You seem a little quiet today," Helen said. "Anything wrong?"

"No," Cassidy lied.

"You're a horrible liar, just like Alexis."

A deep sigh preceded Cassidy's response. "I think Alex and Claire are planning to try and apprehend someone today."

"She told you that?"

"More or less. She called early this morning right before I took Kenzie to school."

"I don't need to tell you that Alexis and Claire can handle themselves, and likely anyone else they encounter."

"No, you don't," Cassidy replied. "That doesn't make the waiting easier."

"You're not used to her being away so much."

"No, I'm not," Cassidy admitted. "To be honest, it's been much harder than I thought it would be this time."

"I understand."

"I miss her."

Helen patted Cassidy's knee. "You're not the only one," she said. "We all do. Are you regretting that she went back to the FBI?"

Cassidy shook her head. "No."

"But?"

"I suppose I got used to our life the way it's been; Alex coming home in the evening, marching off to soccer games and track meets together. It's selfish of me; I know it is. Sometimes, I wish it could be that way forever."

"Mm. It's not selfish," Helen disagreed. "Selfish would be holding her back."

Cassidy sighed. "Dylan asked me about what Alex used to do."

"You mean at Carecom?"

Cassidy shook her head. "At the CIA. He overheard you and mom talking about Dad and Nicolas."

"What did he hear?"

"He didn't say—enough to ask questions and draw some conclusions."

"What did you tell him?"

"The truth, just not all of it."

"That's what has you worried."

"Not worried. Sometimes, I wish our lives were less complicated."

Helen laughed. "I'm sorry," she said. "I'm not laughing at you. I've had that same thought so many times over the years."

"Really?"

"God, yes and God, forgive me, sometimes I look at Nicky and Barb and I envy their innocence."

"Nick must have some idea about his father and Alex, particularly with Jonathan in the equation."

Helen smiled. "Oh, I'm sure he does. He's never asked and I've never offered details."

"Neither has Alex."

"Sometimes, I envy their world, Cassidy—only sometimes. I loved Nicolas for who he was. I love Alexis for who she is. I would never want to change Nicky or his world. But, I wouldn't want to live in it either."

"No?"

"Would you? Honestly? I don't know. I used to think I didn't agree with the decisions Nicolas and Alexis made."

"And now?"

"Someone has to make those decisions. Someone has to be willing to take those chances. Don't get me wrong; I'm sure I would have issues with many things they've done. I know they both made their choices for the right reasons. I wish the life they chose wouldn't come with so much pain at times, but pain comes in its own time anyway."

"Yes, it does," Cassidy agreed.

"I guess, I prefer seeing the world as the messy place it is. Maybe that's because that's all I've ever known. It isn't better from where I sit, but it is colorful," Helen laughed. "It isn't selfish to look at the grass on the other side of the fence and envy it every so often. We all do it. The important thing is that you tend the lawn on your side, and remember to appreciate it." She chuckled. "Even if it is full of weeds from time to time."

Cassidy smiled and looked back over at her children. She was grateful to have Helen Toles in her life. Having Helen in the family had meant the world to Alex. Helen's presence had strengthened their family. In many ways, Cassidy saw her mother-in-law as the glue that held them all together. While Cassidy adored her mother, over the years, she had often confided her deepest fears in the woman beside her. She was worried about Alex. She was concerned about Dylan. She still had moments when she struggled to connect with her father. Helen provided both stability and solace for Cassidy. She was like a mother, but more than that, she was a friend.

"I'm glad that you are here today," Cassidy said.

"Why? Think I can get those two under control?"

"If anyone can, Mom—it's you."

"True," Helen agreed. "Alex and Claire will be fine," Helen said. "Neither of them will want to miss out on the chance to drive the other crazy."

Cassidy laughed. "You caught that too, huh?"

"They're more alike than they think," Helen observed candidly.

"Yes, they are."

"And, neither wants to endure your wrath," Helen joked.

"True."

"YaYa!" Abby ran over.

"Yes, my pumpkin?" Helen addressed her granddaughter.

Abby put her hand on Cassidy's stomach. "Kenzie says we get anudder sister."

"Oh, did she?" Cassidy asked.

"Yep!" Connor called from behind his sister.

"And, what makes Mackenzie think you will have another sister?" Cassidy wondered.

"'Cause, she knows stuff," Connor explained.

Cassidy raised her brow. "Is that so?"

"She's smart, Mommy," Abby said.

Helen had to hide her face. Mackenzie was, without any doubt, the most precocious of her grandchildren. She suspected that Connor might give his parents a run for their money in time as well, but she kept that suspicion to herself.

"Well," Cassidy said. "What if you have another brother?"

"Nope," Abby replied.

"No?" Cassidy questioned.

Connor shook his head. "This is a house of women," he said seriously.

Cassidy's jaw dropped at the statement.

Connor shrugged. "Kenzie says so," he explained with a grin. He grabbed his sister's hand and pulled her along toward the tire swing.

Helen burst out laughing. Cassidy shook her head and laughed along. "Where does she come up with this stuff?" Cassidy wondered.

"She's creative," Helen said.

"That's one way to describe it."

"Oh, she has a lot of you in there," Helen said. "I know she's a lot like Alexis. She is, but she's articulate beyond her years. That, I think, she gets from you."

"I'm not sure I'd say that."

"I would," Helen said. "Have you thought any more about writing?"

Cassidy sighed.

"You used to talk about writing a book. Why don't you?"

"Funny you should bring that up."

"Oh?"

Cassidy smiled. "Candace asked me if I'd consider working as a speech writer for her."

"You should!"

"I don't know," Cassidy shook her head. "I've never done anything like that."

"What do you mean? You campaigned for years for Christopher."

"I did, but…"

"Did someone else write your speeches?"

"No," Cassidy said. "I had input, but no."

"Uh-huh."

"This is different," Cassidy said. "Candace is on the world stage. She deserves the best people on her team."

"Seems to me that's what she's asked for."

Cassidy chuckled. "There are people far better qualified than me."

"Really?"

"Yes."

Helen shrugged. "Well, I don't know Candace Reid well, but she seems to me like someone who knows how to discern talent."

Cassidy sighed.

"Do you respect her?"

"Candace?"

"Yes," Helen replied. "Do you respect her?"

"Completely," Cassidy said. "She's one of the most intelligent and thoughtful people I know."

"Oh…"

"Oh, just say it."

Helen looked at Cassidy. "Then I suppose she would be intelligent and thoughtful enough to know you might be able to help her."

"I don't know."

"What is it?" Helen wanted to know. "Would you have to travel?"

"No."

"Okay. So, is this because you're afraid you won't be successful or is it because you're afraid you might love it too much?"

"I…."

Helen nodded. "I know you, Cassidy—as well as I know my daughter, I think. You can love this family and support them and still have something for yourself."

Cassidy sighed.

"It's your decision. Don't regret not trying," Helen advised.

"You think I should accept."

"I think you want to. I think it's something you can do that is completely for you, and I think maybe you need that now more than ever."

Cassidy reached across the short distance and squeezed her mother-in-law's hand. "Thank you."

"Cassidy, you already know what I am about to say, but I'm going to tell you anyway. I know that your mother and I tease you and Alexis endlessly. You'll learn as the kids grow that it is part of claiming playful parental revenge," she winked. "But don't ever doubt that I love you every bit as much as I love Alexis, and I know that your mother feels the same way about my daughter as she does about you. We have a different vantage point than either of you do. We watched you grow up. And, one thing I do know, Alexis was floundering until she found you—not in her career, but in herself."

"She's not the only one."

"Mm. I know that," Helen said. "Some people just fit. They are meant to find each other. That doesn't happen for everyone. There's a big difference between loving someone and living your life with them. You can love and never be able to live with a person. You can live with a person most of your life and never be in love with them. I've seen both. The thing about loving someone the way you love Alexis is that you can sometimes forget that they love you just as much. Don't give up yourself, Cassidy. I did that for too many years. As much as I love my children, and as much as I loved their father; I forgot that there was a me behind it all for a long time. I know you love your children. I know how much you love Alexis. One day, your children will need you differently, and unfortunately, one day you might be parenting them at a distance without Alexis by your side. I hope that day is a long, long time from now, but no one knows better than me that the day will come for one of you. Alexis has always had something outside this home to fall back on. You need that too."

Cassidy's teeth tugged at her bottom lip in a futile effort to stem her emotions. Nothing in the world meant more to her than her family. That was the truth. Still, Helen's words reverberated in her chest. She did need something to fall back on, something to remind her from time to time that she was not just Mom or Alex's wife or someone's daughter. "Sometimes, I worry I've forgotten how."

Helen smiled. "How to be just Cassidy?"

Cassidy nodded.

"Oh, I think you'll find she is right where she's always been," Helen said. "I realized the day Alexis brought you home that I had let myself slip away somehow. You're not me. You're much stronger."

"I don't think…"

"You are," Helen said. "Alexis has always been one to look for a challenge to master."

Cassidy chuckled.

"This family is no exception," Helen added.

Cassidy laughed.

"That's been her nature since the moment she came into the world. Yours is not the same. You're a guide," Helen observed. "That's what teachers do in the end. That's what parents do in the end. They learn how to communicate in a way that others understand. It allows them to nurture. That's you."

"Maybe you should have been a teacher," Cassidy said.

"Me? No. I'm a cook. I feed people."

Cassidy rolled her eyes. "You're a lot more than a cook."

"The truth is, Cassidy, I'm not sure what I was meant to be. I spent so long away from myself, I lost sight of it. I know you don't think that's what you're doing. You need something for you. Don't deny yourself that."

Cassidy leaned over and kissed Helen on the cheek. She sat back and enjoyed watching the twins for a few minutes as she processed her mother-in-law's thoughts. "You know," she said.

Helen looked over at her. Cassidy's eyes remained focused on Abby and Connor. "My kids aren't the only ones who were lucky enough to get two moms." She smiled and looked at Helen. "I think you're wrong."

Helen was stunned.

"You are a teacher. I see what you can't. I have a different vantage point," she winked and turned her attention back to the playful children skipping through the yard. She'd noted tears were gathering in Helen's eyes. Without a word, Cassidy reached over and took the older woman's hand, content to sit in companionable silence.

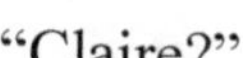

"Claire?"

"Yeah, I'm here."

"How's Jameson holding up?" Alex asked.

"Seems okay to me."

Claire's response didn't surprise Alex. Jameson Reid grew up in a law enforcement family. She had two brothers, which meant she could hold her own physically, and Alex had learned from their visits that Jameson possessed a quiet confidence.

"I take it he hasn't shown yet?" Claire guessed. She heard Alex sigh. "He will."

"Unless he got spooked."

"Nah. He's probably playing Patty Cake in his basement by himself," Claire replied. "Give him time. He'll show."

"I hope so."

"Hey," Claire softened her tone. "He'll show. You said it yourself; he can't resist. Besides, did you see that piece on the news this morning? I'll bet he did. He's coming, Alex."

"Just stick close to Jameson."

"I think I might worry about him more than JD."

"JD?" Alex asked.

"That's her name; right?"

"You like her," Alex surmised.

"She's real," Claire said honestly. "And, she's no pushover, Alex. Pretty sure she could do what we do if she wanted."

"Probably so," Alex agreed.

"Even without us, he'd be getting more than he bargained for with her."

Alex snickered. *Probably so.*

"You just make sure you don't tip his ass off following him here."

"You want first crack, huh?"

"You have no idea," Claire said.

"I'll let you know," Alex promised.

"I'll be waiting for your call," Claire replied sweetly.

"Fuck you, Brackett."

"So much fucking with you, Toles. No wonder Cass is pregnant every time I see you."

Alex laughed. "Goodbye, Claire."

Claire placed her phone in her pocket and laughed. "She is so easy."

"Nothing yet?" Jameson asked.

"Nope. He'll be there."

Jameson nodded.

"You know, your wife is going to kick your ass when she finds out how close you're letting him get," Claire said.

"No, she won't. Well, maybe a little," Jameson laughed.

"You seem calm. It's not every day you let a serial killer into your home."

"I guess not," Jameson replied. "I heard what Alex said. If he makes the move toward me, if he starts to chatter; it gives you even more to nail his ass to the wall. That's if I don't pull out my nail gun and beat you to it."

Claire grinned. "You're not as mild-mannered as people think; are you?"

Jameson shrugged. "I am as long as you don't hurt someone I love."

Claire nodded. She looked around the kitchen. "Big kitchen."

"Big family," Jameson replied.

"How come you offered?" Claire asked curiously. "To do this; I mean?"

"Shell is Candace's daughter," Jameson replied. "That makes her my daughter—as strange as that might seem to some people."

"Nah, I've seen strange," Claire said. "That ain't it."

"I can only imagine. You? Why do you do this?" Jameson asked.

"Don't know if I can answer that. It's just kind of the thing I always seemed destined to do."

"Catch criminals?"

Claire laughed. "More like find a way to cause trouble without going to jail."

"Married?" Jameson asked.

"Me? No."

"Really?"

"Do I seem like the marrying kind?" Claire asked.

"Is there a kind?"

"If there is, it isn't me."

Jameson nodded and turned to start a pot of coffee.

"Oh, no. Alex does that all the time," Claire said.

"Alex does what?"

"Nods her head and goes to do something else when she thinks I'm nuts."

"Does that happen often?" Jameson asked.

"Pretty much."

"I don't think you're crazy."

"You don't?" Claire asked.

"No. I swore I'd never get married."

"What changed?"

"Candace."

Claire chuckled. "Just like that?"

"I don't know," Jameson said. "Coffee? I'd prefer a beer, but something tells me that's frowned upon."

"Got any?" Claire asked.

"Beer?"

"Yeah."

"In the fridge."

Claire made her way to the refrigerator and pulled out two bottles. "Pour that shit out," she gestured to the coffee cup in Jameson's hand. "Tell me you can hold one?"

"I think I mastered that in the ninth grade."

"Good." Claire popped off the caps with a key and handed Jameson a beer. "Now, if we both survive this nightmare nursery rhyme, I will buy you a shot to celebrate."

"And, if we don't?"

Claire held up her beer and clicked it against Jameson's. "We will."

"You sound sure."

"Hell, serial killers are nothing compared to marriage."

Jameson lifted her beer. "Here's to survival mode."

"Is that what you call it?"

"What?" Jameson asked.

"Marriage," Claire said.

Jameson laughed. "Something tells me we'll need more than this for that conversation."

Claire shrugged and took a pull from her beer. *Definitely.*

Alex sat in the back office at Candace's Campaign

Headquarters nervously drumming her fingers on the desk.

"Should I know that tune?" Jane Merrow asked when she walked in.

"You're here."

"In the flesh," Jane replied.

"Thanks."

Jane nodded. "Always happy to help."

"Does that mean me or Candace?"

"Both," Jane said. "I am curious, Alex; why not just arrest him here?"

Alex groaned. "There's more than one reason," Alex said.

"Enlighten me."

"You have to promise not to tell Candace."

Jane nodded. "Let me guess; the powers above don't want a take-down of a serial killer in her campaign office."

"Something like that."

"I figured as much. What else?"

"The best evidence we have against this guy is what we found in that house yesterday. If that body is Brad Lawson—between that and the trophy case in the basement it's a pile of circumstantial evidence."

"And, that's the problem, I gather."

Alex shrugged. "You know the drill, Jane. This isn't the CIA. The FBI still operates in the courts and the court of public opinion. It's just as political as what we did together. The difference is the outcomes end in a court of law. Juries like forensic evidence. I've got nothing in that department but hope."

"Explain."

Alex sighed. "Well, Claire and I collected a few things in that house we think are likely to have the killer's DNA on them. The best possibility was a Coke can in the basement. Just so happens we have a few soda cans from a place we think he frequented—a place where he could visit his burial plots undetected. It's a long shot. If there is

DNA from the can in that house that matches even one of those cans we found in the woods…"

"And, if that matches this person you expect will show up here, you'll have some compelling evidence."

Alex nodded.

"And?" Jane asked.

"Well, if we get him on tape making a play or even some type of backhanded confession…"

"Oh, Alex."

"I know. I hate this. This office has people coming and going all day. It's a risk to pursue him here. This plan is the best chance to get him without having anyone else compromised."

"Including Candace."

"Yeah," Alex admitted.

"What about Jameson?" Jane asked.

"Claire's with her."

"Whose decision was that?" Jane inquired.

"Mine."

"Is that so?"

Alex groaned. "She won't let Jameson get hurt, Jane and she won't let this asshole slip past us either."

"You don't need to convince me," Jane said. "I've been at this a long time, Alex. I've seen this from both sides of the street—if you know what I mean."

"I do. So, why the questions?"

Jane smiled. "Based on that drumming and the expression on your face when I walked in here, you needed to hear yourself say that. It's not me, Alex—it's not Candace or Jameson, or Claire or anyone of the agents out in that office behind us that need to trust you—it's you."

Alex sighed and began to massage her temples. "There are risks. We both know it."

"There are always risks, Alex. You know that better than

anyone."

"Thanks. That makes me feel so much better," Alex rolled her eyes.

"You're welcome."

"Remind me not to call you when I need a confidence boost."

Jane laughed. "If you didn't think this was the right course, we wouldn't be standing here. Stop second-guessing yourself. Doing that will only increase the risk to everyone."

Jane was on point. Alex was about to continue the conversation when the door opened.

"He's in the parking lot," Agent Robbins said.

Alex nodded. Alex looked at Jane. "Showtime," she said.

CHAPTER TWENTY-ONE

Michelle took a deep breath.

Agent Robbins whispered in her ear. "Relax," he tried to calm her. "If he senses you are nervous, play it off as Jane Merrow being here today."

Michelle looked at the agent beside her and smiled. "Thanks."

Robbins nodded and stepped away, heading back to where a coffee maker was kept. It would give him a line of sight to the suspect and Michelle.

Michelle moved to a large bulletin board and began pinning volunteer names to it.

"Hi," a voice called to her.

Michelle turned and met the gaze of the man she knew as Brad Lawson. "Hey. I'm glad you are here."

"Really?" he asked.

Michelle smiled and finished pinning a cut-out to the board. *You can do this, Shell. Just like it was yesterday.* She stepped up to him. "I was hoping you'd show. I looked to find your number, but we don't seem to have one here for you."

"Yeah, I sort of dropped my cell phone a few days back. I need to replace it."

Michelle nodded.

"You were going to call me? Need somebody to change a lightbulb again or clean a chimney?" he asked.

"Close," Michelle said. She reached into her pocket. "I mentioned you to JD..."

Alex watched and listened carefully to the conversation taking place in the other room. She smiled. "She's good," Alex said.

Jane stood over her shoulder watching the scene unfold. "She has a future."

"In the FBI?" Alex asked without diverting her eyes from the screen in front of her.

"No."

"Always recruiting," Alex commented. "Bring it home, Shell. Bring it home."

"Your step-mother?" Brad asked.

"Yeah. She called me early this morning. Wondered if you had any carpentry skills."

"I can handle a saw."

Michelle forced herself not to shiver. "I don't have any idea what she's up to. My sister and her kids took off for the weekend. I guess that gave JD the bright idea to bite off more than she can chew with some project," she laughed.

He tipped his head.

"Her number is on that card," Michelle explained. "If you're interested. I hate to lose you, but she pays better," Michelle joked.

Alex chuckled. "She pays better? Nice, Shell."

"What do you think?" Jane asked.

"If he doesn't take the bait, we take him. I'm not risking losing him again."

Jane nodded.

"Did you get that Robbins?" Alex asked.

Agent Robbins picked up the phone on the table in front of him and answered Alex. "Understood."

"Lots of people here today," Brad commented.

"Oh, yeah," Michelle glanced around the office.

"Sudden surge?" he asked.

"No, just sort of happens when someone is occupying the back office," she gestured with a nod.

He brightened. "Your mother?"

"No," Michelle shook her head. "Safe to say she's tied up at the Capitol."

He grinned. *Tied up?*

"Jane Merrow is fielding some press calls and meetings today."

"You're kidding?"

"Nope. She's good friends with my mom."

"Huh."

"Like I said," Michelle continued. "I'd love you to stay and help me manage all the excitement, but JD pays better. In other words, she pays money, not just bad coffee."

He smiled. "She doesn't have a crew?"

"JD?" Michelle laughed. "JD likes to do everything herself. She should build herself a doghouse for the trouble it gets her in."

He chuckled. *Oh, I'm sure we can arrange that.* "I'll give her a call."

"Bingo," Alex commented. "Robbins, I'm on my way to the car. Johnson, you have the make on his?"

"Yep, he arrived in a 2012 Toyota Camry—black. License plate, 203 XDG Connecticut. It's registered to a Jennifer Benjamin."

"Son of a bitch!" Alex replied. "Smart bastard. It's registered under his wife's maiden name." She picked up her jacket and headed for the back door.

"Be careful, Alex," Jane said.

Alex nodded. "Keep an eye out in case he circles back," Alex said. "Robbins will be here. Johnson and I will tail him to Schoharie."

"Just be careful," Jane repeated.

"I promise."

Jameson picked up the phone. "Hello?"

"Um, hi. Shell gave me your number. We met briefly the other night…"

"Oh yeah, Brad; right?"

"Yeah. She mentioned you might need some help with something."

"I could. I seem to have taken on a little more than I bargained for."

"What kind of project?"

"Well, it's supposed to be a surprise. Our grandson and our son have taken to building forts all over the house," Jameson explained. "I started the framework—a fort of sorts, but I think I might have been too ambitious for a weekend project. Candace's daughter will be back Sunday, and if I leave a mess, I'll probably be forced to live in the little shack I've yet to finish."

Brad chuckled. "What kind of help do you need?"

"I have a lot of wood out in the old barn. Someone to help me carry it out here. "I've done most of the cutting. It's the piecing together that seems to be tripping me up. Two hands and two feet aren't fast enough. I called my cousin. Seems he's tied up with another project. If you're interested, Shell can give you the address. It's about a forty-five-minute ride from there; well, unless you drive like Shell. Then it's half an hour."

"You need help today?" he asked.

"I needed help yesterday if you ask my wife," Jameson said. "The sooner, the better. I'm happy to kick a couple of hundred bucks your way if you have the time."

Brad smiled. "Sure, I have plenty of time."

"Great. Shell will give you directions," Jameson said. "I'd better get back to it."

"Sure. I'll head your way shortly."

"Sounds good," Jameson said.

Claire smiled. "Shit, you almost made me believe you were building a fort."

Jameson moved to the back door and opened it. She pointed a short distance away.

"Holy shit," Claire said.

"I figured it'd be better to have something when he arrived."

"When the hell did you do that?" Claire wondered.

"I got here at about six this morning and started."

"By yourself?"

Jameson chuckled. "You might have given me an excuse to start something I've been meaning to."

Claire shook her head. Jameson had framed out what looked to be a play castle not far from the back of the house. "You did that in less than six hours?"

"Been doing it a long time."

"We need to meet with the team and position them."

Jameson nodded. "Like I said, I know every nook and cranny on this property."

"Good," Claire said. "I looked at your drawing. I've got some ideas. You're the expert. We've got less than an hour and fifteen people to position. Let's take the tour."

Alex pulled her car over and let the Toyota Camry make its final turn out of her sight,

She pulled out her phone. "He's coming to you now," she said.

"Understood," Claire replied. "We're ready," she promised.

"As we planned?" Alex asked.

"Better," Claire replied. "Jameson really does know every inch of this place. Upstairs in her son's room," she told Alex. "Corrigan is up there, Alex. Everything is set up. You should have eyes and ears the whole time."

"Is Jameson wearing a wire?"

"Yeah. Not easy to place in that tank top," Claire chuckled.

Alex rolled her eyes. "You're both taken."

"Yeah, doesn't mean I didn't enjoy it."

Alex chuckled. She appreciated Claire's moment of levity.

"Be careful," Alex said.

"Worried about me?" Claire asked lightly.

Alex sobered. "I'd like to keep my partner around."

Claire closed her eyes for a second. *Me too.* "You too," she said.

Alex hung up the call.

"You okay, Toles?" Agent Johnson asked.

Alex nodded and began to pull the car back on the road. "Just realizing something," she said. *Be careful, Claire.*

Jameson wiped some sweat from her brow and started to make her way toward the car pulling up the driveway.

Claire watched from her position in the top of the barn. *Just be cool, JD.*

"Hey," Jameson waved. Brad stepped out of the car. "Thanks for making the drive."

"Thanks for the chance to make a few bucks."

"Believe me; it's well-worth the investment."

"Pretty hot out today for May, huh?" he commented. His eyes raked over Jameson's body.

Jameson smiled despite feeling her stomach roil. *Gross.* "It is."

"So, you want to show me what you've got?" he asked.

Claire rolled her eyes as Jameson's conversation unfolded in her ear. "And, people call me obvious?"

"You are," Alex's voice came over the com. "You're also crude."

"Nice of you to join us, Agent Toles," Claire said.

"Thanks for the invitation. How's your view?" Alex asked.

"From up here, I can see everything out there."

"Good. What's Jameson's plan?" Alex asked. She watched the computer screen in front of her as Jameson led their suspect to the backyard.

"She'll get him working a bit. Hot day—cold beer."

"She's going to bring him in the kitchen?" Alex asked.

"Nope. Too confined. She'll bring him to me."

Alex sighed. *The barn—good plan, Claire.* "Good plan, Brackett."

"I know."

Alex snickered. "Going silent until he moves."

"Understood. Buy you one of Jameson's beers later," Claire said.

Alex smiled. "You're on."

"Any news?" Candace asked.

"He's at the house," Jane told her over the line. "That's all I know."

Candace sighed.

"They'll be okay, Candace."

"I believe you. For some reason, I still feel sick."

Jane understood that emotion. She had felt it more than once as a military wife, a First Lady, and as a CIA operative. She did believe that today's outcome would find everyone they cared about returning home safely. She also knew that didn't mean they would return unscathed.

"Hang in there, Governor. This will pale by comparison one day."

"Not a ringing endorsement for the job I'm applying for," Candace quipped.

Jane laughed. "You're the fool who put in the application."

"Thanks."

"Any time, Madame President."

Candace snickered. "From your lips to the Republicans ears."

"One can hope. Try and relax. I'll bet the next call you get is from Jameson."

"I hope so."

"How old are these kids?"

Jameson laughed. "Four and five; why?"

"Big playhouse."

"They won't stay four and five," she pointed out.

He heaved a long 2x4 onto a pile and wiped the sweat from his face with the back of his hand. "Right, but don't you think they'll outgrow it?"

Jameson finished nailing two boards together and leaned against the structure. "Maybe. I don't know. I thought I'd outgrown castles and nursery rhymes."

Alex sat up. "Holy shit! She's baiting him."

He cocked his head slightly. "You thought you outgrew them?"

"Yeah," Jameson said. "Until I started reading them to the kids. I don't know; it brought back lots of memories, I guess." She looked at the frame of her creation. "Sometimes, I would finish reading to one of the kids or I'd hear Candace reading to them and I'd find myself remembering my mother doing the same thing with me. Funny."

"What's that?" he asked.

"I thought I'd forgotten all the words and stories; you know?" Jameson said. "Spencer, our grandson—he loves *Old King Cole*." She laughed. "Maybe that's why I wanted to build this. He's four. He and my son are always making up some story about a castle. I think he wants to be Old King Cole," she explained.

Claire grinned. Jameson had told her the same story while Claire got her set up with a microphone. Claire had suggested looking for the opening to tell Brad or Jack or whoever the hell this guy really was the tale. *Perfect, JD—perfect.*

He shrugged.

"What? Not a fan of *Old King Cole?*" Jameson asked. She directed him to help her hold another board in place while she fastened it.

"A merry old soul?" he laughed.

"That's what they say," Jameson said as she hammered a nail in.

"And his fiddlers three," he said. "Not every nursery rhyme is a fairy tale," he told her.

"Don't like fairy tales either?" she asked.

"I love fairy tales. They seldom have the ending you see in a movie."

"Oh, I don't know," Jameson replied. "Mine has had a pretty happy ending." She moved to fasten the other end of the board. "To tell you the truth, I feel a bit like Old King Cole a lot of the time, emphasis on the old—and the merry," she said. She finished her task and looked at him. "Thanks. It is hot. I think I could use something cold. You? I have some beer in the barn if you're interested."

"Did King Cole drink on the job?" he asked.

"If I am him—yes," Jameson replied.

He nodded.

Jameson removed her tool belt and directed him to follow her. She had made it her mission to focus on the project at hand. For Jameson, that was building the playhouse. It allowed her to fall into a groove with the man beside her. Now, as they approached their appointed destination, Jameson began to feel the gravity of the situation pressing in. This man was not an extra hand or a comrade. He was a killer; a killer who was likely setting her in his crosshairs as they walked.

Claire watched as Jameson's gait slowed slightly. "You've got this, JD. Keep going. Just get him in the barn."

Alex listened as Claire mused aloud. It was evident that Claire and Jameson had spent time talking. Alex had noticed Jameson's pace slow as well on the screen. She could only see Jameson's back now, at least, until Jameson entered the barn. She suspected Claire could see Jameson's expression as well. There would have been no safe way to give Jameson ears. They could hear and see her every move; Jameson was deaf and blind. She had to trust that Alex and Claire were prepared. "I wish she could hear us."

Claire sighed. "She knows we're here. Time for you to move closer, Toles."

"I won't have eyes," Alex said.

"I'll be your eyes," Claire promised.

Alex looked at Jill Corrigan. She nodded. "Go," she told Alex.

"It's Claire's call," Alex said. She could almost hear the gasp of surprise of everyone listening. "She says when to move and where. Not before her direction."

Corrigan nodded. "That's you, Agent Brackett."

Claire took a deep breath. Alex's words meant one thing—she

trusted Claire. "Understood," Claire said. "On my call."

Jameson opened the cooler that she had placed in the barn and handed her helper a beer.

"Thanks," he said.

Jameson took a seat on a pile of wood. "You think my King Cole story is silly."

He took a long pull from the beer in his hand and looked at the bottle. "No," he said. "I'm a bit more like Simple Simon."

Claire moved carefully toward the ladder she had pulled up to the upper level of the barn. She sprawled out flat, looking through a crack between boards at the figures below. *"Stay steady, JD. He's following those breadcrumbs we talked about.*

"Simple Simon the pie man?" Jameson chuckled before taking a sip from her beer.

He grinned. "Simple Simon wasn't the pie man," he told her. "He met the pie man going to the fair."

Jameson nodded. "And, that's you?"

"No. Later Simple Simon goes fishing," he said.

"Yeah? I don't remember this one? Does he catch anything?"

He smiled. "No. He wants to catch the whale. But, all the water he had got was in his mother's pail."

Jameson tried to understand his pun. "Doesn't he prick his finger or something?"

"He does. You see, Simple Simon is innocent. He's a curious boy."

"So, you were curious as a kid."

He lifted the beer bottle in his hand to his lips again and swallowed greedily. He wiped his mouth with the back of his hand

and offered Jameson a sickening smile. "Curiosity is a funny thing," he said. "Simon wants to try everything, but at every turn, someone like Old King Cole stops him."

"This is it," Claire said. "Be ready." *He's telling you, JD. He's telling you.*

"Claire," Alex's voice called cautiously. "He's cracking."

"Trust me," Claire said.

Alex took a deep breath. *I do. It's him I don't trust.*

"How did I end up in your story?" Jameson asked. *Claire, I hope you are there.*

He inched closer to her. "How do we all end up in each other's stories?" He looked her in the eye. "Take Little Tommy Tucker who sings for his supper," he said. "Or, what about Little Miss Muffet? They all have something in common. Someone takes something from all of them," he said. "They think they are safe. They're curious, hopeful, minding their own business until something stops them in their tracks. Tommy Tucker has no knife. He has no wife," he explains. "Miss Muffet? A spider takes over her tuffet. There are no happy endings," he said. "We're all living in The House That Jack Built."

"Go!" Claire said.

He reached behind him and picked up a hammer from the ground. "You're just the latest resident," he whispered to Jameson.

Jameson's stomach flipped over violently. She anticipated his move and lifted her hand to grab his. Their motion sent them both falling backward, leaving him hovering above her.

"Fuck the ladder," Claire said. She jumped through the small opening in the floor. She landed with a small thud on what she imagined was a rolled-up tent. "On the right, Toles. On the right! They're on the ground!"

Alex drew her gun and started into the barn. A small army of agents followed on her heels. "Where!" she asked.

"Behind the woodpile."

Jameson struggled to match the strength of the man above her. She caught a glimpse of Claire behind him. *Thank God.*

In less than a second, Claire had grabbed the hand holding the hammer. She whisked the man off Jameson and threw him to the ground. "Son of a bitch." He got up before Claire could draw her weapon and cocked his arm to swing the hammer at her. She ducked.

Alex ran up behind the man as cries of "FBI!" rang out behind her. Her focus remained squarely on the man. For a split second, she considered firing her weapon. Her foot seemed a better option. She landed a kick squarely to the middle of his back. He tipped and Claire's fist sent him backward onto the ground with a thud.

Alex held her gun on him. She shook her head. "FBI," she said. "John Carter, you are under arrest for the murder of Kaylee Peters…"

Claire heard Alex reading the suspect his rights. She moved a few short paces to where Jameson was finding her feet. "You okay?"

Jameson nodded.

"You did good," Claire said. Jameson stared at the scene unfolding a few feet away. Claire took hold of her arm. "JD," she said. "You did good. Go call your wife."

Claire's words finally pulled Jameson's focus away from the organized chaos in the barn. She nodded. Claire watched her walk away and sighed. An approaching voice caught her attention.

"The legend," he said when Alex spun him around, his hands cuffed behind his back. Alex stared at him passively. He laughed. "What's the matter, Agent Toles? Ding Dong Bell," he said. "How'd you like the well, pussycat?"

Alex's expression remained unchanged. "Your rhymes are over, Carter. We know everything."

He laughed again. "You haven't begun."

"Candace?"

"Jameson? Are you all right?"

"Other than really sweaty, I'm fine."

"Alex?"

"They got him."

"Jameson?"

Jameson closed her eyes. "I don't want to talk about it—not right now."

"I'm coming home."

"Candace…"

"Don't bother," Candace said. "I'll see you in a couple of hours."

Jameson set her phone on the table and sighed.

"Hey," Claire poked her head in the kitchen.

"Hey."

Claire stepped in. "Afraid I'll have to take a raincheck on that shot," she said. Jameson smiled weakly.

Claire took a deep breath. It wasn't in her nature to reassure people. She had seen the hint of ghosts in Jameson's eyes. And, Claire Brackett knew a thing or two about ghosts. While Claire was sure that the conversation in the barn had unsettled Jameson, she suspected the experience had conjured old demons and fears.

"I told you; you did good," Claire said.

"Glad it worked."

"Listen, JD, shit like this? Dealing with people like that asshole in the barn? It messes with you. He's not just sick," Claire said. "He's an asshole without a conscience. I get it. You were out there just working for two hours—talking. You know why you're there, but he makes you forget for a minute. You think maybe, just for a second he's not the guy you know he is. Then, just when you think he's someone else, he shows you his true colors. I've lived it," Claire said.

Jameson sighed. "How could I be so comfortable?"

"How do you think he managed to lure all those women?"

"Hey," Alex peeked inside. "Sorry. We gotta' roll," she said to Claire.

"I'll be right there," Claire replied.

Alex nodded and offered Jameson an understanding smile.

Claire waited until Alex had shut the door to continue her thought. "Killers are people, JD. The worst of them are the most charming. It's what makes them sinister. You held your own. You looked him in the eye. That takes more than guts. It takes resolve. Don't second guess anything you said or did."

Jameson nodded. "I don't know how people end up like that."

"People will say they're sick. Maybe. Maybe someone fucked with their life at some point. That's not what makes them kill for pleasure."

"Then what does?"

Claire shrugged. "I don't know," she admitted. "You have a soul, so you think everyone else does. Maybe sometimes that piece is just missing." She reached out and put a hand on Jameson's shoulder. "Raincheck on shots and marriage?"

Jameson smiled. "I look forward to it."

"Me too."

CHAPTER TWENTY-TWO

Alex looked through the glass at the man in the interrogation room.

"Do you want to beat the shit out of him as much as I do?" Claire asked.

Alex nodded. "You have that journal?"

"Yeah. I've got it."

"Good. Let's go talk to Mr. Carter."

"You think this is funny?" Alex asked.

The man in the chair across the table sat back and shrugged. "You said you know everything."

"And, you said we haven't begun. So? Enlighten me." Alex picked up the journal. She opened to the first passage. "The rose is red, the violet is blue, green is grass, where I lay you," she read.

He stared at the table smiling.

"That's your first? Pretty simple stuff. Did you write that before or after you killed Monica Leibowitz?"

He laughed raucously.

"Something funny?" Alex asked.

"You think I killed my cousin?" He kept laughing.

Alex waited, sensing he was about to continue. "I didn't kill that kid," he laughed. "She was a little young for my taste."

"But, you lured her," Alex said.

"Aww, she liked Badly Bradley. Had a crush on him. I helped him out. Watched Gordo and Badly Boy take turns with her even."

Alex felt her skin grow cold. *Gordo? Gordon. Fuck.*

He looked at Alex and grinned. "Didn't see that one coming, I guess."

"Gordon Daniels?" Alex asked calmly.

"Met him, huh?" he guessed. "Oh, yeah; he's quite the polished chap these days. You flip through the book. Look for Wee Willie Winkie," he laughed. "Gordo. Poor kid."

Alex steadied her breathing. "Why kill Brad Lawson?"

He shrugged and laughed again. "Why not? S'pose you'd have to ask Wee Willie about that one."

"His body was in the barn at your parents' house."

He laughed.

"Are you trying to tell me Gordon Daniels killed Brad Lawson?"

"I'm not trying to tell you anything. You already know everything anyway."

Alex nodded. "Why would Gordon Daniels want Brad Lawson dead?"

He sighed dramatically. "I would suppose he didn't want Brad rattin' on his ass."

"But, you weren't worried about that?"

"Why would I be? Badly Bradley didn't know Jack."

Alex thought for a moment. "He knew BJ."

"Right."

"How many women have you killed?" Alex asked stoically.

"How many pages in that book you've been reading have been filled?" he replied.

"Forty-two."

"Hum. Forty-two? I'd say Forty-two minus one."

Claire watched from the viewing room. She shook her head. "We need to detain Sergeant Daniels," she said.

Assistant Director Bower nodded. "I'll make the call. You don't sound surprised. You believe what he's saying in there?"

"He's got no reason to lie," Claire said. She turned and looked at her superior. "He just admitted to murdering forty-one women. No reason he'd lie about Monica Leibowitz or Brad Lawson." She turned back to watch and listen to Alex.

"So, you didn't know Lawson was dead when you assumed his

identity?"

"Bradley," he laughed. "No. Bradley was no businessman," he explained. "He ran his daddy's business into the ground. Served a purpose for us both. He got out of debt and…"

"And you got your freedom. Must've been convenient then, Daniels killing Lawson."

"Convenient? Willie boy, he hated Bradley almost as much as he hated me."

"Why?"

"Well, Bradley left him with my cousin."

"Monica?"

"Yeah. Things got a little outta' hand," he grinned. "She got skittish. Willie Winkie put her to sleep. Bradley?" He shook his head. "He freaked out and ran off. Left Willie all by his lonesome to take care of things. Had some issues a few days later. I fixed it for him."

"That's how you got the idea to put the women in the Moriarty's yard."

"Yeah. Kinda went to hell after their kid stepped in. Had to find another place. Lots of places out there."

"Why Kaylee Peters?"

He stared at her.

Alex watched him closely. "She saw something?"

"She saw enough that day."

"Where did she see you?"

He chuckled. "I see everything, Agent Toles."

"You mean from Flat Rock."

He shrugged. "Good place to have a drink with your buddies."

"And, you saw Kaylee getting close to something."

"You haven't turned over all the stones," he surmised.

"Why don't you tell me what stones to overturn?"

"Where's the fun in that?"

Alex held her anger in check. "Why does Daniels hate you?"

"Well, Bradley left his ass in the lurch, but the thing about

Bradley is, he always would save mine—was that way since he pulled me out of that same well you fell down when I was a kid."

"And, you paid him back by letting Daniels kill him?"

He shrugged. "Wasn't my decision. I told you; I didn't kill him. Not my rhyme."

"No? Why would Gordon put Lawson in your barn?"

He laughed. "Probably thought it suited him. Maybe he just wanted to put you all onto me. Keep you away from his little indiscretion."

Alex nodded. "BJ," she addressed him.

He looked up at her.

"Crow Electrical, that's named after the movie *The Crow*."

"Right."

"Why?"

"Everything has its place in the house that Jack built," he replied seriously. "Everything comes back, Agent Toles." He nodded. "Look at me. Look at you standing there." He shook his head. "What are you trying to avenge?" he asked her.

Alex stared at him.

He grinned. "You're thinking that you're the white hat catching the bad guy. Everybody's avenging something or someone. Everybody's in the rhyme. When you were at the bottom of the well, what did you hear?"

Alex made no reply.

He nodded. "I heard my mother's voice singing to me. Know what she sang? She sang, 'Diddle, diddle dumpling, my son John.' Over and over she sang that. Except she sang, "Fell in a hole, now he's gone.' That was after she threw me down it for breaking a glass."

Alex shook her head. "What do you want, Carter? Sympathy?"

"Nah. I don't need sympathy. I told you. Everybody's got a rhyme, Agent Toles—me, Badly, Willie—you. Even that pretty redhead behind the window over there," he gestured to the mirror on the wall. "Even Old King Cole and the governor. You all want something, and there's always somebody ready to take it from you."

Alex chuckled and turned on her heels.

"Don't like the answer?" he called after her.

She turned back to him. "It's not an answer," Alex said. "It's an excuse."

He laughed. "I guess, I'll see you in court."

Alex shut the door and stepped beside Claire. "I'll see you in hell, Jack."

"Nah," Claire said. "Hell's got a special place for his kind."

Alex sighed.

"Bower made the call to pick up Daniels."

Alex stared at Jack Carter. He sat smiling at them as if he could see them plain as day.

Claire shook her head as she looked at him. "Do you think that's what started it? You think he watched Daniels strangle Monica and that kicked him off?"

"No," Alex said. "And, I'll bet Gordon Daniels has more blood on his hands than Monica Leibowitz's and Brad Lawson's."

Claire nodded. "Assholes." She turned to Alex. "Give you a lift home?"

"You're driving?"

"Hell yeah, you look like shit."

Alex shrugged.

"What about him?" Claire asked.

Alex stared at the man in the other room. "What about him?" she said.

Claire shrugged. She'd be content to let him rot forever in that chair. She opened the door for Alex to step through. "So, do you think marriage is scarier than chasing serial killers?"

Alex burst out laughing at the seriousness in Claire's voice.

"I'm serious!"

Alex shook her head. "Give me the keys."

"Why?"

"I'm driving."

"Why?"

"You must be drunk," Alex said. She took the keys from Claire's hand and walked past her.

"I'm not drunk! Alex!"

Alex held up the keys and rattled them.

"Toles!

Alex laughed. *She is so easy.*

Alex walked through the front door, set down her bag and fell back against the wall.

Cassidy made her way into the hallway and smiled at the familiar sight. "Long day, I guess."

Alex opened her eyes. She watched as Cassidy approached and stepped into her arms. For the first time in weeks, Alex felt herself take a full breath. "God, I missed you."

Cassidy let her head fall against Alex's chest. Her arms wrapped around Alex's waist tightly. "I'm glad you're home."

"Me too."

"Is it over?"

Alex sighed heavily.

Cassidy pulled back. "Alex?"

"It's over in the sense that he's out of the picture."

"But?"

"It's never really over; is it?"

Cassidy cupped Alex's cheek. "It is for you, at least, it is for now."

"Sorry, I missed taco night."

"You didn't."

Alex tipped her head in question. She had intended to be home much earlier. She had also needed to decompress before facing her family.

"Claire called me."

"She did?"

"Yeah. She said she thought you needed a little time to unwind and maybe a beer or a whiskey before coming home to the Brady Bunch."

Alex smiled.

"I postponed taco night until tomorrow; assuming you'll be here."

"I'll be home in time," Alex promised.

Cassidy took Alex's hand. "I also understand she made you eat."

"Maybe I made her eat."

Cassidy laughed. "Nice try, love," she said as she led Alex up the stairs. She noted the slowness of Alex's step. "Your back?"

"Yeah. I sort of kicked something."

"You kicked something? Why? What did you kick?"

Alex shrugged.

Cassidy nodded. "I wonder how he's feeling."

"I hope it hurts like hell," Alex mumbled.

"You want me to run you a bath?" Cassidy asked when they stepped into their bedroom.

"Why? Do I need one?"

"Well…"

Alex laughed and pulled Cassidy back into her arms. "Wash my back?"

"Is that all you need help with?" Cassidy teased.

"I'm sure there are some harder to reach places you could…."

Cassidy pulled Alex down to her and kissed her soundly.

"What was that for?" Alex asked.

"I love you, Alex. I'm glad you're home."

"I love you too." Alex kissed Cassidy's forehead.

Cassidy heard Alex gasp slightly. It was an occurrence she had come to recognize signified a back spasm. "I'll wash your back," she said. "The only hard to reach place either of us is going is to bed."

"That's exactly what…"

"To sleep."

Alex smiled. "I'll make it up to you."

"There's nothing to make up, Alex."

Alex watched as Cassidy headed into their bathroom. She closed her eyes for a moment and savored the feeling of home.

"Alex," Cassidy called. "Get in here before you fall over."

"She might be right on that one," Alex muttered.

"I am right."

Alex laughed. Home was the reason she could face people like Jack Carter and still have hope for humanity. Avenge? Revenge? Alex sighed. Jack Carter was right about one thing; the story was only beginning. He was wrong about everything else as far as Alex was concerned. Maybe every person was part of a rhyme. Eventually, they made the choice what the rhyme would sound like. Life wasn't about what happened to you. It was about what you made happen for you—what you tried to do for others.

"Alex!"

"Coming," Alex promised. *You could've built any house you wanted, Jack—any house at all. Look at me.*

"Claire?"

Claire shrugged.

"What are you doing here?" Hawk asked. "I thought you'd be passed out at your apartment. What are you doing in DC in the middle of the night?"

"Can I come in?"

"Of course, you can come in."

Claire followed Hawk through the door. Hawk was surprised

to see Claire's eyes glistening when she turned back around.

"Hey," Hawk took Claire into an embrace. "Rough day, huh?"

Claire's head fell softly onto Hawk's shoulder.

"Want to talk about it?" Hawk asked.

Claire stepped back a pace. "That depends on which 'it' you mean."

Hawk's confusion was evident.

"Do you still want to?" Claire asked.

"Do I still want to what?"

Claire sucked in a nervous breath. "Get married—to me, I mean."

Hawk studied Claire for a moment. She wondered what might be driving Claire's emotional questions.

"I get it," Claire said.

"No," Hawk reached out and took Claire's face in her hands. "I'm just wondering what you're thinking." She searched Claire's eyes. "I wouldn't have asked if I didn't mean it, Claire."

Claire nodded. "I don't know that I'd be any good at it."

"It?"

"You know, the married thing."

Hawk smiled. "I don't know that I will be any good at it either," she said. "I do know that I'd like to try."

Claire bit her bottom lip gently. "People like us don't tend to grow old, Hawk."

"Well, chasing double agents, drug lords and serial killers does tend to lower one's life expectancy," Hawk agreed.

Claire closed her eyes.

"That's what scares you," Hawk suddenly realized. "You're afraid that you'll bank on forever and I'll leave you alone somehow."

"No…"

Hawk pulled Claire to her. "Claire," she whispered soothingly. "I can't promise you that nothing will ever separate us. I can promise you that I don't want it to. We've been at this for five years. I haven't chosen to leave yet."

"It isn't always our choice," Claire said.

"No, I guess, it isn't. Denying yourself something you want won't change that."

"I think, I do."

"You do what?" Hawk asked.

"Want to try," Claire said.

Hawk brought their lips together gently. "Are you sure?"

Claire nodded. "Not very romantic, huh?"

"I wouldn't say that."

Claire managed a shaky breath. "I never thought I could love anybody after…"

"I know."

"And now? Hawk, I can't imagine being with anyone else."

Hawk smiled. "Neither can I."

"I can't even flirt effectively anymore," Claire said.

Hawk laughed. Claire would always be Claire. "So? Will you, Claire? Will you marry me?"

Claire nodded. "But…"

"But?"

"Just Alex and Cassidy with us."

Hawk smiled. "I'm sure that can be arranged." She leaned in and kissed Claire lovingly. Claire fell into her arms gratefully. Hawk wondered if anyone would believe how sensitive Claire Brackett was underneath all her banter and all her bravado. She held Claire close. *I think more people realize than you want to admit, Sparrow—far more people than you ever wanted to imagine.*

EPILOGUE

Cassidy stood in the doorway chuckling. Claire was standing over the baby's crib. She was biting her bottom lip so hard, Cassidy feared she might put a hole in it.

"I have to hold it?" Claire groaned.

"For a few minutes—yes."

"What if I drop it?" she asked.

Cassidy laughed. *It?* "You were a trained spy. I think you can handle holding a baby."

"Alex's baby," Claire corrected Cassidy. "Are you sure you want me to do this?" she asked.

"Cass, could you give me a minute with Claire?" Alex stepped into the room.

Cassidy smiled, leaned in and kissed Alex on the cheek. "Go easy on her," she whispered. "I'll see you downstairs," she told Claire.

"It's kinda like a little jail cell," Claire said as she looked in the crib.

"Well, trust me when I tell you, they all seem to find an escape route sooner or later."

Claire frowned. The baby gurgled.

Alex grinned and shook her head. She grabbed Claire's arm gently.

"What did I do?" Claire asked.

Alex shook her head. "Do you know why we asked you to be a godparent?"

"Not a clue. My amazing wit?"

Alex nodded. "I asked Cass when she told me she was pregnant if it was a boy if we could name him Brian." She looked back in the crib and smiled. "Cass swore it'd be a boy," Alex laughed. "She was right every time."

"Uh.... Alex?"

"Until now," Alex laughed. "Mackenzie will never let her live that down."

"I'm not sure what this has to do with…"

"I was a little disappointed when we found out it was a girl," Alex confessed.

"Really?"

"Not because I cared that we were having another daughter," Alex said. "I just… Part of me wished that I'd asked to name Connor, Brian," she explained.

Claire nodded.

"Cass? I'll never forget it. She didn't miss a beat. She just smiled at me and said, 'What do you think of the name Fallon?' I lost it for a minute," she admitted.

"He was a good guy, Alex," Claire said. "I know how much he meant to you."

"He did. He was my partner," she said. "I'll never replace him."

Claire nodded sadly.

"No one is replaceable. To tell you the truth, I think that's part of the reason I didn't want to do it anymore."

"You mean, why you quit Carecom?"

Alex nodded. "I didn't want to lose another partner."

"I understand."

"It's kind of crazy if I think about it."

"What is?" Claire asked.

"Well, having a partner is a lot like being married. It's not the same relationship. There are a lot of similarities. You depend on that person to steady you, to let you vent, to make you laugh." Alex smiled at Claire. "I never thought I would have a partner like Fallon again."

Claire smiled, but Alex could see the disappointment in her eyes.

"Maybe that's a good thing," Alex said. "No one thinks it's crazier than me," she said with a chuckle. "I don't say it. I didn't say it to him. He just knew. I just knew. It was an unspoken understanding. Maybe you need to hear it. I know you think that we asked you to do this because Cass wanted it. That's only partly true," Alex said. "You're my partner, Claire. When I leave this house, you're the person I count on the most. The truth is, you haven't let me down yet. I know you love Cass. I know she loves you. That's different. She's like the mom you lost. I get that. Me? I'm your equal."

Claire shook her head. She wasn't certain she'd ever feel equal to Alex Toles. "I don't want to fuck it up."

"You mean being Fallon's godmother or being my partner?"

"Either."

"You won't."

"How can you be so sure?"

"I know you. You don't give up on anything you care about," Alex said honestly. She reached into the crib and picked up her daughter. Alex smiled at Claire and handed her the baby.

"What are you…"

"If you ever doubted that I trusted you, you can stop right now," Alex said. She started to walk away.

"Where are you going?" Claire called after her.

"I'll see you downstairs," Alex said. "With Fallon."

Claire's mouth fell open. She looked at the baby in her arms. "Your mothers are nuts." Fallon gurgled. "Yeah, right there with you, kid."

Alex walked down the stairs chuckling.

"Where's Claire?" Hawk asked.

"Oh, she'll be along any minute." Alex made her way to Cassidy and put an arm around her.

Cassidy looked up the stairs and saw Claire making her way toward them. "You're making her go to church and carry Fallon down the stairs?"

Alex shrugged.

"Evil," Cassidy laughed.

Claire made her way cautiously down the stairs with her charge.

"Mom!" Mackenzie yelled.

"You want to get it or shall I?" Cassidy asked Alex.

"I'll go," Alex said.

"Mom!"

Cassidy shook her head. "Patience is not her virtue."

Helen snickered. "Takes after Alexis."

Dylan walked up and kissed Cassidy on the cheek. "Do you want me to drive Claire and Hawk over?"

"Sure."

"Does that mean you are taking her back?" Claire looked at Cassidy hopefully.

Cassidy grinned. "Why? You looking for practice?"

"Me?" Claire's eyes flew open. "Hell no!"

Cassidy laughed and took Fallon from Claire's arms. "Go with Dylan," she said. "We'll see you there."

"Yeah, why couldn't you give me the one who can drive already?" Claire asked.

"Probably because I am leaving in the fall," Dylan said.

"Exactly!" Claire said.

Cassidy rolled her eyes.

"Mom!" Mackenzie ran toward Cassidy.

"Yes?"

"Mom says I can go with YaYa."

"YaYa and Grandma are taking the twins, Kenz. I thought you wanted to go with us."

"Then, can I do with Dylan?"

"Dylan just left with Claire and Hawk," Cassidy said.

Mackenzie sighed. "Well, can I go with Grandpa?"

"Grandpa left earlier. Why don't you want to go with us?" Cassidy asked.

Mackenzie stared at her mother.

"Because she hates when I sing to Fallon in the car," Alex said as she descended the stairs again. "I must be off key or something."

"You sing old people music," Mackenzie said.

Cassidy couldn't help but giggle.

Rose put an arm around Mackenzie. "Come on, Kenzie. "We'll squeeze you in between Abby and Connor. YaYa has that Ariana person you like on her iTunes."

Alex stared at her mother in disbelief.

"What?" Helen said. "It has a good beat." She offered Cassidy a wink and waved goodbye, shuttling her three grandchildren along.

"What just happened?" Alex asked.

"We've been out-hipped by our mothers, love."

Alex shook her head. "Unbelievable."

Cassidy kissed Fallon's head. "I need to make a quick call before we leave," she told Alex.

"Candace?"

"I sent her some revisions. I want to be sure she got them."

"I'm proud of you; you know?" Alex said.

"Yeah?"

"Yeah. I don't know how you do it."

"Do what?" Cassidy asked.

"Manage all of us and help Candace."

Cassidy smiled. "I don't always manage it, Alex. I don't do any of it alone," she reminded her wife. "I do love it—all of it." She kissed Alex on the cheek. "I'll be right there."

"I'll buckle in the wee one."

Cassidy nodded. She heard Alex humming James Taylor to their daughter as she walked through the kitchen to the garage. "Old people music." She laughed. "I'm not sure anyone can get old living with this brood," she mused before lifting her phone. "Candace…"

"The jury heard closing arguments in the case against John 'BJ' Carter today. Carter is accused of killing forty-one women between 2005 and 2018. While he confessed to the killings, his lawyers have attempted to prove that he did not understand his actions at the time, laying claim to the idea that his fractured personality prevented him from understanding the difference between right and wrong."

"Carter's case is tied to another, isn't that right?"

"That's right. Marine Sergeant Gordon Daniels testified against Carter in court this week. Daniels plead guilty earlier this month to two counts of second-degree murder amid a slew of lesser charges in a plea deal that required his testimony against Carter."

"Any sense of where the jury might be?"

"What I can tell you is that it's unlikely John Carter will be seeing the outside of four walls in his lifetime. Even a not guilty verdict by reason of insanity is bound to see him confined to a state institution for the rest of his life. Something that is cold comfort for his victims' families. There are still eight women whose remains have yet to be found."

"Unreal," Jameson said.

Candace turned off the television. "He's not ever getting out."

"Neither are any of those women."

"Forget about him, Jameson."

Jameson shook her head. "That is one of the only things I will never be able to promise you," she said.

Candace nodded. "Well, at least you can take comfort that people like Alex and Claire are out there."

"I do."

Candace smiled. Her phone buzzed. *Speaking of.* "Hi, Cassidy. Yes, I got it…"

BOOKS BY NANCY ANN HEALY

THE ALEX AND CASSIDY SERIES:

Intersection

Betrayal

Commitment

Conspiracy

Untold

FALLING THROUGH SHOOTING STARS

Coming Soon: *ALL THE WAY HOME*

BOOKS BY JA ARMSTRONG

THE OFF SCREEN SERIES (Addy and Emma)

Off Screen

The Red Carpet

Dim All the Lights

Writer's Block

Casting Call

Intermission

Waiting in the Wings

Script Doctor

THE BY DESIGN SERIES (Candace and Jameson)

By Design

Under Construction

Solid Foundation

Rough Drafts

New Additions

Renovations

Building Blocks

Road Blocks

COMING IN JULY 2017: Campaign Trail

COMING IN NOVEMBER 2017: Commander in Chief

THE SPECIAL DELIVERY SERIES (Brooke and Tess)

Special Delivery

Small Packages

Handle with Care

Late Arrivals

COMING 2017: Best Practice

THE FIRST COURSE SERIES (Carrie and Devon)

First Course

Main Dish

COMING CHRISTMAS 2017: Sweet Things

Visit www.thebumblingbard.com for more information

CPSIA information can be obtained
at www.ICGtesting.com
Printed in the USA
LVHW05s1545020518
575706LV00015B/945/P